WIT'CH FIRE

WIT'CH

FIRE

Book One of the Banned and the Banished

James Clemens

THE BALLANTINE PUBLISHING GROUP | NEW YORK

For my parents, Ronald and Mary Ann, who encouraged my dreams and gave me the home and the world to make them real.

A Del Rey® Book
Published by The Ballantine Publishing Group

Copyright © 1998 by Jim Czajkowski

All rights reserved under International and Pan-American Copyright Conventions. Published in the United States by The Ballantine Publishing Group, a division of Random House, Inc., New York, and simultaneously in Canada by Random House of Canada Limited, Toronto.

http://www.randomhouse.com/delrey/

Library of Congress Cataloging-in-Publication Data
Clemens, James.
Wit'ch fire / James Clemens. — 1st ed.
p.   cm. — (The banned and the banished ; bk. 1)
ISBN 0-345-41705-4
I. Title. II. Series: Clemens, James. Banned and the banished ; bk. 1.
PS3553.L3927W56   1998
813'.54—dc21   97-48402
CIP

Cover design by David Stevenson
Cover illustration by Brom

Manufactured in the United States of America

First Edition: July 1998

10 9 8 7 6 5 4 3 2 1

ACKNOWLEDGMENTS

First and foremost, I wish to thank Terry Brooks, John Saul, and Don McQuinn for their kind words and support at the Maui Writers Conference and for their help in introducing me to the Del Rey family. And, of course, I must thank John and Shannon Tullius, directors of MWC, for bringing us all together in the first place among the gardens and waters of Wailea.

I owe Kuo-Yu Liang, associate publisher of Del Rey, a debt of gratitude for taking a chance on a new author—and I can't find nearly enough words to thank Veronica Chapman, editor-supreme (I think that should be her new title), for honing the novel into its present incarnation. Thanks also to my agent, Pesha Rubinstein, for her willingness to take up my banner.

Likewise, I would be remiss if I didn't acknowledge a group of people who had to trudge through every page of every draft of this novel, and without whose comments, critiques, and words of encouragement, this novel would never have seen the light of day: Judy and Stephen Prey, Caroline Williams, Dennis Grayson, Chris Crowe, Ron Ball, Nancy Laughlin, Jeffrey Moss, and Dave Meek—or known collectively and affectionately as "The Warped Spacers."

And finally, two folks have been my right and left hand during the entire production of this world and its characters. They have shared my dreams and my heart. I owe all my worlds, imaginary and real, to them. My eternal love and thanks to Carolyn McCray and John Clemens.

FOREWORD TO WIT'CH FIRE,
by Jir'rob Sordun, D.F.S., M. of A.,
director of University Studies — U.D.B.

First of all, the author is a liar.

Do not proceed deeper into this work without first accepting this fact and holding it firmly in mind as you grasp this translation in hand. The author will try to confuse your mind, to cloud your reason. Beware of his many traps.

For five centuries, this document has been outlawed. At one time, the mere perusal of its first page warranted execution.[1] And even in this enlightened time, many scholars still believe every copy of the Kelvish Scrolls ought to be destroyed. I, *too,* am of that circle of scholars.

So why, you must wonder, am I writing the foreword to this vile first document?

Simply, because I am practical. Banning, burning, and outlawing the texts have not eradicated their existence.[2] Handwritten copies, memorized translations, pages written in secret code, and many other nefarious incarnations of the Scrolls survived the purges. Over the recent decades, it was sadly realized that the only practical way to deal with this abomination was by regulating it and thereby limiting its access to only those with prior instruction and study. By doing so, its lies, deceptions, and half-truths could be debunked.

For this reason, this version of the Scrolls has been released for postgraduate studies *only*. Your instructor has been properly trained and licensed in the safe reading of this first text. *Do not scrutinize*

---

[1] *Laws of Oppression,* by Prof. Sigl Rau'ron, University Press (U.D.B.), p. 42. "In Arturian times, followers of the banned texts were often hunted down, their eyes burned out with hot coals, and their intestines gutted for public display. Even worse punishments were sometimes employed."

[2] "Deceit among the Scholars," by Jir'rob Sordun, *New Uni Times,* Vol. 4, issue 5, pp. 16–17. "In one heretic sect, pages of the Scrolls were tattooed in hidden places on a person's body. And annually the group would unite and read the text off each other. Such was the fervor to avoid the banning."

the book without this instruction. Do not read beyond your prescribed schedule as outlined in the syllabus. Do not share this with a friend or family member unless they are attending the same class.

For more than a decade, this manner of control has kept the rumors and curiosity about the Scrolls to a minimum. There is nothing like dry academia to bleed the thrill from a banned document.

This translation of the first Scroll is to our knowledge one of the few that reflects the true original. There are scores of bastardized translations in other countries and lands. But in your hand is a direct translation, written almost three centuries ago, of the original text. Where the actual handwritten scroll disappeared to and who wrote it still remains a scholarly mystery.[3]

So here in your hands is the closest approximation to the true abomination you are likely to encounter. Only a select cadre of postgraduate students are allowed to attend this instructed reading. It is both an honor and a responsibility. After you have completed the reading of this text, you will undergo a vigorous class on how to conduct yourself when queried about the book.

And you, dear student, will face questions from the uninitiated!

So beware! Much curiosity still surrounds this document among the poor and uneducated public, and one of your main goals is to weaken this curiosity. We will teach you methods to calm the curious and turn interest into a yawn.

Proceed with caution. And remember at all times, in your waking hours and in your dreams . . .

The author is a liar.

---

[3]*The Mystery of the Lost Scrolls,* by Er'rillo Sanjih, Vulsanto Press, p. 42. "The last recorded mention of the original handwritten copies was back some two centuries. But even this mention by Lord Jes'sup of Argonau is questioned by Scroll scholars as simple bragging."

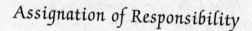

Assignation of Responsibility

This copy is being assigned to you and is your sole responsibility. Its loss, alteration, or destruction will result in severe penalties (as stated in your local ordinances). Any transmission, copying, or even oral reading in the presence of a nonclassmate is strictly forbidden. By signing below and placing your thumbprint, you accept all responsibility and release the university from any damage the Scroll may cause you—or those around you—by its perusal.

_____

Signature

_____

Date

Place Thumbprint Here:

*** **WARNING** ***

If you should perchance come upon this text outside of proper university channels, please close this book now and alert the proper authorities for safe retrieval. Failure to do so can lead to your immediate arrest and incarceration.

YOU HAVE BEEN WARNED.

WIT'CH FIRE

This is the way the world ended,

and like grains of sand cast into the

winds at Winter's Eyrie,

this is the way all other worlds began.

WORDS, WRITTEN IN BLACK INK ON PARCHMENT, ARE A FOOL'S PARA-dise, and I, as a writer, know this only too well. Pronunciations change; meanings mutate; nothing survives intact the ravages of blind time.

So why am I writing this? Why pursue this folly? This is not the first time I have told her damned story. I have written of her many times, in many incarnations. One time, virginal in her honor. Another time, evil without soul or conscience. I have por-trayed her as a buffoon, a prophet, a clown, a savior, a hero, and a villain. But in reality, she was all these and none. She was simply a woman.

And for the first time, I will tell her true story. A truth that may, with luck, finally destroy me. I still remember her promise, as if only a single heartbeat has passed. "Curse or blessing, little man? Do with it what you want. But when the marching of years weighs too heavy, tell my story . . . Tell my *true* story and you will find your end."

But can I? So much time has passed.

A thousand tongues, mine included, have distorted the events with each telling, twisting them detail by detail, word by word, each storyteller embellishing his favorite parts. Like starving curs on a meat bone, we tear at its substance, dragging it through the grime, fouling it with saliva and blood, until nothing but a ragged remnant of the original survives.

As I put ink to paper, my hand shakes. I sit here in this rented room and scrawl each word with a sore wrist. Around me are piled stacks of crumbling parchments and dusty books, bits and pieces of the puzzle. I collect them to me, like dear old friends, keeping them close at hand and heart, something I can rub with my fingertips and smell with my nose, some tangible evidence of my distant past.

As I hold a pen poised, I remember her final words, each a knife that cuts jaggedly. Her sweet face, the sunlight off her shorn red hair, the bruise under her right eye, the bloody lip that her tongue kept touching as she fought out her final words to me . . . and I remember the sadness in her eyes as I laughed at her folly. Damn her eyes!

But that was later, much later. To understand the end, you must first know the beginning. And to understand even the beginning, you must understand the past, the past that had disappeared into myth long before she was born.

Let me show you, if I can find it: a parchment that tells of the creation of the Book itself, the tome that would destroy a girl and a world.

Ah, here it is . . .

PROLOGUE

[Text note: The following has been determined to be an excerpt from L'orda Rosi—The Order of the Rose— *written in the high Alasean tongue almost five centuries before the birth of she who will be known as the Wit'ch of Winter's Eyrie.]*

MIDNIGHT AT THE VALLEY OF THE MOON

Drums beat back the stillness of the winter's valley, snow etching the landscape in silver. A hawk screeched a protest at the interruption of its nighttime nesting.

Er'ril leaned his knuckles on the crumbling sill and craned his neck out the inn's third-story window. The valley floor was dotted with the fires of the men who still followed the way of the Order. So few campfires, he thought. He watched the black shadows bustling around the firelight, arming themselves. They, too, knew the meaning of the drums.

The night breeze carried snatches of shouted orders and the scent of oiled armor. Smoke from the fires reached toward the heavens, carrying the prayers of the soldiers down below.

And beyond the fires, at the edge of the valley, massed a darkness that ate the stars.

The hawk screeched again. Er'ril's lips thinned to a frown. "Silence, small hunter," he whispered into the moonless night. "By morning you and the scavengers will be feasting your bellies full. But for now, leave me in peace."

Greshym, the old mage, spoke behind him. "They hold the heights. What chance have we?"

Er'ril closed his eyes and let his head hang lower, a sick tightness clamping his belly. "We'll give him a bit longer, sir. He may yet find a weakness in their lines."

"But the dreadlords mass at the entrance to the valley. Listen to the drums. The Black Legions march."

Er'ril turned from the window to face Greshym with a sigh and sat on the sill, eying the old man. Greshym's red robes hung in tatters on his thin frame as he paced before the feeble fire. The old mage, his dusty hair just wisps around his ears, walked with a bent back, his eyes red from the fumes of the hearth.

"Then pray for him," Er'ril said. "Pray for all of us."

Greshym stopped and warmed his backside by the fire while frowning back at him. "I know what's working behind your gray eyes, Er'ril of Standi: hope. But both you and your Standi clansmen are clutching empty air."

"What would you have us do? Bow our heads to the dreadlords' axes?"

"It will come to that soon enough." Greshym rubbed the stump of his right wrist, almost accusingly.

Er'ril remained silent, his eyes caught by the sight of that smooth stump. He should not have pressed the old man some six moons ago. Er'ril remembered the Gul'gothal dog that had trapped the two of them and a handful of refugees in the Field of Elysia.

Greshym seemed to notice his stare. He raised his stump toward the flickering flame. "Listen, Boy, we both knew the risks."

"I panicked."

"You were frightened for the children, what with your niece among the townspeople."

"I shouldn't have pushed you. You told me what would happen if you tried to renew." Er'ril bowed his head, picturing the late afternoon sunlight slanting across the fields of tallac. He again saw Greshym raise his right fist to the heavens, begging for the gift of Chi, his hand vanishing in the fading sunlight as the ritual began. But this time, when the old mage pulled his arm back down, instead of his hand reappearing richly coated in red Chyric power, Greshym pulled back only a stump.

"It was my choice, Er'ril. Put this aside. It was you who saved all our hides that day."

Er'ril fingered the scar on his forearm. "Perhaps . . ." After Greshym's maiming, he had lunged at the Gul'gothal beast, tearing the creature to bloody ribbons. Even now, he was unsure if rage or guilt had driven his wild stabs. Afterward, he had been covered in steaming blood and gore; the children had shied from him in fear—even his niece—as if he were the monster.

Greshym snorted. "I knew it would happen. The same fate befell the other mages of the Order." He shoved the sleeve over his stump, hiding it away. "Chi has abandoned us."

Er'ril raised his eyes. "Not everyone has suffered the same fate."

"Only because they have held off renewing." Greshym sighed. "But they will. They will be forced to try. Eventually even the hand of your brother, Shorkan, will fade. When I last saw him, the Rose had already waned to a feeble pink. Barely enough power for one decent spell. Once that is gone, he will be forced to reach into Chi himself, to try to renew; then he, too, will lose his hand."

"Shorkan knows this. The academy in the neighboring valley—"

"Foolish hope! Even if he should find a student who is

still bloodred, of what use is one child's fist? It would take a
dozen mages fresh to the Rose to drive off the force out
there. And what of the other hundred battles going on
across our lands? We're besieged by the Gul'gothal dreadlords from all fronts."

"He has a vision."

"Posh!" By now, Greshym had returned to face the fire.
He held silent for several breaths; then he spoke to the embers. "How could three centuries of civilization vanish so
quickly? Our spell-cast spires that once reached to the very
clouds have toppled to dust. Our people rage against us,
blaming us for the loss of Chi's support and protection.
Cities lie in ruin. The feasting roar of the Gul'gotha echoes
across the countryside."

Er'ril remained silent. He had squeezed his eyes closed
when a horn suddenly trumpeted across the valley—a Standi
horn! Could it be?

Er'ril swung to the window and almost fell through as he
leaned out into the night, one ear cocked to listen. The horn
blared again, and even the distant drums of the Black Legion seemed to falter a beat. Er'ril spotted a commotion by
the northern campfires. He squinted, trying to pierce the
night's blanket. A roiling of activity disturbed the fire pits;
then for just a heartbeat, outlined by the camp's cooking fire, he saw the rearing of a chestnut stallion. It was
Shorkan's steed!

The dark swallowed away the sight before Er'ril could
tell if the horse was mounted by one or two riders. Er'ril
struck the sill with his gloved fist.

Greshym was already at Er'ril's shoulder. "Is it Shorkan?"

"I believe so!" Er'ril pushed away from the window.
"Hurry below! He may need assistance."

Er'ril did not wait to see if Greshym followed as he
rushed from the room and pounded down the wooden steps
of the inn, leaping from the last landing to the main floor.
Once his feet hit the planks, he charged across the common

room. Makeshift beds lined the wall, with bandaged men occupying nearly all of them. Normally, he would stop beside a bed and place a hand on a knee or exchange jokes with one of the injured, but not now. Healers stepped aside as he burst across the room, and a posted guardsman swung the door wide to allow him outside.

The frigid night air burned his lungs as he flew through the portal and across the inn's porch. As he reached the icy mud at the foot of the porch, he heard the thundering of heavy-shod hooves approaching fast. Flickering torches around the entrance did little to illuminate the horse's approach; no sooner had he sighted the flaring nostrils and wild eyes of the stallion than it was upon him. The rider yanked back the reins. The steed buried its forelimbs to the pasterns in mud as it heaved to a halt. Foamy spittle flew from its lips as it shook its mane, and huge plumes of white blew into the black night from its feverish nose.

But Er'ril gave no more than passing notice to the savagely exhausted horse. Where he might ordinarily blast the foul rider who would so poorly treat such a beautiful beast, tonight he knew the rider's urgency. He raised a hand to his brother.

Shorkan shook his head and slid off the horse, landing with a groan but keeping his feet under him. He clapped his brother on the shoulder. "Well met, Brother. Give me a hand with my friend."

For the first time Er'ril noticed the small second rider who had been mounted behind his brother. The small figure shivered in a borrowed coat over a set of nightclothes. Blue lipped and pale faced, the towheaded boy could be no older than ten. Er'ril helped the boy off the sweating horse and half carried the trembling child up the steps to the porch.

"We've a warm room and hot ko'koa on the third floor," Er'ril said over his shoulder to his brother. Shorkan was passing the reins of his stallion over to a groomsman. Er'ril saw the pain in his brother's eyes as the horse limped away.

Both brothers bore the gray eyes and thick black hair of their Standi heritage, but Shorkan's face, even though he was the younger of the two, wore deep-etched lines of worry at the corners of his mouth and eyes. Er'ril wished he could shoulder more of his brother's burden, but he was not the one chosen by Chi to bear the gift of the Rose. Er'ril could only offer the strength of his arm and the edge of his blade to aid their cause.

"Quick then. Up to the room." Shorkan tipped his head, listening to the drums from the heights. "We've a long night ahead of us still."

Er'ril led the way inside and to the stairs, the boy stumbling beside him. At least some color was returning to the child's face as the heat from the fireplaces warmed him. His pale thin lips reddened, and his cheeks bloomed with a rosy warmth. From under straw-colored hair, his blue eyes, rare for these parts, stared back at Er'ril.

Shorkan studied the number of beds as they passed through the common room. "More injured?"

"Skirmishes at the valley ridges," Er'ril explained.

Shorkan merely nodded, but a deeper frown buried his lips. He gently nudged Er'ril up the stairs faster.

Once in the room, Er'ril found Greshym where he had left him — still warming his backside by the fire.

Shorkan stalked into the room. "I'm surprised to find you still here, Greshym."

The older man stepped aside to allow room for Shorkan by the fire. "Where else would I be?" Greshym said. "You've boxed us into this valley, trapped us."

"You've followed me this far, Greshym, on blind faith of my word. Trust me a little farther."

"So you keep saying." The old man pointed with his chin. "Let's see your hand, Shorkan."

"If you must." He shoved his right hand toward the old man. It had a slightly ruddy hue to it, like a fresh sunburn.

The old man shook his head. "Your Rose fades, Shorkan."

Greshym eyed the boy who was sneaking closer to the warmth of the fire. He grabbed the boy by the shoulder once he was within reach. "So you found one of the students?" He reached down and lifted the sleeve of the man-sized overcoat to expose the child's right hand. It was as pale and white as the boy's frightened face. "What's this? You failed?"

Shorkan gently freed the boy from Greshym and placed an arm around the child's shoulders. He positioned the boy closer to the fire and patted him on the head. "He's left-handed." Shorkan scooted the left sleeve of the coat up to expose the child's other hand. It glowed bright red, as if the boy had dipped his hand, wrist-deep, into a pool of blood. Whorls and eddies of various red hues swam across his tiny palm and the back of his hand. "Being left-handed saved his life. One of the dog soldiers made the same mistake and let him slip through the initial slaughter. He hid in an apple barrel. The rest of the academy is a slaughterhouse."

"So there are no others?" Greshym asked. "Of what use is one child's power against an army of the Gul'gotha? I was hoping you would have found a teacher still bloodied and fresh to the Rose, someone with knowledge."

"None. Even the headmaster fled."

"That sounds like Master Re'alto," Er'ril said sourly. "I never trusted the weasel."

Shorkan turned away from the fire. He nodded toward the window, where the drums could still be heard. "It is of no matter. We will all be slaughtered by the morning."

"What?" Er'ril stepped up to his brother. "What of your vision?"

Greshym snorted. "What did I tell you?" he mumbled.

"Trust me, Brother. Tonight doesn't concern our mere survival here. It concerns the fate of our future."

"What future?" Greshym said. "This child is probably the last full-bloodied mage in all the lands of Alasea."

"You speak the truth, Greshym. With this child ends the

reign of Chi. The world is heading into a black age, a grim time where men will be forged in blood and tears. It was foretold by the sect of Hi'fai, those of the Order who trace the paths of the future."

"Doomsayers!" Er'ril said. "Heretics. They were cast out."

"Bad news was never well received, least of all by those in power. But they spoke the truth." Shorkan pointed out the window. "The drums announce the clarity of their visions."

"But we are still a strong people," Er'ril said. "We can survive."

Shorkan smiled thinly at his older brother. "You also speak the truth, Er'ril. But Alasea will still fall, and her people will be subjugated by the Gul'gotha. It is the time of darkness for the land. Like the cycles of the sun and moon, night must follow day. But with our actions here, we may create a future sunrise. We will not see it, nor will our great-grandchildren, but someday, a new sun will have a chance of rising. To ignite that future dawn, a piece of this sunlight must be passed down to our descendants, from us."

"But how?" Er'ril said, eying the small child. "How?"

"The Hi'fai sect foretold a book."

Greshym retreated to the lone bed in the room. "The Book? Shorkan, you are a fool. Is this why you brought me along?"

"They were your words, Greshym—when you once belonged to the Hi'fai."

Er'ril paled and took a step away from the old man.

"It was a long time ago," Greshym said. "When I was still new to the gifts. I dismissed the sect ages ago."

"Yet I am sure you still remember the prophecy. Others in later years confirmed your visions."

"It is madness."

"It is the truth. What were your words?"

"I don't remember. They were foolish words."

"What were they?"

Greshym covered his eyes with his one good hand. His voice seemed to come from far away.

> " 'Three will come.
> One injured,
> One whole,
> One new to the blood.
> There,
> Forged in the blood of an innocent
> At midnight in the Valley of the Moon,
> The Book will be made.
> Three will become one
> And the Book will be bound.' "

Shorkan sat on the bed next to Greshym. "We have studied your words. Now is the time."

Greshym groaned. "There's much you don't know. You're young to the blood. I have studied other scrolls, texts since burned when the Hi'fai were cast out. Not all was committed to parchment."

Shorkan gripped the old mage's shoulder. "Speak, Greshym. Free your tongue. Time runs short."

Greshym lowered his head and mumbled quietly,

> " 'Blood will call her,
> Book will bind her.
> Bound in blood,
> She will rise.
> Heart of stone.
> Heart of spirit.
> She will rise again.' "

Silence blanketed the room. Only the crackling of the fire intruded.

Er'ril's hand drifted to the pommel of his sword. "I thought her myth."

"Sisa'kofa," Shorkan said, releasing his grip on Greshym's shoulder, his eyes narrow with worry. "The wit'ch of spirit and stone."

Er'ril began pacing the threadbare rug. "Legend has her destroyed by Chi for daring to wield the blood magick. All women are cursed to bleed with each moon as punishment for her atrocities. How could this abomination rise again?"

Greshym shrugged. "That's why we held our tongue. Not all visions surrounding the Book are bright."

"A grim vision indeed," Shorkan said. "Maybe with time, we could discern other prophetic visions to shed some light on your words. But midnight closes in on us. It must be now, or we will lose the chance forever."

Greshym sighed. "Yet dare we risk it?"

"Even with visions, the future is blind to us." Shorkan stood up from the bed, the wood of the frame creaking in protest. "We must work with the tools at hand. Our order is at its end. By creating this book, a small piece of our magick can be preserved. I say we still proceed."

"I'll follow your lead, Shorkan. What else can I do?" the old man said, exposing his stump.

"Come then." Shorkan helped Greshym to his feet. "By the fire."

Er'ril watched as his brother gathered the boy to him, and the three mages set up a warding circle of candle drippings before the fire: strong warding for strong magick. Er'ril stepped back.

Shorkan twisted his neck to acknowledge Er'ril. "You, too, will play a role in this venture, Brother, a vital role. When we are finished, a bright flash of white light will burst forth, and wild magick will still be loose in the room. You must quickly close the Book to end the spell."

"I will not fail you," Er'ril said, frowning, a sick emptiness worming into his chest. "But magick is your heart, Brother. Why not close the Book yourself?"

"You know why, or at least suspect it. I can see it in your eyes," Shorkan said quietly. "The forging of this text will destroy the three of us. We must become the Book."

Er'ril tensed, his suspicions realized. "But—"

"Midnight fast approaches, Brother."

"I know the hour is late! But . . . but what of this child?" Er'ril nodded toward the boy. "You will sacrifice him. Does he not have a say?"

"I was born to this, armsman," the boy said, speaking for the first time, his words calm and sure. Er'ril realized he still did not know the boy's name, though his accent suggested he was raised in one of the coastal townships. "Chi guided me to the apple barrel to hide when the dreadlords attacked. This is meant to be."

"The boy and I have already spoken of such matters," Shorkan said, stepping from the circle and putting his arms around Er'ril. He squeezed him tight. "Fear not, big brother. It must be done."

Er'ril tightened his own arms around his brother and remained silent, afraid his voice would betray the depth of his despair.

After too short a time, Greshym cleared his throat, placing his spent candle on the mantel. Er'ril released his brother after a final firm hug.

"What will act as the totem for the Book?" Greshym asked, wiping wax from his fingers on his robe. Er'ril noticed the old man stood taller, less stooped—almost his old self. It had been many months since the elder mage had wielded magick. "The totem, too, must be warded by the heart of a forger."

Shorkan pulled out a battered book from a pocket of his riding vest. Er'ril recognized the rose etched in gold-lined burgundy on its cover, the edges of the paint flecking away in places from age and tired use. It was Shorkan's diary. "I have carried this at my breast for three years."

He rested the book in the center of the circle and reached

to his waist and removed a gilt-edged dagger, a sculpted rose prominent on the butt of the hilt. Greshym slipped a matching dagger from a fold in his robe. Then the older mages looked to the boy.

"I don't have mine," he answered their stares, eyes wide. "It's back at the school."

"It's of no matter," Shorkan consoled. "Any knife will do. These fancy blades are just ceremonial."

"Still, it would be prudent to maintain proper form," Greshym said. "This is a powerful spell we weave."

"We have no choice. The night wears thin." Shorkan turned to his brother and held out his hand. "I'll need your dagger—the one Father gave you."

With an emptiness still aching in his chest, Er'ril snapped the buckling and freed his dagger. He laid the ironwood hilt in his brother's palm.

Shorkan gripped the knife, seeming to weigh its balance, then spoke firmly. "Er'ril, step three paces back from us. Do not approach, no matter what you see, until the burst of white light."

Er'ril did as instructed, stumbling back as the three knelt within the protective circle of wax. Shorkan passed his rose-handled knife to the boy, keeping his father's dagger for himself.

"Let us prepare," Shorkan said.

Er'ril watched his brother slice a thin bloody line across his right palm. Greshym did the same to his left palm, holding the hilt in his teeth. Only the boy held his dagger still poised, unbloodied.

Shorkan noticed his hesitation. "The knife is honed fine. Cut fast, and only the smallest sting will be felt."

The boy still held the dagger frozen.

Greshym spat his own knife from between his teeth into his bleeding palm. "This must be done by your own will, Boy. We can not take this burden from you."

"I know. This is my first time."

"Quick and clean," Shorkan said.

The boy squeezed his eyes tight, face tensed in a wince, and drew the blade across his palm. Blood welled into his cupped palm. Eyes bright with moisture, the boy turned to Shorkan.

Shorkan nodded. "Good. Now let it begin."

All three reached and placed bloodied palms upon the book, fingers touching each other, entwined like tentative lovers. Shorkan intoned, "As our blood mingles, so do our powers. Let the three become one."

Er'ril watched as the intense redness of the boy's hand spread to the other two mages, until all hands glowed a deep rose. A slight breeze began swirling through the room, stirring a few strands of Er'ril's black hair. At first, Er'ril thought it simply a wind from the open window. But this breeze was warm, like a whisper of spring.

All three mages had heads lowered in prayer, lips moving silently. As they prayed, the breeze began whirling faster and faster, hotter and hotter. And as the wind swept through the room, it drained color from the circle, drawing substance from the wax ring. Er'ril could now see the sweeping wind buffeting him, swirls of hues mixing and gyrating. As the wind gained a richness of texture, the contents of the wax circle became duller, bled of their substance.

In the fading ring, only the book itself remained substantial, still crisp with color as it rested in the center of the circle. Even the mages, crouching by the book, had become crystalline statues, translucent and vague.

The wind grew fiercer. His eyes stinging, Er'ril had trouble standing before the gale as its hot breath attacked him in swirls of color. He leaned into the storm.

Suddenly Er'ril saw his brother, still only a translucent figure, burst to his feet within the circle.

"No!" Shorkan screamed at the ceiling. With his yell, the diary flew open, and a blinding light fountained upward from the pages, bright as a sun for a heartbeat, then collapsing back to nothing, swallowed into the pages of the book.

Er'ril rubbed away the afterimages of the burning light from his eyes.

The boy, who like the others was just a translucent outline, scrabbled away from the book, backing toward Er'ril.

Shorkan spotted him. "Halt!" he yelled.

The boy ignored him and continued, pushing to the edge of the wax ring. There, he met resistance, having to lean and shove against an invisible barrier. But he was stronger than the barrier, and as he pushed past the wax ring boundary, parts of his body became substantial again.

But what was coming through wasn't human!

As the boy crossed the warding, his body changed from a translucent figure of a boy to a hulking, shaggy-limbed beast.

Shorkan called to his brother, "Stop him, Er'ril, or all is lost! We are deceived."

Before Er'ril could react, a fiery gale exploded from the circle, flipping him across the room and onto the bed. The room plunged into darkness as the candles and fire were snuffed out by the force of the wind.

After the burst, the wind instantly died away, as if someone had slammed a door shut on a winter's storm. Er'ril searched the darkened room. He was alone.

Suddenly the fireplace flamed back to life, a still-glowing ember reigniting the blaze. Blinking in the sudden light, Er'ril spotted his brother's diary, open on the rug. No light emanated from its pages.

Where was the beast? Where was his brother? Er'ril scrambled up from the bed and cautiously surveyed the wind-ravaged room, clothes and traveling bags flung to all corners, chairs overturned.

As he stepped from the edge of the bed toward the open book, something grabbed his ankle from behind and yanked, toppling him to the rug. Rolling onto his back, he blindly kicked at his assailant, a heel striking flesh with a satisfying thud. The grip weakened on his ankle, and Er'ril ripped his leg free. Leaping away from the hidden assailant, Er'ril rolled on his shoulder to face his opponent, pulling to a crouch as he swept out his sword.

From under the bed, it crawled free, pursuing him—the beast that had once been a boy. Amber eyes, slitted black, spat hate toward him as the were-creature hissed. Straightening from a lumbering crouch to its full shaggy height, it stood easily as tall as Er'ril, but massed at least twice what he did. Mats of black fur hung from it like drapes of hoary moss. But its daggered claws and razor teeth drew most of Er'ril's attention. It lumbered toward him, its foul stench preceding it.

Er'ril backed, raising the tip of his sword. As if his motion were a signal, the creature leaped at him. Er'ril dodged to the right, under one of its sweeping arms, and dragged the edge of his long blade across the beast's flank as he passed.

Ignoring its howl, Er'ril leaped atop the bed, seeking a better position to attack. Whirling to face the monster, his sword readied to parry a second attack, Er'ril froze. No attack came. The beast lumbered away from him.

It was going toward the book!

No! Er'ril leaped toward the beast, sword aloft in both hands. He used the force of his plummeting weight to plunge the sword deep through the center of its wide back, driving the sword through to the wooden planks beneath the creature. The beast spasmed, its neck snapped back, and its mouth opened in a silent scream. The creature collapsed forward, Er'ril landing on top of it.

Er'ril rolled clear and grabbed for his dagger. His hand froze on the empty scabbard. He had given Shorkan his knife! But the beast remained limp on the floor, dead.

Breathing heavily, one eye on the monster, Er'ril crept around its limp bulk and stepped to the open diary. Shorkan had told him he needed to close the book to complete the spell. But after all that had occurred, had something gone wrong? Had the transformation failed?

Er'ril knelt by the diary. He saw that his brother's scrabbly handwriting filled the exposed pages. The book had not changed.

Er'ril felt fresh tears well up in his reddened eyes. Had his brother lost his life for nothing? Gently he reached down and touched the cover's edge—the only token of his lost brother, his lost family, his lost land. Closing his eyes, he flipped the book closed, completing his dead brother's wish.

As the book clapped shut, a cold shock jerked through Er'ril's body and sprawled him across the floor. Lights danced across his vision for several heartbeats, and the room spun and tilted cockeyed. Finally, his vision focused again. The first sight was of the beast now transformed back into a boy. Er'ril's sword thrust up from the child's back as he lay in a widening pool of blood that reached to the diary itself.

My gods, what have I done? Er'ril felt an icy claw around his heart. What trickery is this? Did I slay an innocent child?

He scanned the room for some insight, panicked that some foul magick had deceived him into murdering the boy.

His eyes settled on the book. Maybe . . .

He reached, ever so slowly, toward the diary. His finger hovered above the cover, then quickly tapped at it, as if teasing a snake. Nothing happened. There was no shock this time.

Biting his lip, he placed his entire palm down on the book. Still nothing happened.

With a single finger, he flipped the cover open. A blank white page stared back at him. He knew his brother had crammed the diary from cover to cover with his scribblings. Again with a single finger, Er'ril fanned through the rest of the book. It was blank—all empty pages.

Er'ril picked up the book, the boy's blood dripping from its leather binding, and flipped to the first page.

As he stared at the white page, words coalesced on the paper, as if a ghost were scribbling across it in red ink. He recognized the handwriting. It was Shorkan's!

"Brother, do you hear me?" Er'ril spoke to the empty air.

The writing continued as if he had never spoken.

"Shorkan?"

Still no response.

Er'ril read the words, and his fists clenched at the book's pages.

And so the Book was forged, soaked in the blood of an innocent at midnight in the Valley of the Moon. He who would carry it read the first words and choked in tears for his lost brother . . . and his lost innocence. Neither would ever return.

Dropping the Book to the floor, Er'ril stared at the boy's blood coating his palms and crashed to his knees in bitter tears.

AND SO THE BOOK WAS FORGED, BY FOOLISH MEN PLAYING WITH POW-
ers they did not fully comprehend. Then again, I would do the
same, so who am I to complain? Just a storyteller, spinning tales
of times past.

Now you know how and why the Book was forged, out of
prophecies, visions, and wild magick.

Answers grow other questions.

What is the Book? What is its purpose? And what became of
its blood-soaked pages?

As I can testify, time marches forward, the past forgotten, the
future dreamed. And questions are answered.

The world spins, like a child's top, marking time. Centuries fly
by like the fluttering of a frantic sparrow's wing—until she ap-
pears. Then I place a finger on the world and slow its spin to a
stop. There she is in the orchard. Do you see her? Now's the time
for her story to be told: she who was prophesied by a one-handed
mage, she who would devour the soul of the world.

Book One

FIRST FLAMES

1

THE APPLE STRUCK ELENA ON THE HEAD. IN SURPRISE, SHE BIT HER tongue, and her foot slipped off the next rung of the ladder. She fell the two yards to the hard ground and crushed a decayed apple, smearing sticky foulness over the seat of her new work clothes.

"Careful there, Elena," Joach called from another ladder, the strap from his apple basket digging into his forehead. The basket on his back was almost full.

She glanced to her own basket, its contents spilled across the orchard ground. With her face as red as the apple that had dropped on her, she stood, trying to reclaim as much dignity as possible.

Wiping her brow, she looked to the sun, which was low on the horizon. Late afternoon shadows stretched toward her. Sighing, she gathered her stray fruit. The dinner bell would be ringing soon. And her basket, even reloaded, was only a bit over half full. Father would be angry. "Head in the clouds," he would accuse her. "Always slacking from real work." She had heard his words often enough.

She placed a hand on the ladder leaning against the trunk of the tree. It wasn't as if she was purposefully avoiding work. She didn't mind working long hours in the fields or orchards. But the monotony of the chores did little to keep her attention from wandering to the numerous curiosities around her. Today she had found a kak'ora bird's tiny nest tucked in the crook of an orchard tree. The nest, long abandoned for the season, fascinated her with its intricate weaving of twigs, dried mud, and leaves. Then there had been the lacy spiderweb she had found, heavy with dew, like a jeweled drape. And the molted husk of a fiddler beetle glued to a leaf. So much to study and admire.

She stretched the ache buried between her shoulders, staring at row after row of apple trees. For just a heartbeat, Elena felt a twinge of suffocation—the "willies" her mother called it. In the past, many workers had whispered of the orchard's smothering touch. The trees consumed the entire high country, blanketing hundreds of thousands of acres, spreading from the distant peaks of the towering Teeth down to the lowlands of the plains. While the orchard wore many different seasonal faces—a spread of pink and white blossoms in the spring, an impenetrable green sea in summer, a skeletal tangle in winter—its very bulk had a constancy that ate the spirit, draining it.

Elena shivered. The branches blocked all the horizons around her. The entwining limbs overhead kept even the sun's touch from Elena's face. When she was younger, she had played among the rows of trees. Then the world had seemed huge, full of adventure and new discoveries. Now, nearing womanhood, Elena finally understood the whispered words of the other workers.

The orchard slowly choked you.

She raised her face. Here was her world. A trap of trees, leaves, and apples. She could find no break in the view. The cloying smell of decaying apples lay thick on the air. The odor crept into one's pores, marking each person like a dog with its scent, claiming you as its own. Elena spun around, drowning in the beauty of the orchard.

If only she had the wings of a bird, she would fly from here. Sail across the plains of Standi, wing over the I'nova swamps, fly among the humped islands of the Archipelago to the Great Ocean itself.

She turned in circles under the boughs of the trees, imagining far-away places.

"When you're done dancing, Sis," Joach called down to her, "you'd better get back to work."

His stern words clipped her wings and tumbled her from the clouds. She stared up at her older brother. His voice rang with echoes of her father. For a moment, Elena could even see her father in her brother's broadening shoulders and strong, sunburned face. When had that happened? Where was the boy who had run screaming with her in imaginary hunts through the orchards?

She stepped back toward her ladder. "Joach, don't you ever want to leave this place?"

"Sure," he said, continuing to pick. "I want my own farm. Maybe I'll stake out some land by the wild orchards near the Eyrie."

"No, I mean leave the valley—leave the orchards."

"Be a townie in Winterfell, like Aunt Fila?"

Elena sighed and mounted her ladder. The orchard had already swallowed her brother whole, his mind and spirit trapped in the tangle of branches. "No," she said, trying again, "I mean leaving the foothills, going to see other lands."

He stopped, a ripe apple in his hand, and turned to her, his eyes serious. "Why?"

Elena slipped the carrying strap across her forehead. "Never mind." Her basket now felt twice as heavy. Nobody understood her.

Suddenly laughter burst from her brother, drawing Elena's attention back.

"What?" she said, expecting ridicule.

"Elena, you're so easy to fool!" Joach's face split with a mischievous grin. "Of course I want to leave this boring valley! Who do you think I am, some doddering farmer? Sheesh, I'd leave here in a bloody second."

Elena grinned. So the orchard hadn't snatched her brother yet!

"Give me a sword and a horse, and I'd be long gone," he continued, his eyes wide with his own dreams.

They shared a smile across the row of trees.

Suddenly a ringing clang echoed across the field: *the dinner bell*.

"About time!" Joach said, leaping from his ladder to land gracefully on the ground. "I'm starving."

She grinned. "You're always starving."

"I'm growing."

Her brother's words were certainly true. Joach had spurted in size over this last season; his fourteenth birthday would come next week. Just a year older than she, he already stood a good head taller. She resisted the impulse to glance down at her chest. The other girls on neighboring farms were already sprouting in all directions, while she, if she took her shirt off, looked not unlike her brother. People had often mistaken them for brothers, even. They had the same red hair, tied in a ponytail in back, the same green eyes above high cheekbones, and the same sunburned complexion. While it was true she had more freckles, longer eyelashes, and a smaller nose, she was still almost as muscular as he. Working in the fields and orchards together since they were children had conditioned them similarly.

But the farm work they did amounted to no more than children's chores. Soon Joach would join the men in the harder labors and grow the chest and arms of a true man, even as he grew in height already. Eventually no one would mistake them for brothers—at least she hoped not. Unwittingly, she found herself staring at her chest and thinking fervently, *the sooner the better*.

"If you are done admiring those baby apples of yours," he teased, "let's get going."

She plucked a fruit and threw it at him. "Get out of here!" She meant to sound abrasive, but her laughter at the end ruined it. "At least I don't keep flexing in front of the mirror when no one's looking."

It was his turn to go red faced. "I wasn't . . . I mean, I didn't—"

"Go home, Joach."

"What about you?"

"My basket is far from full. I think I'd better work a little longer."

"I could pour some of my apples into your basket. Mine's over-flowing anyway. That way it'll look like we did the same amount of work."

Knowing her brother was trying to help her, she still felt a twinge of annoyance. "I can pick my own apples." Her words came out more acerbic than she had intended.

"Okay, I was only trying to help."

"Tell Mother I'll be back before sundown."

"You'd better be. You know she doesn't like us out after dark. The Cooliga family lost three sheep last week."

"I know. I heard. Now get going before they run out of mutton. I'll be fine."

She saw her brother hesitate for a heartbeat, but his hunger won out. With a wave, he headed away, marching between the rows of trees, back toward the house. Quickly swallowed up by the trees, even his scrunching footfalls faded to silence.

Elena climbed to the top of the ladder and pushed her way up to the more heavily laden branches. In the distance, she spied the multiple trails of chimney smoke rising from the town of Winter-fell, hidden deeper in the valley. Her eyes tracked the black, smudged columns until they faded to faint haze high above the valley, where winds blew the smoke toward the distant ocean. If only she could follow . . .

As she stared, her father's words returned to her, his voice gruff: *Your head's always in the clouds, Elena.*

Sighing, she tore her gaze from the sky and leaned her belly against the ladder for balance. This was her life. Using both hands, she grabbed apples and dropped them over her shoulder into her basket. Experienced fingers judged if the apples were ripe enough to pluck, pausing here, picking there, until all the mature apples from the local branches rested in her basket.

As she worked, her shoulders began to ache again, shooting complaints down her back. But she did not stop. Swatting at the flies that circled about her, she climbed up another rung to reach fresh branches, determined to fill her basket before sundown.

Soon the ache in her shoulders spread like a weed to her belly. She shifted her position on the ladder, thinking the rungs were bruising her midriff as she leaned. Suddenly a sharp cramp gripped her gut. She almost lost her balance, but a quick hand on the ladder stopped her plummet.

Eyes narrowed, she held on to the ladder, waiting for the pain to subside. It always did. For the past few days, she had been suffering from bouts of cramping. She had kept silent, attributing it to the number of blisterberries she had been consuming. The season was short, and the purplish berries had always been her favorite. Cramping or not, she couldn't resist their sweet nectar.

Breathing sharply between her clenched teeth, she rode out the pain. Within a few heartbeats, it faded back to a dull ache. Resting her forehead against her arm, she allowed herself a few deep breaths before continuing.

Glancing up, she spotted a sight that made her forget about her belly. The late evening sunlight pierced the canopy of leaves and blazed on a beauty of an apple, exceptionally large, almost the size of a small melon. Ah, how her mother prized these large, succulent apples for her pies. Even her father would be doubly pleased if she returned with her basket full and this trophy of an apple.

But could she reach it?

Stepping up another rung, one more than her father normally allowed them to climb, she strained an arm upward. Her fingertips brushed the bottom of the apple, setting it to swinging on its stalk.

Blast! If Joach were here, he could have reached it. But this was her prize. Pressing her lips together, she carefully eased herself up another rung. The ladder teetered beneath her. Hugging the trunk with one arm, she stretched the other toward the prize. Her hand inched toward the large fruit as her shoulder throbbed.

With a triumphant grin, she watched her hand slide into the sunlight outlining the apple. Or at least she intended to. As her hand slipped higher, it vanished as it struck the edge of the sunbeam. Thinking the sun-dazzle had momentarily blinded her, she did not immediately panic.

Instead, her stomach cramped viciously, her lower belly flaring with agony as if someone had dragged a rusty dagger through her innards. Gasping, she stumbled down a rung, clutching tree and ladder in a huge embrace.

A hot wetness seeped between her thighs as she hung there. Believing the pain had loosened her bladder, she glanced down in disgust. But what she saw there caused her to slip down the length of the ladder and land in a crumpled pile at its foot.

Rolling into a seated position, she again examined herself. Blood! Her gray pants were soaked in the crotch with seeping blood. Her first thought was that something had cut her up inside. Then it dawned on her, and a small smile played about her lips. Something she had heard about, had been hoping for, had finally happened: her first menstra.

She, Elena Morin'stal, had become a woman.

Stunned, she sat there and raised a hand to her forehead. Before she could touch her damp brow, her right hand drew her eyes.

It was swamped in blood, too!

A thick redness coated the entire surface of her hand like a ruby glove. What had happened? She knew she hadn't touched herself down there. Besides, she wasn't bleeding that much.

I must have cut myself on a ladder nail during the fall, or maybe on a sharp broken branch, she thought.

But there was no pain. Instead there was an almost pleasant coolness. She wiped her hand on her khaki shirt. Nothing wiped off. Her shirt was still clean. She wiped harder. Still nothing.

Her heart began to race, and stars danced across her vision as she started to panic. Her mother had never warned her of anything like this associated with a woman's first menstra. Maybe it was some sort of woman's secret, kept hidden from men and children. That had to be it! She forced her breathing to slow. It obviously didn't last. Her mother's hands were normal.

She took several cleansing breaths. It would be okay. Her mother would explain this nonsense. She stood up, and for the second time that day, righted her spilled basket and gathered her stray apples. The last apple she spotted was the giant trophy apple. She must have grabbed it before she fell. What luck! She touched her right earlobe in proper deference to the spirits for this boon. "Thank you, Sweet Mother," she murmured to the empty orchard. Here lay a good omen as she started her womanhood.

Bending over to retrieve her prize, she watched her bloodied hand close upon it and remembered the moment when her hand had vanished, disappearing in a blaze of sunlight. She crinkled her brow and dismissed the thought. It must have just been the light playing tricks on her tired eyes.

Her hand clamped on the apple. Mother would make a fine pie out of this. She pictured the warm apple and cinnamon oozing from a fresh slice of pie.

As she lifted her trophy, the apple quaked in her palm as if it were alive, then promptly withered and dried to a wrinkled, parched mass. Pulling her lips back in disgust, she dropped it. As the apple hit the ground, it flashed up in a flame bright enough to blind her eyes. Elena raised her arm across her face, but the light just as quickly vanished. She lowered her arm cautiously. All that was left of the apple was a tiny mound of ashes.

Holy Mother of Regalta!

As she backed away from the black pile, the dinner bell again clanked from across the orchard, startling her but also setting her in motion. Abandoning her basket, she fled across the orchard.

BY THE TIME ELENA REACHED HER FAMILY'S FARMYARD, ONLY THE last rays of the setting sun still glowed in the western sky. Shadows lay thick across the packed dirt between the horse barn and main house. Leaping over the irrigation ditch, she burst from the last row of trees.

A wagon loaded with day workers trundled toward her, heading for the town road. Raucous laughter carried across the yard. The mule driver, Horrel Fert, waved her out of the way. "Move it, lass," he called to her. "I've got a boot full of hungry men here needin' to git to their dinners."

"And our ale! Don't forget our ale!" someone called from the back of the wagon. His comment triggered another spate of laughter.

Elena hopped to the side of the yard. The train of four mules leaned into their harnesses and pulled the creaking wagon past her. She began to raise her right hand to wave to the departing workers, then lowered it, hiding it behind her back, suddenly ashamed of her stained hand. If the red color was a mark of budding womanhood, she suddenly felt awkward at declaring her change before the rowdy men. She even found her cheeks blushing at the thought.

As soon as the wagon lumbered past, Elena darted across the yard, but not before hearing one of the men declare to another, "That girl's an odd one. Always running about. Not right in the head, I wager."

Elena ignored the insult and continued toward the back door of her house. It wasn't anything she hadn't heard before. The children at school were even crueler with their tongues. Elena had always been a tall, gangling child, dressed in old homespun hand-me-downs from her brother. She endured being the butt of much joking, often crying herself home. Even her teachers thought her somewhat slow, believing her daydreams to be evidence of a dull mind. This judgment hurt, too, but over time, Elena's heart had grown thick-enough calluses.

Isolated, with only her brother and a few youngsters from neighboring farms for companionship, Elena had discovered the joys of exploring on her own. She had rooted out many wonderful places in the surrounding foothills: a rabbit warren where the does and bucks would feed freely from her hand; an anthill as high as her head; a lightning-struck tree that was hollow inside; a patch of mold-frosted headstones from a long-lost cemetery. She would

often return exhausted from a day of roaming, bramble scratched
and muddy, with a wide grin on her face.

Frowning now, Elena slowed her running as she neared the
back door.

As much as she enjoyed her explorations, she could not ignore
that lately a certain discontent had crept around her heart. She
found her eyes lingering on far horizons. Her hands itched for
something she could not name. It was as if a storm were building
up in her bones, waiting to burst free.

Elena climbed the back steps. As she reached toward the door
handle, her eyes caught the ruby glow of her stained palm in the
last rays of the sun. And now this! What did it mean? Her fingers
trembled as they hovered over the brass door handle. For the
first time, she sensed the true depth and breadth of the strangeness
that could lie beyond her orchard. She closed her eyes, suddenly
fearful.

Why would she ever want to leave her home? Safety was here,
and all those who loved her. Here were lands as comfortable as
worn flannel on a cold morning. Why seek more?

As she shivered on the doorstep, the door burst open before her,
startling her down a step. In the doorway, her father towered with
Joach's shoulder clutched in his large hand. Both the men's eyes
widened in surprise to find Elena on the stoop.

"See," Joach said sheepishly, "I told you she'd be right in."

"Elena," her father said, "you know you're not supposed to be
in the orchards alone after dark. You need to think—"

Elena flew into her father's arms.

"Honey?" he said as he closed her up in his thick arms. "What's
wrong?"

She buried her face into her father's chest, never wanting to
move from his arms. More than the thatched roof and warm
hearth, here was her home.

2

THE TWILIGHT GLOOM DEEPENED UNDER THE THICK BRANCHES OF
the orchard trees. Rockingham pulled his cloak tighter around his
shoulders and stamped his feet. The night always grew so cold in
this cursed alpine valley. He hated this assignment from his supe-
riors. Stuck in a backwater village of backwoods bumpkins—and
these frigid winters! Nothing like the sunny climate of his island
home . . .

As a cold breeze bit at his thin cloak, Rockingham pictured his
home in the Archipelago. The beaches, the moist heat, the sunsets
that took hours to dim over the ocean swells. As he remembered
the home he had left so long ago, a trace of memory whispered at
his ear: long blond hair and laughing eyes . . . and a name . . . a
woman's name. But who? He tried to grasp the memory firmer,
but it fluttered away like a frightened bird. What was he forgetting? Then, a frigid gust snatched at his riding cloak, its icy touch
distracting him from his reverie. Rockingham clutched the wind-
whipped material to his exposed neck.

Making noises of impatience in the back of his throat, he
watched the near-blind seer swirl a finger in a mound of cooling
ashes beside an overturned apple basket. The old man raised his
nose to the night breeze that swept between the rows of trunks,

for all the world like a hunting cur checking an invisible trail. He then raised the soiled finger to his crooked nose.

"She bleeds," the blind man said, sniffing at his finger, his voice like old sheets of ice breaking and grinding against one another.

"Of whom do you speak, Dismarum? Why did you force us from town?"

"The one the master seeks—she has come at long last."

Rockingham shook his head. Not this nonsense again! A whole night's rest disturbed for this old man's fantasy. "She's a myth!" he said, throwing an arm up in disgust. "For how many centuries has the Dark Lord tried to imbue a female with his powers and failed? During my tenure at Blackhall, I saw the result of the exalted one's effort: the misshapen creatures howling from the dungeons. It's impossible. A female cannot wield magick."

"Not impossible. She is here."

Rockingham kicked the basket nearby, scattering red fruit across the ground. "You said the same last year. We splayed that girl's entrails across the altar and found you were wrong."

"That is of no matter."

"Tell that to the townspeople of Winterfell. Her screaming almost set them to riot. If it wasn't for the battalion of dog soldiers, they would have driven us to the fields."

"Thousands can die, as long as we catch the right one." Dismarum clutched Rockingham's elbow with a bony claw. "I have been waiting for countless years. Old prophecies, whispered from the past, told me she would come to this valley. I came here a young man, when your great-grandfather was still an infant in swaddling . . . and I have waited."

Rockingham pulled his elbow free of the iron grip. "Are you sure this time? If you're wrong, I will personally relieve you of your tongue, so I don't have to listen to your lies anymore."

Leaning on a gnarled poi'wood staff, the blind seer turned his milky globes in Rockingham's direction. Rockingham jerked a step back. Those eyes seemed to penetrate to his spine.

"She is here," Dismarum hissed.

Rockingham cleared his throat. "Fine. I'll collect a squadron from the garrison in the morning and have her arrested."

The old man turned those ghostly eyes from him, his ancient fingers pulling the cowl of his cloak over his bald head. "It must be tonight."

"How? This girl's parents aren't about to let us drag her into the night. These farm folk are not as cowed as the rabble in the cities. They're still a damnably independent lot."

"The master has granted me your aid, Rockingham. I requested you. You will be enough."

"Me? Are you telling me that you're the reason I was yanked from Blackhall and assigned to this blighted valley?"

"I needed someone like you, prepared by the master."

"What are you babbling about?" the soldier demanded.

Instead of answering, the old man whipped out a long dagger, flashing silver in the moonlight, and stabbed it into Rockingham's lower belly, just above the groin. Stunned, the younger man fell back, but not in time to stop the seer from slicing clean up his belly, splitting him like a fish.

Stumbling to his knees with a moan, Rockingham clutched his slit belly, trying to dam in the loops of his intestine. "Wh-wh-what have you done?"

With one hand still holding the bloody dagger, Dismarum pointed with his other limb, an arm that ended in a blunt stump. "Go, my children. Seek her out. Be my eyes. Be my ears. Destroy those that stand in our way!"

Weakening, Rockingham fell to one hand, his other arm clutched around his belly. Something writhed in his gut, like coals stirred in a fire. His agony flared. He fell to his side with a squeaking cry, giving up his grip.

As darkness began to blot out his vision, he saw them leave his belly, thousands of them: white wormlike grubs. As they poured and rolled into the night air, they seemed to swell and stretch until each was an arm's length long and as thick around as his thumb.

They squirmed in a fetid mass over and around him, some burrowing into the soil and disappearing away. Blackness swallowed the sight from him as he died.

Only the old man's words followed him into oblivion. "Seek her out, little ones. She will be mine."

3

ELENA SIGHED AS SHE SANK INTO THE HOT BATH, STEAM RISING TO THE raftered ceiling, the scent of berries pungent in her nose from the crushed leaves Mother had added to the tub.

"The hot water will cleanse you, and the herbs will ease your cramping," her mother assured her as she poured another hot pitcher into the tub. "But you must stay here until the water begins to cool."

"I'm not going anywhere," Elena answered. She rolled back and forth in the hot water, letting sore muscles stretch and relax. The strangeness of the day's events had faded, bled away by a meal of roasted duck accompanied by the dry mumblings between her parents across the dinner table on the best place to barter for a new bull. The revelation of her first menstra had drawn far more attention from her family than her stained hand. It all now seemed like a bad dream.

"Tomorrow I'll send Joach to announce the party," her mother said, her eyes adrift with plans. "I'll have your Aunt Fila arrange for the cake and send your father out for more cider. Do we have enough chairs? Maybe I'd better take the wagon to the Sontaks' and borrow some of theirs. And then I should make sure—"

"Mother, I don't need a party," Elena said, but secretly she was thrilled. Everyone would know she had become a woman. Smiling, she slid down under the waters, then resurfaced, wiping water from her eyes.

"Pish, we must have a party. You're my only little girl." A certain sadness crept into her mother's eyes. Elena remained silent. She knew her mother was remembering the stillborn girl birthed two years after Elena. Since then her mother had been unable to get pregnant. Now streaks of gray coursed through her auburn hair, and many wrinkles were etched where her skin was once smooth. For the first time, Elena realized that her mother was getting old. She would have no other children besides Elena and Joach.

Her mother ran long fingers through her graying tresses and gave a soft sigh. Her eyes focused back to the present and on Elena's right hand. "Now, Elena, you're sure you didn't fool with any of Grandma Filbura's paints?" She picked up Elena's ruby-coated hand in her own and turned it back and forth. "Or maybe accidentally splash some rugger's dye from the workshed on it? You know I don't like you kids playing in there."

"No, Mother," she said, pushing higher in the tub. "I swear. It just suddenly turned red."

"Maybe some prank of Joach's."

"I don't think so." Elena knew Joach well. The shock on her brother's face when he had first seen her stained hand had been genuine.

"Then maybe one of the neighbor's kids. Those Wak'lens are always brewing mischief."

Elena slipped her hand free of her mother's and picked up the horsehair-bristled brush. "So this isn't some women's mystery?" she said, scrubbing at her palm. "Something secret to do with becoming an adult?"

Her mother smiled at her. "No, my dear, it's just some prank."

"Not a very funny one." She continued scrubbing, but the bloody stain remained.

"They seldom are." Her mother brushed Elena's cheek with

her palm, but her gaze remained on Elena's hand, small wrinkles of worry whispering around her lips. "I'm sure it will fade. Don't fret about it."

"I hope it's gone by the party."

"If not, honey, you could wear my dressy gloves."

Elena brightened. "I could?" She stopped grinding the brush across her flesh; her skin was beginning to burn. Maybe she'd just leave it be. She had always fancied wearing her mother's long satin gloves. They would look spectacular with her party dress!

"Just finish cleaning before the water cools. We'll talk more about the party later." Her mother stood and straightened her robe. "It's getting late. Make sure you drain and rinse the tub before you go to sleep."

"Yes, Mother," she said with an exasperated sigh. She wasn't a child anymore.

Her mother kissed her on the top of her head. "Good night, sweetie. I'll see you in the morning."

Slipping from the bathing chamber, her mother closed the door on the animated ruckus coming from the main room. Joach was still getting a tongue-lashing from Father for leaving his sister in the orchard alone. Elena could imagine Joach's expression—dutifully subdued. She knew her father's harsh words breezed past Joach with hardly a sting.

She smiled. With the thick oaken door shut, all she heard was a low murmur. She leaned deeper into the steaming water, content, her worry about the burning apple just a distant throb. It had to have been some sort of trick. Suddenly she was glad she had failed to mention the apple. It seemed so silly now that she was home, just some silly prank.

Still . . .

She held her hand up in the lamplight. The light seemed to absorb into her hand, and the color appeared to swirl in whorls across her skin. She remembered how she had been thinking about warm apple pie when the apple had suddenly heated up and dried to a wrinkled crisp.

It seemed almost magickal.

She waved her hand across the steamy air, pretending to cast spells and perform evil magick.

Grinning at her whimsy, she imagined herself one of the ancient darkmages from those old stories told around campfires, stories of times before Lord Gul'gotha came across the Eastern Sea to rescue her people from chaos.

The mythical stories of the wild magick were whispered at night and sung in songs: of the silver-haired elv'in people and the giants of the highland; of A'loa Glen, the thousand-spired citadel of black magick sunk under the seas ages ago; of the og'res of the Western Reaches, who spoke like humans but burned with hatred for humankind; of the mer-creatures that swam among the Blasted Shoals far to the east. Elena could recount hundreds of such stories told to her as she grew up.

In her head, Elena knew it was all wives' tales and pure invention, but her heart still thrilled at the old stories. She remembered sitting in her father's lap, her tiny fists clutched to her throat, as her Uncle Bol recounted "The Battle for the Valley of the Moon." He had prefaced the story by telling her in hushed tones that this very valley was where the battle had taken place. "And the town of Winterfell was only a small crossroads," he said in a furtive whisper, "with a shabby stable and a drafty inn." She had laughed at such a thought. Only a small child at the time of the telling, not even yet allowed in the fields, she had swallowed every word from her uncle as if it were true. She smiled now at her foolishness. How the adults must have laughed at her gullibility.

Well, she was no longer a child.

She lowered her hand back to the water and blushed. She knew she was too old to be fantasizing about such follies. She was a woman today. These stories were all fantasy. Magick was not real. It was all the mummery of carnival tricksters and scoundrels.

In school, she had been taught her land's true history. How, five centuries ago, the Gul'gotha had crossed the sea and brought civilization to her land and people. How they had brought reason and logic to destroy her ancestors' pagan rites. How her people had once practiced human sacrifice and worshipped invisible spirits. Then the king of Blackhall, the Lord Gul'gotha, had come. A tumultuous time followed as his lieutenants offered peace and knowledge to her barbarous ancestors. Blood was shed as the hand of peace was offered. But eventually truth and wisdom prevailed, and the trickster mages were destroyed. An age of logic and science began, wiping out myth and barbarism.

Frowning, Elena rubbed the barley soap through her hair, tired of pondering dry lessons from school. She had more important things to consider. What should she wear to the party? Should she wear her hair up like an older woman?

She pushed the sudsy locks atop her head. She hated it that way, preferring to let it flow free, but she was entering womanhood, and it was coming time to stop acting like a little girl. With soap trailing down her neck, she let her hair drape to her shoulders.

And what about Tol'el Manchin, the blacksmith's handsome apprentice? She pictured his curly black hair and ruddy complexion—and his arms! The months of working the forge's bellows had grown muscles that the other boys were jealous of. Would he come to the party? Surely he would, wouldn't he? Elena felt her heart begin to beat faster. She would ask her mother to let her wear her grandmother's shell necklace. It would be grand with her green dress.

Elena glanced down at her wet torso. Only the barest hint of developing womanhood interrupted the rivulets of bathwater draining across her chest. There wasn't much there to attract the eye of Tol'el. Others in her class were already murmuring about underclothes and the tenderness of blossoming growth. Elena reached to her chest and pressed firmly. Nothing. Not even a hint of the ache the other girls whispered about.

Maybe it would be best if Tol'el didn't show up for the party, maybe even best if the party was canceled. Who was going to believe she was a woman?

Elena suddenly shivered as a stray draft blew across her

exposed back. The bathwater was quickly losing its heat. Elena sank to her shoulders, the tepid water still warmer than the chilly bathing chamber. Why couldn't the bathwater stay hot a bit longer? A twinge of ire flashed through her. Couldn't she at least have a few more moments of steamy bliss? She sank deeper into the cooling water.

As she lay there, she pictured herself soaking in the hot springs of Col'toka. She had read about them in a school text: volcanic springs deep in the snowy Teeth. As she dreamed about their mineral-rich waters, her own soapy tub seemed to warm with her thoughts. She sighed, a smile playing about her lips. This was nice.

As she continued to recline in the bath, picturing in her mind the steam-choked chambers of Col'toka, her bathwater continued to warm, soothing at first, then becoming surprisingly hot! Elena's eyes fluttered open.

Her skin began to redden from the heat. She sprang to her feet in the water. Bubbles started to rise along the edge of the tub. Her lower legs and feet began to scald. Elena leaped from the tub just as the water began to roil with steam and bubbles.

As Elena backed away, the water erupted over the edge of the tub, hissing as it splashed to the oaken floor. The room swelled with choking steam. Elena's naked bottom bumped into the bathing chamber's cold door, startling her to action. She fumbled for the handle. What was happening?

Swinging the door open, she stood in the doorway, a call to her mother frozen on her lips. At that moment, the remaining water blew from the tub in a final explosion of steam. Elena was thrown forward by a wall of superheated air and flung naked into the next room.

She landed on a rug and slid across the floor, the loose rug bunching up under her. As she came to rest, she noticed she was not alone in the room. Her father had sprung from the couch where he had been enjoying his evening smoke. Her brother sat frozen in a chair by the fire, his mouth hanging open.

As she sat up, her father's pipe dropped from his slack lips and clattered to the floor. "Elena, girl, what . . . what did you do?" he asked.

"I didn't do anything! The water just kept getting hotter and hotter." Elena began to feel the sting of her scalded skin, and tears welled up in her eyes.

Joach stood up and stomped out the burning tobacco that had spilled from his father's pipe before it scorched the rug. He seemed to concentrate fully on his chore, his cheeks blushing slightly. "Elena, don't you think you'd better grab a towel?"

Elena glanced at her naked form, and now a sob of embarrassment escaped her throat.

Just then her mother clattered down the stairs in only her nightgown, her robe clutched in one hand. "What happened? I never heard such a noise!" Her eyes settled on Elena's crumpled form and grew wide. She hurried over to her daughter. "You're red as a boiled potato. We need to get some salve on those burns."

Elena allowed herself to be bundled up in her mother's robe. But even its soft cotton was like coarse burlap against her tender skin. Wincing, she pushed to her feet.

Her father and Joach had stepped to the bathing chamber entrance. "The tub is cracked," her father said, his voice thick with shock. "And the wax on the floor has bubbled up from the planking. It looks like someone tried to set the place on fire." He turned questioning eyes toward Elena.

"Whoa," Joach said, shaking his head, his eyes wide. "You did some damage, Sis!"

"Hush, Joach!" Her father turned to face her fully. "What happened here?"

Her mother put a protective arm around Elena. "Now, Bruxton, I won't have you pointing fingers. She's hurt. And besides, how could she do such a thing? Do you see any wood ash or smell coal oil?"

Her father grumbled under his breath.

"Elena is already shook up enough. Leave her be. We'll solve this in the morning. Right now she needs medicine."

Elena leaned into her mother's arms. What truly had happened?

How could one explain a tub of water suddenly trying to boil you alive? Elena had no real answer, but in her stomach, she knew somehow she was to blame. She remembered the burning apple, and her head began to ache. The whole day had been one mystery after another.

Her mother gently hugged her. "Let's go upstairs and treat those burns."

She nodded, but already the worst of the stinging was beginning to fade. Glancing down at her palms, she noticed that the stain on her right hand had faded from a deep purplish red to a ruby color that hardly stood out from her singed arms. At least the scalding had boiled away a fraction of the dye—a small blessing considering her sore skin and the ruined bathing chamber.

"SO WHAT REALLY HAPPENED?" JOACH WHISPERED. HE SAT CROSS-legged AT the foot of Elena's bed. He had snuck into her room after her mother had finished smearing her arms and back with medicinal balm.

Clutching her pillow in her lap, Elena sat with her knees almost touching her brother's. "I'm not sure," she said, keeping her voice quiet in the dark room. Neither of them wanted to attract their parents' attention. Elena could occasionally hear her father's rough voice echo up from below. She cringed with each of his outbursts, shame burning her cheeks. They were not a rich family, and it would cost much to repair the ruined bathing chamber.

Suddenly, her mother's voice carried up to them. "They said she might be the one! I must tell them!"

Her father's voice rose higher. "*Woman,* you'll do no such thing! That side of your family is daft! Fila and Bol—"

Joach nudged her with his knee. "I've never heard them so mad."

"What do you think they're talking about?" Elena strained to listen, but her parents' words had lowered back to a murmur.

Joach shrugged. "I don't know."

Elena felt tears beginning to well in her eyes. She was thankful for the darkness that hid them.

"I'm surprised that cracking the tub got them so upset," Joach said. "Heck, I've done worse than that. Remember when I fed Tracker that basket of hazelnuts Mother was going to use in Father's birthday cake?"

Elena couldn't stop a smile from coming to her lips. She wiped at her eyes. Tracker, their stallion, had suffered from diarrhea all night, and their father had spent his entire birthday shoveling the barn clean and walking the horse to keep it from getting colic.

"And the time I told the Wak'len kids that you could touch the moon if you jumped from the top branches of a tree." He snickered in the dark.

Elena punched his knee. "Sam'bi broke his arm!"

"He deserved it. No one pushes my little sister in the mud."

Elena suddenly remembered that day two years ago. She had been wearing the flowered dress Aunt Fila had given her for the midsummer celebration. The mud had ruined it. "You did that for me?" she asked, her voice a mix of shock and laughter.

"What are big brothers for?"

Elena again felt tears beginning to threaten.

Joach slid from the bed, then leaned over and hugged her. "Don't worry, El. Whoever is playing these pranks on you, I'll find out. No one messes with my little sister."

She hugged Joach back. "Thanks," she whispered in his ear.

Straightening up, Joach slunk to the door. He turned to her just before slipping from her room. "Besides, I can't let this mysterious prankster get the better of me! I've a reputation to uphold!"

4

DISMARUM KNELT IN THE DAMP WEEDS IN THE MOONLIT ORCHARD, A cowled figure, crooked as a rotten stump. Not a single bird called this night; not an insect whirred. Dismarum listened, both with his ears and with his inner senses. The last of the mol'grati had snaked into the soil, worming their way toward the distant homestead. The ragged-edged wound in dead Rockingham's belly had long stopped steaming into the night as the carcass chilled.

Pressing his forehead against the cold dirt, Dismarum sent his thoughts to his creatures. He received their answer back like the singing of a thousand children's voices, a chorus with one message: hunger.

Patience, my little ones, he sent to them. *Soon you shall feast.*

Satisfied with their progress, Dismarum stood up and stumbled over to Rockingham, feeling with his one good hand, seeking his dead guide, his weak eyes of little use in the dark. His fingers settled on Rockingham's frozen face. Squatting beside the dead man, Dismarum unsheathed his knife. He tucked the hilt in the crook of his stumped arm, then pricked a finger with the dagger's blade. Ignoring the twinge from his sliced finger, he sheathed his dagger and turned to Rockingham. Using his bloodied finger, he painted

Rockingham's lips with blood, like an undertaker preparing a corpse for viewing.

Once done, Dismarum leaned over and kissed Rockingham's bloody lips, tasting salt and iron. He exhaled between the cold, parted lips, huffing out Rockingham's cheeks, then slipped his lips to the dead man's ear. "Master, I beg you hear my call," he whispered into the cold ear.

Dismarum leaned back, waiting, listening. Then it came: The air grew frigid around him; he sensed a malignant, icy presence. A noise like a wind rushing through dried branches escaped the dead lips. Then words trickled up from Rockingham's black throat.

"She is here?"

"Yes," Dismarum answered, his eyes closed.

"Speak." The word echoed, as if from a dank well.

"She has ripened, bloodied with power. I smell it."

"Get to her! Bind her!"

"Of course, my lord. I have already sent the mol'grati."

"I will send one of the skal'tum to aid you."

Dismarum shivered. "That won't be necessary. I can—"

"It is already on its way. Prepare her for it."

"As you command, Master," Dismarum said, but he could already sense the receding presence. The wintry orchard seemed sultry in the wake of its passing. Still, Dismarum pulled his cloak snugly around his shoulders. It was time to go. The mol'grati should already be in position.

Dismarum lowered his hand to Rockingham's belly, his palm sinking into the gelatinous wound, clotted blood slipping between his fingers. He sneered, revealing the four teeth still rotting in his black gums.

Kneeling beside the carcass, he grabbed handfuls of dirt and hurriedly stuffed them in Rockingham's wound. After adding thirteen handfuls, Dismarum used his good hand and the stump of his one arm to pull the edges of Rockingham's wound together.

Holding the clammy edges, he whispered the words taught

him by his dread master. An ache developed in his own belly as he
recited the words. The last words were spoken in a push of agony,
as if he were giving birth. He squinted at the almost unbearable
pain as the last syllable stumbled from his tongue. His old heart
hammered in his breast. Mercifully, though, the agony subsided
with the last word.

Leaning back, Dismarum ran a hand over Rockingham's
wound. The edges were now sealed together, healed. He placed a
finger on his dead guide's forehead and spoke a single word.
"Rise!"

The carcass jerked under his finger, spasmed almost a handspan above the cold dirt, then settled to the ground. Dismarum listened as a single ragged breath escaped Rockingham's cold lips.
After several heartbeats, a second rasping gurgled out, then a
third.

Dismarum pushed to his feet, struggling up with his staff
gripped tight in a single fist. A cow lowed mournfully from a
nearby field. He stood silently as Rockingham struggled, gasping
and choking, back to this world.

After several racking coughs, Rockingham pushed to a seated
position. He raised a tremulous hand to his belly and pulled his
ripped shirt over his exposed midriff. "Wh-what happened?"

"Another fainting spell," Dismarum answered, his attention
aimed toward the distant dark homestead.

Rockingham closed his eyes and rubbed at his forehead. "Not
again," he mumbled as he rolled to his knees, then slowly to his
feet. He pawed at the trunk of a tree to steady himself. "How long
have I been out?"

"Long enough. The trail grows cold." Dismarum pointed a finger toward the farmhouse. "Come." The old seer began walking,
thumping his staff with each footfall. Exhaustion from the use of
his master's black art made his limbs as weak as a hatchling's. He
noticed that Rockingham remained standing by his tree trunk.

"The night grows thin, old man," Rockingham called to his
back. "Maybe we should return to town and come back for the

wench in the morning. Or at least let us ride—the horses are near enough—"

Dismarum turned his cowled face toward Rockingham. "Now!" he said with a hiss. "With daybreak, we must have her shorn and trussed. The master left explicit instructions. She must be bound while the moon still glows."

"So you say." Rockingham shoved off the tree like a boat leaving a safe harbor. He stumbled toward the seer as Dismarum turned to follow the trail of the mol'grati. Rockingham continued to blather. "You've been reading too many scribblings of madmen. Wit'ches are from stories to frighten children. All we'll find at this farm is a frightened farmgirl, her hands thick with calluses from working the plows. I'm losing a night's slumber in this mad pursuit."

Dismarum stopped and rested on his staff. "You'll lose more than slumber if she slips our net tonight. You've seen in the master's dungeons how he rewards failure."

The seer allowed himself a moment of satisfaction as Rockingham shuddered at his words. Dismarum knew that Rockingham had toured the nether regions of Blackhall and seen the twisted remains of those who once walked under the sun. His talkative guide now followed silently as Dismarum led the way.

The seer appreciated the silence. He could have left the feeble man stiffening in the cold orchard, but besides harboring the mol'grati, Rockingham still had many other uses. Back at Blackhall, the master had splayed Rockingham open upon his blood altar and imbued him with the darkest of his arts. Dismarum still remembered the man's screaming that midnight, how he bled from his eyes in pain, how his very back broke as he writhed on the bloody stone. Afterward, the master had put him back together again, piece by piece, then wiped the fool's memory of the long night. Forged into a tool of the master, Rockingham had been granted to Dismarum to aid in his vigil of the valley.

Dismarum glanced sidelong at Rockingham. He recalled one particularly odious rite, made at the stroke of midnight during

Rockingham's forging, requiring the slaughter of a newborn babe. The infant's innocent blood bathed both the altar and Rockingham's exposed, beating heart. He remembered the tool imbued into Rockingham at that moment—something so dark that even the thought of it now sent a shiver through the milky-eyed seer.

Somewhere over the hills, a dog howled into the night, as if catching a brief scent of the thing hiding inside Rockingham.

Oh, yes, there was much more that Rockingham would yet do.

5

ELENA COULD NOT SLEEP. HER BURNS CHAFED WITH EVERY SLIGHT movement. Her mind still swam with the frightening events that had occurred in the bathing chamber. As much as she would like to believe herself blameless in the destruction of the room, in her heart she knew better. This concern, too, kept her eyes open, far from slumber.

What had happened?

Her mother's words kept running through her head. *She might be the one.* There had been fear, rather than pride, in her mother's voice.

Elena slipped her hand for the hundredth time from under her blanket and held it up. In the dim light, the stain on her right palm appeared darker. The salve her mother had slathered over her arms glistened in the weak moonlight sifting through her bedroom's curtains. The sweet scent of wit'ch hazel drifted strong from the balm. Wit'ch hazel. The very air she breathed spoke her fears.

Wit'ch.

Her Uncle Bol, always a storehouse of old stories and tales, had kept her and her brother shivering in their bedrolls when out on hunting trips, tantalizing them with stories of wit'ches, og'res, and the faerie folk—creatures of both light and dark, fantasy and folklore. She remembered the serious set to Uncle Bol's lips and his intense eyes, highlighted in the cooking fire's glow, as he spoke his tales. He seemed to believe what he was telling and never winked slyly or raised his eyebrows in exaggeration. It was the earnest way he spoke, his voice low and rumbling, that was the most disquieting aspect of his stories.

"This is the true story of our land," he would say, "a land once called Alasea. There was a time when the air, land, and sea spoke to men. Beasts of the field were the equals of those who walked on two legs. The forests to the distant west—what were even then called the Western Reaches—gave birth both to creatures so foul as to turn you to stone dare you see them, and to creatures so wondrous you would fall to your knees just to touch them. This was the land of Alasea, your land. Remember what I tell you. It may save your life."

And then he would talk late into the night.

Elena struggled to conjure up some of Uncle Bol's humorous stories to ease her worries, but her troubled mind kept dredging up darker tales—stories with wit'ches.

Elena rolled to her side in her tiny bed, the soft cotton ticking scratching at her legs. She pulled her pillow over her head, trying to block out the old stories and new fears, but it didn't help. She still heard the hooting of a barn owl from the rafters of the nearby horse barn. She threw her pillow back from her face, clutching it to her chest.

The barn owl repeated his protest, and a heartbeat later, the flutter of heavy wings could be heard flapping past her window as the owl began its nightly foraging. Nicknamed Pintail, the owl earned its lodging by keeping mice and rats out of the grain bins. Nearly as old as she, Pintail had roosted in the barn's rafters for as long as Elena could remember and began his hunt at the same hour every evening.

Though the bird still hunted, age had dulled the poor creature's vision. Worried about the bird's well-being, Elena had been sneaking scraps out to the old owl for nearly a year.

Elena listened as Pintail flapped past her window, finding some small solace in this familiar ritual. She let out a rattling sigh, releasing the tension from her body. This was her home; here she was surrounded by a family that loved her. In the morning, the sun would shine, and like Pintail's, her own daily routine would begin again. All these wild happenings would fade away or be explained. She closed her eyes, knowing now that sleep was possible this evening.

Just as she started to drift off, Pintail began screaming.

Elena bolted up in her bed. Pintail continued to scream. Not a hunting challenge or a territorial warning, this was a wail of agony and fear. Elena flew to her window, pulling the curtains wide. A fox or bobcat might have caught the bird. She clutched her throat with worry as she scanned the farmyard below.

The horse barn stood just across the yard. She heard the mare and stallion's concerned nickering. They, too, knew this owl's screeching was cause for alertness. The yard below was empty. Just a wheelbarrow and a stone-chipped plow her father was repairing stood on the packed dirt.

Elena pushed open her window. Cold air swirled her night-clothes, but she hardly noticed as she leaned out. She squinted and tried to pick out movement in the shadows. There was nothing.

No! She took a step away from the window. Just at the edge of the empty pen that housed the sheep during shearing season, a shadow moved. A figure—no, two figures—stepped from the darkness under the branches of the orchard trees into the feeble moonlight that limned the yard. A cowled man with a crooked staff and a thin man who stood a head taller than his bent companion. Somehow she knew they weren't lost travelers but something darker, threatening.

Suddenly Pintail flew screeching into the empty yard, just a handspan above the head of the taller man. The man ducked slightly, raising an arm in alarm. Pintail ignored him and swooped across the open space, banking sharply as he struggled with something caught in his claws. Elena felt a moment of relief that Pintail was all right.

Then the owl twisted in midair, flailing, and tumbled toward the ground. Elena gasped, but before the bird hit the hard dirt, Pintail spread his wings and halted his fall, sailing upward again—right toward her! Elena stumbled a few steps back from the window as the bird swooped to the windowsill and landed hard, his beak open in a scream of rage.

Elena thought at first that the owl had caught a snake, but she had never seen a snake so sickly white before, like the belly of a dead fish. It writhed within the grip of the bird. Pintail was obviously struggling fiercely to restrain the creature, and from the bird's screeching, the fight was obviously causing the bird harm. Why doesn't Pintail just drop the foul thing? she thought. Why keep carrying it?

Then Elena knew. She saw the snake thing worm itself deeper into the owl's chest. Pintail wasn't carrying the thing; he was trying to dislodge it. Pintail's frantic claws were trying to stop it from burrowing deeper inside him. Pintail rolled a huge yellow eye toward her, as if asking for help.

Elena rushed forward. Pintail teetered on the sill, trying to balance with one claw, struggling with the loathsome creature. Just as her hand reached out to her friend, it became too late. The snake broke free of Pintail's claws and drove the rest of the way inside the bird. The owl froze, its beak stretched open in agony, and fell backward, dead, out the window.

"No!" Elena lunged to the window, leaning on the sill, searching for Pintail. Below, she spotted his broken body collapsed on the packed dirt of the yard. Tears rolled down her face. "Pintail!"

Suddenly the ground beneath his body churned like quicksand. Elena screamed as hundreds of the monstrous snake creatures writhed in a mass up from the dirt and swallowed the bird. Within two heartbeats, all that was left was a scattering of thin white bones and a skull whose empty eye sockets stared back at her. Her knees weakened as the worms disappeared back into the soil. Somehow she knew they were lying in wait, still hiding and hunting for more meat.

With tears in her eyes, she again spied the two travelers on the far side of the yard. The cowled one, using his staff as a crutch, began to hobble across the treacherous yard, apparently feeling no threat from the foul beasts that lurked beneath the dirt. Then he stopped and raised his face toward Elena's window. Shivering, she bolted from the opening, suddenly fearful of those eyes settling upon her. The fine hairs on the back of her neck tingled, sensing danger.

She must warn her parents!

Elena ran to her bedroom door and threw it open.

Her brother was already in the hall. Joach rubbed at his bleary eyes, dressed in only his underclothes. He pointed toward the farmyard. "Did you hear that darned screeching?"

"I must tell Father!" She grabbed her older brother's arm and dragged him toward the stairs leading back to the first floor.

"Why?" he said in protest. "I'm sure they heard it, too. It's just ol' Pintail tangling with a fox. He's tough enough for ten foxes. He'll be fine."

"No, he's dead."

"What! How?"

"Something bad! I . . . I don't know."

Elena continued to pull Joach with her down the stairs, afraid to let go of her brother, needing his touch to help control the screaming in her chest. She rushed down the stairs and through the den toward her parents' room. The house was dark and hushed, the air heavy, as before a summer storm. Panic welled in Elena, her heart thumping loudly in her ears. She pushed Joach toward the table. "Light a lantern! Hurry!"

He ran to the tinderbox and obeyed her order.

She flew to her parents' bedroom door. Normally she would knock before entering, but now was not the time for manners. She burst into the room just as Joach ignited the oiled wick. Light flared, casting her shadow across her parents' bed.

Her mother, always a light sleeper, awoke immediately, her eyes wide and startled. "Elena! My dear, what's wrong?"

Her father pushed up on one elbow, squinting groggily in the lantern's light. He cleared his throat, a look of irritation on his face.

Elena pointed toward the back door. "Someone's coming. I saw them in the yard."

Her father sat straighter in the bed. "Who?"

Her mother laid a hand on her father's arm. "Now, Bruxton, don't think the worst. It might be someone lost or needing help."

Elena shook her head. "No, no, they mean us harm."

"How do you know that, girl?" her father said, throwing back the sheets. Dressed in only his winter woolens, he clambered from the bed.

Joach stepped to the doorway, a lantern in his hand. "She says Pintail's dead."

Tears welled up in Elena's eyes. "There's some sort of . . . creatures. Horrible things."

"Now, Elena," her father said sternly, "are you sure you didn't just dream—?"

Suddenly a pounding erupted from the back door.

Everyone froze for a heartbeat, then her mother spoke. "Bruxton?"

"Don't worry, Mama," her father said to her mother. "I'm sure it's just like you said, someone lost." But her father's light words did not match his lowering brows. He pulled hurriedly into his pants.

Her mother slipped from the bed and into her robe. She crossed the room and circled Elena in an arm. "Your father will take care of this."

Joach followed her father with the lantern as he crossed the den. Elena, trailing from a safe distance with her mother, noticed her father pick up the hand ax they used to shave logs into kindling for the fire. Elena leaned closer to her mother.

Her father passed through the kitchen and approached the back door with Joach beside him. Elena and her mother stayed by the kitchen hearth.

Her father hefted the ax in one hand, then yelled through the thick oaken door, "Who is it?"

The voice that answered was high and commanding. Somehow

Elena knew it was not the cowled one who spoke, but the other man, the taller figure. "By order of the Gul'gothal Council, we demand access to this house. To refuse will result in the arrest of the entire household."

"What do you want?"

The same voice came again. "We have orders to search the farmstead. Unbar the door!"

Her father turned a worried look to her mother. Elena shook her head, trying to warn her father.

He turned back to the door. "The hour is late. How do I know you're who you claim to be?"

A sheet of paper was shoved under the door at her father's bare feet. "I bear the proctor's seal from the county's garrison." Her father signaled for Joach to pick it up and hold it in the lamplight. From across the room, Elena saw the purple seal on the bottom of the parchment.

Her father turned and whispered toward them. "It looks official. Joach, leave the lantern and take Elena upstairs. Both of you stay quiet."

Joach nodded, obviously nervous and wanting to stay. But as always he did as his father directed. He placed the lantern on the edge of the table and crossed to Elena. Her mother gave her a final squeeze, then pushed her toward her brother. "Watch after your sister, Joach. And don't come down until we call you."

"Yes, ma'am."

Elena hesitated. The flickering lantern light skittered shadows across the wall. It was not the speaker that gave her pause, but the other, the cowled man who had yet to speak. She did not have words for the cold sickness around her heart as she remembered the face that had tried to spy her in the window. So instead she stepped back to her mother and gave her a longer hug.

Her mother patted her hair, then pushed her back. "Hurry, sweetheart. This doesn't concern you. Now you and Joach scoot upstairs." Her mother attempted a reassuring smile, but the fear in her eyes destroyed the effort.

Elena nodded and backed to her brother, her eyes still on her parents in the kitchen.

Joach spoke behind her. "C'mon, Sis." He placed a hand on her shoulder.

She shivered at his touch but allowed herself to be led away. They backed across the den to the shadowed foot of the stairs. The lantern in the kitchen, like a lonely beacon across the dark house, highlighted her parents. From the stairway, Elena watched her father turn away and begin to lift the rusted iron rod that barred the door against brigands. But Elena knew that what stood outside the door was much worse than thieves.

It was this fear that kept her bolted to the foot of the stairs. Joach tugged at her arm and tried to coax her up. "Elena, we have to go."

"No," she whispered. "They can't see us here in the shadows."

Joach didn't argue, obviously wanting to watch, too. He knelt beside his sister on the first step. "What do you think they want?" he whispered at her ear.

"Me," she answered, also in a whisper, without even thinking. Elena seemed to know this was true. All of it was somehow her fault: the change in her hand, the burned apple in the orchard, the exploded bathing chamber, and now this midnight visitation. There were too many strange happenings to be mere coincidence.

"Look," Joach whispered.

Elena focused back to where her father swung the kitchen door open. He continued to block the threshold, the ax still in his hand. She heard their voices.

Her father spoke first. "Now, what is all this commotion?"

The thin man stepped to the doorway, now highlighted in the lantern. He stood just a few fingers shorter than her father, but not as broad in the chest, and he had a small paunch of belly protruding from a torn ruffled shirt. He wore a riding cloak and black muddied boots. Even from across the house, Elena could tell the cloak was from an expensive clothier, not something purchased in the village. He rubbed at a thin brown mustache under his narrow nose, then answered her father. "We've come concerning an offense. One of your daughters has been accused of a . . . um, a foul deed."

"And what offense might that be?"

The speaker glanced over his shoulder and shifted his feet, as if needing assistance. The second figure now approached the doorway. Elena saw her father stumble back a step. The lantern light revealed a figure cloaked in a coal black robe topped by a dark cowl. A staff was planted in the dirt beside him. Using a skeletal hand, the occupant of the robe kept the edge of the cowl pulled between his face and the lantern light, as if the brightness stung. His voice creaked with age. "We seek a child—" He held up his bony hand. "—with a bloodstained hand."

Her mother let out a sharp gasp that was quickly stifled, but the old man's face twisted toward her, the lantern light now shining into the cowl. Elena suppressed a gasp herself as those eyes turned toward her mother—they were dead eyes, like the dull globes of stillborn calves, opaque and white.

"We don't know what you're talking about," her father said.

The cowled one collected up his staff and retreated to the dark yard.

The younger man spoke. "Let us not disturb your entire family. Come out here where we can talk in private, perhaps settle this matter without a fuss." He bowed slightly and extended a hand toward the farmyard. "Come, it's late and we could all use sleep."

Elena watched her father take a step toward the door and knew what awaited her father in the yard. She remembered Pintail's body being torn by the beasts that lurked under the soil. She darted up and meant to run to the kitchen, but Joach caught a fist in her nightclothes and yanked her back.

"What do you think you're doing?" he hissed at her.

"Let go!" She struggled with Joach, but he was much stronger. "I must warn Father."

"He told us to stay hidden."

She spotted her father stepping to the doorway. Oh, dear goddess, no! She ripped out of Joach's grip and ran to the kitchen. Joach pursued. The three adults turned to her as she burst into the lantern light.

"Wait!" she called. Her father had stopped at the threshold, his face reddening with fury.

"I thought I told you—"

Behind her father, the younger intruder grabbed her father's shoulders and shoved him outside. Elena screamed as her surprised father flailed and toppled down the three steps to the hard dirt. Her mother rushed the man, a kitchen knife raised in a fist. But her mother was too old and the man too quick; he snatched her mother's wrist and wrenched her around.

Joach yelled in fury, but the man sneered and shoved her mother through the door to land in a crumpled pile beside her father. Joach, spittle flying from his mouth, flew at the intruder. The man swung a cudgel from inside his cloak and clubbed Joach on the side of the head. Her brother collapsed to the wooden floor with a crash.

Elena froze as the man's eyes settled on her. She saw his eyes twitch toward her right hand, the one stained red. Then his eyes grew wide.

"It's true!" he said and took a step away through the door. He glanced out to the cowled one in the yard. "She is here!"

Her father had struggled to a standing position by now. He stood guard over his wife as she nursed her left arm and pushed to her knees. "Don't you touch my daughter!" her father spat at the intruders.

Joach, his forehead bloody, rolled to his feet and stood between Elena and the door, swaying slightly.

The old man hobbled toward her parents. "Your daughter or your life," he creaked, his voice like serpents in the dark.

"You're not taking Elena. I'll kill you both if you try." Her father stood firm under the old one's gaze.

The robed figure simply raised his staff and tapped the ground twice. With the second strike, the dirt at her parents' feet erupted explosively, the cloud of mud obscuring her parents. For the first time in Elena's life, she heard her father scream. The dirt settled, and she saw her mother and father coated in the white worms that had attacked Pintail. Blood flowed freely from them.

Elena screamed, falling to her knees.

Her father swung toward the doorway. "Joach!" he screamed. "Save your sister! Ru—" Further words were choked shut as the worms climbed in his mouth and throat.

Joach backed into Elena, pulling her up.

"No," she said, a mere whisper. Then louder, "No!" Her blood ignited with fire. *"No!"* Her vision turned red, and her throat constricted shut. She flew to her feet, quaking, her fists clenched. She was dimly aware of Joach, wide-eyed, stumbling back from her. All of her attention was on the yard, on her parents writhing on the churning dirt. Suddenly she screamed, sending all her rage out from her.

A wall of flame burst forth and blasted into the yard. The two foul men tumbled out of the fire's path, but her parents could not move. Elena watched it envelop her mother and father. Her ears, still humming with energy, heard her parents' screams end as if a door was shut upon them.

Suddenly Joach grabbed her around the waist and propelled her back from the kitchen into the dark den. The kitchen wall was on fire. Elena collapsed into his arms, spent, a mere rag doll now. Joach struggled with her weight. The room filled with smoke.

"Elena," Joach said in her ear, "I need you. Snap out of it." He began coughing in the oily smoke. The fire had spread to the curtains in the den.

She labored to get her feet under her. "What have I done?"

Joach stared at the flames behind him, tears shining on his cheeks in the firelight. He looked forward, searching.

Smoke choked the air. Elena coughed.

Joach took a step toward the front door, then stopped. "No. They'll expect that. We need another way out."

He suddenly pulled her toward the stairs. Elena felt pinpricks returning to her numb limbs. She started to shake with silent sobs. "It's my fault."

"Hush. Upstairs."

Joach pushed her to the staircase, then prodded her up the steps. "C'mon, El," he whispered urgently in her ear. "You heard them down there. They're after you."

She turned to him with tears in her eyes. "I know. But why? What did I do?"

Joach didn't have an answer. He pointed to the door to his room. "In here."

She spied the window at the end of the hall and shook free of Joach. "I didn't see what happened. I need to see." She stumbled toward the window.

"Don't!"

Elena ignored her brother's urgent whisper. She reached the hall's end. The thick-paned window did not open but had a wide view of the farmyard below. She leaned her forehead against the cold glass. Below, only steps from the rear door, lit by the flames, she saw what was left of her mother and father. Smoke billowed across in waves.

Two sets of scorched bones, entwined in each other's arms, lay on the brown dirt, skulls touching each other. The old man stood a few paces away. The fringe of his robe smoldered. He had an arm raised, pointing toward the front of the house.

Joach stepped behind her and pulled her from the window. "You've seen enough, Elena. The fire spreads. We need to hurry."

"But ... Mother and Father ..." She looked toward the window.

"We'll mourn for them later." Joach helped her to his bedroom. He pulled open his door. "Tonight we need to survive." His next words were ice. "Tomorrow is soon enough for revenge."

"What are we going to do, Joach?" she said as she entered his room.

"Escape." In the shadowed room, she could still see the firm set to his jaws. How could her brother remain so hard? A few tears had escaped him, nothing else. "We need warmer clothes. Grab my wool overcoat." Her brother slipped into his pants and a thick sweater her mother had knitted him for last Winter's Eve. She remembered that holiday night, and fresh tears began to flow. "Now," Joach said.

She grabbed his long coat off the hook in his closet and pulled into the thick warmth. She hadn't realized how cold she was until the warmth of the jacket embraced her.

Her brother stood by his bedroom window. "El, how's your balance?"

"I'm doing better. Why?"

He waved her to the window. The view looked out on the side of the house. A huge chestnut tree spread its thick branches far and wide, tickling both the eaves of the house and the roof of the horse barn. Her brother pushed the window wide. "Do as I do," he said, as he climbed onto the sill.

He leaped out, caught a thick branch in his hands, and swung up onto a thicker limb. He had obviously done this before. He twisted around and waved her forward.

She climbed onto the narrow sill. Her bare toes clung to the wood. She looked down at the dirt far below. If she should fall, a broken bone was the least of her worries. It was what lay under the dirt that made her teeter on the sill.

Her brother whistled like a warbler, drawing her attention back to him. She leaped out the window and caught the same branch he had. Joach helped pull her onto the thick bough beside him.

"Follow me!" Joach said, his words low, fearful of drawing the others' attention. She heard voices from the front of the house, followed by a crash of glass. She followed him through the limbs of the tree, ignoring the tinier branches that snatched at clothes and flesh.

Through the branches of the tree, they crossed the treacherous yard. As they reached the smaller branches, the limbs began to bend under their weight. Joach pointed to the open door of the barn's hayloft. "Like this." He ran down a thin branch and jumped across the empty space. He landed with a roll on a tufted pile of hay. Instantly on his feet, he was at the door again. "Hurry!" he hissed toward her.

She took a deep breath and ran. She must do this! And she might have succeeded if a branch hadn't snagged a pocket as she leaped. The coat ripped, spinning her in midair. She flailed as she flew and could not suppress a scream. Still yelling, she collided with the barn just below the door to the loft.

Before she could fall, Joach had a handful of the overcoat's collar in his grip. She hung in the coat from his arm. "I can't pull you up," he said, straining. "Reach up and grab the edge! Hurry! They're sure to have heard you!"

With her heart clamoring in her ears, she struggled to grasp the edge of the hayloft opening. Only her fingertips reached the wooden lip. But it was enough. With her fingertips pulling and Joach yanking on the coat, they managed to haul her into the loft.

Both winded and gasping for air, they pushed through the hay to the ladder leading down.

Elena paused at the top rung and pointed to the dirt floor of the barn. "What if the worms are down there, too?"

Joach pointed to the stallion and the mare in their stalls. "Look at Tracker and Mist." The two horses, agitated from the commotion, eyes white and rolling with fear, were still alive. "C'mon." Her brother led the way, scrambling down the ladder.

Elena followed, piercing her right hand with a thick splinter as she slid down. She picked the piece of wood from her palm, noticing that the ruby stain had faded to a slight pink, almost the same color as her other hand.

Joach had already thrown the stall doors wide, and the two horses snorted warily as they stepped out, upset at the smoke. Her brother tossed her a set of reins and a bit. She ran a fast hand down Mist's neck, calming her, and slipped the bit and reins in place. They didn't have time for saddles.

Joach leaped atop Tracker and sidled over to help pull her onto Mist's bare back. Once seated, he crossed to the door at the rear of the barn and used his toe to kick loose the latch. The doors swung open, facing the edge of the orchard. Joach held a door wide to allow Mist passage.

As Elena guided Mist outside, she scanned the dark space between the barn and the trees. Clouds had masked the moon, and the air was thick with smoke. Just as she was turning Mist toward the trees, light bloomed from behind Joach. Elena swung in her seat and gasped. Behind her brother, at the corner of the barn, the cowled man stepped into the rear space. His partner held a lantern high.

"Elena, go!" Joach swung his horse to face the two men. "I'll hold them off."

Elena ignored him and watched the old man raise his crooked staff and strike the packed dirt. With this sharp impact, the ground swelled around the two men and spread in a wave, like a pebble dropped in a pond. The wave of churning soil raced toward Joach. Momentary glimpses of thick white bodies roiled in the dirt. "No! Joach, run!"

Joach saw what sped toward him. He yanked on Tracker's reins, twisting the horse's neck around. Tracker whinnied in panic, fighting for a moment, then danced in a circle and began to leap away from the pursuers. But the horse moved too slowly. The advancing edge of the corrupt wave swallowed the mount's hind legs.

Elena watched as the rear of the horse sank into the soil as if into mire. The mud turned black with blood. Tracker reared up and screamed in pain, his eyes bulging. Joach held tight to the reins. The horse crashed to the ground. The hooves of his forelimbs dug deep into the packed dirt, trying to drag his rear limbs out.

Joach urged the horse on, but Elena knew it was futile. The predators in the soil could rend flesh from bone in mere heartbeats. Elena raced her steed toward the struggling pair. She pulled up fast in front of Tracker. With an arm wrapped in the reins, Elena had to fight to keep Mist in place before the panting, wild-eyed stallion. "To me!" she screamed to her brother.

Joach recognized the futility of his position. "Leave me! Go!"

"Not without you!" Mist skittered back a step. The wave, momentarily delayed by the meal of the horse, now rolled toward her. Tracker's forelimbs became trapped in the churning soil. "Jump!" she yelled to her brother.

Joach clenched his fists on the reins, frozen in indecision. Then, with a shake of his head, he fought to his feet on the bucking horse. Cartwheeling his arms for balance, he leaped from Tracker's back and landed hard on his belly across Mist's rump. His sudden weight set fire to the horse's legs. Mist leaped away as if struck by a whip.

Elena let Mist run, only guiding her enough to point her toward the dark orchards. Elena was busy with her other arm, trying to keep her brother on horseback.

The three plunged into the grove of apple trees.

6

THE JUGGLER, BARE CHESTED, WEARING ONLY HIS BAGGY TRAVELING trousers, stepped to the edge of the stage and set down his pan. Each town was the same, one blurring into the next, the same vague faces staring up from the audience. He had been on the road now for eight years, alone, with only his memories for company. And still those memories crowded him too closely.

A few in the audience mumbled and pointed fingers toward him. He backed a safe distance from the edge. He knew the fingers pointed to his right shoulder, where his arm should have been.

The juggler tossed his four knives in the air, slicing the pipe smoke of the room into thin ribbons. He watched the first tumble back toward his left hand and, with practiced indifference, snatched the hilt and returned the knife aloft with a flick of the wrist. He sent the remainder chasing after the first. The spinning blades caught the flame of the torches and blazed back to the audience clustered up to the inn's rickety stage.

Appreciative *ooh*'s and *ahh*'s echoed thinly from some in the audience, but most of their attention was on the quality of the ale being proffered by the inn and the promptness of the service. With one eye on his knives, the juggler watched a harried barmaid wallowing through the crowd, a platter laden with sloshing glasses balanced about her head. She wore the plastered smile of the overworked.

He nodded briefly to acknowledge the clink of a coin in the pan at the foot of the stage. It's how one earned a living on the road.

"Hey, buddy!" someone yelled from the stage's apron, his voice slurred with a generous lubrication of ale. "Careful there with those fancy pig pokers, or you might lose your other arm."

Someone else cackled from near the back of the room and answered the drunken man. "Careful there yourself, Bryn. You're standing awful close to those whirling knives. He might just clip off that ugly woolyworm under your nose you call a mustache."

The audience roared at the jibe.

The insulted man—who was balding and had a thick, curled and waxed mustache—pounded a footboard of the stage. "Oh, yeah? Well, Strefen, at least I'm man enough to grow one."

This was not a good sign. Not that the juggler expected this altercation to worsen into anything more than an exchange of insults. But when the audience found more entertainment among the tables than on the stage, he would catch few coins in his pan. He needed to gain their attention. These days, even a one-armed juggler sometimes warranted no more than passing interest.

He let a knife fall to the floor, feigning loss of control. The blade struck into the wooden stage with a *thunk* and sank deep into the board. This caught the audience's eyes. Nothing like failure that could be ridiculed to draw attention to oneself. He heard the beginning of derisive laughter bubbling from the crowd. Then each knife, one at a time, supposedly toppling uncontrolled, landed its blade tip into the hilt of the one below it—*thunk, thunk, thunk*—ending up with all four knives stacked in a row on top of each other.

The tower of knives waved slightly back and forth in front of the stunned guests of the inn. A smattering of claps spread into a moderately enthusiastic applause. The tinkle of a few coins in his pan accompanied the acknowledgment.

Each copper bit, which could otherwise be spent on ale, was hard won. If he wanted to purchase dinner tonight, he still needed more of a take. He seldom earned enough to put a roof over his head in the evening, but he was used to sleeping under his horse.

He swung to the side of the stage and opened his satchel. He retrieved his next trick—a set of oiled torches. He grabbed the three in his fist and lit them from a flaming brand in a brazier. They flared to life. The audience responded with a hush when each torch burned a different color—a deep green, a sapphire blue, and a red deeper than ordinary flame. He had learned this trick, which used an alchemy of special powders, during his years in the Southlands.

A few claps erupted behind him.

He turned to face the audience with the torches raised high and flung them upward, almost to the rafters of the inn's common room. As they cascaded down, showering a trail of light, he caught them up and returned them toward the roof.

The applause was now vigorous, but his ear still only heard a few coins tapping into his pan. So he sent the torches even higher, his biceps bulging with the effort until his body shone under a thin oil of sweat. A few women *ooh*'ed to the left of the stage, but he noticed from the corner of his eye that they were staring at his physique and not the cascading torches. He had learned that there were other ways to earn a living on the road, and he was not above showing his wares.

As he worked the torches, he flexed his shoulders, displaying his wide chest and ample musculature. Black haired and gray eyed, with the ruddy complexion of the plainsmen of his home, he had been known to juggle more than knives and torches to earn a room and a bed.

More coins were flipped into his cache.

With a final flourish, he bowed with all three torches still aloft. The audience gasped, as usual, as the torches tumbled toward his bowed back. He noticed one of his buxom admirers raise a concerned hand to her mouth. Just as the torches were about to hit, he performed a standing flip and caught each torch one at a time, sailing the torches into a waiting bucket of water. Each sizzle of vanquished flame accelerated the clapping. When he was done, the audience was on its feet clapping and thumping tabletops with mugs.

He noticed his pan was still filling with coins. He kept bowing until the audience calmed and the coins stopped flowing. With a final wave, he collected his knives and pan and leaped from the stage. The crowd still murmured appreciatively, and a few patrons patted his back as he moved through them. He pulled on his leather jerkin, still too heated from his performance for the thick cotton undershirt he normally wore.

By eyeballing the pile of coins, he knew he would eat well tonight, and with luck, he might just have enough left over to pay for a room at the inn. If not, he spotted a few ladies who still had an eye fixed on his bare chest. There *were* other options.

The innkeeper slid his fat belly down the bar toward him, his chubby face pinked by the heat of the room to the color of a pig's rump. He wore the wine-stained smock that seemed the usual attire for the owner of an inn of this quality. Pushing back the four hairs that still adorned his head, he swung his wide nose to the juggler and plopped his thick paw on the scarred wood of the bar. "Where's my cut?" he said in a wheeze.

The juggler counted out the proper percentage of coins to pay for his use of the stage. The innkeeper's eyes watched each copper descend into his meaty palm. The juggler expected him to begin licking his lips at any moment, the lust was so evident in the keeper's eyes.

"That's all?" he said, shaking the fistful of coins. "I saw those coins filling your pan. You're holding out on me."

"I assure you, your percentage has been met." The juggler stared the innkeeper square in the eye.

The innkeeper backed down with a grumble and swatted a barmaid out of his way as he returned to his post farther down the bar. Another barmaid, a comely lass with thick blond hair in braids, slipped a glass of ale in front of him while the innkeeper had his back turned. "Enjoy," she whispered to him with a slight smile and lowering of lash. "Something to cool the fire in you until later." She continued to the next customer with only the briefest glance back at him.

No, his horse would definitely be sleeping alone tonight.

He collected his glass of cold ale and twisted around to lean on the bar and watch the next performer mount the stage. This was a tight crowd, and after his performance, he pitied the young boy he saw climbing the steps to the stage.

Not *boy*, he realized once he saw the performer straighten from placing a pan by the apron of the stage. She was small, and the gray trousers and plain white shift she wore did little to highlight her feminine attributes, the few that there were. At first he thought her barely past her first bleed, a sapling of a woman, but once she sat on the stool and faced the crowd, he knew he was wrong. Her face, young with a buttered complexion and a rosebud for lips, belied the look in her violet eyes: a sadness and grace that could only come from the passage of many hard years.

The crowd, of course, ignored her as she slipped a lute from a cloth case. The tables grew raucous below her with the din of wine orders, friends carousing, the clink of glasses, the occasional guffaw. Pipe and torch smoke thickened the air. She seemed a petal amidst a raging storm.

The juggler sighed. This was not going to be a pleasant sight. He had seen other performers pelted from the stage with soiled napkins and the crusts of bread.

But the small woman positioned the lute against her belly, leaning over the instrument like a mother with a child. The wood of the lute was thickly lacquered, almost appearing wet in the sheen of the torches. It was the reddest wood he had ever seen, almost black, and the grain of the wood whirled in tiny pools upon its surface. This was an expensive instrument to be carting through the backwoods.

The crowd still ignored her. He heard an argument break out

concerning who would win the cider contest at the local fair next month. Fists flew and a nose was broken before the combatants were pulled apart—all over cider. Well, he supposed that during his travels he'd witnessed other ridiculous fights that had ended worse than a split lip and a bloodied, battered nose.

He sipped from his ale, letting it slide down his throat. He allowed his eyes to close halfway just as the woman on the stage strummed her first chord. The music, for some reason, seemed to cut right through the chatter and settle in his ear like a nesting bird. She repeated the chord, and the crowd began to settle, the voice of the lute drawing eyes back to the stage.

He widened his own eyes. The bardswoman looked out, not to the crowd but farther, somewhere other than here. He watched her shift her fingers slightly on the neck of the instrument and saw the nails of her other hand strum down the strings. The new chord was a sister of the first. It echoed across the room as if searching for those first notes. The crowd settled to a silence, afraid to disturb this quest.

With the lull, the woman began to play. The sweetness of the music spread across the room, speaking of happier times, brighter times than the cloudy day that had just ended. The juggler watched her fingers dance across the wood and strings. Then she did the most remarkable thing: She began to sing. Her voice started low, barely detectable from the honeyed chords, but as she played, her voice raised as a harmony to the other. Though he did not understand the tongue she sang, he sensed the meaning. She sang of years, of the turning of seasons, of the cycle that all life followed.

The crowd sat stunned in their chairs. One man coughed, and his neighbors glared at him as if he had spat the foulest offense. But the rest ignored him and stared slack jawed toward the stage.

She continued, oblivious to their reaction. Subtly her voice changed, and the chords began to moan more than sing. She now warned of danger, of the time when the cycles of life are threatened. She sang of beauty destroyed and innocence shattered. Drums could be heard behind her voice and the strike of her chords.

The juggler found himself wanting to console her, to tell her all was not lost. He watched her fingers slow on her lute as her song again shifted to a new rhythm, the beat of a fading heart. Slower and slower the chords stretched across the aching room. Patrons leaned toward the stage, trying to keep her from stopping. But stop she did, a final brush of nail on string, then nothing. Only a single note of her voice hung in the air. Then this, too, faded with her breath.

The room was deathly still, no one wanting to be the first to move. The juggler inexplicably felt a tear roll down his cheek. His hand did not move to wipe at it. He let it fall. Many other eyes in the room were wet and cheeks damp.

He expected this to be the end, but he was mistaken. A whisper of a chord began to drift again from her lute. Her fingers did not seem to be even moving. It was as if the lute itself were singing. The music wafted through the room, brushing the many moist cheeks. Then her throat sang the final passage—of one alone, the last of the brightness standing among the ruin. Her music drew further tears from the juggler, as if her song were specially for him. But he was also aware of the many others in the room touched by her music, other souls attuned to her rhythm. Then with her final chord, firm and clear like a bell, and with the last whisper of her song, she offered them all one consolation, one word: *hope*.

Then it ended. He watched her shift from her stool and stand.

The crowd took the breath it had been holding and released it in a single gasp. A murmur of surprise followed by clapping ensued. There was a rush to the stage to rain coins into her pan. Before he knew what he was doing, the juggler found himself standing before her pouring the coins from his own pan into hers.

He glanced up to the stage and found her violet eyes staring back at him. She was cowering at the back of the stage, apparently intimidated by the frenzy around her and the calls of praise. She held the lute clutched to her chest.

Suddenly there was a commotion from the door to the inn. A man burst into the common room. "There's a fire burning at

Bruxton's place!" he yelled to the crowd. "The orchard's afire!"
The audience erupted in response.

But the juggler ignored this all, his eyes still fixed on the lute
player. The fire was of no concern to him.

She darted to the front of the stage, to him. The bardswoman
knelt until she stared directly into his gray eyes. "I need you, Er'ril
of Standi."

7

The fires lit the horizon behind Elena. Smoke blacker than the night rolled toward them between the rows of trees, and a crackling roar growled down the ridgeline. She tried to urge Mist to a faster pace, but the horse began to founder, sweating fiercely from its panicked run.

"We need to rest her, El!" Joach yelled from behind her. "Mist can't keep up this pace."

"But the fire!"

"We've a good lead! The winds here will slow the flame." He reached from behind her and pulled on the reins. Mist slowed to a walk.

Joach rolled off the mare and swung the reins forward to guide the horse. Mist huffed thickly into the night, her nostrils flaring, eyes wide and frightened. The smoke and the roar of the fire kept her skittish, hooves dancing, wanting to run again.

Elena patted her neck and climbed off the horse, too. Joach was right. Mist would run until her heart burst if given her head. She took the reins from her brother and kept Mist walking.

Joach laid a palm on the horse's wet flank. "She's overheated. We can't ride her again tonight. But I think we made enough of a head start."

Elena stared back at the fiery heights. She remembered the flames consuming her home, then leaping to the horse barn, and a heartbeat later, burning embers blew from the barn's roof into the trees, igniting the dry orchard. After the drought of summer, the undergrowth was ripe tinder for the torch, and the fire spread with an unnatural speed.

She had watched her world burn to ash, set to flame by her own hand. Unconsciously, she rubbed at the scant remainder of the stain on her right palm.

Joach noticed the tears that had begun to flow across her cheeks, but he misunderstood. "El, we'll get out of here. I promise."

She shook her head and waved to the growing fire. "I killed them." She again pictured the wall of flame rushing toward her parents.

"No." Joach laid a hand atop hers on the reins. "You didn't, Elena. You saved them from horrible pain."

"Maybe they could've survived."

Joach shuddered. "Mother and Father had no chance. I saw how quickly those snake monsters devoured Tracker. Even if they did somehow survive, I don't think . . . I don't think it would've been a blessing."

Elena hung her head, silent.

Joach raised her chin with a finger. "You're not to blame, El."

She twisted away from her brother's touch and turned her back to him. "You don't understand . . . I . . . I . . ." Her tongue resisted admitting the guilt in her heart. "I wanted to leave . . . I wished it." She swung back to him; tears ran hot across her cheeks. She pointed to the flaming orchard. "I hated this place . . . and now it burns by my hand!"

Joach took her in his arms and held her tight as she shook with sobs. "El, I wanted to leave, too. You know that. All this is not your fault."

She spoke to his chest. "Then who is to blame, Joach? Who caused all this?" She stepped from his embrace and held up her right fist. "Why did this happen to me?"

"Those are questions for another time. Right now, we need to reach Millbend Creek." He stared back at the flames cresting the ridge behind them, flames licking up toward the moon. "If we can cross the creek, we should be safe from the fire. Then maybe we can think."

Elena bit at her lower lip, suddenly afraid of the answers she might yet discover, knowing that Joach's words of consolation might prove hollow and that what occurred this black night might yet be laid at her feet. She sniffed and rubbed her nose.

As Mist nickered in fear beside her, Elena ran a hand over the mare's quivering nostrils. "Shh, sweet one, you'll be fine," she whispered to the horse.

Suddenly, Mist jerked back, almost ripping the leather reins from Elena's fist. The startled girl was lifted off her feet as the horse reared, neighing in terror. Mist bolted down the slope, dragging Elena with her.

"Whoa, Mist! Whoa!" Elena scrabbled to get her feet under her. Bushes, twigs, and stone tore at her coat and knees.

"Let her go, Elena!" Joach called in pursuit.

But Elena was not about to let this one piece of her home disappear into the night. She clenched the reins tight in both fists. As she bounced and ran along, she managed to plant a foot on a boulder, then yanked savagely on the leather reins. Mist's head flew backward, and the horse's rump flipped forward down the slope. Elena threw the reins around the trunk of an orchard tree and secured them, praying the bridle would not snap. Thankfully, it held. Mist floundered, then fought back to her feet.

Joach slid to a stop next to her. "What was that all about?"

"Shh!" Elena said.

Through the roar of the fire, a new noise grew. At first just a whisper, then more clear. The beating of heavy wings, like someone waving a thick rug, approached.

Mist nickered and pulled against the reins, eyes rolling to white. Elena found herself ducking lower, and Joach crept under the branches of an apple tree.

Both scanned the sky. Smoke obscured the stars, but the cloak of soot swirled as the winged creature beat past. It was something large, with a wingspan longer than two men. Just the tip of one wing—a bony structure spanned by membranous red folds—poked through the smoky shield for a heartbeat, then disappeared again.

The sight iced Elena's blood. What flew this night was not a denizen of the valley, but something that roosted far from here, far from the view of good men. It flew toward the fire.

After it passed, Joach spoke first, his voice a whisper. "What was that?"

Elena shook her head. "I don't know. But I think we'd better hurry."

ROCKINGHAM PRESSED A HANDKERCHIEF OVER HIS NOSE AND MOUTH while holding a burning torch as far from his body as possible. His throat ached with soot and smoke. He flipped the torch into a dry hawthorn bush at the edge of the orchard. The bush blew into flame as he danced back to the hard dirt yard of the homestead.

He stumbled to where Dismarum leaned on his staff. The seer held one hand up in the air, testing the wind. "One more." Dismarum pointed to a pile of dead leaves raked near the edge of the field.

"I've lit enough fires," Rockingham said, wiping ash from his hands onto his pant leg. Sweat and smoke marred his face. "The whole hillside is ablaze."

"One more," the seer said again, pointing to the pile. His dark robe, singed black at the edges, swirled in the night breeze.

Damn this one's cursed eyes, Rockingham thought. He stayed rooted where he stood. "The fire already burns fierce enough to flush the children out of the orchard hills and into the valley floor. We don't need to scorch the whole mountain."

"Let the valley go to ash. All that matters is the girl."

Rockingham wiped his face with his handkerchief. "The orchards are this valley's livelihood. If these farm folk even get a hint that we spread this fire—"

Dismarum spoke to the fire. "We blame the girl."

"But the townsfolk, they'll—"

"They'll be our net. The fire will force her to Winterfell."

"And you expect the townspeople to capture her if she shows her face? If these bumpkins think she burned the orchards, you'll be lucky to get her back in one piece."

Dismarum pointed his staff to the stack of dead leaves. "She must not escape us a second time."

Rockingham grumbled and grabbed another torch. He lit it from a small fire still sputtering in the husk of the burned barn and crossed to the pile of raked leaves. He shoved the flaming torch deep into the mound. As he backed away, rubbing his hands together to remove the grime, the parchment-dry leaves instantly bloomed with flame, snapping and growling hungrily.

He coughed at the thick smoke billowing from the pile. Suddenly, a fierce gust of wind blew toward him, and a tumble of flaming leaves swirled around him like a swarm of biting flies. He swatted at the burning embers, his expensive riding cloak singed in several places. "That's it!" he yelled, stomping a flaming twig under his heel. "I'm heading back to town!"

Smoke stung his watering eyes. His nose, clogged with soot, itched and burned. He sneezed a black foulness into his handkerchief. Waving an arm through the smoke, he tried to spot Dismarum through the smudged curtain. "Dismarum!" he called.

No answer.

The old man had probably hobbled to the road. Rockingham fought his way across the smoky yard, using the smoldering skeleton of the homestead as a guide through the haze. He coughed and spat into the dirt. Then his foot hit something soft. Startled, he jumped back a step, then realized it was Dismarum. The old man was kneeling in the yard, his staff dug deep into the dirt. Rockingham noted a flash of pure hatred in the seer's milky eyes, but the venom was not directed at Rockingham but at something behind him.

Rockingham froze, suddenly awash with the overwhelming sensation of cold eyes drilling into his back.

He swung around. What he saw through the smoke forced him to fall screaming to his knees beside Dismarum.

The beast towered just beyond the flaming pile of leaves, scabrous wings spread wide, eyes stung red in the firelight. Standing twice as tall as Rockingham but thin as a wraith, its translucent skin was stretched taut over bone and gristle. The spasms of four black hearts could be seen in its chest, pumping black rivers through its body. The fires illuminated other internal details, a churning and roiling foulness. Rockingham's stomach seized in nausea, and even with the fire's heat, a cold sweat pebbled his forehead. The creature's wings beat a final time, again sending a flurry of burning embers toward him. Then the wings pulled back and folded behind the creature's thin shoulders.

The beast stalked into the yard, its clawed feet gouging the packed dirt. Its bald head and muzzle swung between the two men, yellow fangs protruding from its black lips. Tall, pointed ears twitched in Rockingham's direction. A hand reached toward him. Daggered claws slid free of fleshy sheaths, a green oil dripping from their razor tips.

Rockingham knew poison when he saw it and knew what stood before him. He had never seen such a creature, but rumors of them were whispered in the halls of the Gul'gothal stronghold: the skal'tum, lieutenants to the Dark Lord himself.

It opened its mouth to speak, baring teeth filed to points. A black tongue lashed out, as long as a man's arm. Its voice was high and sibilant, with a hissing quality to its words. "Where isss the child? Where isss the child the overlord seeksss?"

Dismarum raised his face, but he still refused to meet its gaze. "She is ripe with power—" He waved a hand to encompass the fire. "—and burned her way past us. She flees through the trees."

The skal'tum lowered its head and lunged closer to Dismarum. It used a talon to raise the old man's face farther into the light. Rockingham watched the seer strain back his neck to keep the sharp tip from piercing his tender skin. "She esscaped? Why was the massster not told?"

Dismarum's voice was as thin and whispery as a reed in a wind. "We have laid a trap for her. We will have her before the sun rises."

"The Gloriouss One wantss her—quickly!" The skal'tum spat in anger, his spittle hissing like a living thing on the packed dirt. "Do not dissplease the masster!"

"She is ensnared in the walls of this valley. We will succeed."

The beast leaned closer to Dismarum, its tongue lapping at the seer's nose. "Or you will sssuffer for your failure." The skal'-tum retracted the talon at Dismarum's throat and pulled its hand away.

The seer bowed his head to his chest. "The Dark Lord was wise to send you. With your help, we cannot fail." But Rockingham recognized the true hatred in Dismarum's words.

The creature cocked its head back and forth, studying the old man like a bird examining a worm. "I know you, old one, don't I?"

Rockingham saw Dismarum shudder, whether with fear or rage he could not tell.

The skal'tum then turned to Rockingham, its red eyes bright with mischief. "And you, fresh one. I remember you."

Rockingham didn't know what it was talking about. He could not have forgotten meeting such a creature, not in a thousand years.

The skal'tum rested a finger on Rockingham's chest; he trembled at the touch, fearing the daggered claw. The creature leaned nearer and cupped the base of Rockingham's skull. Suddenly it whipped forward, pressing its black lips tight to his. *No!* Its tongue snaked between his lips as he tried to scream. Rockingham fought the intrusion, but the skal'tum held him firm as it probed deeper. He spasmed in its grip; his throat constricted, and his heart thundered blood past his ears.

Just before Rockingham's mind snapped, it ended. The skal'-tum pulled back and stepped away. Rockingham fell to his hands and knees, spitting and gagging.

The skal'tum spoke above him. "I can taste her spoor in you."

Rockingham vomited into the weeds.

8

THE JUGGLER PUSHED INTO THE ROOM BEHIND THE BARDSWOMAN. Sixteen coppers did not buy much, he noted. The sleeping quarters were dark, but the chambermaid crossed to the lantern and flamed the wick. Light did not benefit the small space. The walls were in need of fresh paint, and the sole bed appeared to be the main source of sustenance for the handful of moths flitting toward the lamplight. The only other piece of furniture was a stained cedar wardrobe off to the side. He stepped over and creaked open one of its crooked doors. Dust and moths escaped. It was empty.

The room was also in need of an airing out, as it smelled of old candle wax and unwashed bodies. But its single narrow window, looking out on the inn's courtyard, had its wooden frame painted shut. Raised voices and the clopping of many hooves rose from the yard three stories below. The orchard's blaze still raised a stir among the townsfolk.

But the fire was of no concern to him.

The juggler waited for the chambermaid to slip out of the room after he graced her palm with a coin. He swung the locking bar in place and stood by the door until her footsteps faded. No other steps approached. Satisfied that no one eavesdropped, the juggler turned to the bardswoman, who had settled her bag at the foot of the bed. She kept the covered lute in her hand and sat softly on the bed's rumpled coverlet. She kept her face slightly tilted away, her straight hair a blond drape between them.

"The name you used—*Er'ril,*" he said, anxious to get to the core of the mystery, "why did you call me by that name?"

"It is who you are, is it not?" The woman, small as a waif, gently placed the lute beside her lap, but she kept one hand resting on the instrument.

He ignored her question. "And who might you be?"

Her voice remained meek, "I am Nee'lahn, of Lok'ai'hera." She raised her eyes to him as if expecting him to recognize the name.

Lok'ai'hera? Why did that stir a memory? He tried to remember, but he had been through so many towns and villages. "And where is that?"

The woman shrank farther from him, withdrawing inward. She slid the lute from its cover. Again the red wood seemed to stir in whirls in the lamplight. "How soon you forget, Er'ril of Standi," she whispered to her lute.

He sighed, tiring of this dance. "No one has called me by that name in hundreds of winters. That man is long dead." He crossed to the window and pulled away the threadbare curtain. Men with torches milled in the courtyard. Many others carried buckets and shovels. A wagon pulled up, and men crowded into the rear. The two draft horses pulling the wagon had to be beat with switches to haul such a load. Er'ril watched the wagon lurch away toward the road. To the west, an orange glow rimmed the foothills.

He suddenly shivered, remembering when he had last stood in this cursed valley. Then, too, he had stared out an inn's window toward fires in the hills.

He spoke with his back turned. "Why do you seek me?"

In the reflection of the glass, he saw the bardswoman bow her head and finger the strings of her lute. The lonely notes softened the hard edges of the room. "Because we are the last."

Her notes continued to draw him from this room, pulling him

to a faraway place. He turned to her. "The last of what?" he mumbled.

"The last whispers of power from the distant past, of Chi."

He scowled. He had come to revile the name of the spirit god who had abandoned Alasea to desecration by the Gul'gotha. His voice hardened. "I bear no such power."

She tilted her head, totally obscuring her small face with the fall of her hair. "You have lived for five centuries, yet you doubt your power?"

"It was all my brother's doing. He did this to me."

She whispered a word. "Shorkan."

Er'ril started slightly at the mention of his brother's name. He raised an eyebrow and looked closer at the woman. "How do you know so much about me?"

"I have studied the old stories." She reached out a slender finger and pulled aside a stream of blond hair to reveal a single violet eye. "And ancient words: 'Three will become one and the Book will be bound.' "

"Old words from a forsaken time."

Her eye narrowed at him. "You are no longer like the man described in the stories. That man rescued the Book, protected it. He searched the lands, trying to raise resistance to the Gul'gothal overlord. That man is rumored still to be roaming the land."

"Like I said, old stories."

"No, the same story." She let her hair fall back over her face. "It continues to this day."

Er'ril sat on the windowsill. "How did you recognize me?"

She cradled her lute in her lap and strummed the strings a single time. "The music."

"What? What does your lute have to do with this?"

She caressed the edge of the lute with the tip of a finger. "Beyond the Teeth, deep in the depths of the Western Reaches, there once stood an ancient grove of koa'kona trees. Do you still know them—the koa'kona, the spirit trees? Or have you forgotten them, too?"

"I remember one that stood in the center of A'loa Glen." His mind's eye pictured the sun setting through the tiered branches of the single koa'kona tree, its blossoms like sapphires in the twilight. "It grew higher than all the thin spires of the city."

Nee'lahn sat straighter on the bed and revealed her face fully for the first time. There was a sudden longing in her voice and eyes. "Does it still flower?"

"No. Last I saw it, the brine of the sea had rotted its roots." Er'ril noticed his words seemed to wound her. "I believe it is dead," he finished softly.

Er'ril saw a tear roll down her cheek. She continued, a sadness edging her words. "The grove was called Lok'ai'hera, the Heart of the Forest. It—"

Er'ril stumbled to his feet, suddenly remembering. Lok'ai'hera! Like a river cresting its banks during a flash storm, the memory came to him. He pictured his father smoking his pipe at the kitchen table, one hand rubbing his full belly. The clarity of the memory weakened his knees. He pictured the spiderweb of broken blood vessels on his father's nose, the way his breath whistled as he pulled from his pipe, the creak of his chair on the plank floor. "My father . . ." he mumbled. "My father once told me about his journey to such a place in his youth. I always thought it a fable. He boasted of nymphs wedded to tree spirits, wolves as tall as men, and trees as thick around as our house."

"Lok'ai'hera is not a fable. It was my home."

Er'ril stayed quiet, picturing his own home. The memory of his father brought back a rush of old images, pictures he had been trying so hard to forget: he and his brother playing hunt-and-seek in the fields, the harvest celebration when he first kissed a girl, the way the plains seemed to stretch forever in all directions. "I'm sorry," he said to her. "What happened to your home?"

Her shoulders wilted. "It is a long tale of a time before your people first stepped upon the land. A curse was placed upon our spirit trees by a foul race called the elv'in." She seemed to draw inward, away from the dusty room.

Er'ril could hear the ancient pain that still ached her heart. "These elv'in of whom you speak," he said, speaking into her silence. "I have heard other tales of the silver-haired wraiths. I thought them creatures of myth."

"Time transforms all truths into mere myths." She raised her eyes to him briefly before again lowering her face. "You of all people should know this, Er'ril of Standi. To most, you are myth and legend."

Er'ril remained wordless.

She continued her story. "Over countless years, we sought a way to stop the death of our trees. But the Blight, the ancient curse of the elv'in, spread. Leaves turned to dust in our fingers; branches sagged, riddled with grubs. Our mighty home dwindled down to a small handful of koa'kona trees. Even these last few were doomed to die until a mage of your people came and preserved the last of our trees with a Chyric blessing. But as Chi's power vanished from the land, the Blight returned. Our homes once again began to die. Trees that had thrived since the land was young failed to flower. Strong limbs began to droop. And with our trees, our people began to die."

"Your people?"

"My sisters and our spirits. We are tied to our trees as you are to your soul. One cannot live without the other."

"You—"

She brushed her fine hair from her face. "I am of the nyphai."

"You're a nymph?"

A tiny scowl scarred her lips. "So your people have called us."

"But my father said you couldn't live more than a hundred steps from your trees. How can you be here, half a world away?"

"He was wrong." Nee'lahn placed a hand on her lute. "We must be near our spirit, not the tree. A master woodwright of the Western Reaches carved this lute from the dying heart of the last tree . . . my tree. Her spirit resides in the wood. Her music is the song of ancient trees. She calls to those who still remember the magick."

"But why? The time of magick is long dead."

"Her song draws others like her, those with traces of magick, to her, as a lodestone draws iron. I have been traveling the countryside playing her music, probing for those with power. Her music allows me to see into the mind's eye of the listener. I saw what you remembered as I played: the towers of A'loa Glen, the fields of your home in Standi. I knew who you were."

"But what do you wish of me?"

"A cure."

"For what?"

"For Lok'ai'hera. I am the last. With my death, so die my people and our spirit. I must not let that happen."

"How am I supposed to help you?"

"I don't have that answer. But the oldest of our spirits and her keeper had a vision on her deathbed."

Er'ril sighed and rubbed at his temple with his one hand. "I am sick of visions and prophecy. Look where it has brought me."

Her voice swelled with hope. "It has brought you to me, Er'ril of Standi."

"You are placing too much significance on this chance encounter."

"No, the evening is full of portents."

"Like what?"

"The elder's dying vision was of Lok'ai'hera sprouting to green life from red fire—a fire born of magick." She pointed out the window. "Fire. And now you—a creature of magick—are here."

"I am not a creature of magick. I am a man. I can be maimed like any other." He pointed to his missing arm. "I can die like any other. Only . . . only the blessed gift of aging is denied me. And that bit of magick is more curse than gift."

"Still, it is enough," she said firmly. "Fire and magick run the night." Her eyes glowed the same color as the jewel-like blossoms of the lone tree in his lost A'loa Glen. "It is a beginning."

9

THE SCREECH OF THE WINGED BEAST SPLIT THE DARKNESS LIKE A butcher's ax. The creature had been tracking them throughout the night. With the cry echoing in her ears, Elena added her weight to help haul Mist up the wall of the dry gully.

Joach's arms strained on the lead as he pulled on the horse. "It has our scent," her brother said between clenched teeth. "We need to leave Mist and run!"

"No!" Elena said fiercely as she slid down the dry streambed to get behind the horse. Mist's back hooves had sunk to the pasterns in the loose dirt, bogging down the horse. Exhausted, Mist did not even struggle to free herself.

Elena fought her way to Mist's rump. She ran a hand across the horse's feverish skin. Sweat dripped and steamed in the cold air from the beast's quivering flanks. "I'm sorry, Mist," she whispered as she reached for the horse's tail. "But I'll not let you give up!"

Elena gripped the horse's tail and hauled it back over the horse's rump, bending it cruelly. "Now move your butt, girl!" She smacked Mist's hindquarter with one hand and yanked harder on the tail with the other.

Mist snorted explosively and bucked herself free of the dirt, throwing Elena to the bottom of the gully. Landing on her backside, she watched with satisfaction as Joach, guiding and pulling on the reins, hauled the horse out of the trap.

A second screech suddenly burst across the foothills. It sounded closer.

"Hurry, El!" Joach called to her.

Elena didn't need his prodding. She was already on her feet and digging her way back up the loose wall of the streambed.

Once up top, Joach pointed. "Millbend Creek is only a few leagues that way."

Elena shook her head. "We need to hide, now! The creature is too near." She grabbed Mist's reins from Joach and pulled the horse in the opposite direction—toward the blazing fire.

"El, what're you doing?"

"The smoke will cloak us better and confuse the nose of the hunter. Now hurry! I know a place we can hide until it loses interest."

Joach followed, his eyes on the burning orchard. "That's if we don't get fried first."

Elena ignored her brother, trying to keep track of familiar markers. The smoke and her thundering heart confused her concentration. Was this the right way? She thought she recognized this area of the orchard, but she wasn't sure. She searched as she raced with Mist in tow. Yes! Over there! That old stone shaped like a bear's head. She wasn't mistaken. This was the place.

Darting to the left, she waved to her brother to follow. Hidden in a wild hollow ahead lay her goal. Suddenly the blanket of smoke obscuring the stars overhead billowed as something huge shot past just a stone's throw from their heads. Elena could almost feel its weight pressing down on her as it flapped over them. It flew toward the gully from which they had just fled.

Joach's eyes were wide in the meager light from the nearby fires as he stared at her. She recognized in them the terror that gripped her own heart. If they had tried to make a dash for the Millbend, they would have been easy targets. Joach nodded for her to continue, no longer objecting to their path toward the flames.

Elena led the way, quickly but as silently as possible. She allowed herself a soft sigh of relief when she spotted the Old Man. Leading Mist, Elena entered the small patch of wild forest sunk in a shallow hollow, an uncivilized oasis among the orderly orchard rows. She pushed through the brambles and led the way to the center of the hollow.

"Sweet Mother," Joach whispered as his eyes first saw the Old Man. "I can't believe it."

Hulking before them stood the dead husk of a massive tree—not one of the spindly trunked apple trees, but one of the ancient giants that towered here long before humans first entered this valley. Eight men with linked arms couldn't reach around its trunk. The top of the tree had long since fallen away, leaving only this ragged stump with a single thick branch pointing toward the sky.

"I found it while exploring," Elena said. She spoke in hushed tones, not to avoid the ears of the winged hunter but in respect for what stood before her. "I call him the Old Man."

She led the way to a long black split in its bark. "It's hollowed out inside, a natural cave. We can—"

A screeching roar of rage exploded across the valley. The hunter had realized that its prey had slipped its snare.

Without another word, Elena and Joach tumbled inside the embrace of the Old Man. Even Mist didn't balk at sliding inside with them. The hollowed chamber in the heart of the wood was roomy enough to have allowed a small herd of horses to enter with them.

The first thing that struck Elena as they sheltered within the tree was the Old Man's smell. The pervading reek of decaying apples under the boughs of the orchard never penetrated the fresh, woody scent of the tree. The air here was redolent with pine oils and a hint of chestnut. Though the tree was long dead, its scent persisted, as if the Old Man's ancient spirit still hovered within the husk of the once proud giant. Even the choking smoke wafting now through the orchard could not push away the Old Man's presence.

Elena reached a palm to rest tenderly against the wood. Somehow she knew the Old Man would protect them this night. As her right hand touched the wood, she felt a cool calmness spread up her arm to her heart. And for just a moment, she thought she heard words whispered in her head, like a voice reaching up from a deep well.

Child . . . of blood and stone . . . a boon . . . seek my children . . .

She shook her head at her foolishness and removed her hand from the tree. Wrapping her arms about her chest, she dismissed the voice. It was just this night of terror echoing in her head.

Joach stepped beside her, and without a word, they each reached a hand toward the other. Joach squeezed her fingers tightly as they both listened to the night. Eventually the screeches faded in the distance. They had fooled the beast and confused its tracking, and it had apparently abandoned its chase—at least for now.

Joach peeked his head out of the tree's heart and surveyed the orchard. "We must leave now," he said. "The fire is on us. We'll be trapped in it if we don't hurry."

Elena nodded, though she regretted leaving the companionship of the Old Man. She led Mist out and was instantly assaulted by the sting of smoke on eyes and nose. She glanced over her shoulder. The fires lit the entire horizon behind her! Its devouring howl rolled toward them from the heights.

"We must hurry," Joach said, pushing through the wall of brambles. "We still have a long way to go to reach the creek."

Elena followed. Soon they cleared the hollow and raced across the orchard. Elena kept glancing behind her. They were hunted again, but this time by roaring flames.

Her last sight of the Old Man was its one outstretched branch. It was afire, like a drowning man in a sea of flames, waving for help.

With tears in her eyes, she turned away. Strange words still echoed in her head: *Seek my children.*

"I CAN'T BELIEVE BRUXTON'S BOY WOULD DO SUCH A THING!" THE wagon driver, a gnarled root of a man, pounded his buckboard with his fist. The other men gathered in the back of the wagon grumbled hot words. Several shook shovels above their heads.

Rockingham leaned over the pommel of his winded horse toward the wagon. "His father sent for the seer." He pointed a thumb to Dismarum, who rode a smaller filly tethered to his mount. The old man bent with his cowl over his face, rocking as if half asleep. "His father sent for us to try to get the boy and girl some help."

"But those children . . . you're saying his father actually caught the two together? He saw the abomination with his own eyes?"

Rockingham nodded. "In the barn. Like dogs, they were, not caring that they were brother and sister."

A satisfying flurry of gasps arose from the rear of the wagon. Rockingham suppressed a twinge of a smile. This was too easy, wicked words to incite the hidden fears of every family. He pulled his riding cloak tighter over his shoulders. Down the dark road ran a cool wind from the mountain heights. Rockingham glanced to the nearby smoldering foothills. The blaze still occasionally spouted plumes of flame as it stretched through the orchards.

A squeaky voice rose from somewhere in the cart. "And when you got there, what happened?"

Rockingham righted himself in his saddle to again face the wagon. "We found the boy with an ax. His mother lay bloody at his feet; his father already long cold on the dirt."

"Sweet Mother!"

Several townsmen pressed thumbs to forehead in a warding against evil.

"And the girl child, she had already set torch to barn and house. The boy came at us with his ax as soon as we appeared. I was forced to guard the blind seer and retreat."

"How could this happen?" the wagon driver said, his eyes wide with shock. "I knew those kids—sweet, they seemed, and polite, with nary a mean streak."

Dismarum spoke for the first time, raising his cowl to face the torchlight of the wagon. "Demons. Evil spirits hold their hearts."

Now almost the entire wagon raised thumbs to foreheads. One

man even leaped from the wagon and ran back toward the distant town. His footfalls faded into the night.

"Bring them to me unharmed," the seer continued. "Do not kill them, or the evil will flee from their dying hearts—perhaps to one of your own children. Beware." Dismarum lowered his cowl and raised a bony hand to wave Rockingham ahead.

Rockingham kicked his horse forward. Dismarum's filly followed. Rockingham called to the stunned wagon behind him. "Spread the word! Search! Bring the tainted children to the garrison!"

As soon as the wagon was hidden by a curve in the road, Rockingham slowed his horse until he rode beside Dismarum. "The trap is set," he said to the old man.

Dismarum remained silent. Suddenly the beating of leathery wings burst from over the tree line. Both ducked as it passed overhead. It continued toward town. "Pray it's a snug trap," Dismarum mumbled as the winged horror faded into the dawning light of the east.

ELENA RODE BEHIND JOACH, HER ARMS WRAPPED AROUND HIS WAIST as he guided Mist across Millbend Creek. As the horse splashed through the wide, shallow creek, an occasional spray of water jetted high enough to wash across Elena's calves. The water's frigid touch reminded her of the winter to come. But Mist nickered boisterously, the water seeming to calm the horse's fears.

"We should be safe once we're across," Joach said, his voice cracking with fatigue and smoke. "The creek is wide, and I doubt the fire will be able to leap the distance. At least, so I hope."

Elena remained silent. She hoped, too. Behind her, the fires spread like fingers of a hand through the orchard, seeking them. At one point the fire had almost trapped them in a dry gully between two foothills. They were forced to mount Mist and race back along their trail, barely escaping the edge of the fire. But, thankfully, at least no sign of the winged beast had appeared again.

By the time they reached Millbend Creek, the moon had already set, and in the east, a pale glow warned of morning.

"Joach," she said, "how much farther to Winterfell?"

"I'm not sure. If only I could see some familiar landmarks through this cursed smoke. But I'd still say we should reach the town by daybreak."

Joach tapped Mist's flanks with his heel to encourage her up the creek's bank to the dry ground. "We'd better walk her again from here." He slid off the mare and raised a hand to help Elena off.

She climbed down and almost collapsed to her knees, her legs so bone tired. Her feet throbbed, and all her joints quaked with exhaustion. She felt raw all over, as if someone had flailed the skin from her body.

Joach supported her. "We could rest for a few breaths, El."

She wiped at her soot-stained face and nodded. Stumbling to a mossy boulder by the creek bank, she sat. Nearby, Mist nosed at some green shoots by the creek and began to pull at them with her teeth.

Joach sighed loudly and plopped on the bank's edge. He leaned back on his hands, staring at the river of smoke flowing across the stars.

She hung her head. Since last afternoon, all she had ever believed in, the very ground she walked on, had become a treacherous bog. Nothing seemed real. Even Joach and Mist, both only an arm's length away, seemed insubstantial, as if they might turn to dust and blow away, leaving her alone among the trees. She hugged her arms around her and began to rock back and forth on her stone seat and shiver. Her tears could not be denied.

She was barely aware of Joach rising from the creek bank and crossing to her. He wrapped her in his own arms and held her, halting her rocking. She still shivered in his grip. He squeezed her tighter and pulled her head to his chest. He did not whisper a word, just held her tight.

Her shivering began to quell, and she leaned into Joach.

She knew it was not only her brother who held her this night. In his close embrace flowed the love and warmth of her mother, and in the strength of his arms were the bone and muscle of her father. No matter what had happened this night, they were still a family.

She wished to remain in his arms until the morning sun crested the mountain peaks, but Mist suddenly huffed loudly and danced away from the river, ears perked in confusion. Joach released his sister and rose to his feet, alert for what had startled the horse.

Elena stood and grabbed at Mist's reins. Joach crouched at the mossy edge of the bank and scanned the creek bed. "Do you see anything, Joach?"

"No, nothing. This night's got her spooked."

Elena could understand Mist's edginess. She crept carefully to stand by Joach's side. She peered upstream and downstream. The creek gurgled over smooth rocks between fern-shrouded banks. Nothing seemed unusual. "Maybe you're right . . ." she began to say, but stopped. She blinked, afraid it was a trick of her tired eyes.

A silver glow, like reflected moonlight, bloomed in a calm eddy of water at the foot of the bank. But the moon had already set. As she stared, the glow swirled contrary to the current.

"What is that?" she asked.

"Where?"

She pointed to the light as its swirling slowed and spread like spilled milk across the water.

Joach glanced to her. "I don't see anything."

"The light in the water. You don't see it?"

Joach took a step away from the edge and tried to pull Elena back, but she stayed rooted in place. "El, there's nothing there."

She stared as the glow thinned to a wavery sheen on the water; then in a wink, it vanished. She rubbed at her eyes. "It's gone," she said quietly.

"What? Nothing was there."

"There was . . . there was something."

"Well, I didn't see it. But considering this night, whatever it was probably meant us harm."

"No." Elena spoke before even thinking but knew that she spoke the truth. "No, it was not a danger."

"Well, I've had enough strange occurrences for one night. Let's go. We've still a long walk to reach Winterfell." Joach peered a final time at the water, then with a shake of his head proceeded downstream.

Elena followed with Mist in tow.

She again pictured the spreading glow. Maybe her eyes had been playing tricks, but for an instant, just before the light had vanished, a single image coalesced, etched in silver: a woman with stars for eyes. Then in a whisper, nothing but dark water and rock again. She rubbed at her sore eyes. A trick of light and exhaustion, that's all it was.

But why, when the image had flashed in the water, had her stained hand suddenly burned like fire as if she had touched the sun? Then in an instant, like the image, the heat, too, had vanished.

And why didn't Joach see the woman or even the glow?

Mist nudged her with her nose. She trudged faster after Joach. There were too many questions. Maybe in Winterfell she would find answers.

10

DAWN CAME COLD TO THE TINY ROOM OF THE INN. ER'RIL LAY wrapped in a blanket on the floor of the room, his knapsack acting as a pillow. He had been awake to see the first rays of the morning sun stir the dust motes in the room to a slow dance. It had been a long evening. He and Nee'lahn had talked well into the night before both finally agreed that a few hours of sleep were needed to face the morning.

Nee'lahn had fallen quickly asleep on the bed, still in her clothes, the lute held to her breast like a lover. Meanwhile, Er'ril found only islands of slumber, and even those few naps were beset with terrible dreams. Finally forsaking even the pretense of sleep, Er'ril had watched the sun dawn into morning.

As he stared at the encroaching light, his thoughts spun on a thousand pins, through old memories, questions, and fears. Why had he stayed with this daft woman? he wondered. After her eyes had closed and her breathing slowed, he could have easily stolen away. But her words kept him trapped in the room. Was there some meaning in his encounter with this nyphai woman, as she contended? Was there some hidden portent in the blazing orchard fire? And why . . . why did he return to this cursed valley?

But he knew the answer to this last question. In his heart, he couldn't hide from what drew him back to this valley. Last night was the anniversary of the Book's binding—and worse yet, the loss of his brother. Er'ril could still picture Shorkan, Greshym, and the boy—whose name he never had learned—crouched in the wax ring as drums beat in the distance. The memory, like a painting whose oil still ran wet, remained vibrant and bright.

Five hundred winters ago, he had stood in a similar inn, the Book firm in his grip, as an innocent's blood pooled at his feet. Unknown to Er'ril, the marching of years had stopped for him at that moment. It took him many turnings of the seasons before he realized the curse bestowed upon him that evening: never to grow older. He had to watch those he had grown to love age and die while he stayed forever young. He had seen in each of their eyes the occasional glimpse of ire: Why must I age and you live? Finally, the pain of witnessing this over and over again had become too great, and he took to the road, to call no place home, no one friend.

Each hundred winters he returned to this valley, hoping to find some answer. When will this end? Why must I live? But so far, no answer came to him. As the land aged, he watched the scars of that fateful night's battle heal in the valley. The people forgot; the dead lay unremembered, their graves unmarked. He returned each century to honor those fallen to the dreadlords' march. They deserved at least one person to preserve the memory of their bravery and sacrifice.

Er'ril knew he could fall upon his own sword and end this curse; the thought had passed through his mind many nights as he lay awake. But his heart would not let him. Who would then remember the thousands who had died this night so many winters ago? And his brother Shorkan, who had died giving the Book life—how could Er'ril abandon his own responsibility when his brother had given so much?

So each hundred winters he returned.

Er'ril heard Nee'lahn stir. He watched her raise a hand and wipe the cobwebs of sleep from her face. Er'ril cleared his throat to let her know that he, too, was awake.

She pushed up on one elbow. " 'Tis morning so soon?"

"Yes," he said, "and if we want to find a seat in the commons to break our fast, we should be about soon. I've heard men bustling in and out all night."

She slipped from the bed, shyly straightening her frock. "Perhaps we could just eat here. I . . . I prefer to avoid crowds."

"No. They only serve in the common room." Er'ril pushed into his boots and stood. He cracked a kink in his neck and peered out the window. To the west, the morning sky was smudged with snaking trails of soot, and a pall of smoke hung thick across the valley roof. Above the heights, thunderheads stacked behind the mountain peaks. A storm threatened, but rain would be a blessing to the valley this day. Er'ril still saw a few spates of flame licking upward. Closer, the foothills were scarred and blackened, with only an occasional shoal of green life.

Nee'lahn stepped beside him and brushed her hair with her fingers. "A foul morning," she whispered, staring out the window.

"I've seen the valley far uglier than this." He pictured the morning after the Battle for Winter's Eyrie. Blood had run red through the thousand creeks, screams echoed off the craggy mountains of the Teeth, and the stench of charred flesh had fouled the nose. No, this was a pleasant morning in comparison. "It will heal," he said to Nee'lahn as he turned from the sight. He shouldered his knapsack. "It always does."

She collected her bag and strapped her lute to it. She joined him by the room's door. "Not always," she said softly.

He glanced at her. Her eyes stared far from the room. He knew she was picturing the blighted grove of her home. He sighed and opened the door.

Nee'lahn slipped out the door into the hall. She led the way down the stairs toward the common room. The voices and loud talk that echoed up from the inn's main room sounded as boisterous as when they had left late last night. Something still had the townspeople all stirred up.

As he and the bardswoman entered the commons, a scrawny man with a shock of red hair and ash-stained clothing stomped a foot on the player's stage. No pan lay at the stage's foot, so Er'ril knew this was not an early morning performer.

"Listen, people!" the thin man shouted to the crowded tables, his voice high and strident. "I heard this from the captain of the garrison himself!"

Someone carrying a shovel yelled to the man, "Forget it, Harrol! First we stanch the fire! Then we'll worry about those children."

"No!" the man argued. "Those young 'uns are *demon spawn*!" He spat the last words toward the crowd.

"So what! Demons don't keep food from my family's mouth. We need to salvage what we can of the season's crop, or we'll all starve this winter."

The man on the stage was now red faced; his shoulders shook. "Fool! It was them kids that set those fires! If we don't find them, they'll keep torching other folks' orchards. Is that what you all want? The whole dang valley ablaze?"

This last argument silenced the protester in the audience.

Nee'lahn had crept into Er'ril's shadow. She looked up at him questioningly. He shrugged. "Just wagging tongues. Sounds like they're looking for a scapegoat."

A grizzled old man at a nearby table overheard his words. "No, my friend. Word's come out of the hills. It was those Morin'stal whelps. Evil's taken their hearts."

Er'ril nodded and offered a weak smile as he stepped away. He pulled Nee'lahn toward the bar, trying to avoid being drawn into local affairs. He slid two stools close for them to sit on.

The innkeeper manned his post behind the bar, but this morning an actual smile played around his usual scowl. The fire was an obvious boon to the inn. Nothing like a commotion to fill his coffers with coin.

Er'ril caught the eye of the innkeeper, who sidled down the bar toward their seats. "Nothin' but cold porridge left," he said as an introduction. Er'ril saw the innkeeper's eyes drift to Nee'lahn. As his gaze drifted over her slight form, he licked his fat lips. She shrank from him. Sneering, the innkeeper turned back to Er'ril.

" 'Course for an extra five coppers, I might be able to scrounge up a bit of blackberry preserve for your little lady here."

"Porridge and bread will be fine," he said.

"Bread's an extra copper."

Er'ril frowned. Since when didn't porridge come with bread? The innkeeper was obviously taking advantage of the crowd. "That'll be fine," he said coldly, "unless you're going to charge us for the spoon."

The ice in his words must have reached the portly man. He backed away with a grumble. When their food arrived from the kitchen, it was fetched by a timid maid, her eyes bloodshot and tired as if she had worked through the entire night. Er'ril snuck her an extra coin. At these prices, few patrons would be tipping the maids this morning. He saw her eyes brighten as she snatched the coin and made it vanish into her pocket, her hands as quick as a carnival magician's.

Behind him, the men continued to argue a course of action. It seemed they were stuck in a stalemate when suddenly their arguments were interrupted.

Two men bustled in from the courtyard, faces flushed from the morning chill. The smaller of the two, gnomish in comparison to his giant companion, walked with a limp and swung his weak leg wide as he marched into the common room. He led a huge shaggy-bearded man with wide shoulders. Outfitted in a heavy, furred jacket and calf boots, the bigger fellow's coal black eyes searched the crowd warily, his lips thinned with threat. He had a rangy look to him, as if the company of people made him edgy.

Er'ril guessed him to be one of the mountain folk, a nomadic people living among the frozen peaks of the Teeth. Seldom did they venture to the lowlands outside of trading season when the passes thawed. To see one so close to winter was rare.

The smaller man waved a fist into the air. "We have news! News!"

Since the previous argument had become a stalemate of grumbles and complaints, all eyes turned to the newcomers, including

Er'ril's. "What have you heard, Simkin?" someone called from the tables.

"Not heard. *Seen!*" The tiny man named Simkin shook his head and proceeded to elbow his way through the crowd, creating a path for the lumbering mountain man. Once he reached the stage, he crawled onto the platform, waving the larger man forward impatiently. With Simkin's added height from his position on the stage, he was now almost eye to eye with the mountain man, able to rest a hand on the tall man's shoulder. Simkin turned to face the crowd. "This fellow saw the demon!"

The crowd broke into dismissive hissing, though a few placed thumbs to foreheads just in case. "Quit your tall tales, Simkin!" someone yelled.

"No listen. It's true!"

"What did he see? Your wife!" The crowd erupted in laughter, though there was a clear vein of nervousness in their response.

"Tell them!" The tiny man poked the mountain man's shoulder with a finger. "Go ahead!" Er'ril spotted a momentary flash of anger in the man's eye at Simkin's poke. One didn't goad the mountain folk.

Still, the bigger man cleared his throat, a sound like bark being ripped from a tree. Then he spoke, his voice as deep as the caverns that burrowed through the icy peaks. "It flew through the Pass of Tears at twilight, near our home. Pale as the fungus that grows on dead trees and wide of wing as three men stretched. As it flew past, its red eyes glowing, our beasts panicked and a woman of my fire gave birth to a stillborn babe."

None dared call a mountain man a liar—not to his face, at least. They were known for the truth of their speech. The crowd stayed hushed at his words.

Er'ril sat straighter on his stool during this exchange, a spoonful of porridge frozen halfway to his lips. Could it be, after so long? None had been seen for centuries.

Someone spoke softly from the back of the room. "You came all this way to warn us?"

The mountain man's voice deepened to a rumble. "I came to kill it."

Er'ril lowered his spoon and was surprised to hear his own voice call to the mountain man. "Was this beast gaunt like a starved child, with skin so thin you could see through it?"

The mountain man swung his beard in Er'ril's direction. "Aye, the fading light cut through it like a knife. Sick, it looked."

Nee'lahn whispered at his sleeve. "Do you know of the creature he speaks?"

Another man spoke from the crowd. "You there! Juggler, what do you know of this beast?"

All eyes were now on him. Er'ril regretted his quick tongue, but there was no way now to take back his words. "It means disaster," he said to the crowd and threw his spoon on the bar. "You have no hope."

The crowd became agitated. Only the mountain man stood quiet among the milling men. His eyes remained fixed on Er'ril, narrowed and determined. Er'ril knew his words had not swayed the giant. The blood of the mountain folk ran with the ice of their peaks and the stubbornness of their granite home. The threat of death seldom shook their resolve. Er'ril turned away from the giant's stare.

Nee'lahn caught Er'ril's eye and leaned closer. "What manner of beast is it?"

His voice was a whisper, meant only for his own ears. "One of Gul'gotha's dreadlords—a skal'tum."

"THE SSSUN RISESS." THE SKAL'TUM STALKED ACROSS THE DANK BASEMENT chamber of the garrison toward Dismarum. It shook its wings like a wet hound in the rain. The rattle of the leathery bones echoed loudly in the room. "Iss all prepared?"

Dismarum shied a step back. The stench in the cell of rotten meat and filth drove him away as much as the threatening menace of the skal'tum. "Rockingham is on horseback. He spreads word of the girl through town. She'll be found soon. She has nowhere else to go but here."

"Pray ssso. The Black Heart hungerss for her. Do not fail him again."

Dismarum bowed slightly and backed toward the door. He blindly reached for the latch and swung the door open. Morning sunlight, barely discernible with his weak eyes, streamed down the nearby stairway and edged through the doorway, spilling in around him. Dismarum smiled inwardly as the skal'tum backed from the light. Unlike some of the Dark Lord's minions, these creatures could survive the sunlight's burn, but the beasts still preferred to avoid its warm touch. Their translucent skin darkened when bared for long stretches of time to the sun. It was considered disfiguring among its foul kind to be so marred.

The seer kept the door open longer and wider than necessary, chasing the skal'tum to the back of the chamber. How Dismarum would relish the chance to stake the beast in the noon sun and see it squirm. His hate for the winged beasts had not been dulled by the years.

Finally, the creature hissed angrily and stepped toward Dismarum. Satisfied that he had pushed as far as he should, Dismarum swung the door closed. For now the creature had its uses, but if the seer were given the chance . . . He knew how to make even a skal'tum howl.

Keeping his hand on the damp stone wall, he followed the hall to the stairway. Torches brightened the stairs enough for him to see rough outlines. Using his staff, he worked his way up the worn steps. As he progressed, his knees ached with exhaustion. He was forced to stop several times to rest. Closing his eyes and breathing hard, he tried to remember what it was like to be young: to see with sharp eyes, to walk without the stitch of pain in his bones. It seemed like he had been old forever, crumbling with hoary age. Had he ever been young?

During one of these breaks, a soldier coming down the stairs almost barreled into him. The officer pushed against the wall to allow him room to pass. "Pardon me, sir."

Dismarum noted the man lugged a feeding bucket for the prisoners in the cells below. It stank of sour meat and mold. Even his weak eyes could see the maggots roiling within the slop.

The young soldier must have noticed the seer's nose curl in distaste. He spoke up, raising his bucket. "Luckily, there's only one prisoner down there. I'd hate to have to haul more of this filth."

Dismarum nodded sourly and continued up the steps, leaning heavily on his poi'wood staff. He wondered who the young officer had crossed to warrant this punishment. There was only one occupant among the labyrinth of cells—the skal'tum. And it wouldn't be feeding on the scraps in the bucket.

He heard the soldier whistling as he descended into the bowels of the garrison. Dismarum continued up into the main hall. Just as he reached the next landing, the young soldier's scream rang up from below, only to be cut off abruptly.

Dismarum sighed. Perhaps the meal would put the skal'tum in a better mood. He climbed the remainder of the stairs without stopping, ignoring his complaining joints. Right now, he wanted to put as much distance as possible between him and the creature below.

Leaning on his staff, he pushed into the main hall of the garrison. The high doors were open to the large courtyard, bathed in morning sunlight, where horses and wagons jostled for space. Soldiers milled among the clopping hooves and creaking wheels. The clang of beaten iron could be heard coming from the smithy on the far side of the yard.

Dismarum turned his back on the doorway and struck out across the hall, stomping his staff on the flagstone floor. More soldiers bustled around him. Swords slapped thighs, and the odor of oiled armor clogged his nose. He proceeded unimpeded through the melee. No soldier dared come within an arm's length of his robed figure. As he passed the three doorways that led to the soldiers' sleeping quarters, he noted the rows of empty cots. All were on duty. On this morning, the streets bristled with armor and blade.

Suddenly a familiar voice called out from behind him. "Dismarum! Hold up, old man!" It was Rockingham.

Dismarum swung to face the man. Rockingham had changed

out of his singed riding clothes and now wore the colors of the
garrison, red and black. His polished black boots climbed to his
knees, and his red overcoat was festooned with brass hooks and
buttons. He had oiled his mustache and finally washed the soot
from his face, but as he approached across the stone floor, Dismarum's keen nose still smelled the smoke on him.

Rockingham stopped in front of the seer. "We may have too
many patrols out," he said.

"How so?" Dismarum asked in irritation, his nerves still jan-
gled by the skal'tum.

"With this much activity, we might spook the boy and girl
away from town." Rockingham pointed out the door. "You can't
walk two steps without bumping an armsman. I'd be spooked
myself to enter this town."

The seer nodded and rubbed his eyes. Perhaps the foolish man
was right. If he weren't so exhausted, he might have realized the
same. "What do you propose?"

"Pull the soldiers back. I've spread the word. The people are in-
flamed. They'll do the hunting for us."

Dismarum leaned hard on his staff. "She mustn't slip our
snare."

"If she shows her nose in town, she'll be nabbed. The fire and
the talk of demons have the townsfolk roused. Every street is
watched by a hundred eyes."

"Then no more hunting." Dismarum swung away. "We'll wait
for her to come to us." As he limped across the flagstone, he pictured the skal'tum crouched in its warren of cells, like a starved
cur awaiting its bone. To think of betraying its lust and the master
it served was a madman's folly.

But Dismarum had waited for so long.

11

FROM ABOVE THE TREE LINE, ELENA SPIED THE RED ROOF OF THE town's mill ahead. By now, the fire had been left far behind, though the smoke still chased her and her brother across the morning sky. The sight of the pitched roof gave renewed vigor to Elena's steps. She caught up with Joach, dragging a protesting Mist by her lead.

"Almost there," Joach said.

"What if Aunt Fila's not at the bakery?"

"She always is, El. Don't worry."

The two of them had already decided to seek out their widowed aunt, who owned and operated Winterfell's bakery. Their mother's sister was a stern woman with a backbone of iron. She would know what to make of the previous night's horrors.

As Elena followed her brother around a bend in the creek, the mill came fully into view. Its redbrick exterior and narrow windows were a comforting sight. She often ran errands here for her mother, collecting a bag of flour or bartering for cornmeal. Its large paddle wheel turned slowly in the deep silver current as the creek plummeted down a short wash. Just beyond the mill stood the Millbend Bridge, a stone span that forded the creek and connected the town road to the wagon ruts that led up into the sparsely populated highlands.

Joach held up a hand to stop Elena from proceeding out from under the canopy of the trees. "Let me see if anyone's at the mill. You stay hidden."

Elena nodded and pushed Mist's nose to back her several steps. The mare shook her head in protest; a hoof stomped the ground. Elena knew the horse itched to get out from under the branches and reach the meadow that still grew green beyond the trees. "Shh, sweet one." Elena scratched Mist behind an ear. Her whispered consolations settled the anxious horse, but not herself.

She watched Joach steal across the open expanse to the mill's door. He tried the iron latch. She saw him tug at it. It was locked. He climbed atop a flour barrel and peered through one of the windows. Then he hopped off, scratched his head, and disappeared around a corner.

Elena hated seeing the last member of her family vanish from sight. What if he never returned? What if she was left alone? Pictures of life without any family bloomed in her head. What if she was the last Morin'stal alive in the valley? She clutched her arms around her chest, holding her breath.

As she waited, a kak'ora bird sang from a nearby branch, a lonely song. The scent of dewflowers, open only during the first rays of the sun, perfumed the morning, strong enough to penetrate even the smoky pall. As she watched for Joach's return, she saw a rabbit burst from hiding in the prairie grass and bound toward the trees. Disturbed by its passage, a flight of butterflies blew into the air. It was as if summer held eternal sway in this little meadow.

She sighed. As horrible as the night had been, she had somehow expected the land to be wildly changed once the sun rose: trees twisted, animals corrupted. But valley life continued undisturbed, like any other morning. Strangely, she found this reassuring.

Life continued and so could she.

Movement near the mill caught her eye. Joach reappeared from beyond the mill and waved her from hiding. Thank you, Sweet Mother! Elena flew forward, wanting to narrow the distance between them as soon as possible, though Mist kept grabbing mouthfuls of grass as Elena pulled her on. When she reached her brother, he shook his head. "Empty. Must be out trying to stop the fire."

"What if Aunt Fila is out, too?" Elena asked as Mist attacked the leaves of a thrushbush.

"No, El. Our aunt's a tough old lady, but the men wouldn't let her battle the flame no matter how much she might kick a fuss. She'll be home."

"I suppose you're right."

"Let's go." Joach led the way to Millbend Bridge. Elena had to keep tugging Mist to get her to follow, but the mare was determined to get a full belly before leaving the meadow.

Finally, she did manage to get the horse on the bridge. The mare's hooves clopped loudly on the stone as they crossed. As they reached the top of the bridge, Elena glanced back to the mill. She spotted a curtain snap shut across a window on the second floor. "Joach, someone *is* in the mill." She motioned to the curtained window.

"Odd. They had to have heard me. I even pounded on a window in back."

"Maybe it was one of the miller's children, frightened while their parents were out."

"I know Cesill and Garash. And they know me. I don't like this." Joach wore a stern expression.

From down the road, the wheels of an approaching wagon clattered toward them. Joach scooted them off the bridge and into the trees on the north side of the road. He pushed Mist back until they were well hidden.

"But it might be someone we know," Elena said. "Someone to help us."

"And it might be one of those men from last night."

Elena bent closer to Mist. From their shadowed hiding place, she could spy the open wagon as it passed. Men dressed in red and black crowded the buckboard and rails—garrison men. She remembered that the thin man from last night had claimed to be from the town's garrison.

Neither she nor Joach called out to the wagon as it clattered past.

Joach motioned for her to slink deeper into the forest. She came upon a deer trail that gave them room to maneuver Mist around. From here, they could just discern the wagon. Soldiers hopped from the back to take up posts by the bridge. Two men marched toward the mill.

"We'd better get out of here," Joach breathed in her ear.

Just as they turned to leave, Elena saw the mill's door pop open. She watched the miller and his wife rush toward the soldiers. She couldn't hear what the miller said, but his arm kept pointing toward the road to town.

"I don't understand," she said.

"Get on Mist." Joach boosted her onto the mare's back. He jumped up behind her. "We need to reach Aunt Fila before anyone else sees us."

"Why? Our family has plenty of friends in town."

Joach shoved an arm toward the bridge. "Like the miller and his wife."

Frightened, she tapped Mist's flanks to get her trotting down the deer trail. "Then what are we going to do?"

"Travel the wood. Aunt Fila's place is closer to the north end of town. We'll circle through the trees that way. There will be less of a chance of being spotted."

She remained silent. As much as her heart railed against his words, her mind knew them to be true. For now, only their family could be trusted. Aunt Fila had a level head and a keen mind. She and her three grown sons would protect them and help straighten all this out.

She kicked Mist to a quicker gait. The sooner they reached Aunt Fila's bakery, the safer they would be. She watched the smoke trail across the sky from the scorched orchards in the distant foothills. What had happened to her valley, to her people?

She remembered her moment of revelation as she stared at the calm meadow by the mill. She had been deluded.

Life was *not* the same in her home valley.

It *had* twisted into a cold and foreign place.

ER'RIL LEFT HIS PORRIDGE ON THE BAR AND NODDED HIS HEAD TOWARD the door. "We'd better strike for the road."

Nee'lahn cowered on a stool beside him. She was obviously still shaken by the rush of men who had crowded around them, trying to force more details of the dreadlord from Er'ril. His assurance that he knew no more than they about the creature, just old stories he had heard on the road, did little to dampen their curiosity. They persisted until finally Er'ril had unsheathed one of his juggling knives and waved away the last of the stragglers from his side.

By now, the talk of the commons had turned to what to do about the demon-spawn children. And this was a feeble discussion since most of the men had already left, thumbing their foreheads in superstition, to protect their own households from the cursed threat.

Only one patron still kept his eyes drilled toward Er'ril. Hunched over a mug of warmed ale, the mountain man did not seem in any rush to leave the inn. His stare made Er'ril edgy.

Er'ril stood up and turned his back on the giant. "We should go," he repeated.

The nyphai did not move. Er'ril reached for Nee'lahn's elbow, but she shied away.

"Can't you feel it?" he continued. "The air is heavy with threat. The town is like dry tinder, and everyone is scurrying about with lighted torches. We need to leave."

"What about the skal'tum?" she said meekly. "Maybe we'd be safer in town until it's killed."

"It won't be killed."

"Why?"

"The skal'tum are protected by dark magick."

A deep voice grumbled from just behind his shoulder. "What is this dark magick you speak of?" Er'ril jumped at the words, startled that so large a man could move so quietly up on him. Nee'lahn's eyes widened in fright.

He turned to face the mountain man, finding himself craning his neck back. "Excuse me, but our words are private."

"I go to hunt a beast that makes you cower," the big man answered with a coarse grumble, his nostrils flared. "If you have honor, you will tell me what I need to know."

Er'ril's cheeks reddened. There was once a time when no one would question his honor. He felt a burn of shame that he had not felt in countless winters.

Nee'lahn spoke from her hiding place behind Er'ril's back. "Perhaps he's right. The man deserves to know."

Er'ril clenched his one fist. "It would be best to leave this matter be, mountain man."

The giant drew back to his full height. Er'ril had not appreciated how bowed the man had been when among the townspeople. Behind him, he heard a maid drop a glass in fright at the sight of his towering bulk. Considered tall himself, Er'ril found himself at eye level with the giant's belly. "I am called Kral a'Darvun, of the Senta flame," he said sternly. "The creature has wounded the fire of my tribe. I cannot return without the head of the beast."

Er'ril knew the fervor in which the mountain folk held honor. Among the treacherous icy passes, trust was crucial to survival. Er'ril pressed his fist to his own throat, acknowledging the oath pledge.

Kral mimicked the motion, a slightly startled look to his eyes. "You know of our ways, man of the lowlands."

"I have traveled."

"Then you know my will. Tell me of this dark magick."

Er'ril swallowed, suddenly embarrassed by the lack of information he could extend to this man. "I don't . . . don't really know. The dark magick's touch came to our land when the Gul'gotha invaded our shores. Scholars of my time believed its pestilence drove Chi away. When Chyric magick faded in the land to isolated whispers, the dark magick grew stronger. I have seen horrors during my travels that would shrivel the bravest man."

Kral's brow crinkled with his words. "You speak of times before my flame ventured from the Northern Waste. How could that be?"

Er'ril balked. He had spoken without thinking. One night of talking freely with Nee'lahn and the years of practiced constraint on his tongue had fallen away.

Nee'lahn spoke behind him. "Before you stands Er'ril of Standi, called the Wandering Knight by storytellers."

Kral's eyes narrowed in distaste, but an edge of fear crinkled at the corners. "You tell tales when I ask for truth."

"He is not myth," she said. "He is the truth."

Suddenly Kral thrust his hands forward and placed both palms on Er'ril's temples. Er'ril knew what this meant and did not fight the large man. Nee'lahn, though, unacquainted with the custom, gasped.

The innkeeper, who had been sweeping broken glass across the common room, called to them. "No roughhousing in here! Take your argument to the street!"

Kral kept his hands steady.

Er'ril remained still as he spoke. "I am the one she named. I am Er'ril of the clan Standi."

Kral closed his eyes for a heartbeat. Then his lids whipped open wide. He stumbled a step away, crashing into a table and overturning it. "You tell the truth!"

The innkeeper, red faced, his jowls shaking, raised his broom. "What did I say? Out before I call the town guard!"

Kral dropped to a knee. A floorboard cracked to splinters under his impact. "No! It cannot be." His voice boomed across the room. Tears flowed to his beard.

Er'ril was shocked by the man's reaction. He knew the mountain people had the ability to read the truth in another's tongue due to some form of elemental rock magick that throbbed from the roots of their mountain home. But this reaction? Mountain men never shed tears, not even when horribly injured.

"You have come!" Kral's voice was a rumbling moan. He sank to the floor. "Then the Rock speaks the truth. My people must die."

12

THE DAMP PANTS WERE TOO LONG, AND ELENA WAS FORCED TO ROLL them up at the ankle. The tail of her green woolen shirt hung to her knees. Joach had stolen the clothes from a shepherd's drying line. As she shoved the locks of her red hair under a hunter's cap, she complained to Joach. "I look ridiculous. Must we really do this?"

They stood hidden under a willow tree, its branches a screen around them. A small brook gurgled past the tree, stirring the branches on one side.

"This'll make it harder to recognize us." She watched Joach scrub his face with his nightshirt. Once clean, he pulled into a ragged jacket with yellow patches on the elbows. "They'll be watching for two on horseback. We should leave Mist tied to the willow tree here."

"I don't like leaving her alone," Elena said. "What if some thief comes upon her and steals her?" Elena purposely straightened her purloined shirt and gave Joach an accusing look.

He ignored her glare. "From here, it's only a short walk to Aunt Fila's. We can send Bertol back for her."

Elena pictured Aunt Fila's hulking son. "Bertol could get lost in his own backyard. What if he can't find her?"

"El, the mare will be fine. There's plenty of grass, and she can reach the water."

"But it's like we're abandoning her."

"We're not. She's safer here than with us."

Her brother was right. Still, she hated breaking up her family. After last night, she found some small security in their closeness. Wearily she patted Mist's flank. "Don't fret; we'll be back soon."

Mist glanced up from where she chewed at the shoots of the scraggly grass that grew under the willow. She flicked her tail at Elena for disturbing her.

"See, El; she's fine."

Slightly hurt, Elena tucked her shirt under her belt. "Let's go," she said with a sigh.

Joach pushed through the sweep of willow branches. He held them wide to allow Elena to duck through, then let them brush back into place. Elena glanced over her shoulder. The mare was just a pale shadow in the tree's shade.

She sniffed and followed after Joach, who had stopped by a thin path. The dirt rut ran from the edge of Winterfell to a swimming hole popular among the town children. The pool, its waters now icy cold, lay abandoned for the season, so the path was empty of prying eyes.

With the sun close to its highest point, the path was bright after the shadows of the forest. As they approached closer to town, the path widened enough for Elena to walk abreast of her brother. She noted how Joach's eyes darted back and forth and how stiffly his legs moved as he hiked. Her brother's nervousness leaped to her. She found her hands tugging at her shirt and adjusting her cap.

"Look," she said, pointing down the path. "There's the butcher's shack." Ahead, buried under the eaves of the forest's branches, stood the icehouse of the butcher. The limbs of the trees helped keep the sun's warmth from its roof.

Joach only nodded and hurried ahead.

By the time they passed the icehouse and reached the end of

the path, both were white-faced and sweating thickly. The town of thatched roofs and brick buildings loomed ahead. Chimney smoke drew black lines into the sky, joining with the haze from the orchard fire. The town seemed uncommonly quiet. Usually bustling with the strident voices of stall merchants and shoppers, the streets ahead were silent except for an occasional shout.

Joach turned to her and offered a sick smile. "Ready? Walk fast, but not too fast."

She nodded. "Hold my hand."

His hand reached for her palm, then froze. "No. We might draw attention. Maybe we should even walk a distance apart."

She found tears coming to her eyes. "Please, Joach. I need you close."

"Okay, El," he said with a relieved rush. It seemed similar emotions warred within him, too. "But we'd still better not hold hands."

She squeezed back her tears and forced her head to nod. Aunt Fila's bakery stood only a handful of blocks from the edge of town. If Elena concentrated, she'd swear she could even smell the baking bread from where she stood. Actually, the whole town of Winterfell greeted her with its familiar smells: the roasting breakfast meats; the hickory wood smoke; the yeasty pungency from the cider mill nearby; even the sweet, loamy smell of horse dung from the unwashed streets and stables. Elena straightened her shoulders. "Okay, I'm ready," she said in a calmer voice.

Joach bit at his lower lip and stepped toward a back street that led into the merchants' quarter. Elena swallowed the hard knot of tears in her throat and followed her brother closely.

The first shop they came to was the butcher's shop. His wares of carved pig, yellow mutton, and headless chickens buzzed with flies. The butcher himself could be seen through the doorway, a bloody cleaver in his hand. His coarse black hair always reminded Elena of a pig's spiky stubble, especially set against the man's pale skin, shining with sweat and oil.

Elena found herself cringing. The butcher, loud of voice and smelling of offal, always made her nervous. He had a way of staring at Elena as if judging the quality of meat on her bones. This being the first shop greeting them upon entering Winterfell, Elena found herself clutching her baggy clothes tighter around her. A sense of unease crept toward her heart.

She and Joach walked on the far side of the street.

As soon as they passed the butcher's shop, a voice spat toward them from a shadowed doorway just ahead, startling them. "You there, boys! Hold it right there!"

Both of them froze.

Joach stepped between her and the speaker. A soldier dressed in a red and black uniform, his sword still sheathed, sauntered from the doorway. His dark hair and brown eyes warned that he was not a local conscript but one of the foreigners manning the garrison. His knotted nose spoke of past fights that Elena suspected were not in the line of duty.

"Where you coming from, boys?"

Joach made a subtle motion for Elena to back farther behind him. "We was out checking our traps, sir!"

The soldier's eyes drifted behind them toward the forest. "Didn't happen to see a boy and a girl with a horse, did you?"

"No, sir."

The man's dark eyes settled on Elena. She kept her head pointed to her feet and her stained hand buried deep in her pocket. "How about you, young 'un?"

Elena, afraid her voice would betray her, just shook her head.

"Then be off with you two." He waved them past with a swing of his chin.

Joach slipped past the soldier with Elena on his heels. She risked a glance behind her and saw the soldier, a hand raised to shade his eyes, surveying the forest's edge. He then drifted back to his shaded doorway.

Neither spoke until they had turned a corner. "So they *are* hunting for us," Joach whispered.

"But why? What did we do?"

"Let's just get to Aunt Fila's."

Though they tried to keep their steps steady, their pace became hurried as they neared the corner beyond which Aunt Fila's bakery stood. Elena nearly had to run to keep up with her brother's frantic steps. Joach swung around the corner first and stopped so short she barreled into his back, pushing him a step forward. Elena could now see around the corner.

Where Aunt Fila's bakery had once stood, smelling of fruited pastries and sugared cakes, only a smoldering skeleton of scorched posts and blackened beams remained. Elena's first thought was that somehow her magickal fire had leaped from the orchards to strike down her aunt's shop. But the milling crowd that sported torches quickly dismissed this worry.

"She's in league with the demon!" someone yelled from the crowd.

"Mark her forehead with an evil eye!" screamed another.

"Anyone related to those cursed whelps should be banished from town!"

"No! Hung!"

Elena saw her Aunt Fila kneeling before the burned bakery. Her face, covered in smoke, ran black with tears. One of her sons, facedown on the cobblestones, lay in a pool of blood.

Elena's vision blurred with tears. Though her fire had not directly burned her aunt's shop, it had still destroyed more of her family. She took a step toward the crowd.

Joach stopped her. "No."

They could have slipped back around the corner and maybe escaped, but Elena's motion and Joach's word drew the eyes of the crowd. Most simply ignored the two children dressed in crude clothes. But Aunt Fila's son Bertol stared with eyes wide in recognition. He raised a finger to them. "There! There's my cousins. See! See, we weren't hiding them in our shop."

One of Aunt Fila's hands flew up toward her son, as if trying to force back his words and his betrayal. Her eyes touched Elena's for a heartbeat, full of sorrow and pain.

The crowd lunged toward them. Joach tried to pull Elena with him, but strong hands suddenly grabbed them from behind.

Elena screamed but could not break free. She and Joach were shoved toward the crowd. Elena stared up into her captor's eyes. It was the butcher. Thick of limb, he held both of them easily. His lips were white with hate, his eyes red with murder.

"Call the guard!" someone in the crowd called as they descended on her and Joach. "We've caught the demon spawn!"

ER'RIL FROWNED AT THE MOUNTAIN MAN, WHO STILL KNELT IN TEARS at his feet. Nee'lahn seemed abashed at his outburst, one small hand covering her mouth. "Kral," Er'ril said, "I know nothing to doom your people. Stand up and put aside this foolishness."

Kral only moaned, his face turned to the floor.

The innkeeper approached with his broom raised across his wide belly. "Out with the lot of you!" He made a sweeping motion with his broom, then pointed its handle at Kral. "Out before that lout passes out on my floor."

Kral pushed to his feet, now towering like a bear over the rotund innkeeper. "Guard your tongue, keep, or I shall nail it to your door."

The innkeeper blanched and took a step away. He raised his broom higher. "Don't ... don't make me shout for the town guard."

Kral started to reach for the innkeeper, but Er'ril laid a palm on his high shoulder. "He's not worth the effort, Kral. Leave the man be." Er'ril tugged the tall man toward the door. It was like moving a boulder settled deep in the dirt. But Er'ril felt the man's shoulder relax, and Kral allowed himself to be pulled from the innkeeper's throat.

Er'ril turned to the innkeeper. "In the future, mind your manners among the mountain folk."

With Kral in tow, Er'ril led the way to the inn's door. Nee'lahn followed them outside, where the cobbled streets were oddly empty except for a pair of soldiers slouched at a corner near two tethered horses. One, with his jacket unbuttoned and his gut hanging over his belt, raised a bored eye toward them, then returned his attention to his companion, who continued to brag of the previous night's gambling.

Er'ril ignored them and turned to Kral. "Here we part ways, mountain man," he said. "You seek the skal'tum, and as much as this may anguish you, I pray you never find it. But for me, I seek only the road to the plains." He turned to Nee'lahn, who still stared toward the guards. She nervously scuffed at a cobble with the toe of her boot. "And what path do you seek, bardswoman?"

Er'ril never did get his answer from Nee'lahn, since a towns-man suddenly rushed to the pair of soldiers from around a corner. "We've found them!" he yelled. "The demon children! We've got 'em caught like rabbits in a snare! Come quick!"

The heavier of the guards pushed off the wall he had been leaning against and nodded to the other soldier. "Go alert the garrison," he said in a bored voice, obviously doubting the agitated man. "I'll check what this fellow has found."

The other soldier nodded and untethered his horse. He mounted briskly and hurried past Er'ril and his two companions, the clatter of hooves deafening until he tugged the horse around a corner.

"Show me what you caught," the remaining guard said.

"It's those Morin'stal whelps, all right," the townsman said, pointing down the street. "Their cousin even confirmed it." He led the way for the guard and disappeared between the tailor's shop and the shoemaker's.

Nee'lahn was the first to speak. "What will they do with those children?"

Er'ril stared down the road to where the townsman and soldier had disappeared. "The town is incensed. Talk of demons in small towns is dealt with brutally. By the end of this day, they will probably beg for death."

"But what if this is all gossip and rumor?" Nee'lahn said. "Then innocent blood will be shed."

Er'ril shrugged. "This has nothing to do with me."

Nee'lahn's eyes grew wider. "If you ignore this, then their blood is as much on your hands as on the townsfolk's."

"I already have blood on my hands," he said bitterly. Er'ril pictured the night of the Book's binding and the young mage slain in a pool of red with Er'ril's sword sprouting from his back like a weed among stones. "An innocent's blood."

"I know your story, Er'ril. That was the past. This is now!" Nee'lahn's eyes narrowed with anger. "Do not let one wrong stain your hands forever."

Er'ril's cheeks heated up—whether from anger or shame, even he couldn't tell.

Thankfully, Kral interrupted. "If these whelps be demon spawn true," he said, "then the skal'tum may be close. I will go see."

Nee'lahn nodded her head. "I wish to go, too."

Both their eyes swung to him. One pair of eyes determined and proud, one pair concerned and passionate. Once he would have felt similar emotions at the thought of children in danger. But what did he truly feel now? He looked inward and found nothing. This disturbed him more than their questioning eyes. What had the endless years done to him?

He faced Nee'lahn and Kral. "Let us find the truth."

ELENA WATCHED JOACH STRUGGLE WITH THE ROPES THAT TIED HIS wrists. Thick ropes secured her hands also, but she stood quietly. What was the use of struggle? She stared at the remains of her aunt's bakery. The circle of townsfolk jeered and mocked. She knew most of them, had schooled with many of their children. Still their faces twisted with hate. Even if she and Joach could shed their bonds, where would they run? This was her home. This was her people.

A small stone flew from the crowd and struck her forehead, causing her to stumble. It stung and blood flowed from the welt. She saw her cousin Bertol reach for another stone, but Aunt Fila slapped his hand. At least one person still cared for her. Tears began to flow, not from the pain, but from all that she had lost.

Joach stopped his struggle, obviously succumbing to the futility, too, and edged closer to her. He had no words.

The butcher strode from the crowd toward them. He reached a hand toward Elena. Joach tried to step between but was cuffed away by a meaty palm. Elena saw blood spill from her brother's lips as he fell to his knees. The butcher ripped the hunter's cap from her head and released the cascade of her red hair. "See," he said. "See the wit'ch! This is the demon that destroyed our lands and murdered good people. Do not be fooled by her pretty face."

The butcher ran a finger across her cheek and down her throat. "Or her innocent body!" He suddenly grabbed her shirt and ripped it open. Buttons danced across the cobbles.

Elena cried out at the violation.

The crowd gasped at the butcher's actions. Joach fought to reach the man, but hands held him down.

The butcher traced a finger along the bare budding of her breasts. "So innocent in appearance!" His voice had become thick and husky. "But so foul its lusts!"

He swung away from Elena. "I can sense her evil trying to worm into me, tempting me with impure thoughts." He faced Elena again. "Back, wit'ch; you will not win me over like you did your brother." The butcher shaded his eyes and backed from her.

The crowd was hushed by the display until Aunt Fila pushed forward. "Enough!" she yelled to the crowd. She crossed to Elena and pulled the torn shirt closed over Elena's chest. Elena could smell the scent of flour and sugar on her aunt's apron. She must have been working in the kitchen when the town rose up and mobbed her bakery. Elena leaned into her aunt's embrace.

Aunt Fila faced the crowd. "She is a child! Can't you see

how terrified she is? Does a demon fear rope and mortal man? What proof is there that she did anything? Words and gossip! That's all."

The crowd still rumbled with anger. "The orchards!" someone called out. "We lost almost a quarter of the crop!"

Aunt Fila did not retreat. She pushed a lock of gray hair from her face. Her words were ice from the mountains. "I have lost more this day than the lot of you put together. It is my son that was cruelly murdered trying to save my shop! It was not the child that harmed me this day, but madness!"

She stabbed a finger at various townsfolk. "What if it was your child up here? Or yours, Gergana? Stop this madness! Look to your hearts!"

The crowd became subdued with her words.

"I know this girl and this boy. There is not an evil bone in their bodies! You know them, too! When has either of them displayed anything but good manners and a sweet countenance?"

"Fie!" cried the butcher. "We all heard talk of what a strange child she is, skulking in the woods by herself. Consorting with demons, I don't doubt! She just now tried to bewit'ch me!"

"Lies!" Aunt Fila pointed a finger toward the butcher, her lips tight with suppressed anger. "There lies your evil. His behavior speaks of his own foulness—not the children's. To assault a small girl in such a manner! That is evil, not the child!"

By now many eyes had turned toward the butcher with disgust. Elena allowed herself a moment of hope that perhaps Aunt Fila would win past this insanity. But then she heard words sound behind her in a voice from a moldy tomb: a familiar voice.

"Good woman, stand back from the girl. She has tricked you, tricked you all. She is a wit'ch, and I will give you proof!"

Elena twisted around to see the cowled figure of the old man who had murdered her parents. Soldiers stood behind him. Elena's knees weakened as his dead eyes settled upon her.

Using his poi'wood staff, the old man hobbled toward her. "Stand back!" he suddenly hissed toward the crowd.

Aunt Fila ignored him and stepped between the crooked man and Elena. "You! You were the one who accused these children!"

Elena's tongue froze with fear. She nudged her aunt's arm with her elbow, trying to warn her away from the man, but was ignored.

The old man waved his staff to his dark partner. "Rockingham, remove this child to the garrison. There, we will conduct our interrogation and prove her demonic heart."

Rockingham strode forward with four guards beside him.

Aunt Fila grabbed Elena's shoulder and tugged her away toward the crowd. "Like you did the Sesha girl two years ago. Her screaming still rings in my ears!" Aunt Fila raised an arm and waved it to the crowd. "Who is willing to give another child to these monsters? This is our valley, our town!"

Around Elena, townsfolk erupted with echoes of her aunt's words. Elena's heart stirred, freeing her tongue. "Aunt Fila! They are the ones who murdered Mother and Father."

The crowd heard her words. A gasp arose from the mingled townspeople.

Rockingham and the four soldiers balked as the crowd grew belligerent. Several townsmen unsheathed knives. Elena saw the town's tailor slice free Joach's ropes. He dashed to Elena's side and untied her bonds. Freed, she rubbed her raw wrists.

"I told you Aunt Fila would help us," Joach said, his face flushed.

Elena noticed Aunt Fila's eyes widen at the sight of her stained right hand. Her aunt reached to cover it. "Keep this hidden," she whispered quickly and drew the oversized shirtsleeve down around Elena's hand. Her aunt then turned her attention back to the brewing altercation.

The soldiers took a tentative step forward but were outnumbered by the townspeople.

"Leave the child be!" someone yelled.

Another raised a knife in the air and cried, "Protect the children!"

Aunt Fila bent to Elena's ear. "You're safe now, dear. Don't fear. I won't let them harm our family anymore."

But Elena hardly heard her aunt's words. Her eyes were glued to the old man. She watched him raise his staff and tap it twice on the cobblestones. No one else took notice of the decrepit man's action. But Elena remembered the signal. It was the same one he had used when he called the white worms upon her and her brother.

"No," Elena's voice squeaked. She clutched Joach's arm, causing him to wince. "We must run!"

But it was already too late.

Someone in the crowd screamed in terror. All eyes turned to the smoke-stained skies.

From beyond the roofline, it came. A huge shape flew into view. Wide wings smote the air. Elena recognized the leathery beat of its wings. Its screech scattered the townspeople, who scurried like mice before a pouncing barn cat. Though previously invisible in the night skies, there was no mistaking the sound of the creature that had plagued her and her brother as they fled through the burning orchard. Now revealed, Elena wished for darkness to return again and remove the loathsome sight from her eyes. Its very image seemed to taint her spirit.

"See!" the robed man screamed. He pointed with his other arm, revealing a smooth stump where his right hand had once sprouted. "There is her demon consort, come to rescue her!"

The crowd erupted with screams, fleeing as the beast dove toward Elena. Only Joach and her aunt remained as it crashed to the street, taloned feet clawing the cobblestones. Through its skin, black blood could be seen churning in thick rivers. It folded its wings back and hissed at the townsfolk crammed into doorways and behind shop displays. Then its poisonous black eyes, glowing with malice, swung toward Elena.

Aunt Fila moved between her and the beast. "Run, children!" she said as she faced the creature. "Seek your Uncle Bol!" Even before Aunt Fila had finished her command, Joach was yanking Elena toward the burned shell of the bakery.

Like a snake, the creature sprang forward and snatched up Aunt Fila.

"No!" Elena cried as it broke her aunt's back, the snap distinct among the yelling. Then it tore Aunt Fila's throat open with pointed teeth and flung her body to the ground. "No," she moaned again as Joach pushed Elena away.

He was too slow. The creature shot out a claw and seized her brother by the neck.

"Joach!" she screamed as her brother was ripped from her side and hauled away choking, his eyes bulging.

13

BOL LEANED OVER HIS DUSTY BOOK. THE WEAK MIDDAY LIGHT SHED only feeble fingers through the grimed window. The single candle on his desk, melted to a nub, waved a small yellow flame. He had been reading all night, striving to glean the knowledge he needed. The stacks of moldy books and rows of cubbyholed scrolls were his only company.

"Fire will mark her coming," he mumbled as he combed white hair from his tired eyes. He squinted at the other words on the page. His lips, hidden under a thick mustache, slowly translated the ancient words. The portents of the Sisterhood spoke of this day. He glanced outside. The windows of his cottage, built high above the valley in a lonesome place called Winter's Eyrie, had glowed red all night with the flames of burning trees.

Poor child. She should have been better prepared, warned.

Rubbing his white beard, Bol turned back to his tome, but as he paused with a finger gently turning a rat-nibbled page, his heart trembled a beat; then a loss larger than his house filled his chest. He placed both palms on his desk, keeping himself from tumbling to the plank floor. An intense sorrow threatened to swallow him away as he felt his twin sister die.

"Fila!" he moaned to his empty room.

Tears rose to his lids and fell to the yellowed pages. Usually so fiercely protective of these fragile texts, he let the salt of his tears smear old ink across the page.

He clutched an amulet through the coarse weave of his shirt. "Fila!" he called again.

And as always, she came to him.

The corner of the room by the hearth glowed softly like a will-o'-the-wisp. The weak glow retreated inward, growing brighter as it shrank in size, until finally it formed the figure of his sister. Dressed only in sweeping eddies of white light, she frowned at him, more exasperated than sad.

"It's time, Bol."

As his tears welled, her image swirled. "Then it's true!" he said.

"No tears." She still wore her no-nonsense grimness. "Are you prepared?"

"I . . . I expected more time, years still."

"We all did. But it begins now. Time to put aside your books, old man."

"You leave me this chore?" he asked pleadingly. "To do alone?"

Her stern look softened. "Brother, you know I have my own role."

"I know: to seek the cursed bridge. But do you truly think you can find it?"

"If it exists, I will find it," she said fiercely.

He sighed and looked upon his sister. "Always the will of cold iron," he said with sadness, "even in death."

"Always the caster of dreams," she answered with a hint of a smile, "even alive."

Their lips formed twin smiles at the old argument, both so alike and yet so different. The pain of loss shone clear in each one's eyes.

Fila's apparition began to grow faint at the edges. "I can't hold here any longer. Watch over her." Her image faded to a vague glow. Her last words trailed as the light was vanquished by the library's shadows. "I love you, Bol."

"Goodbye, Sister," he mumbled to a room far emptier and lonelier than before.

ELENA RUSHED TOWARD HER STRUGGLING BROTHER. TIME SEEMED TO thicken and slow like sap in a winter's maple. She watched Joach's face turn a purplish hue, his throat closed in the claws of the skal'-tum. Elena leaped and grabbed at the creature's wrist, a cry trapped in her chest. Blind with fear, she dug her fingers into its clammy skin, refusing to lose her brother to the beast. *"Let go!"* she shrieked to the world.

In answer, her hand burst with flame. Heat like the touch of molten rock flowed from her fingers. She clenched her fist and found her fingers flowing through the beast's wrist—through skin, muscle, and bone.

The creature howled and tugged its arm away, pulling back only a seared stump. Screeching, panicked by its maiming, it tumbled away from Elena and her brother.

Joach stumbled forward, pawing the severed hand from his neck. He threw it to the street. "Sweet Mother!" he blurted and dashed to Elena's side.

Elena's eyes flashed to her hand, expecting to see blackened bones and burned flesh, but all was normal—not even a hint of the red stain remained. Was she free of that curse?

"Run, El!" Joach cried. He hauled Elena toward the charred beams of the bakery.

But the howling beast was not the only menace on this street.

Joach skidded to a stop and pulled Elena to him. Between them and refuge stood the cowled man leaning on his staff. He wore a smile, as if this all served his purpose perfectly.

"Come to me, child. I've waited long enough." With surprising speed, he whipped the heel of his staff toward Elena's head.

Elena, her mind still muddled by the flow of power through her hand, could not quite comprehend the danger.

She stood frozen until Joach knocked her aside. With a gasp, she fell to the street, her knee striking the hard cobblestones. From the corner of her eye, she saw the staff smite Joach a glancing blow on the shoulder.

She scrambled to her feet, roused now, and began to flee. Joach, however, failed to follow. Elena swung to a stop and stared. Her brother's upper body tried to heave his legs into motion, but like two rooted trees, his legs would not obey.

He looked up, eyes filled with horror, and saw that Elena had stopped running. "Go!" he yelled.

She stumbled back as she saw the bewit'ching spread through her brother's body. Now even his arms couldn't move, and in a heartbeat, his neck and head froze in position. Only a single tear rolled down his cheek.

"Do you abandon your brother, child?" The old man beckoned to her with a gnarled finger. "Come!"

TOWNSPEOPLE FLED PAST ER'RIL AS HE FOUGHT HIS WAY TOWARD THE screaming. Like a rock in a fast-flowing river, he was buffeted by elbows and knees and could make no headway. Finally, Kral pushed forward and used his large bulk to forge a path ahead.

One of the townspeople, Er'ril judged him a butcher from his bloody apron, tried to pound Kral aside. But with a shrug of the mountain man's shoulder, the heavy man flew far. His head hit the brick wall, and he fell limp to the ground. Kral ignored him and continued on.

"Run!" another townsman called to them. "The demon has come!"

Kral gave Er'ril a stern stare, then hastened his pace forward. Er'ril, with Nee'lahn in his shadow, followed in the mountain man's wake. After several heartbeats, the street emptied around them, the crowd now fleeing behind.

"Use caution, Kral," Er'ril said softly. "We're close."

They crept to the next corner and used a farrier's wagon for cover. Er'ril peered over the edge of the cart to the street beyond.

His blood went cold. Only a stone's toss away, before the burned-out skeleton of a building, stood a beast he had hoped never to see again. Wings stretched taut in pain, the skal'tum howled and held a wounded arm to its chest.

Wounded? Er'ril slunk back under cover. Who could harm such a beast?

Er'ril saw Kral begin to pull the ax from his belt. It was too small a weapon against a dreadlord. Er'ril raised a palm toward the mountain man, warning caution and patience. Kral's brows knitted heavily.

Nee'lahn knelt beside them, peering down the street from under the wagon. "There are the children," she whispered, pointing between the spokes of the wagon's wheel. "Who is that man, the robed one?"

Er'ril looked and spied the two youngsters crouched before a cowled figure near the edge of a scorched building. Though the cowled one's face was hidden in shadow, Er'ril recognized the black robe. His lips thinned with menace. "A darkmage."

"Come to me, child," the robed figure said, his voice finally carrying to them as the shrieking of the skal'tum waned. "Or your brother dies."

The skal'tum stalked toward the young people. Its voice cut through the air like a thrown dagger. "Give me the boy. I will rip his limbss, one by one, from his body as the other brat watchess."

Another man, dressed in the red and black of the garrison, quaked by a rain barrel. "Do what the master's beast says, Dismarum! We don't need the boy."

"Still your tongue, Rockingham," the one called Dismarum spat. Whatever look the darkmage gave the man caused him to pull farther behind his barrel.

The skal'tum repeated his demand. "Give me the boy! I will taste his young heart."

"Demon!" Kral growled beside Er'ril, his voice thick with venom. Before Er'ril could raise a hand to stop him, Kral leaped forward over the wagon, his ax already raised above his head.

The skal'tum twisted to face the sudden assault.

The darkmage retreated toward the shadows of the burned building, his hand reaching for the young girl still frozen in place.

Fool of a mountain man! Before Er'ril could ponder his own response, his feet and heart betrayed him. He found himself springing after Kral, his own sword drawn, prepared to join the battle.

ELENA'S EYES WERE FIXED ON JOACH'S. THOUGH SHE WAS NOT BE-wit'ched like him, she could not flee. Other ties held her trapped to this spot. She refused to leave her brother's side, even when the cowled man reached a clawed hand toward her.

But before his fingers could touch her skin, an elbow suddenly struck her chest and threw her backward. A one-armed swordsman thrust between her and the old man. Tall, wide-shouldered, with the ruddy complexion of the plains people, he raised his sword. "You won't have her, darkmage!"

Before the cowled man could react, the winged beast screeched, drawing all eyes. The swordsman shoved Elena down as a wide wing ripped over their heads. "Flee, girl!" he yelled in her ear.

But her legs did not obey. Her heart, still attached by invisible bonds to the frozen Joach, would not budge. She crouched numb in the street.

Cringing, Elena saw a giant attack the winged monster, wielding an ax in a blurring pattern of honed edge and muscle. The winged demon retreated from his assault.

Suddenly a new hand rested on her shoulder. She looked up into the concerned face of a tiny woman.

"Come with me. Leave Er'ril to rescue your companion."

She shook her head. "My brother!" was all that came to her tongue, an arm pointing toward Joach.

But the woman was stronger than she appeared and pulled Elena to her feet.

"Nee'lahn!" the swordsman called. He crouched on one knee, his sword raised toward the robed figure. "Get her to safety!"

The woman called Nee'lahn laid an arm over her shoulders and whispered in her ear. Her words, almost a soft song, were unintelligible, yet somehow pierced through the cloud in her mind. They reminded her of the words whispered to her by the Old Man in the orchard. Elena found the woman's song freeing her legs, and she allowed herself to be guided away from the battle.

NEE'LAHN COAXED THE GIRL TO THE WAGON'S SHADOW. COULD THIS be the one? the nyphai wondered. She sang in the child's ear, words she had been taught to woo the minds of humans. She brushed a strand of red hair from the child's face and stared into eyes the color of green growth. Could it be?

Once the girl was safely hidden, Nee'lahn returned her attention to the street. Er'ril had climbed back to his feet, and now the darkmage cringed from the sword's touch. Er'ril kept the cowled one from slipping away, but Nee'lahn noticed that they were both watching the battle raging between the skal'tum and the mountain man.

Kral attacked savagely, his swings wild and furious. But every strike was simply repelled by the beast's tough skin. No blood was shed.

Yet even though Kral's ax simply bounced off the creature, Nee'lahn noticed that the skal'tum appeared shaken by its previous injury. It kept the stumped arm far from harm, using wings to protect its flanks.

"Drive the skal'tum into the sunlight!" Er'ril called to his large companion. "There, you can wound it!"

With a furious feint, Kral switched the direction of his assault and soon had the creature retreating toward a square of sunlight. But the skal'tum seemed to realize the approaching danger and began to fight back. Its intact hand swiped black claws at the axman. Kral danced back. Quick and agile on his feet, the mountain man managed to escape injury, but he also lost ground. The beast now stood farther from the sunlight.

The skal'tum screeched in satisfaction, regained its confidence, and continued to thrust toward Kral, driving him around, almost toying with him. Soon their positions were reversed. The mountain man, sweating fiercely now, backed step by step toward the sunlight. Kral gasped for air, bent in exhaustion.

The beast spread its scabrous wings wide in victory, then swooped for the kill.

Nee'lahn raised a hand to her mouth in fright.

Kral suddenly darted backward with amazing speed—into the sunlight!

The creature drew up to the square of bright light and hissed at Kral. The beast balked at the sun's touch, staying just behind the shadow line. It stalked in a circle around the mountain man.

"There'ss nowhere to run, little man-thing," it said with laughter on its tongue.

Nee'lahn realized the creature was correct. The area of sunlight was a square island. Shadow lay on all sides. And in the shadows waited the beast.

Kral searched around, desperate for a solution.

Nee'lahn did the same. If the mountain man should fall, Er'ril would be trapped between the dreadlord and the darkmage. That must not happen! She twirled on one heel and grabbed up the tin top of a pickle barrel. Darting into another patch of sunlight, she caught the sun's reflection in the tin and tilted it so the sun's rays reflected into the face of the skal'tum.

The beast screamed and tried to dart away. Nee'lahn angled the tin to keep the beast in the light.

Kral seemed to realize his advantage and plunged forward with a bellow of rage. He swung his ax at the monster, striking the beast square in the neck. Exposed to the sun, the skin of the beast lost its dark protection. The blade sank home.

The beast stumbled back, pulling free of Kral's weapon. It clutched its neck as a river of black blood flowed from between its claws. Swaying on weakening legs, it tried to unfold its wings but instead fell forward into the sunlight, its foul blood hissing and bubbling as it stained the cobblestones.

Kral crossed to the collapsed creature, his ax raised high above his head.

Er'ril did not watch Kral finish with the skal'tum. He turned his full attention back to the darkmage. The sight of the black robe sickened his stomach. How could any man give himself to the black magick that had poisoned the land? Er'ril felt his blood heat with an anger he had not felt in over a century. He found it a not unpleasant sensation.

"Your pet is dead, mage!" he spat at the hunched man. "Release the boy, or suffer the same fate."

With his cowl bowed, the mage crept behind the boy and leaned heavily on his staff as if exhausted. "You interfere in matters you could not begin to comprehend."

The darkmage raised his other arm, revealing the stump of a wrist. Shadows rushed to the mage and flowed up his robe to his arm. The darkness then pulsed to his empty wrist and congealed there. Like a black rose budding, an ebony fist grew atop his stump, formed of black shadows. "And you make threats that you cannot possibly fulfill."

Er'ril's eyes narrowed. "Just test me."

The darkmage opened his malignant fist. Fingers that drank the light stretched out. "One final time: Give me the girl. You don't know what she is, what she means."

"I refuse to do your bidding, foul one." Er'ril raised his sword but held his position, fearful of injuring the frozen boy.

The darkmage switched his staff to his black fist. From his loathsome hand, the darkness swept down the gray wood until the entire shaft flowed with shades of night.

As Er'ril prepared for battle, the cowled figure instead put his hand of flesh on the boy's shoulder.

"Leave the boy be!" Er'ril shouted, and rushed the man, determined to stop him before he harmed the youth.

The darkmage threw his head back, his cowl falling away, and for the first time, he stared Er'ril full in the face. Their eyes met, freezing Er'ril's heart.

No! Er'ril stumbled to a stop. This could not be! His sword slipped down, scraping the cobblestones.

The robed figure raised his staff and struck the street. Blackness erupted up from the cobblestones to swallow mage and boy. The voice of the darkmage echoed up from the shadows. *"Er'ril, have the ages taught you nothing?"*

In a blink, the well of shadows vanished like a black flame extinguished. Where the boy and the mage had stood, the street now lay empty.

Er'ril sank to his knees as the young girl shouted behind him, her cry full of anguish and tears.

Er'ril, though, barely heard her. His eyes still saw the face of the darkmage. It was a familiar face: the same broken nose, the uneven cheekbones, the thin lips. And then there was the stumped wrist.

He remembered the man crouched with his brother in a warding of wax drippings so long ago—the night the Blood Diary had been forged.

The darkmage's true name tumbled from Er'ril's lips. *"Greshym!"*

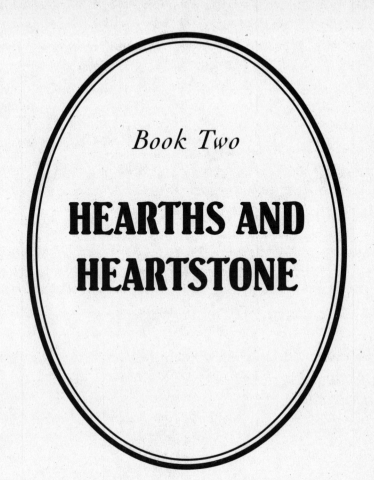

Book Two

HEARTHS AND HEARTSTONE

14

TOL'CHUK SIFTED THROUGH THE STONES IN THE GULLY, WHICH WAS bone dry from the summer's drought. He glanced to the thunderheads building like an army beyond the peaks of the Teeth. The summit of the tallest of the mountains, the Great Fang of the North, swirled in black cloud. Soon the gully would be roiling again with muddy water from the stormy mountain heights.

He turned his attention back to the scree of boulders. Thunder rolled down from the perpetually frozen summit. He must hurry before the rains began. But low cliffs blocked the sun's light, making it harder to spot the yellowish glint of scentstone. And this gully, dry all summer, had been carefully picked through for many moons.

He fingered the boulders apart, his grayish claws scraping each rock, searching for the characteristic color. His nostrils splayed wide as he hunted for the burning odor of raw scentstone.

There were more likely spots to find such rocks, but Tol'chuk preferred this route. Due to the scarcity of scentstone here, none of his people were around. Tol'chuk liked the isolation, free of the taunts from the other og'res. Especially now, with his magra ritual—the ceremony marking him as an adult among his tribe— beginning tomorrow. He needed a scentstone for tonight's preparations, one picked out by himself on the eve of his magra.

He bent to a thick plate of stone and dragged a claw along it, gouging its surface. He sniffed his nail: no, just sandstone.

As he lowered again to push through the rubble of the wash and scree, a rock the size of a melon struck him in the shoulder, knocking him to the boulder-strewn ground. He landed hard and rolled to his side.

Fen'shwa leered over the lip of the cliff.

A sneer cracked Tol'chuk's thick lips to expose his smooth, yellowed fangs. He pushed to his feet. With his back bent, his head reached only halfway up the cliff. He kept one hand knuckled on the ground for support. He twisted his neck and frowned toward his enemy.

Fen'shwa squatted like a craggy boulder by the cliff's edge, his wide yellow eyes bulging. Bent like Tol'chuk, balancing on the callused knuckles of one hand as was custom for the og'res, his bristled, straw-colored hair crested the top of his head and trailed in a spiky stream down his arched back to disappear under his leather coverings. He smiled, his chipped fangs exposed. A winter older than Tol'chuk, he was always baring his teeth, displaying the chips on his fangs that marked him as having mated.

All the females worshipped Fen'shwa, brushing their full rumps against his sides as he lumbered past them. No female brushed against Tol'chuk in invitation, no matter how much he kept his back bent and knuckled as he walked. Tol'chuk knew he was ugly. Smaller than other adult og'res, his eyes were too almond shaped, and slitted, rather than the bold circles of Fen'shwa. His nose also stuck out too far, and his fangs were too short to excite a mate. Even his hair did not bristle on its own. Tol'chuk was forced to use beeswax to make it spike. But no matter how much he tried to hide it, everyone knew his shame.

Fen'shwa reached for a stone with his free hand and hefted it. "I'll chip those teeth for you, half-breed!" he said with glee.

Tol'chuk burned at the insult. "Fen'shwa, you know the law. I am magra, not to be disturbed."

"Not until the sun sets!" He threw his stone, but Tol'chuk

dodged it easily enough. As much as his mixed breeding scarred his appearance, it gave him agility.

Fen'shwa picked up another rock, this one larger than the last. His eyes narrowed with menace.

"Leave me be, Fen'shwa."

"You fear! You are not og're in your heart!"

Even though Tol'chuk was used to ridicule, this was too foul an insult to leave unanswered. To call an og're a coward! Tol'chuk put aside his charade and straightened his back until he towered on two legs—something no og're could ever do. It was this ability that forged his name: *Tol'chuk*. In the ancient tongue it spoke his half-breed status and his shame: "He-who-walks-like-a-man."

Now erect, his head stretched to the height of the cliff. He saw Fen'shwa wince in disgust at the sight of his back straightening. Fen'shwa drew the rock back, preparing to attack.

Without thought, Tol'chuk shot his hands out and grabbed Fen'shwa's supporting arm. He dragged him, shocked, over the edge of the cliff and threw him to the bouldered floor of the gully. Tol'chuk instantly regretted his sudden action. Fen'shwa was not an og're to provoke.

Fen'shwa landed on his face in a sprawl across the rocky grade. Thick skinned and wide boned, Fen'shwa immediately scrambled up. Tol'chuk stepped back as Fen'shwa rolled to his feet. He sneered at Tol'chuk and raised a finger to his bruised lip. Fen'shwa probed his mouth, his eyes widening with shock as his finger came out bloody. A fire grew in Fen'shwa's glare, his eyes dilating until the yellow in them became black.

Tol'chuk had never seen such rage!

Fen'shwa howled a battle cry, his bellow washing down the gully. Tol'chuk now saw the reason for the fury. One of Fen'shwa's fangs had been broken off by the fall, a disfiguring injury that could cost the og're significant rank among the tribe.

Fen'shwa screamed again in rage and leaped for Tol'chuk's throat.

Tol'chuk ducked and rammed the bony crown of his head into

the midriff of his attacker. The force of the impact knocked the air from Fen'shwa's chest. Gasping, Fen'shwa flew back, landing hard on his backside.

But Tol'chuk's attacker was an experienced fighter, in training with the warrior clan. Fen'shwa rolled back to his feet and lashed out with his callused hand, grabbing Tol'chuk by the ankle. Yanking on Tol'chuk's leg, Fen'shwa toppled him to the ground.

Tol'chuk tried to bear the brunt of his fall on his shoulder. But his efforts still resulted in a crack to his skull. Pinpricks of light swam across his vision. Blurry eyed, he saw Fen'shwa leaping on top of him. Tol'chuk tried to roll away but failed.

Fen'shwa landed on him and immediately began kicking at Tol'chuk's exposed belly. Tol'chuk writhed, trying to limit the damage. Fen'shwa's back claws dug ribbons of skin, while his front claws jabbed at Tol'chuk's eyes.

Tol'chuk fought to free himself, but Fen'shwa outweighed him. If he could not break away soon, he would be gutted. Tol'chuk grabbed for Fen'shwa's wrist, but from the corner of his eye he spotted Fen'shwa's other hand slipping a hart-horn dagger from his belt.

When og'res struggled for mates, matching claw to claw, it was considered deceitful to use a weapon. Thick of hide and hard of bone, seldom did these mating contests result in the death of an og're. Within a tribe, og're did not kill og're. Only during a tribe war, when the og're clans fought for territory, were weapons employed. It took a weapon to kill an og're.

Fen'shwa raised his dagger, his eyes still aflame with hatred. "Half-breed," he said between clenched fangs, blood flowing from his lips. "Today you haunt us no more!"

This pause to gloat was Fen'shwa's undoing. Tol'chuk realized Fen'shwa planned to do more than just bloody him. Tol'chuk grabbed a boulder in each of his hands and slammed them together against Fen'shwa's ears. Tol'chuk heard the crack as rock met skull. The simultaneous blows at the only weak spots on an og're's skull were dramatic.

Tol'chuk only meant to stun Fen'shwa, to knock him unconscious until his reason returned. As the rocks struck, blood fountained from his attacker's nostrils, spraying Tol'chuk with its heat. He watched Fen'shwa's eyes roll to white and heard his breath gurgle on swallowed blood. The dagger tumbled from Fen'shwa's fingers. His body followed the knife to lie limp on the boulders. Tol'chuk pushed the rest of Fen'shwa's bulk off his legs and scrambled up. Blood flowed across the boulder from Fen'shwa's nose and open mouth. His chest did not move.

Tol'chuk stood stunned, unable to breathe. What had he just done? Og're must never kill og're within a tribe!

He raised his hand and saw the bloody rock still clutched there. A corner had broken away when it struck Fen'shwa's skull. A yellow glint sparked from the rock's heart.

Scentstone.

The rock tumbled from his numb fingers.

MOGWEED STOOD AT THE EDGE OF THE GREEN FOREST THAT WAS THE Western Reaches. He slouched against a trunk, reluctant to leave his forest home. A breeze shook the dry leaves overhead, rattling them like the husks of dead beetles. Beyond the trees to the east, the wide expanse of climbing foothills seemed naked, covered only in yellow meadow grass. And beyond the foothills and open meadows climbed the peaks of the Teeth, the mountains he must cross to reach the lands of man. Mogweed felt the rough bark with his cheek. But how could he leave here?

He raised a hand and stared at the thin fingers and smooth skin. He shuddered at the sight, then glanced to the clothes hanging from his body. A huntsman had shown him how to wear the strange garments. Gray leggings over linen underclothes, and a red coat over a gray wool shirt. He wore them correctly. Still, each stitch and weave of the fabric chafed against his tender skin. And the black boots were the worst. He refused to don them. Instead he carried them in a leather sack on his back. As long as he was in the forest, he would feel the loam between his toes!

He knew that once he left the shadow of the trees he would

have to put the boots on his feet. He needed to appear to be a man. Once dressed, only his eyes would betray his heritage. With slit pupils instead of round, his eyes spoke his true nature.

He stood there, one arm against the tree, until he was nudged by a nose. "Quiet, Fardale. I need a moment to prepare." He glanced down in irritation at the treewolf.

As massive as a man, Fardale sat on his haunches, his tongue lolling from the side of his mouth. His dense black hair, frosted with browns and grays, seemed like the dappled forest shadows given form and life. The wolf's pricked ears listened to the forest around them. His raised muzzle sniffed the air, checking for danger.

Mogweed's nose crinkled with bitter envy. Fardale's thick black fur was the only clothing he needed. No further adornment was necessary to complete his disguise. To almost anyone, Fardale would appear to be an ordinary treewolf, again except for his eyes. Like Mogweed's, his pupils were slitted, too, more like a forest cat's than a wolf's. Their eyes were a sign of their true heritage: *si'lura*.

Fardale glanced toward him, their amber eyes meeting. A slight glow seemed to warm toward Mogweed from the treewolf's eyes. Vague feelings formed in his head, whispers of thoughts and images from his wolf brother: *A sun setting. A hungry belly. Legs wanting to run.* Mogweed knew the meaning in these images. Fardale warned that daylight waned and that they still had much ground to cover before nightfall.

"I know," Mogweed answered aloud. He, too, could speak with the whisper of his soul, as Fardale had done, as all si'lura could, but his tongue needed practice. He would be among men shortly and must perfect his disguise if they were to make their journey safely. He shuddered again. "But I hate leaving home."

Images answered: *A mother's teat, heavy with milk. The scents of the forest, varied and thick. Dappled shadows burned away by raw sunlight.* Fardale also regretted abandoning their forest home.

But they must. The elder'root of their clan had ordered it, and his words must be obeyed.

Still ... Did they *truly* need to listen to the ancient one's command?

Mogweed took a deep breath and dropped his pack to the dirt. He bent and fished out his boots. Sitting at the edge of the forest, he slipped his boots over his feet, cringing as each foot sank into its leathery coffin. "We could just stay," he said to his companion, his voice a bare whisper. "Live as outcasts."

Fardale growled, and the wolf's thoughts shot deep into him: *A poisonous tree frog. A pond scummed over with algae. A hoary oak rotted with yellow molds.* The forest was poison to them now. To refuse the elder'root would bring no joy to them in the forest.

Mogweed knew Fardale spoke the truth, but still a fire grew in his belly. "I know, Fardale! But they've banished us! What do we owe them?" His words were etched with heat, but he kept most of his rage penned up within his breast. This was another reason he spoke with his tongue. He did not want Fardale to sense the true depth of his fury.

Fardale raised to his paws and lowered his head threateningly. His eyes glowed red: *A trapdoor spider. A littermate attacking another. A crow stealing a mottled egg from a nest.* Fardale still accused him.

"I was just trying to free us of the curse," Mogweed answered. "How could I know it would turn out so horribly?"

The wolf turned his head away, breaking eye contact, signaling the end of the conversation.

Mogweed blushed, not with shame, but with anger. Damn you, he thought. Fardale had been a choking yoke around his neck for long enough. The urge to leave the wolf behind and go out alone to seek his fortune among the human race thrilled through him.

Why did he need his own people anyway? They had always shunned him! He might better find his fortune among humans. Mogweed found his feet pulling him out from under the limbs of the trees and into the midafternoon sunshine.

He glanced around him. Free of the protective trees, the sky was so wide, so huge! Mogweed's feet stumbled to a stop. He crouched before the big sky. Like a massive weight, it seemed to crush him toward the ground. He turned back to Fardale. "Are you coming?" He tried to sound acerbic, but fear laced his tremoring words. Going out into such a wide world without someone to lean on terrified him. For now, he still needed Fardale—but only for now.

Fardale slipped from the forest's shadow. The wolf's slitted eyes scanned the horizons calmly, the sight having little effect on him. He simply padded across the rocky soil, his fur reflecting the sunlight in oiled sheens.

Mogweed's eyes narrowed. Fardale was always the cool one, the brave one, the noble one. One day, Mogweed hoped to see him break and prayed he would be the one to cause it.

Mogweed watched Fardale casually lumber past and continue into the barren foothills. With his neck still slightly bent away from the large sky, Mogweed followed his twin brother, cursing his sibling's stout heart.

One day, dear brother, I will teach you to fear.

15

Tol'chuk carried the limp form of Fen'shwa in his arms. He stood upright, his back straight, needing two arms to cradle the heavy body. As he approached the village, he saw several females rooting for grubs in the thin soil. When they spotted him, their noses cringed with disgust at Tol'chuk's upright posture. Og'res normally used their backs and only one arm to haul tree trunks or other heavy objects, leaving the remaining arm to support their lumbering gait. Shocked by the sight of him, it was only when he continued closer that the females spied his burden. Eyelids flew wide, and a cacophony of bleating arose from their throats. The females fled, loping away. The musky scent of their fear still hung in the crisp highland air.

Tol'chuk took no notice, but trod up the worn path toward his tribe's caves. His back and arms burned with exertion, but this was a small price for his atrocity. He had committed the worst violation of og're law: An og're never kills a fellow tribe member. During war, og'res could kill og'res of other tribes, but never of one's own.

As he had stood over Fen'shwa's bloody form, he had considered running, such was his shame. But by doing so, Tol'chuk would dishonor his dead father. And his birth was already enough of a disgrace for his family. How could he add to it by such cowardly actions? So he had collected Fen'shwa and begun his hike toward their caves, determined to face his tribe's punishment.

Ahead, at the foot of towering granite cliffs, Tol'chuk spotted the black hole of his tribe's home, easy to miss among the shadows clinging to the craggy and pocked rock face. The females had already alerted the village. Near the entrance to the caves, a crowd of og'res clustered—almost the entire tribe, even the bent backs of the old and the scurrying feet of the young. A few oak staves of the warriors bristled among them. Silence stood like a tribe member among his people. One weanling pulled a thumb from his tiny mouth and pointed at Tol'chuk, but before the child could utter a sound, his milk mother clamped a large hand over his mouth. No one spoke when the dead walked among them.

Tol'chuk was thankful for the silence. He would soon face those many questioning eyes again and speak his crime aloud, but first, he had a duty he must discharge.

Tol'chuk's heart beat hard in his chest, and his legs began to shake. But he did not falter a step before his people. If he should hesitate, he might lose his momentum, and the growing fear could catch hold of his heart. So he forced each foot to follow the other and marched toward his home.

One thick-limbed adult og're burst through the wall of onlookers. He leaned on an arm as thick around as a tree trunk. He raised his nose to the wind carrying toward him from Tol'chuk. Suddenly the huge og're froze, his muscles tensed like a rocky ridge. After seasons of living in dim caves, og'res' vision weakened as they aged, but their keen sense of smell grew more acute. The adult og're raised his face to the cliff walls surrounding him and bellowed his grief, the sound shattering the silence. He had recognized the scent of Tol'chuk's burden.

Fen'shwa's father knew his son.

Tol'chuk almost stopped. How could he confess his guilt? The muscles of his jaw ached as he clenched his teeth together. He kept his eyes fixed on the hole in the cliff's face and continued his march.

Fen'shwa's father galloped toward him, his thick rear legs hammering the stone escarpment. He slid to a stop, showering Tol'chuk with a flurry of loose shale. He reached his free hand over to touch his son's limp arm as it dragged along the ground. "Fen'shwa?"

Tol'chuk ignored him, as was the custom among his people. The grieving were not to be seen. He continued to march toward the yawning entrance. But Tol'chuk's silence was answer enough to the father. His son was not just injured—Fen'shwa was dead. Behind him, Tol'chuk heard a keening wail from the father's throat. He saw the other members of his tribe turn their backs on the grieving father.

Now stumbling with both exhaustion and fear, Tol'chuk swept through the parting crowd of og'res. No one touched him, no one hindered him: Let death pass quickly by. He carried his burden through the entrance into the darkness of the caves.

The roof of the large common chamber stretched beyond the reach of even the scattered cooking fires. But fingers of rock dripped from the ceiling to point accusingly toward him. With his head bowed, he worked his way through the cooking section of the village. A few females stood hunched by their fires, wide eyes reflecting back the twitching flames of their hearths.

He crossed the living areas of the various families. Smaller entrances jutted off the common space to the private warrens of each family. Males of the tribe poked their heads out suspiciously as he passed, fearful that someone sought to steal one of their females. But when they saw what he carried, they disappeared back inside, fearful that death might hop into their warren.

As he passed the opening to his own family's caves, no og're peeked outside. He was the last of his family. His home caves echoed emptily since his father had gone to the spirits four winters ago.

Tol'chuk ignored the familiar scent of his home. He knew where he had to go before he could rest his responsibility—to the cavern of the spirits.

He continued to the deepest and blackest section of the cavern.

Here a slitlike opening cracked the back wall of the cavern from floor to ceiling. For the first time during his trek, he dragged to a stop, frozen by the sight of that opening. The last time he had neared this dark path had been when his father had fallen during a battle with the Ku'ukla tribe. Tol'chuk had been too young to go with the warriors. When they returned, no one told him his father had died during the fight.

He had been playing toddledarts with a child still too young to fear and loathe him when they had dragged his father's speared body past him. He had stood there stunned, a toddledart in his hand, as they hauled the last member of his family into the black crack on its journey to the cavern of the spirits beyond.

Now Tol'chuk had to walk this path.

Before his legs grew roots of fear and locked him in place, he pulled his burden closer to his chest and continued. He was forced by the bulk of his burden to turn sideways to edge into the narrow slit. He squeezed down the black path, holding his breath. Sliding his back on one wall, he traveled the well-worn path until a weak blue glow flowed from beyond a bend in the corridor ahead. The light seemed to sap the strength from his legs and arms. His resolve faltered. He began to quake.

Then a voice whispered from ahead. "Come. We wait."

Tol'chuk stumbled in midstep. It was the voice of the Triad. He had hoped to drop the body in the spirit chamber and slip off to confess his atrocity to the tribe. The Triad were seldom seen. These ancient ones, blind with age, dwelled deep within the mountain's heart. Only for the most solemn ceremonies would the Triad crawl from their residence beyond the spirit caves to join the og're tribe.

Now the three ancient og'res waited for him. Did the Triad already know his foulness?

"Come, Tol'chuk." The words trailed to him from ahead like an eyeless worm searching for light.

Tol'chuk dragged his feet toward the voice. He held the air trapped in his chest. His grip on Fen'shwa's body grew slippery with sour sweat. Finally, the narrow path widened, and the stone walls pulled back. He was able to twist forward again and walk straight.

With his arms trembling under Fen'shwa's weight, he heaved into the chamber of the spirit. The cavern, lit by blue-flamed torches, stretched away to a black eye on the far side, the entrance to the Triad's domain. No og're except the ancient ones and the dead traveled that path.

Tol'chuk trembled at the edge of the cavern. He had only ventured to this chamber once in his life—during his naming ceremony when he was four winters of age. That day, one of the Triad had branded him with the cursed name *He-who-walks-like-a-man*—a shame he had had to bear for twelve winters now.

He had hoped never to step into the spirit-wrought cavern again, but Tol'chuk had been taught the custom. The og're dead were left in this chamber, away from the eyes of the tribe. What became of their bodies was never even whispered or questioned. To talk of the dead could draw tragedy to a hearth.

The deceased were the Triad's concern.

Tol'chuk took a single step into the chamber. In the center of the cavern, the three ancient ones hunched like rocky outcroppings sprouting from the stone floor. Naked and gnarled, more bone than flesh, the trio waited.

A voice rose from one of the Triad, though Tol'chuk could not say which one spoke. It seemed like the words flowed from all three. "Leave the dead."

Tol'chuk meant to lower Fen'shwa's body gently to the stone, to offer as much respect to his slain tribe member as possible so as not to offend the gods. But his muscles betrayed him, and Fen'shwa's body tumbled from his exhausted arms. The skull hit the stone with a loud crack that echoed across the chamber.

Cringing, Tol'chuk bent his back into proper og're form. His duty done, he began to step back toward the narrow path, away from the Triad.

"No. That path is no longer open to you." Again the voice

carried through the air from all three og'res. "You have harmed one of your tribe."

Tol'chuk stopped. His eyes fixed on the worn rock. The ancient ones knew of his violation of the law. Words slipped from his lips. "I didn't mean to kill—"

"Only one path is open to you now."

Tol'chuk raised his head just enough to spy the hunched forms. Three arms were raised and pointed toward the distant black eye, the tunnel that no og're except the Triad entered.

"You walk the path of the dead."

MOGWEED HID IN THE SHADOW OF A HUGE BOULDER AND STARED EAST toward the mountains. Fardale, with his keener senses, had gone ahead to scout the route forward. After crossing the golden meadows of the low foothills, they had reached a more rocky and treacherous terrain. Gnarled oaks and an occasional spray of pine dotted the higher foothills, but spiked hawthorn bushes covered most of the dusty ground. Luckily, after struggling through rocky gulches and up steep cliffs, Fardale had come upon a more hospitable path leading up to the peaks. The trail was a welcome sight. Ever cautious, Fardale insisted on investigating the trail before trusting it.

After the day's journey, Mogweed's clothes stank of sweat and clung awkwardly. He picked at them and wondered how humans tolerated living in the drapings. He closed his eyes and willed the change, wishing for the familiar feel of flowing flesh and bending bone. But as usual, nothing happened; the manlike form persisted. He swore under his breath and opened his eyes and looked east. Somewhere out there lay the cure to the curse on both him and Fardale.

Sweating from the climb, he stared longingly at the cold snow that tipped the tallest peak on the horizon, snow that even the hottest summer sun had failed to melt. The mountain, called the Great Fang of the North, towered over its many brethren. The range of craggy peaks, named the Teeth, ran from the frozen Ice Desert in the north to the Barren Wastes of the south, splitting the land in two.

Raising a hand to shade his eyes, Mogweed searched the range of mountains south. Somewhere thousands of leagues away rose this Fang's twin sister, the Great Fang of the South. From here, the southern Fang remained beyond the horizon. Even though countless leagues separated the peaks, rumor had it that if someone stood on the top of each Fang they could speak to one another. Even whispers could be sent back and forth, spanning the distance.

Mogweed frowned at such a preposterous notion. He had more important concerns than a child's fantasy. He hugged his arms around his chest and stared with a bitter expression at the wall of peaks, beyond which stretched the lands of the human race— territories he feared to tread, but knew he must.

Clouds began to build among the peaks, caught on the crags as the wind blew eastward. The snowy tip of the Great Fang was blotted out as black clouds churned. Lightning played among the thunderheads. If he and Fardale were to cross the Teeth before winter set its frozen hand upon the land, they needed to hurry.

Mogweed searched for his brother among the scraggly trees and brush. What was keeping that fool? A worry gnawed at his stomach. What if his brother had run off, abandoning him to this barren countryside?

As if he had heard him, Fardale suddenly appeared at the foot of the rocky slide. Anxious, panting from a sudden run, dancing on his paws, Fardale stared up toward Mogweed, requesting contact. Mogweed opened up.

Even from here, the wolf's eyes glowed amber. Fardale's thoughts whispered in his head: *The stink of carrion rotting in the sun. Racing legs pursued by gnashing teeth. An arrow's flight through the open sky.* Hunters approached.

Men? Even though he appeared a man himself and would likely have to interact with men during the long journey ahead,

Mogweed was in no hurry to meet any. He had secretly hoped to avoid the eyes of men, at least until they had passed through the Teeth.

Mogweed slid down the rocky grade to join his brother. "Where do we hide?"

Racing legs. Pads cut by sharp stone. Fardale wanted them to run—and quickly.

Mogweed's legs ached. The thought of fleeing through this rugged terrain sapped his will. He sagged. "Why can't we hole up somewhere until they pass, then return to the trail?"

Razor teeth. Claws. Wide nostrils swelling for scent.

Mogweed tensed. Sniffers! Here? How? In the wild forest, the beasts traveled in packs. Ravenous in their appetites, the creatures used their keen sense of smell to track down isolated si'lura and attack. He had not known the beasts could be domesticated by humans. "Where do we go?"

Fardale swung around and bounded up the trail, his tail flagging the way.

Mogweed hefted his pack higher on his shoulder and took off after his brother. His tired joints protested the sudden exertion. But the thought of the slavering sniffers and the beasts' shredding teeth drove Mogweed past his aches.

As he rounded a bend in the trail, he saw Fardale stopped just ahead, his nose reading the air. Suddenly the wolf darted to the left, abandoning the trail.

With a groan, Mogweed pushed past a bramble bush, thorns tearing at his clothes, and followed his brother. Scrambling up a steep slope of sharp stones and loose dirt, Mogweed soon found himself crawling on all fours like his wolf brother. The footing was treacherous. Mogweed kept slipping and losing hard-won ground.

Gasping between dry lips, Mogweed stared up to the crest of the slope. Fardale had already reached the top and stood with his muzzle raised to the breeze. Damn this awkward body! Mogweed dug his raw fingers into the dirt and clawed his way upward.

Slowly he fought the slope, careful where he placed each toe and hand. As he worked, a familiar buzzing bloomed behind his ears. Fardale sought contact. Grimacing, Mogweed raised his eyes to meet his brother's.

Fardale was crouched at the lip of the ridge, his eyes aglow. With the contact established, his brother's images flowed into him: *Teeth slashing at heels. A noose of hemp strangling.* The hunters were closing in.

Fear igniting his effort, Mogweed scrambled up the last few spans of the slope. He crawled up next to his brother. "Wh-wh-where are they?"

Fardale turned away and pointed his nose east toward the mountains.

Mogweed searched. The trail they had left wound among the steep foothills, a worn track disappearing into the wilder country of the peaks. "Where—?" He clapped his lips shut. He spotted movement on the trail, much closer than he had expected!

Men dressed in forest green, with bows slung over their shoulders and sheaves of arrows feathering their backs, marched down the trail. Mogweed melted lower. Three sniffers, attached by leather leads and muzzled in iron, strained against their master's yoke. Even from this distance, Mogweed could see the wide nostrils fanning open and closed within the iron muzzles as the sniffers drank the scent of the trail. Bulky with muscle and naked of fur, with skin the color of bruised flesh, they fought their leashes. Claws dug at the trail. Mogweed saw one pull back its lips in a snarl as another bumped into it, revealing the four rows of needle fangs that gnashed between powerful jaws.

Mogweed lowered himself closer to the ground. "Go!" he whispered to his brother. "What are you waiting for?"

Suddenly a shrieking wail erupted around them, echoing through the hills. Mogweed knew that wail. He had heard it sometimes at night coming from the deep forest. A sniffer screamed for blood!

Fardale's eyes glowed toward him. Images intruded: *A weanling pup scolded for mewling at night, revealing a hidden den. A nose glued to a trailing scent.* The sniffers had caught Fardale's scent on the upper trail.

Mogweed bit back a venomous rebuke as Fardale sprang away. He raced after his brother's tail. The run was a blur of scraped skin and bruising falls. Screams chased them, but from how far behind was impossible to judge.

Using an old dry creek bed as a trail, Fardale led the way higher into the foothills. The water-smoothed rock that lined the dry bed made slippery footing. Mogweed's boots betrayed him, and a heel twisted on a teetering stone. He fell to his knees, his ankle flaring hotly.

Mogweed fought back to his feet as a wail erupted behind him. The beasts were getting closer! Fardale danced anxiously just ahead. Mogweed tried to put weight on his injured foot, but red agony flared up his leg. He tried hobbling across the uneven surface and fell again. "I can't run!" he called to his brother.

Fardale raced to him and sniffed at his boot.

"Don't leave," Mogweed moaned.

Fardale raised his eyes to meet Mogweed's. *Two wolves, back to back, protecting.*

A scream echoed from behind them and was answered by another wail, closer still.

"What are we to do?"

A pack chasing a deer over a cliff. A flight of ducks taking to wing.

"What?" Fardale made no sense. Had his brother already been in this wolf shape too long? Was the wildness of the wolf overtaking his si'lura soul? Mogweed winced with pain, his shoulders hunched up in trepidation. "You send gibberish!"

A she-wolf leads a litter. Fardale twisted away and started to climb out of the shallow creek bed. He glanced behind to Mogweed.

Mogweed pushed up onto one leg, using just the toe of his other boot for balance. He snatched a handful of Fardale's tail. Between his hopping and Fardale's yanking, he scrambled out of the creek bed. But it took time, and Mogweed's lips were pulled thin with pain. Once up, he collapsed against the trunk of a pine, gasping. "Maybe we should stay put," he said. "Climb a tree. Wait for the hunters. In these forms, they may not know us as si'lura."

Fardale's eyes narrowed. *The eye of an owl. Flesh torn from bone.*

Mogweed groaned. But, of course, Fardale was right. These were forest men of the Western Reaches, not so easily tricked. Their only hope lay in avoiding men until they crossed the Teeth. It had been hundreds of winters since their people had ventured out of the forests and into the eastern lands. With luck, men on the far side of the Teeth would have forgotten the si'lura.

A scream echoed up from the lower washes of the creek bed.

Racing legs! The scent of the nearby pack. A mother's teat near one's nose.

Mogweed shoved off the tree. He hobbled beside his brother, one hand planted on Fardale's shoulder for support. It was slow progress, but as his brother had hinted, they didn't have far to go.

Fardale helped Mogweed over a rise to where even the thorn bushes failed to grow. Beyond the rise, only granite and shale spread before them, weatherworn rock where once an ancient glacier had carved a path through this region. Steep hills of gray rock were etched with black crevices.

The barren sight sucked hope from Mogweed's chest. "No," he whispered to the tumble of rock and shale. His brother was crazy! He stumbled back from the blighted area. "I would rather take my chances with the sniffers." Mogweed turned eyes of disbelief toward Fardale.

A fledgling caught in a tanglebriar, its young blood sucked through piercing thorns until it lay still. Behind lay certain death. *A raging river beyond which the pack howled.* As dangerous as it may seem, ahead lay a chance.

Suddenly a wail erupted behind them, and now even the crashing of hunter's boots could be heard. A voice called out, echoing up from the hidden creek bed. "Lookie here! See them tracks! Looks like them shape-shifters climbed out right here. C'mon,

Blackie. Git at 'em!" The crack of a hand whip and the howl of the sniffers speared through the thin air. "Git them damn shifters!"

Fardale's eyes drilled into Mogweed, full of satisfaction. Fardale had been proven right. The keening frenzy of the sniffers had alerted the forest hunters to what scent had caught the beast's attention: si'lura. Or in the foul, thick-tongued language of the humans—shape-shifters.

A moan escaped Mogweed's clenched teeth. Why had he ever left his forest home? He should have just stayed and tried to make the best of it. So what if he remained an outcast? He would at least have survived.

But in his trembling heart, Mogweed knew the journey was necessary. The thought of being forever trapped in this one shape for all time scared him more than the howling sniffers or what might lie ahead.

Balanced on one boot, weak words tumbled from Mogweed's lips. "Go . . . let's go."

With Fardale's shoulders for support, Mogweed and his brother crossed the threshold of thorn bushes and entered the land of scarred rock, a land all those of the Western Reaches knew to avoid: the land of the og'res.

16

Tol'chuk balked at stepping farther into the chamber of the spirits. He stood silently with Fen'shwa's body sprawled at his feet. The trio of ancient og'res slowly swung and marched with bent backs toward the distant tunnel. Words trailed back to him from the Triad. "Follow. This is your path now."

Tol'chuk had known he'd be punished for his assault on Fen'shwa. Og're law was strict and often brutal. But this? He stared at the black eye in the far wall, the entrance to the path of the dead. He now regretted his choice in returning Fen'shwa's body. He should have just fled into the wilds.

The last of the skeletal old og'res crept within the far tunnel. A single word echoed to him. "Come."

Advancing into the chamber of the spirits, Tol'chuk straightened his back and pulled upright. He had dishonored his tribe and no longer deserved to appear as an og're. The need for pretense had died with Fen'shwa. He stepped over the body of his tribe member and crossed the cavern. Torches of blue flame hissed at him. His many shadows writhed on the walls as he passed, like twisted demons mocking his gait.

At the entrance to the tunnel, before his fright could drive him away howling, he bowed his head and pushed into the darkness.

The scrape and shuffle of the ancient og'res led him farther into the bowels of their mountain home. No torches marked the walls here, and after rounding a bend in the tunnel, blackness swallowed him up. Only the scrape of claw on stone guided him forward.

Down this stone throat, his dead father's body had been swallowed, dragged by the Triad to the land of the spirits. Now, like his father, it was Tol'chuk's punishment to travel this path. He was as dead as Fen'shwa to his people.

What lay at the tunnel's end was known only to the Triad. For as far back as Tol'chuk could remember, the members of the Triad had never changed. He had once asked his father what happened if any of the Triad died. His father had boxed him aside and mumbled that he didn't know since no member of the Triad had died during his lifetime.

Tol'chuk knew little else about the three elders. To speak of them was frowned upon. Like mentioning the name of the dead, it was considered sour luck. Still, the Triad were a constant in the life of the tribe. Old and crookbacked, the three og'res guarded the spiritual well-being of his people.

Only they and the dead knew what lay at the end of this black tunnel.

Tol'chuk's feet began to slow as dread clutched his heart. His breathing rasped from his constricted throat, and a pain began to gnaw at his side. He crept more slowly down the twisting course as the air grew warm and dank. A whispering odor of salt and crusted mold penetrated his wide nostrils.

As he continued, the tunnel closed more tightly around him, as if trying to grab him and hold him from retreating. His head scraped the stone of the ceiling. Its touch sent shivers through his skin. He bowed his head away from the roof. The tunnel continued to lower as he wound into the depths of the mountain's heart. Finally, Tol'chuk was forced to hunker down and use the knuckles of his hand for support, returning again to an og're's shuffling gait.

Tol'chuk's knuckles were scraped and raw from crawling by the time a greenish light began glowing from the tunnel ahead. As he dragged himself forward, the light grew. He squinted in the light after so long in darkness.

The end of the tunnel must be near.

Deeper down the tunnel, the path began to widen again, and the source of the glow became clear. The walls of the tunnel crawled with thousands of thumb-sized glowworms emanating a pale green glow the color of pond scum. The worms undulated and throbbed, some in bunches tangled like roots, some on solitary trails that left an incandescent slime.

The mass of worms on the walls thickened and spread. As he continued, even the floor eventually churned with their grublike bodies. Dark splotches of crushed glowworms marked the footprints of the ancient og'res. Tol'chuk followed, trying to place his feet in the same steps as the others. Squashing the worms with his bare feet disgusted him. The sight of the writhing bodies made his stomach tighten.

With his attention on the worms, he was well into a large cavern before he was even aware of leaving the tunnel. Only the guttural intoning of the Triad drew his attention. The three og'res were huddled in a group, facing each other with heads bowed.

His eyes glanced beyond the Triad, and beheld a towering arch of ruby heartstone. Tol'chuk fell to his knees. Heartstone was a jewel that the mountain seldom released to the miners. The last heartstone discovered, a sliver of jewel no larger than a sparrow's eye, had caused such a stir among the og'res that a tribal war had begun for its possession. That war had killed his father.

The towering span dwarfed the three og'res huddled before it. Tol'chuk gawked at the bulk of heartstone, his neck straining back to see the distant peak of the arch.

Carved into countless facets, the surface reflected back the worm glow into countless colors, hues so stunning that his rough tongue had no way of describing them. He stood, basking in the light.

Where before the oozing sheen of the glowworms had sickened him, the reflected light now stirred something deep in his chest, penetrating even to the red core of his bones, and for the first time in his life, Tol'chuk felt whole. He sensed his spirit in every speck of his body. The bathing glow, like a cascading waterfall, washed clean the shame he felt in his body. He found his back straightening more fully than he had ever allowed it. Muscles knotted since he was young unclenched. He found his arms raising as he stretched his back up.

He was not a half-breed, not a fractured spirit. He was whole!

Tears coursed down his face as he sensed his complete spirit and the beauty his skin and bone hid. He breathed the radiant air deeply, drawing the reflected glow into him. He never wanted to move from where he stood. Here he could die.

Let the Triad cut my throat, he thought. Let my lifeblood sweep the worms from around my feet. Bone and muscle were just a cage, while his spirit buried within could not be sundered by ax or dagger. It was whole and always would be!

He wanted nothing more of life than this moment, but others intruded.

"Tol'chuk."

His name only skittered at the edge of his awareness, but like a pebble dropped into a still pool, the word rippled away his sense of well-being.

His name was repeated. "Tol'chuk."

His neck twisted in the direction of the voice. As he moved, his tranquility shattered. He shook his head, searching for what he had lost. But it failed to return. The heartstone arch continued to spark and glint, but nothing more.

Tol'chuk's back began to bow, muscles knotting, as he discovered the three pairs of eyes studying him.

"Now it starts." The Triad's voice was more a moan than words.

Tol'chuk bowed his head. His heart thundered in fear.

One of the Triad crossed to him. He felt his wrist gripped by the bony paw of the og're. Tol'chuk's hand was raised, and something cool and hard was placed in his palm. The og're backed away.

"See," the Triad commanded. Again the word seemed to come from all three, like a hiss of wind between narrow cliffs.

Tol'chuk glanced to what lay heavy on his palm. It was a chunk of heartstone the size of a goat's head. "What . . . what is this?" His own voice sounded so loud in the chamber that Tol'chuk bowed his head from the noise.

The answer swirled from the clustered og'res. "It is the Heart of the Og'res, the spirit of our people given form."

Tol'chuk's trembling hand almost dropped the stone. He had heard whispers of this rock. A heartstone that conveyed the spirits of the og'res to the next land. He held the rock out toward the Triad, straining for them to take it away.

"Stare." Their eyes seemed to glow in the worm light. "Stare deep within the rock."

Swallowing to wet his scratchy throat, he raised the stone toward his eyes. Though it glinted a thick red hue, it failed to spark and shine the way the arch did. He stared at the rock and failed to see anything of consequence. Confused, he began to lower the stone.

"Search beneath its surface," their voices hissed again.

Tol'chuk clenched his face and narrowed his eyes. He concentrated on the heartstone. Though of exceptional size, it seemed an ordinary jewel. What did they want of him? If they wanted him dead, why fool with this? Just as his eyes started to turn away again, he spotted it. A flaw in the core of the rock. A black blemish buried deep within the jeweled facets. "What is—?" Suddenly the flaw moved! At first he thought he had shifted the stone himself. But as he watched, he saw the dark mass buried deep in the stone spasm once again. Frozen with fear, this time he knew he had not moved.

He squinted and held the rock higher to the light. He now saw what the layers of jewel tried to hide. Deep in the rock was a worm. It could be a cousin of the wigglers coating the cavern walls, but this one was as black as the flaming oil found in pools deep under the mountain. What was this creature?

As if the Triad had read his thoughts, an answer was given. "It is the Bane. It feasts on the spirits of our dead as they enter the sacred stone."

Three arms pointed to the Heart. "That is the true end to the path of the dead—in the belly of a worm."

Tol'chuk's lips grimaced to expose his short fangs. How could this be? He had been taught that the og're dead, assisted by the Triad, passed through the stone to a new world and life. He hefted the stone with its black heart. He had been taught a lie! This is where it all ended. "I don't understand."

The Triad continued. "An og're, many lifetimes ago, betrayed an oath to the land's spirit. For this betrayal, we were cursed by the Bane."

Tol'chuk lowered the heartstone and hung his head. "Why tell me all this?"

The Triad remained silent.

A deep rumble shook the mountain roots, thunder from the distant top of the peak, what the og'res called "the mountain's voice." The threatening winter storm had finally struck.

As the echo died away, the Triad's words flowed again. "You are magra, of proper age. Even the mountain calls for you."

He raised his eyes toward the ancient og'res. "Why me?"

"You are og're and *not* og're. Spirits of two peoples mix in you."

"I know," Tol'chuk said. "A half-breed. Og're and human."

The trio of og'res swung their eyes toward one another, quietly conferring. Tol'chuk's ears strained toward them. Vague whisperings escaped their huddled mass, lone words and scattered phrases: ". . . lies . . . he knows not . . . the book of blood . . . crystal fangs . . ." A final phrase slipped to his ear: ". . . the stone will kill the wit'ch."

Tol'chuk waited, but no other words reached him. His heart thundered in his chest. He could not stand silent. "What do you want of me?" His words boomed in the quiet cavern.

The trio turned three sets of eyes on him, then their answer flowed to him: "Free our spirits. Kill the Bane."

MOGWEED AND FARDALE HUDDLED UNDER AN OUTCROPPING OF ROCK. The shelf of stone offered little shelter, but the late afternoon storm had struck so suddenly and savagely that no other refuge could be found in these barren lands of the og'res.

Arms of lightning grabbed the mountain peak and shook the rock. Booming thunder crushed them both deeper under the stone roof. Whistling winds swept down from the heights, driving a hard rain.

After the hunters had balked at following them into the og're land, Mogweed had assumed that the only risk of death lay in a chance meeting with one of the hulking denizens of these barren peaks.

He had not thought to worry about the weather.

Tiny freezing drops stung Mogweed's exposed skin like the bite of wasps. "We must seek a better shelter," Mogweed said as Fardale shook his thick coat. "We'll freeze to death by nightfall."

Fardale kept his back to Mogweed, staring out into the rain-swept gullies and cliffs. He seemed oblivious to the cold rain sluicing down from the cloud-choked skies. Like the feathers of a goose, his fur simply shed the rain, while Mogweed's clothes absorbed the dampness and held its cold touch firm to his skin.

Mogweed's teeth chattered, and his swollen ankle throbbed in his soggy boot. "We need at least a fire," he said.

Fardale turned his eyes to Mogweed, their amber glow more cold than warm. An image coalesced, a warning: *An eagle's eye spies the wagging tail of a foolish squirrel.*

Mogweed pulled farther under the rocky overhang. "Do you really think the og'res would spy our fire? Surely this storm has driven them deep within their caves."

Fardale scanned the rocky terrain silently.

Mogweed did not press his brother. The cold was much less a

threat than a band of og'res. Mogweed slipped his bag from his shoulder and plopped it on the floor of their shelter. He crouched down in an alcove farthest from the wind and the rain and hugged his knees to his chest, trying to offer the smallest target to the bitter gusts. For the thousandth time this day, he wished for even an iota of his former skills.

If only I could change into a bear form, he thought, then this rain and cold would be nothing but an inconvenience. He stared at his brother's shaggy figure and grimaced. Fardale had always been the luckier of the twin brothers. Life had smiled on him with even his first breath. Born first, Fardale had been declared heir to their family's properties. To match this position, Fardale was gifted with the tongue of an orator, knowing the exact thing to say when it needed saying. Whispers of his potential to become elder'- root of the tribe were soon bandied about. But Mogweed always seemed to say the wrong thing at the worst time and chafed his clansfolk with each movement of his tongue. Few sought his company or council.

All this, while grating, was not what had truly bothered Mog- weed about his brother. What drove Mogweed to shaking rages was Fardale's simple acceptance of their cursed birth.

Born as identical twins in a world of shape-shifters, their birth had been a cause of excitement and celebration. Twins had been born to the si'lura before, but never identical ones. Mogweed and Fardale were the first. No one was able to tell them apart, not even their parents. Each brother was the exact twin of the other.

Among the clan, the brothers were initially a novelty and a de- light. But the brothers had soon learned that whenever one twin altered his form, his brother's body would spontaneously warp to match and maintain their identical natures, whether this change was welcome or not. This led to an ongoing war of control. If one twin should let his concentration weaken, his form was open to unexpected shifts by the other brother's will. In a world where freedom of form was simply a matter of life, Mogweed and Far- dale were chained together by birth.

Where this burden in life was simply accepted by Fardale,

Mogweed had grown bitter, never content to stomach their fate. He had devoured old texts of their people, searching for a way to sunder the chains that tied brother to brother. And eventually he had discovered a way, a secret known only to the ancient si'lura of the deep forest.

Mogweed sighed aloud. If only I had been more cautious—

From an ancient worm-eaten text, he had discovered a little-known fact of si'lura nature: When two si'lura lovers were entwined in mating, neither partner could shift at the peak of their passionate fire. Mogweed had pondered this revelation for many moons. He sensed that a key to freeing himself from Fardale's yoke might lie in this small fact. Then a plan began to swell in his mind.

He knew that his brother had been courting a young female, the third daughter of the elder'root. Most si'lura over time developed a predilection for a certain form, and she had a preference for the shape and speed of the wolf. This young she-wolf, with her long legs and snow-white fur, had caught Fardale's eye. Soon talk of a union was in the mouths of many gossips.

As his brother's romance bloomed, Mogweed clung to shadows. Here, perhaps, lay a chance. He studied, plotted, and waited.

One night, under a full moon, his patience won out. Mogweed crept after his brother and from the cover of a nearby bush watched Fardale's dalliance with the lithe she-wolf. His brother nuzzled and coaxed the young female, her white fur aglow in the moonlight. She returned Fardale's affection and soon stood for him. As Mogweed spied, Fardale mounted her, at first tenderly, with sweet nips at her ears and throat, then with rising passion.

Mogweed waited until a characteristic howl escaped his brother's throat—then acted. Mogweed willed his own body to shift into that of a man, praying that his brother would be locked by his throes of passion into his present wolf form.

His plan succeeded . . .

Under the rocky overhang in the land of the og'res, Mogweed stared at the pale skin of his hands.

His plan had succeeded *too well*!

That cursed night, Mogweed had shifted into the form of a man, while Fardale had remained a wolf. But Mogweed soon learned that the cost of breaking their identical natures came with a price—a steep price.

Neither brother could shift again. Both brothers were eternally trapped in these separate shells.

If only he had been more cautious . . .

Nearby, Fardale growled in threat, drawing Mogweed's attention fully back to the present. His brother's hackles were raised, and his ears were pulled flat to his lowered head. The rumbling growl again flowed from Fardale's throat.

Mogweed scooted closer to his brother. "What is it? Og'res?" Even bringing the name to his lips caused a tremble to shiver through him.

Suddenly a black-skinned creature stalked from out of the sheets of rain directly in front of them. An iron muzzle hung loose around its neck, and a broken chain dragged behind it. It lowered its head to match Fardale's stance, its claws dug into the rock.

A sniffer!

It must have escaped the hunters and continued its own hunt. Mogweed backed behind Fardale, but the wolf offered little protection. Fardale weighed only a fraction of the snarling predator's massive bulk, a mewling pup before a bear.

The beast's shoulders bunched with thick muscle. Free of the iron muzzle, the sniffer opened its jaws, exposing rows of jagged teeth. It howled at them, its cry challenging the thunder among the mountain peaks.

Then it lunged.

17

Tol'chuk pushed the heartstone clutched in his hand toward the closest of the ancient og'res. His own heart felt as heavy in his chest as the rock in his hand. "I don't know what you ask. How can I possibly destroy the Bane?"

The trio stood stone-still and silent. Three pairs of eyes studied him. He felt as if his very bones were being read and judged. Finally, words droned toward him. "You are the one."

Tol'chuk did not want to dishonor his tribe's elders, but surely they were mad with age. "Who? Who do you think I am?"

He received no answer, just their unblinking stare.

The leagues of rock over Tol'chuk's head seemed to press down at him. "Please. I am only half og're. The task you ask should be given to one of the warriors, a full-blood. Why me?"

Words again flowed to him. "You are the last descendant of the Oathbreaker, he who betrayed the land and cursed our people with the Bane."

Tol'chuk felt his arms weaken. Would his shame never end? Not only was he cursed as a half-breed, but if the Triad spoke true, he was also the offspring of the corrupt og're who had damned his people. He found no words to answer this accusation, only denial, his voice a whisper. "This . . . this cannot be true."

The granite of the mountains edged the Triad's tone. "You, son of Len'chuk, are the end of an ancient lineage. The last of the Oathbreaker's seed."

"But . . . what do you mean I am the *last* of his seed?"

"At your naming, an old healer examined you. Your mixed blood has corrupted your seed. You cannot father og're offspring."

Tears threatened to well; so many secrets. "Why was I not told all this?"

His question was ignored. Their next words had the bite of command in them. "You are the last. You must restore the honor to your blood by correcting your ancestor's betrayal."

Tol'chuk closed his eyes and clutched the black-hearted stone in his hand. His tongue caught in his throat. "What did this oath-breaker do?"

The Triad withdrew inward again, necks bent, conferring among themselves. After several silent heartbeats, a whisper of words passed to him. "We do not know."

"Then how am I to correct it?"

The words repeated. "We do not know."

Tol'chuk's eyes crinkled in confusion. "Then how am I to find out?"

"You must leave our lands with the Heart. Seek your answers beyond the Spirit Gate."

Tol'chuk heard nothing past the word *leave*. His shoulders shuddered at the thought. This was what he had most dreaded when he killed Fen'shwa: banishment. To be forced to leave his homelands for the larger world, a world that hated and feared his people. Tol'chuk shrank under their stares. "Where do I go?"

Three arms raised and pointed fingers to the massive arch of ruby heartstone. "Through the Spirit Gate."

Tol'chuk's brows bunched. It was solid rock. How could he pass through there?

"Come." Two of the ancient og'res crossed to the arch. One took up a post by the left foot of the arch, while another crossed slowly to the right foot. The third member of the Triad took Tol'chuk by the wrist and guided him toward the open arch.

"What am I supposed to do?" Tol'chuk asked in a tremulous voice.

The og're beside him spoke. Broken from the others, his voice had a trace of warmth, more like a stern father. "Before the Bane appeared, the Gate collected the spirits from the Heart and carried them to the next world. Like the spirits, you must hold your desire firm, and the Gate will take you where you need to be. It is foretold that when the last descendant of the Oathbreaker crosses through the Spirit Gate, he will find the path to free our spirits."

Tol'chuk nodded to the arch. "But I'm not a spirit. I can't pass through solid rock."

"You need not be a spirit."

"Then how?"

No answer was given, but a low intoning arose from the og'res bowed at each foot of the sweeping stone arch. The thrumming of their voices seemed to sweep to Tol'chuk's marrow. He felt a slightly giddy sensation. His ears buzzed, and the heartstone in his hand resonated to the og'res' humming. As he watched, wide-eyed, the wall of rock contained within the heartstone arch changed. It still appeared outwardly the same—hard granite—but Tol'chuk knew it was now an illusion, like the phantom reflection of a cliff in still water. It had the appearance of rock but was no more substantial than the thin film that watersprites skimmed across on a calm pond.

As the throbbing hum grew, the heartstone in his hands drew toward the Spirit Gate like a mate seeking the warmth of a touch on a cold night. The stone's gentle tugging urged his feet to follow. Tol'chuk found his legs obeying. With his ears still pounding to the intonations and hum, Tol'chuk barely noticed the old og're leave his side. Tol'chuk proceeded alone toward the arch.

But words trailed to him from the lone member of the Triad behind him. "Listen to the heartstone. Though blackened, it is still our Heart. Listen, and it will guide you when it can."

The words wormed through to his fogged mind, but meaning failed to penetrate. He ignored the words. As he stepped close to the Gate, the vibrations swept all thoughts aside. He opened himself to its touch, trusting the Gate to take him where he needed to be. Blind now, he took the next step—the first step on his journey to free his people—on faith.

As he passed through the veil of the Gate, the thrumming in his ears vanished in a heartbeat to be replaced with the ear-splitting howl of a hunter seeking blood.

MOGWEED SCUTTLED BACKWARD AS THE SNIFFER SCREAMED AND lunged. Fardale burst from under the shelf of rock, his fangs bared. A roaring howl exploded from the wolf's throat. Mogweed had never heard such a noise from his brother. The howl iced the blood and froze the heart. Even the sniffer balked in midcharge.

Wolf and sniffer now stood only a span apart. Each beast, head lowered, sought a weakness in the other.

Mogweed crouched motionless in his hiding place. A bolt of lightning struck a scraggled pine a league up the mountain, splitting the air with thunder. Rain swamped both combatants. The sniffer towered over Fardale, its bulk twice that of the wolf. The razor-edged teeth, daggered claws, and sheer ferocity of the beast left little doubt of who would walk away from this fight. The only unanswered question was if Mogweed could escape while the sniffer sated its hunger on Fardale's corpse. Mogweed searched for a way to slip unseen from the overhang.

Suddenly, without warning, as if obeying some instinctual signal, both combatants flew at each other. The snapping of jaws and spurts of furious growls escaped the blur of black fur and bruise-colored skin. Claws and teeth ripped flesh.

Mogweed sought to escape his hole, but as he neared the edge of the overhang, he was forced to dance back as the fighters tumbled near. With the combatants so close, Mogweed saw gouts of blood matting down Fardale's fur. How much of it was Fardale's own was impossible to judge. But it was clear the fight could not last much longer.

Like the ebbing of a tide, the growling battle rolled away from Mogweed's hiding place, freeing a route of escape. Mogweed edged from the security of the overhang, meaning to make his run. The cold rain again attacked the skin of his face with its rough affection. Mogweed ignored its bite. He kept one eye focused on the fight and the other on the dark path that led away among the rocks. Just as he began to turn his back on his brother, motion hooked his eye.

A large boulder tumbled from above to crash near the two fighters. Its cracking impact startled the combatants. Wolf and sniffer paused in midfight, bloody teeth poised at throat and belly.

Suddenly the boulder reached out and grabbed the sniffer.

It wasn't a boulder but an og're! Mogweed dashed back under the overhang and crammed himself into the darkest corner. Fardale scrambled in retreat, hindered by a broken forelimb that hung crooked and limp. Standing on three legs, the wolf stood guard at the entrance to the shelter, protecting Mogweed from this new threat.

From his hole, Mogweed watched the sniffer, one of the most savage predators of the Western Reaches, torn to raw-edged pieces at the hands of the og're.

Once finished, still tangled in the entrails of the sniffer, the creature twisted toward them, its blunt face scarred by splashes of black blood, its yellowed fangs bared. Steam plumed from its wide, squashed nostrils. It boomed, in a crude approximation of the common tongue shared by many of the land's peoples, "Who be you trespassers?"

TOL'CHUK SHOOK AS HE CROUCHED AMONG THE SHREDDED REMAINS of the woodland beast, fighting his blood lust. His claws ached to rend the wolf who still stood near, and his tongue ran thick with saliva. The odor of blood, with its hint of iron like freshly mined

ore, tinged his thoughts. He had heard warriors of his tribe speak
of the *fer'engata,* the fire of the heart, during battles, of how the
scent of an enemy's blood could ignite an og're to further savagery,
until all control was lost.

Tol'chuk felt his heart thundering in his chest, the real thunder
crashing around him only a pale imitation of his blood's booming.
Blood called for blood.

He fought the instinct. Now was not the time for blind actions.
Such a path he had followed earlier in the day, and now Fen'shwa
lay dead in the chamber of the spirits. His shoulders trembled, but
he had control of his mind.

Since he had seen the small man-thing crawl under the shelf
of rock, his wolf guarding him, Tol'chuk spoke in the common
tongue used in trading with other mountain races. Tol'chuk
struggled with his words. An og're's throat was not built for the
subtleties of common speech. The og're language was more gesture, posture, and a guttural grunting. Still, Tol'chuk knew that
there must be some reason for the Spirit Gate sending him here.
He remembered the Triad's words: The Gate would send him
where he needed to be. The appearance of a man in the lands of
his people had to be significant. Humans had not ventured into
this territory in ages. The skulls of the last still adorned the warriors' drum chamber. So Tol'chuk fought his tongue to form the
words needed. "Who be you?" he repeated. "What seek you in
our lands?"

The only answer he got to his questions was a low growl from
the wolf—not a threat or challenge, but a tentative warning.

Tol'chuk sensed from the wolf's answer that the pair meant
him no harm, only wished to be left alone. But he also knew that
their meeting here was not mere chance. This encounter was meant
to be.

"Do not fear," he said calmly and slowly. "Come. Speak."

His soft words seemed to confuse the wolf. Tol'chuk saw the
wolf glance back into the shadowed hole under the overhang.
When the wolf's eyes settled on his own again, Tol'chuk noticed

something strange. The wolf's eyes, glowing a soft amber, had pupils slitted like his own—as unnatural for a wolf as his own eyes were for an og're. Tol'chuk also sensed an intelligence behind those bright eyes equal to his own.

All at once, strange images formed in Tol'chuk's head like suddenly remembered dreams.

A wolf greets another wolf nose to nose. Welcome to the pack.

18

MOGWEED STAYED CROUCHED DEEP UNDER THE OVERHANG. FARDALE must have struck his head on a rock during the battle with the sniffer. The creature out there was *not* si'lura! He refused to risk moving any closer to get a better look at the og're's eyes as Fardale insisted. He was not about to put himself within arm's reach of the beast. He was determined to stay hidden until he died of starvation, rather than have his limbs rended as the dead sniffer's had been.

But the og're's next words gave him pause. "How be it that your wolf's thoughts are in my head?" the og're said in a voice that sounded as if he had a throat packed with grating stones. "What trick be this?"

The og're could hear Fardale? Mogweed found himself creeping forward just enough to peek out from the shelter. The rain had stopped, and a few breaks in the clouds brightened the streaming landscape. He glanced toward the og're, who stood only a few steps away. A wary expression clouded the og're's rocky features. Wearing only a leather loincloth and a pack strapped to its leg, it hunkered among the shreds of the sniffer. It looked like drawings he had seen of og'res, but this one did not seem so twisted and misshapen as the etchings had suggested. Perhaps the drawings had been exaggerated. This was the first og're he had ever seen—if it was an og're!

He saw the slitted eyes. Fardale was right. Si'lura perhaps . . . but this creature was huge. Si'lura could not swell their mass when altering form. Flesh was flesh. A si'lura's weight stayed the same no matter which form was chosen: deer, wolf, bear, man, rok'eagle. The bulk of the si'lura stayed the same.

Fardale glanced back to Mogweed. His brother's eyes glowed with curiosity. Fardale's thoughts intruded on Mogweed: *A wolf recognizes the howl of its pack.*

So the og're *was* sensing his brother's touch! Mogweed crawled forward. How was this possible? The og're was at least three times their weight. No si'lura had ever come close to matching this size.

"Come out, little man. Do not be afraid. I will not eat you."

Mogweed noticed the og're's eyes had picked him out of the black shadows. The og're stared directly at him now. Its vision must be keen, heightened by life in the caverns.

"Come." The voice boomed.

Mogweed stayed where he was, still partially hidden behind Fardale's form. But the og're's words had somewhat calmed the terror around his heart. He loosened his tongue. "What do you want of us?" he called out, his voice a mere squeak when compared to the og're's.

"Come out. I then see you better."

Mogweed tensed. Fardale turned his eyes on his brother. *A hawk with a broken wing can't fly. Forest cats prowl in the bushes.* Fardale hinted that they would need help if they were to pass through og're lands.

Fardale hopped on his three legs closer to the lumbering creature, leaving space for Mogweed to climb out. Still Mogweed hesitated. He knew he had no choice, but his legs refused to budge.

"I will not harm you, little man. My word be my heart." The beast tapped a bloody claw to its chest. The og're's words had a trace of sorrow and weariness. It was more the voice than the words that finally freed Mogweed's legs.

He climbed from under the overhang and straightened to face the og're. Its flat, crushed face, with huge nostrils and thick lips, caused Mogweed's mouth to twist in disgust. Its mountain of muscle and bone trapped Mogweed's tongue.

Fardale nudged his brother with his nose. Mogweed swatted him away. What did you say to an og're?

Fardale huffed loudly and squatted on the wet rock. The wolf turned his gaze on the og're. Mogweed sensed the mosquito itch of a sending. But Fardale's thoughts were not directed at him. Mogweed watched the og're reach a claw up and scratch its thick brow. It shook its head.

"A valley far away?" the og're mumbled. "What be that?"

Mogweed spoke, realizing what his brother had attempted. His voice squeaked. "It's the wolf's name: Distant valley, fardale. He communicates with images."

"Wolves do that?"

"No." Mogweed's confidence grew when it seemed the og're was not going to attack. "He is not a wolf. He is my brother. I am called Mogweed."

"I be Tol'chuk." The og're nodded his chin in greeting. "But how be this wolf your brother?"

"We are si'lura—shape-shifters. We can speak through our spirit tongues to one another."

Tol'chuk stumbled back a step. His voice cracked across the stone. "You be tu'tura! Deceivers. Stealers of babies!"

Mogweed cringed. Why were his people so persecuted? A twinge of anger penetrated his fear. "That is a lie! We are simply a people of the forest, and much maligned by the other races. We harm no one and live our lives peacefully."

Mogweed's words sunk visibly into the og're. Mogweed saw Tol'chuk narrow his eyes in thought. When he spoke again, his voice was softer. "I hear truth in your words. I be sorry. I hear bad stories."

"Not all tales are true."

The og're sagged, and his shoulders slumped. "I be taught that many times today."

"We only mean to pass through here. That beast you killed drove us into your lands. Please let us pass."

"I will not stop you. But you will not survive in our lands alone. The og're tribes will hunt you down before you clear the pass."

Mogweed winced.

"Even now, the beast's screams echo to my brothers." He pointed to the sprawled carcass of the sniffer. "Soon its blood will draw many, many og'res. Then they will eat you."

Fardale pulled back to his feet with the og're's words. He hopped closer to his brother.

Mogweed's breath caught in his throat. Og'res would be swarming through here!

Tol'chuk seemed to sense Mogweed's panic and spoke softly. "This night, I must leave my lands. If you like, I can come with you. Protect you and help hide you in these lands."

Travel with an og're? Mogweed's mouth was sand-dry. Fardale faced him. Mogweed opened to his brother's sending.

A pack grows stronger as it grows in size.

Mogweed found himself nodding, but he could not take his eyes from the long fangs of the og're before him. Let's just hope, he thought, that the pack doesn't get eaten by one of its members.

TOL'CHUK STARED ACROSS THE FIRE AT THE TWO BROTHERS. THEY HAD traveled well into the night before finally stopping to rest the few hours until daybreak. The wolf-brother already lay curled with his nose tucked under a sodden tail. The splinted forelimb stuck out and pointed at the crackling fire. Tol'chuk watched his even breathing. Fardale was fast asleep.

Movement caught Tol'chuk's eyes. The other brother lay wrapped in a blanket on the far side of the fire, but from the open eyes reflecting the firelight, this brother did not sleep. The one called Mogweed had remained wary of Tol'chuk throughout the journey.

"You need sleep," Tol'chuk said in a low voice, still struggling with the common tongue. "I guard. I do not need much sleep."

"I'm not sleepy." But Mogweed's voice cracked with exhaustion. The man's eyes were bloodshot, and bruised crescents outlined them.

Tol'chuk studied him. How frail was the human race. Such tiny arms, like budding sapling limbs, and a chest so small he wondered how a man could catch his breath. He spoke to Mogweed, urging sleep. "Hard day tomorrow. There be two more days of long travel to cross the pass and leave my people's lands."

"And then what?"

Tol'chuk's brow furrowed with grooves. "I know not. I seek answers. When I found you, I hoped for some sign, some meaning to our meeting. But you be just lost travelers."

Mogweed yawned, his jaw stretching wide. He mumbled to the fire. "We, too, seek answers."

"To what?"

"Why we can't shift."

"You cannot change?"

"No. There was . . . an accident . . . and we became stuck in these forms. Like you, my brother and I are on a journey, to try to find a way to free our bodies. We seek a city of trace magick among the lands of the humans, a city named A'loa Glen."

"The trip you take be a dangerous one. Why not be happy with the way you are now?"

Tol'chuk saw Mogweed's lips curl in disdain. "We are si'lura. If we remain in one form longer than fourteen moons, the memory of our si'lura heritage fades until we become that form. I do not want to forget who I am or where I came from—and most of all I don't want to stay a man!" Mogweed's voice had risen enough to cause Fardale to stir in his slumber.

This was obviously a sensitive matter to Mogweed. Tol'chuk crinkled his face, then rubbed his chin with a claw. When he

spoke next, he changed the course of their talk. "Your wolf . . .
I mean your brother . . . he sends me the same picture over
and over: A wolf sees a fellow brother. Over and over. I do not
understand this picture."

Mogweed hesitated. The silence stretched. If it weren't for the
reflection of the fire revealing Mogweed's staring eyes, Tol'chuk
would have thought him asleep. Finally, Mogweed spoke. "Are all
og'res like you?"

This question startled Tol'chuk. Were his deformities so obvious that even another race could spot his ugliness? "No," he finally said. "I be a half-breed. Human and og're blood mix in me."

A trace of bitter amusement laced the small man's next words.
"You are wrong, og're. You are not half human. You are half
si'lura."

"What be this you speak?"

"I know of hunters and other humans of the Western Reaches.
The blood of humans does not flow through you. No race of the
many lands can hear a si'lura's spirit tongue. Yet you can. Your
eyes . . . they are the same as ours. You must have si'lura blood, not
human."

Tol'chuk sat rock-still. His heart slowed its beat, and the
ground suddenly chilled his bones. He remembered the Triad's
hushed response when he had spoken of his mixed blood. The
words "he knows not" had flowed from them. If the Triad had
known of his true heritage, why hadn't they told him?

Tol'chuk shuddered. Mogweed's words had the scent of
truth—especially after seeing how weak and small the race of humans grew. A female of the human race could not withstand the
mating with an og're. The og're females, while weighing no more
than a man, were squat and thick with bone. A human female
could not withstand the mount and forcefulness of an adult rut-
ting og're. Even some of the toadish og're females were crushed
and broken under excited males. That's why a male kept a harem
of the small females: If one was crushed, there were always others.

Tol'chuk lowered his head into his hands, his mind spinning. A si'lura altered into the form of an og're female could have survived his massive father. But did she do this deliberately, or had she become fixed in og're form and forgotten her si'lura past? Tol'chuk would never know. She had died giving birth, or so he had been told. But what was true?

Mogweed must have sensed Tol'chuk's shock. The man's tongue clucked in his throat, obviously fearful he had offended him. "I . . . I'm sorry if—"

Tol'chuk held up a hand to quiet him, his jaw frozen. Words stayed buried in his throat. He only stared in silence at the two brothers across the fire. Here, too, was his tribe. He saw the fearful look in Mogweed's eyes. And here, too, like his og're home, was a place he would never be fully accepted. The og're half of him would always offend and terrify this new tribe.

Tol'chuk watched Mogweed burrow into his blankets and pull a woolen corner over his head. Tol'chuk sat numb. The fire offered no warmth this night. He stared at the few stars winking through the breaks in the clouds. The fire popped as it devoured the bits of wood.

He had never felt so alone.

THE NEXT AFTERNOON, TOL'CHUK REGRETTED HIS COMPLAINTS OF lonely solitude. Suddenly the mountain paths were too crowded. Mogweed's words had kept Tol'chuk's thoughts grinding throughout the night. Only the morning distraction of breaking camp interrupted his shock. It was this roiling consternation and lack of rest that weakened Tol'chuk's keen wariness. Before Tol'chuk could hide his companions, three og'res had rushed them from a leeward slope of the mountain trail.

He stared at the three og'res of the Ku'ukla clan, the very tribe that had killed his father in the raids. Thick with muscle and scar, these three had seen many battles and were well hardened by war. The leader of the pack towered over Tol'chuk.

"It's the half-breed of the Toktala clan!" grunted this giant of an og're. He pointed an oak log that he carried in his free hand in Tol'chuk's direction. "Seems even a half-breed can capture a bit of game on these trails."

Tol'chuk stepped in front of the cowering Mogweed. Fardale, listing on his three good legs, remained near the thick thigh of Tol'chuk. The wolf growled toward the band of og'res. Tol'chuk kept one hand knuckled on the wet stone to maintain as much true og're form as possible. If he were to have any chance of surviving this assault, he must not provoke their disgust. Relieved to use the og're language again, he forced his tongue to its most masculine guttural. "These are not blood meals. They are under my protection."

The leader pulled back his lips to expose his fangs in an expression of amused menace. "Since when does an og're do the bidding of a man? Or is the half of you that is human overwhelming the og're?"

"I am og're." Tol'chuk allowed a hint of fang to slip free of his lips, warning that the words of the leader threatened retribution.

This show, though, only seemed to amuse the huge og're. "So the son of Len'chuk thinks himself better than his father? Do not threaten the one who sent your father to the spirit cave."

Tol'chuk stiffened, and his neck muscles bunched up. If these were true words spoken, here stood his father's killer! He remembered the Triad's words that the Heart would guide him where he needed to be. Tol'chuk fully exposed his fangs.

At this action, the amusement lighting the leader's eyes died away, leaving only a sharp menace. "Do not bite more than you can swallow, little half-breed. Even this insult I'll ignore and let you live—if you give your catch over to us." The leader's eyes pointed to the wolf and Mogweed. "They'll make a tasty stew."

Though they spoke in the og're tongue, some meaning must have been transmitted to Mogweed. Or maybe it was the hungry lust in the leader's eyes as they settled on the small man. Either way, Mogweed moaned and pulled farther behind Tol'chuk. Fardale stood stiff, but his growl thickened.

"They are under my protection," Tol'chuk repeated. "They will pass unharmed."

"Only strength of arm will decide that!" spat the leader. He slammed the oak log on the trail. The thud echoed off the peaks around them.

Tol'chuk glanced at his own empty hands. He had no weapon. He bared his empty hand. "Claw to claw, then."

The giant og're cackled. "The first law of war, half-breed. Never give up the high ground." He kept the log.

Tol'chuk's brows lowered. What chance did he have against this armed opponent? "So this is the honor of the Ku'ukla clan."

"What is honor? Victory is the only true honor. The Ku'ukla clan will rule all the tribes!"

As the leader huffed and prepared to attack, Tol'chuk rapidly scanned the trail for a weapon—rock, stick, anything. But the night's rain had washed the trail clean of debris. He had no weapon.

Then he remembered. No, he had one weapon: a stone. He fumbled his thigh pack open and removed the huge heartstone.

The leader spotted the rock in Tol'chuk's hand. The giant's eyes widened with recognition. "Heartstone!" Obvious lust trembled the og're's limbs. "Give it to me, and I will allow all of you to pass."

"No."

A bellow of rage exploded from the leader, and he raised the oak log high. Tol'chuk pushed Mogweed and Fardale aside. Facing the giant, Tol'chuk prepared to use the stone as a weapon. He had killed earlier with rocks, perhaps he would prevail here.

But he would never be given the chance to find out. As he raised the Heart of the Og'res, a shaft of sunlight pierced the clouds overhead and struck the stone. The sun's touch on the stone burst into a thousand colors.

Tol'chuk winced at the bright light. Shading his eyes against the radiance, Tol'chuk saw the leader bathed in the Heart's glow. A soft smoke drew forth from the giant's body and maintained the shape of the leader for a single breath. Then, like a hearth's soot drawn up a chute, the wispy smoke was sucked to the stone and vanished into its radiance.

As the smoke disappeared, the clouds closed overhead, and the sun vanished. The stone lost its luster.

Tol'chuk and the other two og'res stood like granite statues as the leader's body teetered for two heartbeats, then collapsed to the trail. The log rolled from his limp claws.

He was dead.

The other two og'res stared with eyes stretched wide. Then, as if on some unseen signal, both turned in unison and fled from the trail.

Mogweed stepped to Tol'chuk. "What happened?" he asked, his eyes also on the stone.

Tol'chuk stared at the corpse of his father's killer. "Justice."

OVER THE NEXT TWO DAYS, MOGWEED NOTICED A CHANGE IN Tol'chuk. They traveled mostly at night to avoid the eyes of other og're tribes. But even in darkness, Mogweed spied how the og're lumbered as if shouldering a heavy burden. The creature seldom spoke, and his eyes had a distant glaze to them. Even Fardale's sendings were ignored by the og're.

So Tol'chuk knew of his heritage. Why did this news so damage the creature?

Mogweed dismissed his concerns about the og're. He was just relieved that the party had crossed out of og're territory and into safer lands this afternoon. The summit of the pass through the Teeth lay just ahead. Beyond the ridge lay the lands of the east— the lands of humans.

Even though nightfall approached and they would soon need to prepare a campsite, Tol'chuk trudged ahead of the others to the cusp of the ridge. Fardale followed at the og're's heels like a trained dog.

Mogweed watched his brother leap with difficulty atop a rock.

The splinted forelimb hindered the wolf but did not stop him. Nothing seemed to slow him down for very long. Mogweed reached to his side and felt the iron ribbing of the muzzle through the leather of his pack. He had scavenged it from the dead sniffer when everyone's eyes were busy elsewhere. It might come in handy if he ever needed to control Fardale. He patted the spot. It was best to be prepared.

Stopping next to the boulder, Mogweed gazed out at the eastern slopes. The shadows of the peaks stretched across the lands as the sun set behind him.

From here, all paths led down.

Fardale raised his nose to the breeze coming from the lower lands. Even Mogweed's weaker nose could pick up traces of salt from the distant sea. Such a foreign and intriguing smell, Mogweed thought, so unlike home. But what also colored the air, almost overpowering the subtler scents, was a more familiar odor. "I smell smoke," Mogweed warned.

"Old smoke," Tol'chuk said, his voice stronger than it had been during the previous days. He seemed to be studying the scent, drawing it deep into his throat. "The fire be at least a day old."

"So is it safe to continue?" Worries of a forest fire slid across Mogweed's skin.

The og're nodded. "And now that we be out of og're lands, maybe it be time we parted ways."

Mogweed started to mumble words of thanks for Tol'chuk's help when suddenly the og're gasped and clutched a hand to his chest.

"What's wrong?" Mogweed asked, searching right and left for danger. Fardale leaped off the boulder and loped to Tol'chuk's side. The wolf placed a concerned paw on the og're's leg.

Tol'chuk straightened his back and lowered his hand to his pouch. He removed from among his belongings the huge jewel that had killed the og're. The stone pulsed a ruby red in the dimness. Its brightness stung the eye. Then, as if it were a coal cooling after supper, the fire receded in the stone until the light vanished.

"What is that? You never did tell us." Mogweed tried to suppress the greed in his voice. The jewel had to be of extreme value. It might come in handy if they needed to barter in the human lands.

"Heartstone." Tol'chuk returned the jewel to his pouch. "A sacred stone of my people."

Mogweed's eyes still stared at the pouch. "That glow? Why does the stone do that? What does it mean?"

"A sign. The spirits call me forward."

"Where?"

Tol'chuk pointed to the spreading vistas of the eastern slopes of the peaks. Fingers of distant smoke climbed into the waning light. "If you will have me, I will journey with you into the human lands. It seems our paths are not yet meant to part. Ahead may lie the answers we both seek."

"Or our doom," Mogweed mumbled.

Book Three

PATHS AND
PORTENTS

19

ELENA STOOD FROZEN IN THE STREET, HER EYES FIXED ON THE SPOT where her brother had stood only moments before. Empty, blackened cobbles now remained. The town lay hushed around her, as if holding its breath. Her ability to comprehend what had occurred had vanished along with Joach. She did not blink as the one-armed swordsman stumbled over to her.

"I'm sorry," he said to her, placing his single hand on her shoulder. His next words flamed with suppressed rage. "I did not suspect the monster's power. Fear not. I will hunt him down and free your brother."

The tiny woman who had earlier pulled Elena to safety joined them. "Er'ril, who was that cloaked one? Did you recognize him?"

"Someone from my past," he mumbled. "Someone I never thought to meet again."

"Who?"

"It is of no matter right now. The townspeople are aroused. It would be best if we fled this cursed valley." Around them, the town was beginning to awaken from the demonic assault. A few calls for arms echoed from neighboring streets.

"What about the girl?" the woman asked.

Elena still stared. From slack lips, she whispered, "My brother . . ."

"We'll take her somewhere safe," Er'ril said. "Then I'll search for what became of the mage and the boy."

The giant mountain man approached and stepped between Elena and her view of the spot where Joach had stood. His intrusion severed some tenuous connection between Elena and the spot. Blackness edged her vision. She swooned to the cobbled street. The swordsman's strong arm caught her before her head hit the ground.

"Er'ril, the child's heart sickens with the horrors here," the woman said. "We need to get her somewhere warm, away from here."

Er'ril spoke near Elena's ear, his breath on her neck as he supported her shoulders. "Nee'lahn, you need to discover if she has any other family."

The word "family" penetrated the blackness around Elena's heart. Her eyes settled on the torn remains of Aunt Fila, tossed like rags in a shadowed corner. Tears frozen in her chest thawed and began to flow. Her breathing dissolved to sobs. Elena remembered her aunt's final words. With great effort she turned to face the swordsman. "I . . . have an uncle. She said . . . told me to go there."

The woman knelt beside her. "Who told you, child?"

"Where is your uncle?" Er'ril interrupted.

Elena forced her hand to point north of town.

"Can you guide us there?"

She nodded.

Suddenly a deep voice barked nearby. "Look what I found here!"

Elena and Er'ril both turned. Elena saw the mountain man reach behind a rain barrel and haul out a thin-framed man dressed in a smudged uniform of the town's garrison.

"Who is that?"

Elena knew the answer to the swordsman's question. She had

seen that pinched face with its manicured mustache and black eyes. Elena fought her tongue loose. "He's the one who k-k-killed my family! He was with the old man."

He was the one named Rockingham.

ER'RIL WATCHED THE TREMBLING MAN DART LOOKS RIGHT AND LEFT, searching for help or a way out. But Kral had the man's cloak wrapped in a boulder of a fist. His other hand braced an ax. Er'ril recognized the thin man as the one who had spoken to the darkmage. "Who are you?" Er'ril demanded.

"I am ... head of the county garrison." Rockingham's voice tried to sound threatening, but his words cracked with fear. His eyes kept darting to the headless carcass of the beast slain by the mountain man. "You would do well to release me."

"This girl says you're in league with the darkmage. Is that true?"

"No. She lies."

Er'ril nodded to the mountain man. There was a way to measure this one's truth. "Test him."

Kral nodded and rested his ax against the rain barrel. He reached up and placed his palms against the man's temples. Rockingham shied away, but Kral pressed firmly. A heartbeat later, the mountain man whipped his hand away as if he had touched fire.

"Does he speak the truth, Kral?"

The mountain man flexed one hand as if it hurt. "I cannot tell. I never felt anything like him. It's as if ... as if ..." Kral shook his head.

Nee'lahn spoke up. "What?"

"It's as if the man himself were *constructed* of a lie. His words were mere droplets in a monstrous ocean of untruths. I can't read him." Kral now held the man at arm's length, as if disgusted at the thought of touching his skin again.

"Do you think—?" A bugle blew stridently from across the town, interrupting Er'ril's next question.

A chorus of horns answered, scaring a flock of pigeons from a nearby roof. The blaring horns sounded from the direction of the garrison. Er'ril was suddenly aware of townspeople beginning to peek out of windows and from behind doors. The town continued to awaken from the shock of the magickal assault.

"Perhaps we should take your advice, Er'ril," Nee'lahn said, "and head out. We have nothing else to gain here."

The horns sounded again.

"My men are on the march," Rockingham said. "Release me, leave the girl, and you may yet live."

Kral shook the man and raised a startled squeak from him.

"I don't think you're in any position to give orders," Er'ril said. "Kral, haul him with us."

Elena stirred. "No! He's evil!"

Er'ril rested a hand on the girl's shoulder; all he needed was a hysterical child. He softened his words. "He may have answers as to where your brother was taken. If we are to find him, this man may know how."

Er'ril watched her swallow her fear and straighten her slumped shoulders. Determination shone in her eyes. She spat in the direction of their prisoner. "Don't trust him."

A spark of respect for the youngster flared in Er'ril. "I don't trust anyone," he mumbled. Er'ril turned to Kral and Nee'lahn. "We'll head north and see if we can find her uncle and maybe some answers on what occurred here today."

Kral nodded and bound Rockingham's wrists. Once finished, he secured the ax to his belt and slipped a knife to Rockingham's ribs. "To keep your tongue from waggling," Kral growled with a humorless grin.

Nee'lahn placed an arm around Elena. "Come, child."

Er'ril led the way north through backstreets and alleyways. The commotion kept most of the townsfolk indoors or patrolling the main streets. Few eyes noted their passage.

BOL STUDIED THE ROOM, RUBBING AT THE THICK MUSTACHE THAT HID his pursed lips. He was just about ready. The piles of books and scrolls had been shoved into cabinets, shelves, closets, and empty corners. He had finally cleared the dining table of his scavenged library. Decades had passed since he last saw the wood of the table; some of the books had left scarred outlines of their bindings on its oak finish. Spots of yellowed candle wax dotted the surface, giving it a pocked, diseased look. He sighed. That would have to do. He was no chambermaid.

Running fingers through his white hair, he smelled the ko'koa simmering on the stove. The lentils for the soup should just about be ready. The roast needed basting but could wait a few moments more. Maybe he should collect an extra bunch of carrots from the garden. Frost would soon be here, and they would go to waste otherwise.

He glanced out the western window to the sun setting behind the peaks of the Teeth. Storm clouds blustered among the mountaintops, blurring the tips with rain. It would be a wet night.

No, the carrots would have to wait. Time ran short.

His hand kept fluttering to the amulet hung around his neck by twisted strands of his sister Fila's hair. She would have done a much better job preparing the meal, but such was not to be. Fate had chosen between the twins, and Fila was snatched. She had her own responsibilities now, leaving Bol the more practical concerns. Who had the worse lot in these matters was yet to be seen. The paths from this room pointed to a thousand different compass points. Like a boulder loosened by centuries of rain and tumbling a path of destruction down the mountainside, there was no turning back—for any of them.

"Fire will mark her coming," he mumbled to the empty room. "But what then?"

A chill slipped past his coarse shirt and woolen undergarments to tingle his skin. He crossed to the fireplace and used a brass poker to stoke the fire to a brighter blaze. He stood before the flames and let his clothes cook in the heat. Why were his old bones always so cold? He never seemed to stay warm these days.

But that was not the real reason he stood idle by the fire. The last of his chores still awaited his attention. He clutched the amulet firm to his chest. "Please, Fila, take this duty from me. You were always the stronger of us."

No answer came. The amulet did not even bloom with its familiar warmth. Not that he expected it. Fila was past the point where this simple trick could reach her. He was alone in his task.

He heated his fingers on the waves of hot air wafting from the hearth, trying in some manner to purify his hands for what he must do. He stared at the tiny white hairs on his knuckles. When had his hands become so old, just parchment-dry skin wrinkled over knobs of bone?

Sighing, he dropped his hands and turned from the fire. If his interpretation of the passages read true, the party would be arriving soon. Bol had built his home as a young man at this exact site for the coming night ahead. The ruins of the ancient school's chamber of worship lay buried under the floorboards. Here is where all would be drawn, and the journey would begin.

He must be as strong as Fila this night.

Bol crossed to a cabinet constructed of impenetrable ironwood. The door was sealed with only one key. He hesitated, then reached and slipped the braided cord from around his neck. He raised the cord and stared at the amulet. Carved of green jade in the shape of a wine pitcher, it contained three drops of sacred water. The water still swam with ancient traces of elemental energies. The amulet had allowed the twin siblings to communicate across long distances and had been vital to coordinating their efforts and plans.

He closed his eyes. As sacred as the amulet was, what stayed Bol's hand was its connection to his dead sister. He was reluctant to let this piece of his sister's memory go. Still . . . He pictured Fila's stern gray eyes and could guess her response to his delay. "Hurry up, old man," she would scold. "You have to let go sometime." She had always been the practical one.

A small smile played at the corner of his lips. He twirled the amulet on its cord and smashed it into the seal of the ironwood cabinet. Jade shards flew across the floor. One piece stung his cheek, like a slap for destroying such delicate artwork.

He ignored the bite on his cheek. The key had worked. The seal on the cabinet was broken. He reached to the cabinet's handle and opened a door that had been sealed tight over two decades ago. A single object lay within the shadowed interior: a rosewood box with flowered traceries of gilt around the edges. Bol did not remove the handsome box but only lifted its hinged top. Resting on a violet cushion of silks lay a dagger older than any of the buildings in the valley, older than most people's memories.

Before fear clutched his hand, Bol grabbed the dagger's hilt and lifted it free of its nest in the box. He held it up to the firelight. Its black blade seemed to absorb the light, while a rose of gold carved on its hilt reflected the fire in blinding exuberance.

Tears threatened to well as he held the dagger, but his hand did not tremble, and the tears never did flow. Bol knew his duty. He was his sister's brother.

"Forgive me, Elena," he whispered to the empty room.

20

A GASP OF JOY BURST FROM ELENA'S THROAT AS SHE RAN UNDER THE branches of the willow to the horse. "Oh, Mist, you're still here." She hugged the horse's neck, inhaling the mare's familiar smell, a mix of hay and musk. Her family's barn had always smelled just like this. She hugged the horse tighter. If she closed her eyes, in a tiny way, she was home again.

Mist nickered and nudged her away, reaching for some tender shoots growing nearby, plainly unimpressed that Elena had returned. This familiar snubbing brought tears to the girl's eyes.

Er'ril spoke behind her, but his words were for Kral. Elena ignored him, still content to place her palms on Mist. The horse stood solid: firm muscle, hard bone, and coarse hair. The mare had not vanished.

"Kral," Er'ril continued, "be careful. Just retrieve our gear and mounts from the inn and head right back here."

"No one will stop me. What about the prisoner?"

"Tie him to the tree for now."

Elena clenched her lips at Er'ril's words and untethered Mist from the trunk of the willow.

"Girl, what're you doing? Leave the horse be." Er'ril's voice snapped with exhaustion.

"I don't want that man near Mist." She pulled Mist's halter and guided the mare to the edge of the canopy of branches. Mist's presence bolstered her confidence. Though she had lost so much, she still had her mare. "And my name is Elena, not *girl*."

Nee'lahn crossed to join Elena, an amused smile on her lips; her violet eyes and honey hair caught splashes of light from between the branches. The small woman's beauty snatched the breath from Elena. When in town, she had thought the woman somewhat plain, but out here among the trees, she seemed to bloom like a forest flower. Elena would even swear the willow branches moved so the small woman's beauties were accented by rays of sunlight.

"She is a handsome mare," Nee'lahn said.

Elena dropped her gaze to her toes, embarrassed by her own gawky appearance. This close, Nee'lahn even smelled of honeysuckle. "Thank you," Elena said sheepishly. "I raised her from a foal."

"Then the two of you must be very close. I'm glad you were able to lead us here to find her." Nee'lahn offered Mist a bite of apple from the wares they had purchased as they snuck from town. Mist twitched back her ears in delight and snatched the entire apple with her thick lips.

"Mist! Mind your manners!"

Nee'lahn just grinned. "Elena, can you find the way to your uncle's as easily as you did here?"

"Yes, he lives in the next valley. Winter's Eyrie, up by the old ruins."

"What?" Er'ril wore a shocked look on his face. Kral had already left for town, and Er'ril had just finished testing Rockingham's bonds and gag. He stalked over to Elena. "Where did you say he lived?"

Nee'lahn placed a hand on Elena's wrist. "She said that he lived near some old ruins. Now quit raising your voice."

The swordsman tensed with the rebuke, his face darkening. "Fine. Now, girl . . . I mean, *Elena,* are these the ruins of an old school?"

Elena shrugged. "We aren't allowed near the ruins; there are lots of poisonous snakes. But Uncle Bol is always poking among the stones, digging up books and such stuff."

Er'ril blew an angry wind from his chest. "Did your uncle ever find anything . . . unusual?"

She shrugged and shook her head. "Not that he ever mentioned, but he sort of keeps to himself."

"Er'ril, do you know the place?" Nee'lahn asked.

He spoke as if his jaws were stuck. "I visited it the last time I was here."

"So you know the way?"

"Yes."

"Then as soon as Kral returns with your horses, we can set out." Nee'lahn turned her back on Er'ril and faced Elena. "While we're waiting, maybe you could tell us how you ended up with those evil men?"

Elena kicked at the soil with her toe, reluctant to rehash the entire story, the pain still too fresh.

Nee'lahn reached up and placed one hand on Elena's cheek. "It's all right now. Er'ril is a skilled swordsman. He won't let anyone harm you. We need to know more if we are to help your brother. You want that, don't you?"

Elena bowed her head and refused to raise her face as she spoke, her voice so low Er'ril leaned closer to hear. "That man and the one in the robe, they came to our farm last night." Elena glanced to her hand, plain now, as she related the events of the previous night. She purposely left out the part about the red hand. ". . . and then Joach and I rode away before the worms or fire could get us. But when we made it to town, they were waiting and we were caught."

"Do you know why they were after you?" Nee'lahn asked.

She lowered her eyes. "I don't . . . No."

From the corner of her eyes, she saw a secret exchange pass between Nee'lahn and the swordsman, doubt clear in both pairs of eyes.

"Maybe I should ask our prisoner," Er'ril finally said. "Twist it out of him."

Nee'lahn frowned. "I think we all—" Elena caught the nod in her direction from the small woman. "—have had enough violence for one afternoon. Why don't we wait until the girl is returned to her uncle, before you begin your . . . um, questioning."

Er'ril frowned but finally sighed. "We should wait for Kral anyway. His skills may yet be useful."

Nee'lahn turned back to her. "Elena, you should rest. We still have a long ride ahead of us."

Elena nodded and moved into Mist's shadow. She fiddled with the mare's halter, trying to look busy. Why had she lied to them? They may not have been able to rescue Joach, but they did save her. She glanced again to her right hand and stared at the plain palm. The red hue had vanished. Gone in the flutter of an eye, just like her brother Joach. She fought back a new wave of tears. As much as she hated the thought of her magickal talent, if the power could return her brother, she would gladly accept the curse again.

Elena lowered her hand.

But it was over now. Wasn't it?

Twilight approached.

Er'ril fought to keep his eyes on the path through the woods and to watch for lurking dangers in the dappled shadows. But his mind kept dragging back the image of the darkmage as he vanished on the street. He could not grasp the implications of this encounter. He tried to shove such thoughts away until a time they could be carefully picked at and studied, but he could not.

How could Greshym be alive? Had he imagined it? No. It was an older face, but Greshym's nonetheless. He tried to pierce the years to that midnight in the inn when the Book had been forged. He remembered the bond between Greshym and his brother. He could still feel the respect and affection he had for the older, wounded mage. How could he balance that with the hatred he felt now? His skin crawled with the memory of the black arts wielded by the mage. Foul trickster! What game have you been playing since ancient times?

And what of the Book? What did this mean?

His horse slowed on a steeper grade of the path, and he kicked at its flank harder than he had meant. The stallion whinnied with surprise and bucked a few steps forward. He patted the animal's neck, calming the beast with his touch. His anger and frustration may have loosened his control, but his horse shouldn't suffer.

Er'ril twisted in his saddle and checked his party. When Kral had returned with the mounts and gear they had left at the inn, Er'ril had set them a hard pace. The innkeeper had tried to stop Kral, screaming that the mountain man was stealing other patrons' property. But when the guardsmen, busy with the riled townsfolk, failed to respond to the innkeeper's summons, Kral had split a table with his ax, and the innkeeper quickly bowed out of the huge man's path. On Kral's return, Er'ril had not wasted the waning hours of daylight, fearing any repercussions from the town's garrison. He had loaded everyone up and led the way to the highlands.

Behind him, Nee'lahn and the child rode together atop the girl's horse. Kral and the prisoner rode one of the mountain folk's huge war chargers. Its fiery eyes and metal-shod hooves marked it as a steed only a fool would try to stop.

Nee'lahn caught Er'ril's glance and nodded forward. "A storm comes. We need to reach Elena's uncle before full night."

Er'ril glanced at the girl. And what role did she play in all this? Surely she was just an unwitting pawn—maybe a virgin for some foul magickal working. He had heard whispers during his travels of such sick deeds. He twisted forward again in his saddle, noting the black clouds obscuring the setting sun. Once free of the girl, he could concentrate on the matter of the mage. With a gentle nudge, he urged his mount to a quicker pace. Retrieving the boy was only a small part in his desire to hunt down Greshym. The darkmage had much to answer for.

As he led the party toward the highlands, the woods began to change. The autumn leaves of the oaks and alders, blazing with the crinkled hues of a smoldering fire, gave way to a green blanket of alpine evergreens. A sea of discarded needles spread yellow waves across the path.

Er'ril did not need a guide. He knew the path to the ruins buried in the valley of Winter's Eyrie. Why would someone build a homestead in such a lonesome and windblown place? In winter, the snows at this height could reach the roof of a two-story house. He knew why the school had been built there: Isolation was necessary when training the initiates to the Order. Besides leaving the students with little to distract them from their studies, the distance from others kept the harm from magickal "accidents" of those new to their arts well away from habitable regions.

But with Chi's abandonment of the land, why live out here now?

Er'ril cantered his horse over a steep rise, his mount's hooves nearly slipping on the slick cushion of pine needles. He paused at the crest of the rise. From the tiny vale ahead, a single plume of smoke trailed into the twilight sky. Black clouds from the mountains beyond seemed to be drawn toward the plume like moths to a candle. The storm threatened. Flares of lightning winked from the clouds.

His eyes followed the smoke to its source. A stone cottage stood in the valley floor, its chimney painting the vale with the smell of wood smoke. His nose tasted the invitation to warmth, and yellow light flickered from tiny windows, adding its welcome.

The horse bearing Nee'lahn and Elena drew abreast of his steed. "That's my uncle's place," the girl stated. "Looks like he's home."

Er'ril flicked his reins to walk his horse forward down the slope toward the cottage. "Let's hope he's ready for guests."

With pinched lips, Er'ril studied the surrounding land and judged escape routes and places from which to fight if the need arose. His training as a campaigner in the wars against the Gul'gotha had become as instinctual as the beating of his heart.

He also studied the homestead of this "Uncle Bol." From the condition of his home, Er'ril lost a certain amount of respect for the man. It was a shambles. Moss crusted the shingles. The doors to a small barn hidden to the side of the cottage lay crooked on their hinges. A small pen containing three goats had holes chewed into the planks of the fencing. Three horned heads poked from these holes and stared toward the newcomers. Nasal bleats insulted them as they passed.

Er'ril shook his head, recalling the order and stateliness of his own family's farm on the plains. He turned his eyes to the heights beyond the cottage. Crumbled stone in unnaturally straight lines crisscrossed the neighboring rise. His mind's eye pictured the rows of halls and dormitories of the Order's school. Ravaged stones gave silent testimony to the ancient place of study.

The door to the cottage suddenly burst open, flinging light toward the trio of horses. A man stood limned in the firelight. "Well, what are you all waiting for? Hurry it up! It's about to storm." The man waved an arm and disappeared back inside.

Elena swung in her saddle to face them all, her face scrunched up. "My uncle's not that good with people."

"But at least he seems to be expecting us," Er'ril said, suddenly wary.

His nervousness grew once they had stabled the horses and entered the cottage. After so long traveling in the chilled highlands, the warmth of the cottage stifled the lungs. But Er'ril ignored this, his eyes instead fixed on the lavishly laden table. Three tall candles sprouted like islands from a steaming sea of foods: spit-roasted beef, steamed red potatoes, a thick bean soup with a loaf of pepperbread as big as his head. Platters of carrots and greens dotted the table among bowls of autumn blackberries. Six cups of ko'koa were set before six tin plates.

"Sit, sit," the white-haired man said. He was setting bowls on the plates for the soup. He stopped to tap a quick kiss on Elena's forehead. "I barely made it in time. Fila would be so angry if I didn't do everything like she ordered."

Elena spoke softly, taking the old man's hand in her own. "Uncle . . . Uncle Bol, I have bad news. Fila's dead."

He slipped his hand from the child's and patted her on the cheek. "Oh, yes, I know. Never you mind. Now, sit! Everything will grow cold."

Er'ril found his tongue. "You were expecting guests?"

The man scratched his head with an ink-stained finger. "Guests? Oh no. I was expecting you, Er'ril of Standi."

21

ELENA WATCHED THE SWORDSMAN PICK AT THE BEEF AND RED POTATOES on his dinner plate, his fork scraping across the tin surface. Elena sat beside Er'ril and caught his narrowed eyes darting wary looks toward Uncle Bol at the head of the table. But Uncle Bol ignored Er'ril, his own attention fixed on Nee'lahn at the foot of the table. Though the firelight seemed to have dimmed her beauty when compared to her appearance in the woods earlier, Uncle Bol's eyes seldom spent much time away from her face. How odd, Elena thought, the way Nee'lahn's beauty waxed and waned.

Suddenly a loud belch rattled the stoneware. Kral balanced on a small chair across the table from Elena and wiped at his bearded chin with the edge of his sleeve. He stared questioningly at all the eyes now focused on him. The mountain man was apparently oblivious to the social affront his eruption might provoke. "What?" he asked, placing his fork on his plate and leaning back and rubbing his packed belly. His head swiveled to face them all. "What?"

Elena held a hand over her mouth to stop a giggle from escaping.

Rockingham, who was digging at his beef with a spoon—the only utensil allowed him—mumbled to himself, "And they tied *me* up." The captured man's ankles had been roped together and secured to a foot of the oaken table for security.

Er'ril cleared his throat and faced Uncle Bol. "Well, it seems that everyone is finished with dinner. Now maybe you would care to enlighten us all on how you knew we were coming, and even knew my name."

"Who would like dessert?" Uncle Bol scooted his chair back with a loud squeak. "In honor of the orchard fire, I made a hot apple pie. Anybody interested?"

"That can wait—" Er'ril started to say, but the four raised hands of his companions stopped him. The swordsman's shoulders slumped, and he sighed loudly. "Fine. Fetch the pie."

Uncle Bol got up and stretched. "Perhaps . . ." His eyes settled again on the small woman's face. "Nee'lahn, wasn't it? Perhaps you could help me in the kitchen."

"Certainly." Nee'lahn wiped her delicate hands on the scrap of linen in her lap, then rose and followed Uncle Bol from the room.

Er'ril tapped at his mug of ko'koa with obvious impatience.

Elena sensed that the swordsman was close to exploding. Ever since Uncle Bol had named him, then refused to answer any questions until they all had eaten, the muscles of Er'ril's neck had grown corded and tight. Though he must be hungry, he had hardly touched the food he had taken.

"Don't be mad at Uncle Bol," Elena said. "That's just the way he is."

Er'ril stopped his tapping and swung to Elena. "Just what is your uncle up to?"

"He'll tell us, but only when he's ready. He used to tell us bedtime stories when he visited. If you tried to hurry his stories along, he would just drag them even longer."

"So I guess we eat pie," he said sullenly.

Elena nodded, chewing at the inside of her cheek. She remained silent about the nervousness she sensed in her uncle. Something was truly bothering him. She had never seen him jump at every noise. A popping log in the fire had practically shot him to the raftered ceiling. And Uncle Bol was normally a robust eater—how he ate so much and stayed so wiry and muscular was

a mystery discussed among the female relatives of the family for
years—but tonight, like Er'ril, he had barely touched the piece of
roast on his plate.

Uncle Bol returned, carrying new plates and forks. Nee'lahn
followed with the spiced apple pie. The aroma of simmering apple and cinnamon swelled through the room. Even Er'ril seemed
to brighten at the smell.

This new delay that seemed to so irk Er'ril only lasted a short
span. The pie plate emptied quickly, and after much sighing in
delight at the sweet taste, the table was surrounded by full bellies.

Uncle Bol stood up. "I hope all have had their fill."

Groans of agreement answered him.

"Then I guess it's time I showed you your rooms for the night.
I'm afraid the men will have to share one room, and Nee'lahn and
Elena the other."

Er'ril raised his one hand. "About those unanswered questions."

Uncle Bol frowned. "Join me, Er'ril, after we get everyone settled, for a smoke by the fire." He turned to Elena. "You join us,
too, honey. There's words I must pass to you."

"What you need to say can be said among my companions,"
Er'ril growled. Kral's and Nee'lahn's eyes glowed eagerly. Rockingham tried to feign disinterest, but failed miserably.

Her uncle rubbed at his mustache. "No, I don't think the
Brotherhood would appreciate that."

"What brotherhoo—?" Elena began, but Er'ril placed a hand
on her shoulder and squeezed her to silence.

"It's been a long time since I could relax with a pipe," Er'ril
said. "I look forward to it." His words had an edge of menace.

"Good! Now let me show you the rooms."

ROCKINGHAM LISTENED AS THE GIANT CLOSED THE DOOR TO THEIR
room. He could not see the mountain man as Kral then stripped
out of his riding gear and climbed onto a cot. The bonds that secured Rockingham to the bed—his hands were tied to the pine

headboard, his feet to the posts at the foot of the bed—limited his motion, blinding him to all but the ceiling and a tiny section of the room. Then the single lamp blew out, and even this cramped view vanished.

Rockingham lay stripped on his back under a heavy blanket. He crinkled his nose. Though he might not be able to see the mountain man, he smelled him. The odor of wet goats crept across the room to wrap around him; it was like sleeping in a barn. He closed his eyes and tried to breathe through his mouth. It didn't help. He tried to roll away on his side, but the ropes stopped him. His bed creaked loudly with his efforts.

"I sleep lightly," Kral growled from the darkness. "Do not test me."

Rockingham stayed silent. What was the use of even trying? The ropes, though not tight enough to chafe, were tied snug.

He lay still and found himself staring toward the rafters of the room. And why would he even want to escape? Where could he go? Not the garrison, that was for sure. Once word reached Lord Gul'gotha that one of his lieutenants had been beheaded and the girl he sought had escaped, his death would be one to terrify the hardest soldier. He had seen what slunk through the bowels of Blackhall's dungeons. He shivered under his thick blanket.

His only options were either to disappear and keep running, hoping the minions of the Dark Lord never found him, or to stay with this group and look for a chance to snatch the girl. She was the key to unlock his dungeon. Recovering her would assuage the wrath of the Lord Gul'gotha.

So he had not fought his kidnapping by the one-armed swordsman. Let them take him far from town—all the better. Don't resist. Let them relax their guard. He could wait. A slight grin came to his lips at the thought of returning to Blackhall with the girl in chains. That was worth waiting for.

As he dreamed of that moment, an itch blossomed in his crotch. Damn that tavern wench and the lice she harbored! He tried to rub his legs together and calm the crawling. It only worsened. To make matters worse, the giant began to snore. Not a whispery nasal whistle, but a throaty rattle full of mucus and phlegm. Each outburst made him cringe in disgust.

Rockingham clenched his eyes closed and squirmed quietly. It was going to be a long night.

The tortures of Blackhall's dungeons now didn't seem quite so bad.

ER'RIL LEANED ON THE MANTEL OF THE FIREPLACE. WHERE WAS BOL? The others had retired to their respective rooms, leaving Er'ril alone with Elena. He watched the girl stare at the fire. As she sat, swallowed by the deep cushioned armchair, she seemed lost in the flames. A profound sadness shone past the exhaustion in her face. For a child so young to be so violently uprooted, she had a determined bearing about her that illuminated the strength of her spirit.

Words of consolation tried to form in his mind, but it had been a long time since Er'ril had had the need to show compassion. He found his eyes settling on the twitching flames. Time did not always grow wisdom, sometimes just calluses.

His reveries were interrupted by the reappearance of the girl's uncle. He had two pipes in his hand. "The tobacco leaf is from the south of Standi, I believe. I thought a piece of home might be nice," he said, passing a pipe to Er'ril.

"Thank you." He raised the pipe to his nose. The smell of cured leaf and powder dried further words. At the back of his throat, he tasted the wide fields of his home. Bol sparked a flame on a stiff taper from the hearth. He lit his pipe, his cheeks bellowing in and out, and he sucked it to flame. Er'ril accepted the burning wick from the old man, but his hand hesitated in igniting the tobacco. He was reluctant to set to flame this reminder of home.

He found Elena staring at him, her sadness palpable. She had lost much more to flame this past day. He touched the wick to his pipe and drew smoke into his chest. Its warmth and familiar taste melted the tension in his body, his knees almost weakening.

"Sit," Bol said, pointing to the only other chair by the fire. The old man remained standing near Elena.

Er'ril dropped, sinking into the goose-down cushions. With some reservation, he removed the pipe from between his lips. "How do you know me? How did you know we would be arriving this night?"

Bol nodded. "You ask questions of the end of the story. To understand the end you must understand the beginning."

"I'm listening." Er'ril returned the pipe to his lips.

"You have already heard me mention the Brotherhood. The Broken Brotherhood, I believe, is their full title. Let me start there."

"What is that?" Elena asked softly.

Her uncle sent a puff of smoke from his chest, forming a perfect ring of gray smoke. As it wafted across the room on the waves of heat from the fire, a tiny smile formed on Elena's lips. "Some of this you may not understand, sweetheart. But at one time in the land, there was an order of mages who wielded white magick. A spirit named Chi granted them this power, which was far stronger than the weak elemental magick inherent in the land. The Order used this power to build a wonderful civilization."

"That's not the story I was taught in school," Elena said doubtfully.

"Not all that is taught is true."

"So then what happened?"

"A long time ago, the magick suddenly vanished at a time when it was most needed. The lands were being invaded by the armies and monsters of the Gul'gotha. The mages and our people fought bravely. But without our white magick, we could not withstand the dark magick of the invaders. Alasea was defeated, its peoples subjugated, and its history destroyed."

"Where did our magick go?"

Er'ril answered that question, spite thick in his voice. "It just abandoned us."

Bol nodded. "Only pockets and pieces of the magick still survived.

The Order, without power, broke apart. But some of this group banded together to try to find and nurture the magick left in the lands. They had to do this in strict secrecy, since the Dark Lord of the Gul'gotha sought to wipe them out. So the Broken Brotherhood was formed."

"A secret society?" Elena asked breathlessly.

Secret was too mild a word, Er'ril thought. To his knowledge only a handful of men still alive today knew of the cabal headquartered and hidden among the sunken remains of A'loa Glen. Few men even knew the lost city still existed, its approach guarded by the trace magick still held close to its heart. Many had sought the mythical city, but only a scant few discovered its whereabouts and dared enter. Those that did never returned.

"But the Brotherhood made a crucial mistake," Bol said.

Er'ril's eyes grew wider. What was this?

Bol continued. "With their eyes so blinded by the powerful energies of Chi, they couldn't appreciate the magick born to the land, even after the loss of Chi."

"But of what use are a few weak tricks eked from the elementals of the land?" Er'ril asked. "Of what use is that against the dark power of the Gul'gotha?"

Bol turned to Elena. "Now you see why the Sisterhood was formed. Men see only degrees of power, while women see the warp and weave of strength's tapestry."

"What is this Sisterhood?" Er'ril asked. "I've lived centuries and never heard a whisper of such a group. Who formed it?"

"It is not an open group like your Brotherhood. One must be born to it."

"What?"

Bol waved the tip of his pipe. "You asked who formed the Sisterhood. One person. You may even know her, *or of her.*"

"Who?" Er'ril sat straighter in his chair.

"Sisa'kofa."

The word was like a brick dropped into his gut. "The wit'ch of spirit and stone!" He remembered when last he had heard the blasphemous name spoken, by Greshym on the night of the Book's forging. The one-handed mage had warned the Book would herald the rebirth of the wit'ch.

"Yes," Bol said. "She is my distant ancestor. Very distant. She was an ancient story even when you were a boy."

"You can trace your lineage to that foul wit'ch?"

"There was nothing foul about her." Bol's cheeks darkened. "She was a woman granted powers equal to, and in some ways surpassing, those of men. She even bore the mark of the Rose. And men could not handle the thought of a woman wielding equal power. Lies were fabricated to discredit her."

Er'ril noticed Elena start at her uncle's words, but his heart pounded too loudly in his ears for him to give her any further attention. "Impossible! Chi never granted his gifts to women."

"Who said anything about Chi?"

"What? Are you suggesting elemental magick is the equal of Chi?"

Bol blew out his cheeks, sending pipe smoke across the room. "At times, yes, I believe so. But it was not elemental magick that shared its power with Sisa'kofa."

"Then what?"

"You are jumping ahead of the story again."

Er'ril bit his tongue to keep from rebuking the old man. Obviously Bol needed to tell the story at his own pace. "Fine. Go on," he mumbled.

"Near the end of Sisa'kofa's lifetime, her magick left her, but not before promising to one day return to her descendant when most needed. Sisa'kofa was warned of a black shadow that would spread across the lands of Alasea. Just when this dark time would occur, she was never told. So Sisa'kofa formed a society of her female descendants. She taught them to prepare for her magick's return. Sisa'kofa sensed the elementals would be critical to the eventual rebirth of light to the land, so she trained her Sisterhood in the use and respect for the elemental spirits."

"How do you know so much about the Sisterhood? You're not a female descendant."

"I was born twin to a female, my sister Fila. Being the first male born twin to a girl, I was allowed into their secrets. My birth was believed to be a sign—that she who gave Sisa'kofa her power would be returning soon. So the Sisterhood prepared, studying all they could." Bol swung his arm to encompass the stacks of scrolls and books. "They searched ancient texts and gleaned portents from the elementals."

"And what was learned?"

"We learned the signs of her arrival and some of the key players—like yourself. We also knew the elementals would be involved. 'Three will come' it was written. But we knew not which ones or who. This Kral is obviously rich in rock magick. And Nee'lahn . . . She's a nyphai, isn't she?"

"Yes," Er'ril said.

"She has the fire of the root strong in her. I could hardly take my eyes from her. But that last member . . . he, too, is steeped in magick, but I couldn't tell how."

"Kral sensed a strangeness about him, too."

"He must be the third." Uncle Bol drew on his pipe, his lids slightly closed, and sent wisps of smoke between his words. He scratched at his beard. "Though there was one oracular text that I thought spoke of the arrival of 'someone from times past and lands lost,' but I must have been mistaken. Unless they meant you, but I didn't think so. Maybe I'm wrong. As I said, much that surrounds the Book is vague."

"You seem to know enough already. So when is this wit'ch supposed to return?"

Bol's eyes grew wide. "Oh, my, she already has. Didn't you know?"

Er'ril sat stunned.

Bol pointed to his niece. Er'ril finally noticed how panicked the girl now appeared. "Born of the line of Sisa'kofa and birthed in fire. There sits your wit'ch."

22

After Uncle Bol declared Elena a wit'ch, silence hung like a stone over the room. Elena tried to worm deeper into the goose-down cushions of her chair. She watched the swordsman's eyebrows climb higher on his forehead, his already ruddy complexion darkening further. His eyes settled on her with such force that Elena felt he peered through to her skin. Her arms rose and covered her chest in a tight hug.

She shrank back from his eyes but raised her right hand to the firelight. "But I . . . I'm not a wit'ch any longer," she said. "It's gone."

Her uncle patted a reassuring hand on her shoulder. "It doesn't work that way, honey."

Er'ril ignored their words. "She is just a child. How can I believe you speak the truth?"

Uncle Bol crossed from Elena's chair to the fire. Elena could tell from the limp in his gait and the way his shoulders hung low that her uncle neared exhaustion. But his voice remained strong. "Doubt? You have been on the road too long, Er'ril. Can you not sense the truth of my words? Why do you think that darkmage tried to snatch the girl? He sensed the power birthed in her."

"You ask me to use the actions of a man with a black heart as proof?"

Her uncle warmed his hands for several long heartbeats and spoke to the flames. "You know I speak the truth." He turned to face Er'ril. "We need the Blood Diary."

"So you know of the Book, too?"

"Of course. How could we not? It's the reason you are all here this night."

Er'ril's pipe hung unused in his fingers, forgotten. "I came to return your niece. That's all."

"No. The winds of fate blew you here where you were needed. The wit'ch and the Book share the same paths."

"My brother said nothing of this wit'ch. He said the Book had to be forged if there was to be any hope of ending this dark reign of the Gul'gotha. He knew not of this *wit'ch*." He said the last word with such disgust that Elena's cheeks reddened in shame.

"We decided Shorkan didn't need to know."

"What are you talking about?"

Uncle Bol puffed on his pipe thoughtfully before continuing. "Where do you think your brother learned how to forge the Blood Diary?"

"I don't know. He mentioned something about old texts."

"The information was spirited to him from the Sisterhood. Unknown to Shorkan, we guided his hand."

"Impossible!"

Uncle Bol shrugged, ignoring the swordsman's doubt. Both men just stared at each other.

Finally Er'ril broke the tense silence. "So my brother and I have been pawns in some game to return the heir of Sisa'kofa to the lands of Alasea. Is that what you're hinting at?"

"No, not at all. Your goal is the same as that of the Sisterhood: to bring the light back to our lands, to drive the Gul'gotha from our shores. But do you expect her—" Uncle Bol nodded to Elena. "—even with the Blood Diary, to be able to singly defeat the armies of the Dark Lord, let alone the Black Beast himself?"

Er'ril's eyes shifted to Elena. The anger in his eyes dissolved away to confusion.

Uncle Bol continued. "It is time the Brotherhood and the Sisterhood united. The Brotherhood created and guarded the Book. The Sisterhood nurtured the elementals and prepared for the return of the wit'ch. Now is the time both must be forged into one cause and purpose—to defeat the Gul'gotha and free our lands!"

Er'ril swung his eyes back to Bol's wrinkled face. "How?"

"The wit'ch and the Blood Diary must be joined."

"And what then?" Er'ril asked bitterly. "What have you foreseen?"

Uncle Bol's next words were whispered, edged with smoke from his pipe. "We don't know. The Blood Diary is a potent talisman. Even its function is shaded in doubts. Portents swirl about it like a whirlpool, so violent that they become impossible to read. Beyond the union of wit'ch and book, nothing can be foretold. Some foresee salvation, others destruction. But most signs somehow point at both."

"If the future is so unclear, why chance bringing wit'ch and Book together?"

"Because if we don't, the oracles are all unanimous on the fate of Alasea. The land will continue following its dark path to a blackness that will swallow not just Alasea, but this world and time itself. The wit'ch and the Book must be united!"

Elena cowered in her chair. How could she possibly be this important? She didn't want to bear such a burden.

Er'ril seemed equally unsure. "So where do I fit into all this?"

"You are the guardian of the Book, the eternal watcher. Now you must extend your protection to include the wit'ch. You must guard Elena and take her to the Book."

"Why risk the child? Why not let me fetch the Book alone and bring it here?"

Uncle Bol shook his head. "You will fail. It has been prophesied. For any hope of success, the wit'ch must be accompanied by the guardian and the three elementals here tonight; that we know. But be warned, even this path is shadowed, and success in reaching the Blood Diary is not assured. The journey ahead is fraught with many dangers."

"And I have no choice in this matter."

"Have you ever? Does this life of useless wandering hold such attraction for you?"

Er'ril lowered his head. "I wish my own life back—before I ever stepped into that inn with Shorkan so long ago."

"That cannot be. But perhaps on this path you will find a way back to the man you once were."

Er'ril continued to hang his head. Elena, even though terrified by her uncle's words, felt a twinge of sorrow for the swordsman. His very bones seemed bowed down with exhaustion and the weight of years.

"Make your choice, Er'ril of Standi."

His words were whispered to the floor. "I will take her to where I hid the Book."

"A'loa Glen?"

He raised his eyes. "Is there nothing hidden from you?"

Uncle Bol shrugged. "I know only hints," he said softly. "Words in books and scrolls. I know nothing beyond this door."

"The journey to A'loa Glen is a long one. And the city is guarded by sorcery. Before I can go there, I will need to retrieve the ward that unlocks the path to the city. I hid it here in the ruins of the old school. Near the—"

Uncle Bol waved the tip of his pipe at Er'ril. "Do not tell me. The fewer who know the better."

A long silence followed these words.

Elena squirmed in her seat. Her mind fought to absorb all she had heard, but most of their words made no sense. Only one thing was clear. Her own fears found voice, and she spoke, cracking the silence among them. "I don't want to be a wit'ch."

Her uncle tried to smile at her in reassurance, but only succeeded in quivering his mustache. The profound sadness in his eyes shocked her. But instead of comforting her, Uncle Bol crossed in front of Er'ril, his back to her. "Earlier you asked for proof of my words." He slipped something from inside his vest. "Do you recognize this, Er'ril?"

Elena could still see Er'ril's face. His mouth dropped open, and words tumbled out. "That's Shorkan's! Where did you find it?"

Elena could not see what was proffered. She tilted her head, but her uncle's back still blocked her view.

"If you remember," her uncle said, "Shorkan had given it to the boy on the night of the Book's forging. When you fled with the Book after slaying the child, we retrieved it. The boy still had it clutched in his dead fingers."

"What do you plan to do with it?"

"What I must."

Her uncle suddenly swung around and faced Elena. He held a dagger in his hand; the black blade glinted in the firelight. Tears were in his eyes. "I never wanted to do this, Elena."

He grabbed her wrist and yanked her hand toward him. A small gasp slipped from Elena's chest. What was he doing? She was too shocked to resist.

"This is an ancient dagger used by the mages to consecrate the Blood Diary during its forging." He dragged the blade's edge across her exposed palm.

Blood welled from the cut before the pain reached her eyes. A sharp cry escaped her throat. She stared in disbelief at the wound.

He pressed the hilt of the dagger into her bloody palm. As the blood soaked the knife, the black blade burst forth with a single flash of white light. As the radiance subsided, the dark blade now shone silver in the firelight.

Uncle Bol fell to his knees before her. "Now it's a wit'ch's dagger."

ER'RIL SAT STRAIGHT IN HIS CHAIR. HIS PIPE HAD FALLEN TO THE floor from his limp fingers, scattering smoldering tobacco across the pine planking. Though he had sensed the truth in the old man's words, to see it happen before him numbed his mind and limbs. Long ago, he had witnessed other initiates receive their first cuts from the masters of the Order, christening them to their magick. The same blinding light had marked their coming to power.

Elena *was* a wit'ch!

He watched the child drop the dagger to her lap and wipe the traces of blood from her hand. No sign of her uncle's cut remained. It had healed without a mark.

Her uncle still knelt beside her. "Forgive me, Elena."

"But I don't want the stupid knife."

"You must take it. You will need it to draw on your magick."

She held up her right hand. "I already told you, it's gone. See, my hand is normal again. The red color faded away."

Er'ril spoke up. He kept his voice small so as not to further upset the child; she seemed close to panic. "Your Rose has faded as you exhausted your supply of power," he said. "You will need to renew."

"I don't want to!" Tears rolled down her cheek.

Her uncle placed his hands on her lap. "I know you're scared, honey. But your aunt Fila is counting on you."

At her aunt's name, her sobs quieted. "What do you mean?" she said between sniffles.

Bol rolled back to his feet. "Come, let me show you something. Aunt Fila left a gift for you."

"She knew about all this wit'ch stuff?"

"Yes, she did, Elena. And she was so proud of how strong you were growing."

She sniffed back the last few tears. "She was?"

Her uncle nodded. "Come with me." Bol turned to Er'ril. "You come, too. This may help you retrieve the ward you hid in the ruins."

Er'ril stood from his chair. Along with Elena, he followed the old man to a nearby case of dusty books. Bol's fingers ran along the spine of bindings like a lover's caress. A sigh escaped his lips. His fingers settled on a carved stone bookend of a dragon's head. He reached and tilted the bookend. A series of slipping pulleys and shifting stones sounded from behind the bookcase. The entire cabinet swung toward them.

"Stand back," Bol warned. He swung the bookcase open like a door to reveal a stone stairway leading down.

Elena's eyes widened with surprise, her wonder overwhelming her tears.

Even Er'ril was intrigued. "Where does this lead?"

Bol reached to a hand lantern resting on a sideboard. He picked it up and adjusted the wick to flame the lantern brighter. "Follow me, and watch your step. The stone is damp and slippery."

Er'ril waved a hand for Elena to follow her uncle while he went last. The stairway, constructed of crude slabs of hewn rock, appeared much older than the stone of the cottage. Spiderwebs wisped in drapes from the low ceiling. The girl and the stooped man passed under the webs, setting them to drifting on currents of disturbed air. Er'ril, taller than the others, kept wiping them from his hair as he managed the slick stairs. He slapped at his neck as he felt the scurry of tiny legs on his nape.

Hearing his slap, Elena looked back at him and eyed him as he rubbed his neck. "Careful. It's bad luck to kill a spider."

"Go on, child." He nudged her forward with a finger. She wasn't the one with spiders in her hair.

ELENA LISTENED AS SHE CREPT DOWN THE LAST OF THE STEPS. HER footsteps echoed back from the stones. She crinkled her nose at the smell of stagnant water and mildewed dampness. Reaching the last step, she paused. Uncle Bol stood several steps ahead of her, his lantern held high. The light revealed a wide chamber, its walls sweeping to either side in a crude circle. Twelve pillars of rock, like stone guards, sectioned the walls. Between the pillars, in alcoves, hung ancient mirrored plates, most with green water stains marring their silvery finishes.

Uncle Bol smiled encouragement. "There's nothing to be frightened of here, Elena."

Behind her, Er'ril nudged her forward. As she crossed to her

uncle, the mirrors reflected back sparks of lantern light and movement. Their own reflections shifting in the mirrors made Elena
jittery. She snuck closer to the swordsman. She kept catching
glimpses of motion from the corner of her eye. One black passageway led away from this chamber toward other dark mysteries.

"What is this place?" Er'ril asked, bringing to voice Elena's
own question.

"We are at the outskirts of the old ruins." Uncle Bol still had his
pipe clenched between his teeth. Its glowing tip acted like a pointing finger. He swung in a circle, encompassing the entire room.
"This was the old chamber of worship for the school. Here young
initiates—your age, Elena—would come to pray and meditate for
guidance from the spirit Chi."

She stared into all the dark shadows. Weren't there supposed to
be poisonous snakes around the ruins? She stepped even closer to
the man with the sword. "Am I supposed to pray to Chi?" she
said, her voice a whisper. "Here?"

"No, sweetheart, Chi is gone. The spirit that gave you your gift
is different."

"How so?" Er'ril asked. He didn't seem the least bothered by
the shifting shadows or the possibility of snakes.

Uncle Bol seemed unconcerned, too. He spoke to Er'ril as
Elena listened for hissing. "Where Chi was more a male spirit and
only communed with men, we believe the spirit that granted both
Elena and Sisa'kofa their powers is more the feminine twin of
Chi." He waved the lantern to the mirrors. "Like the mirror
image of Chi."

"But Chi granted his gifts to many men," Er'ril said. "Why does
this spirit only choose this little girl—Elena—to be its instrument?"

"That has been much debated, while the writings of Sisa'kofa
ponder that very question. The best answer the Sisterhood could
settle on was that Chi, like all men, can spread his seed far and
wide, so he could bring many men into his flock. This other spirit,
more like a woman, has only one seed at a time to cherish and
nurture. That seed was Sisa'kofa in the past and Elena today."

"So this spirit is weaker than Chi," Er'ril said.

Uncle Bol frowned at Er'ril, the tips of his white mustache drooping down. "It takes both a man and a woman to birth a child. Who is stronger and who is weaker in this union? It is just sides of a coin."

Er'ril shrugged. "Words for dreamers."

"What is this spirit?" Elena asked, becoming slightly intrigued but still watching for snakes. "Where did it come from?"

"Much is still unknown, honey. That's what I hope your aunt Fila may discover."

"But Aunt Fila is dead. How can she help now?"

Uncle Bol placed a hand on her cheek. "Aunt Fila is special. Our lineage, even before Sisa'kofa, has always been blessed with a unique connection to the elemental spirits. Even your own mother, Elena."

"My mother?"

Bol nodded. "You know how she could always tell the sex of an unborn child or when a cow would calf."

"Yes, all the neighbors used to come to her."

"Well, that was her special skill."

"And Aunt Fila had special skills, too?"

"Yes, and her skills were strong. Your aunt Fila could fold and knead the magick of the elementals like the bread in her bakery. She could wield many sorceries."

Tears again appeared in Elena's eyes as she thought of her parents, of her brother, and of Aunt Fila. "Why did she have to die?"

"Hush, sweetie . . . don't cry. Let me show you something." Uncle Bol led her to an alcove between two pillars.

Elena followed, noticing that this was the only section of the wall upon which a mirror did not hang. The alcove, lit by the hand lantern, was not constructed of stacked stones like the walls, but was carved from the rock of the hillside. It contained a pedestal supporting a basin of water. As she watched, a small drop of water rolled down the damp rock wall to dribble into the basin.

"What is this?" Er'ril asked behind her.

"It was a bowl used for ablutions by the initiates. The hands of many ancient mages used this bowl to wash before meditating."

Elena squeezed forward and had to tiptoe to peer into the water. "What does this have to do with Aunt Fila?"

"This water, seeping from springs deep in the hills, is steeped with elemental powers." Uncle Bol glanced over her head to Er'ril. "I don't think the school's mages, blind to the elemental spirits, even knew what strength flowed through this water. Maybe they somehow sensed it and so intuitively built their chamber of worship here."

"What does it do?" Er'ril asked.

"As water can carve paths in stone, so this water can carve paths between people. Both Aunt Fila and I had amulets that contained drops from this water, and it allowed us to communicate across distances." Uncle Bol slipped a small jade amulet in the shape of an alchemist's vial from his vest pocket. It hung from a gray twisted cord. He offered it to Elena.

She carefully lifted the amulet into the lantern light. "Thank you. It's beautiful!"

Uncle Bol bent and kissed Elena on her forehead. "It's a gift from Aunt Fila. In fact, the cord is braided with her hair." He reached down and removed a tiny sliver of jade acting like a cork in the vial. "Now go fill it with water," he said, pointing to the basin.

Elena looked at her uncle questioningly, then crossed to the tiny pool and dipped the amulet in. The water's cold stung her fingers. She lifted the vial free, and Uncle Bol passed her the jade stopper.

"Cork it snug," he said.

Elena did so, her brows knit tight as she worked the jade sliver in place. "Now what?" she asked.

"With this amulet you can talk to Aunt Fila. You must just hold the amulet tight in your hand and wish it so."

A trickle of fear dripped down her back. She loved her aunt, but . . . "I can speak to her ghost?"

"Yes. Her body may be gone, but her spirit lives. I, myself, cannot reach her with my amulet any longer. The elemental power alone is not strong enough to breach the distance to the spirit realm. But Aunt Fila believed you could succeed."

Elena's eyes were focused on the amulet. "How?"

"Cross to one of the mirrors. You need a reflecting surface. Then gaze inside as you hold the amulet firm and speak Fila's name. Try it."

Elena scrunched up her face and stepped to a mirror in a neighboring alcove. She slipped the cord over her head and clutched the amulet in her palm, its sharp edges pinching her skin. Pressing her fist to her chest, she stared into the mirror. Splotches of green water stains marred her reflection, giving her a diseased appearance.

"Think of her and speak her name," Uncle Bol whispered beside her. His voice sounded so hopeful, and sad at the same time, that she could not refuse him. In her mind's eye, she pictured her aunt's stern expression and the way her hair was always pulled back into a tight knot. "Aunt Fila?" she said to the mirror. "Can you hear me?"

With her words, Elena felt the amulet stir, much like a chick shifting in an egg just before hatching. But nothing else happened. She turned to Uncle Bol. "It's not working."

His eyes narrowed, and his shoulders slumped. "Maybe she's too far."

"Or maybe she was wrong," Er'ril said. "We should—"

The bookcase door slammed shut above them, startling Elena. She jumped, and her fist reflexively clamped, piercing her thumb on a sharp edge of the amulet.

The lantern rocked in Uncle Bol's hand, casting shadows to and fro. He and Er'ril stood stunned for a frozen heartbeat.

Suddenly a new light burst forth into the room. It came from the mirror in front of Elena. Her eyes, drawn by the light, saw a sight she never expected to see again, her aunt Fila! The old woman was draped in waves of light, and stars winked behind

her. The starry view reminded Elena of something she had seen
before.

But before Elena could ponder this, Aunt Fila spoke, a panicked look blooming across her aunt's face. "Run!" She pointed a
ghostly hand toward the single dark corridor leading out from the
chamber and deeper into the ruins. "Flee! Now! Leave the cottage
and escape to the woods!"

23

With his pillow covering his ears, exhaustion finally consumed Rockingham, and he fell into a fitful slumber. He dreamed he stood on the edge of a cliff above a dark, choppy surf. As he watched the white-tipped waves crash on black rocks below, he somehow knew he dreamed. Clouds and rain blotted the horizon as a storm brewed far out to sea. As is often the case in dreams, the time of day was unclear; the quality of light was such that a change felt imminent. But whether the light was due to wax brighter as in early morning or to wane into darkness, he was unsure. The only thing he knew for certain was that he recognized this place. He had stood here before. He remembered the salt in his nose and the breeze on his face. The Dev'unberry bluff, on the coast of his island home!

A smile appeared on his face. It had been many years since he had returned to the Archipelago. Even this nighttime fantasy was a welcome visit. He soaked the air deep into his chest, and if he squinted . . . yes, he could just make out the Isle of Maunsk in the distance, nearly swallowed by roiling clouds.

Suddenly, as he viewed the neighboring island, a feeling of dread clutched his heart. He glanced quickly behind him as if expecting some creature of nightmare to be pouncing toward him, but the rolling green hills stood empty.

What was this fluttering of his heart? This was his home. What should he fear? He stared at the view off the cliffs. The sweep of ocean, wind, and rain seemed strangely familiar, more than just a memory of home. This very picture—the distant island disappearing into cloud, the crash of angry water at his feet, the sting of spray on his cheek—not only had he stood here before, but he had stood *at this exact moment before*. But when?

He tried to organize his thoughts, but a rising panic rattled him. He had a sudden urge to run. But before he could act on this thought, his feet began to move on their own, not carrying him away to safety, but toward the edge of the cliff! As in many dreams, he could not stop. It was as if his body were a carnival puppet through whose eyes he peered. He could not stop his feet as they continued forward. As he fought, he watched his right foot step into open space.

Now he remembered! Not only had he been here before, he had done this very thing. A welling pain escaped his breast in a scream as his body tumbled off the cliff. "Linora!"

As the water-churned rocks flew toward his face, words tolled in his head, in a cold, familiar tongue, laced with black humor. Dismarum's voice said, "Don't worry, Rockingham, I'll catch you again." Laughter echoed as he hit the waves.

Rockingham sprang awake in the old man's cottage, tasting blood in his mouth. His underclothes were drenched in sweat as if he had run a long race. He struggled to sit up, but the ropes held him.

Suddenly a rough hand clamped over his mouth. He tried to scream, but the palm blocked all sound.

"Silence or die," someone whispered in his ear. Rockingham felt the blade of a knife at his throat. He stopped struggling. The weapon lifted from his neck and sliced his ropes free.

Rockingham pulled his arms down and rubbed his wrists. The bulky shadow of the mountain man loomed beside his bed. "Get dressed. Hurry!" Kral growled at him.

He noticed the small woman, Nee'lahn, fully dressed and peering through the tiny window. "Quickly!" she said. "Both are inside. The way is clear. Once we reach the horses, we can draw them after us."

"What is going on?" Rockingham asked as he tucked his shirt into his pants. He bent to his boots.

"Skal'tum," Kral answered.

Rockingham sped his efforts, pouncing into his boots. Now was not the time to be caught by the Dark Lord's lieutenants. He had no bargaining chip. "Where is the girl . . . and the others?"

Kral ignored the small man's question. He pushed him toward the window, not knowing why the woman had insisted on hauling the prisoner along. Rockingham should have been left to the teeth and claws of the beasts. But Nee'lahn had insisted.

Nee'lahn slowly worked the window open. Crashing sounded from below. "Do you think they're safe?" she whispered.

He stayed silent, unsure and reluctant to voice his fears. If only he had sensed the approach of the beasts earlier. Kral had found himself with only enough time to hurry down and kick the cellar door shut before the first skal'tum had begun digging at the cottage's door. He had barely escaped back up the stairs himself.

"Will they be hidden long enough for us to get to the horses and draw the monsters away?" Nee'lahn asked, propping the window open.

"The cellar door is well disguised."

"Still, we must hurry!" With the window now wide open, she climbed through the frame onto the thatched roof.

Kral picked up the prisoner and shoved him over the windowsill. The thin man rolled across the roof, almost tumbling from the edge. Kral wormed through the window next, having to blow all the air from his wide chest to give him room to squeeze through the narrow frame. His belt caught for a difficult moment on the sill before finally popping free and allowing him to scoot the remainder of his bulk through to the roof.

"Like a cow giving birth," Rockingham commented to no one. His flippant words, though, could not hide the wary crinkle of his brow or the way his eyes kept darting to all corners of the roofline.

Nee'lahn stood at the roof's edge. The horse barn with its crooked doors and sparse thatching stood just a stone's throw from her. "We could jump from here," she whispered. "Or work our way to the back of the house and climb down the woodpile."

As answer, Kral leaped from the roof to land with a muffled thud on a heap of dead pine needles. He waved the others down. Nee'lahn pointed for Rockingham to go first, obviously distrusting the man. He did not need goading. The speed with which he slipped to the edge of the roof suggested he, too, did not welcome an encounter with what tore through the lower rooms. He hung from the roof's edge for a moment, then let go to land near Kral.

Nee'lahn adjusted her pack and glanced down to them. Kral took a step forward to catch her if needed. As she hesitated a breath at the edge, a splintering crash erupted from the bedchamber behind her.

"Hurry!" Kral called. But he need not have spoken. Nee'lahn had already launched from the roof.

The word "Run!" blew from her lips as she landed on her feet. Before Kral could get his large bulk moving, she was off and darting for the horse barn. She flew like a fluttering leaf. Kral thudded after her, herding Rockingham ahead of him.

He heard glass shatter behind him, and the explosion of burst planks. He twisted his neck and saw a dark form driving through the window above, claws scrabbling at the thatched roof. It seemed trapped, but from the way it thrashed, it would be free in a heartbeat. He drove faster, shoving Rockingham forward. The townsman stumbled, but Kral caught his shoulder and kept him on his feet.

Kral saw that Nee'lahn had already disappeared into the horse barn. By the time he reached the crooked door with its cracked rawhide hinges, the woman had two of the horses—the girl's gray mare and the plainsman's chestnut stallion—already in tow. His own war charger, Rorshaf, would not allow the woman near and stood snorting and digging an iron-shod hoof into the dried manure. His black flanks heaved in excitement, apparently sensing the foul beasts afoot. Kral clucked his tongue twice, and Rorshaf settled his hooves.

Nee'lahn slid bareback atop the chestnut stallion and tossed the reins of the small mare to Rockingham. Kral noted with satisfaction that she had tied a lead from the mare to her stallion, not trusting the prisoner to stay with them. The mare fought Rockingham's mounting, but Kral—busy with his own beast—could not fault the man's garrison training. He stayed on the back of the horse and managed to gain control.

Kral tossed his saddle and packs atop Rorshaf and yanked the strap to secure it. In a heartbeat, he was mounted. He patted one of his packs at his thigh. Its fullness told him that no one had disturbed its contents.

He led the way to the barn door and kicked it wide.

A large shape crashed to the dirt and rock before him. His war charger, who would run through fire with nary a flinch, reared and snorted in fright. Kral twisted his fist in the reins and fought to keep his seat.

Before him, with wings swept wide, stood another of the Dark Lord's lieutenants. The skal'tum hissed at the rearing horse and blocked the way forward. Kral finally, with a savage yank on the bit, convinced Rorshaf to keep his hooves planted. The other horses and riders had edged back deeper into the ramshackle barn. But in there lay no safety; this beast would not be stopped by rotted and warped boards. Kral kicked Rorshaf forward, and for the first time since broken to the bit, his stallion refused his command. He kicked again with more heel. The horse ignored him, terror holding it frozen.

Kral leaned forward in his saddle, his pommel digging into his stomach, to reach his mount's ear. *"Rorshaf, partu sagui weni sky,"* he clucked in the tongue of the crag horses, a language all mountain folk knew as well as their own. Kral was the best of the Whisperers in his clan. Some said he was born to the fire speaking the language of the crag horses. Still, as skilled as he was, it took all his coaxing to work the fear from Rorshaf's heart and to get his mount to attend him.

The war charger began to respond to Kral's hands on the reins. Kral tapped his flanks, and the horse edged a few paces closer to the skal'tum.

The winged beast's ears swiveled forward and back, gauging the situation. The claws of its feet had dug deep into the soil. A greenish ooze dripped from the daggered tips of its claws as it opened and closed its fists. Fangs showed from between thin lips, and in the scant moonlight, its eyes were black pits with red-hot coals glowing deep within. The motion of the horse drew the monster's full attention.

"Where iss the girl child?" the skal'tum spat toward him. "Give her over, and we will let you die quickly."

Behind its words, Kral sensed fatigue in the beast. Its breathing rasped across the empty space. It had labored hard to arrive here so quickly. With luck, Kral might be able to distract the monster long enough to allow the others to escape. He thumbed free his ax from his saddle harness and pulled it to his lap. Kicking his horse to a lunge, he sped directly at the beast. A roar barreled from his throat in a battle cry of his clan. Kral swung his ax high.

As Kral had hoped, exhaustion and surprise forced the skal'tum back two steps before it could rise to its full height. It was enough; there was room enough for a horse and rider to slip behind Kral and out to the dark woods. "Go!" he screamed at the others. He did not have to call twice. A rush of thundering hooves passed behind his mount's rump. He dared not follow their progress, his eyes fixed upon the claws and teeth of the skal'tum.

The skal'tum, though, saw some of its prey scurrying away. It lunged at Kral just as the last of his companions raced past behind him. A lightning swing of his ax bounced back a flash of poisoned talons from his face, and a downward bat of his hickory handle knocked away a clawed kick at his mount's belly. Kral guided his horse with slight movements of his legs and shifts of his weight. Rorshaf became an extension of his own body. Where horse and man met became a blurred line of muscle and will.

The skal'tum backed a step, its chest heaving with exertion. "You fight well, man of rock. But the night iss mine."

Kral danced his ax in his hand, but it was a useless show of skill. He knew his fight with the beast was hopeless. As his previous battle with this beast's brethren had taught him, dark magick protected the skal'tum from harm. With the sun far from rising, Kral could not maintain this stalemate. Sooner or later, a claw or fang would slip through his defense. His best hope was to buy time for Nee'lahn and the garrison man to escape, then lure this beast away from the cottage—if he lived that long.

The skal'tum waited, its breathing becoming less labored as it rested. It was in no hurry to finish him off, toying with him. Apparently it knew the child it sought was not among those who had escaped on horseback. Kral sat straighter in his saddle. He had given Nee'lahn and the others time enough to flee. If he was to die here, let him die swinging his ax and on the back of the steed he had raised from a foal. He swung his ax above his head, meaning to challenge the beast to lunge. It did—cursed predictable beast!

Now to bait it away from the cottage.

Kral reared his horse, iron-shod hooves striking back the foe. Still hanging on the back of the reared stallion, Kral signaled Rorshaf to twist around. The horse spun on its hind legs and crashed back down, jarring Kral forward across the pommel. The skal'tum now stood behind them, screaming. The mountain man kicked his horse forward, attempting to race for the tree line beyond the corner of the cottage. But after only a handful of paces, Rorshaf ground to a halt, his hooves digging grooves in the rocky dirt. The sudden stop caught Kral by surprise. He struggled to compensate but could not stop his body from tumbling over the head of his mount. He landed with a roll and avoided a snapped bone. Pulling to his knees, Kral looked ahead to what had spooked Rorshaf.

A second skal'tum stalked from the front of the cottage and blocked his escape to the trees. Kral heard the sibilant laugh of the first skal'tum behind him. "Come back, little one. We are not done playing."

As Bol struggled to pry a torch from the crumbling stone of the wall, Er'ril prepared to mount the stairs and investigate the crashing commotion echoing from the cottage above.

"Stay your feet, plainsman!"

Er'ril turned to face the speaker, the ghost in the mirror. The swirling bands of light swelled and ebbed over the stern figure of the old woman. He spoke to the mirror. "I have companions in danger up there."

"They are not your concern," she said coldly, her eyes narrowed. "You were guardian of the Book, and now must be guardian of the one for whom the Book was forged. You must get Elena to safety. Time has not dulled the Black Heart's lust. Now go!" Her bright image in the mirror fluttered like a candle flame in a breeze, her final words stuttering. "The dark magick ... snaking in the cottage ... weakening my link. Flee ... while you still can! Do not fail me, Er'ril of Standi."

Then her ghost vanished and darkness reclaimed the chamber. Only the blue-flamed torches weakly beat back the blackness.

In the silence, the girl edged closer to Er'ril's side. An exceptionally loud crash boomed from above, startling her, and she clutched at his hand. He squeezed in reassurance, her hand a hot ember in his palm. How could this child be a wit'ch? Wit'ches were legends of evil: crook-backed crones buried deep in swampy lairs, or beautiful women with raven hair who lured men to their doom on midnight visits. Er'ril studied the woman-child. In the torchlight, her eyes were glassy with fear, her lips slightly parted as she held her breath. One hand twisted a curl of hair by her ear. He squeezed her hand again. Evil or not, *this* wit'ch was under his protection.

Bol had finally freed one of the torches from its bracket and pointed it to the only hall leaving the chamber.

"This way." He passed the torch to Er'ril.

With only one arm, Er'ril was forced to pry his hand from Elena's tight fingers to accept the flaming brand. The girl's hand, free now, snatched the edge of Er'ril's leather jerkin and clung there.

Bol raised his lantern. "Come. I have explored these ruins and know them well."

"Do you know a way out to the woods?" Er'ril asked.

The old man's words were whispered as he turned and began

to lead the way toward the black hall. "I once did. But these ruins have a way of tricking an eye."

Er'ril, with Elena attached to his side, followed Bol into the dark passageway leading from the chamber. The passage was revealed to be an ancient hall of the school. Hewn stone crumbled in dampness, and mold grew thick across the stone walls. An occasional alcove or niche they passed contained statuary so worn by dripping water and age that the forms had melted into hunched masses that seemed to menace the passer.

Er'ril noted that Elena kept well clear of these dark spaces, and every noise triggered a gasp from the girl. As she walked beside him, her feet stumbled in exhaustion. He heard her mumbling under her breath, words spoken to the floor in a disjointed fashion— something about snakes. Er'ril's lips tightened to a frown. It must be over a day since the child had slept. They needed to get her somewhere to sleep and recuperate. The dangers facing this youngster were more than just physical.

He wanted to put his arm around the girl, but he was fully occupied supporting the sputtering torch. For the first time in a long time, he regretted the loss of his other limb.

Ahead, Er'ril saw Bol hesitate at a junction of three crumbling halls. The subterranean ruins of the old school were a maze of crisscrossing stone halls and collapsed chambers. At first, Bol had been marching through this warren of tunnels with confidence, but as they proceeded he stopped more and more to scratch his head and squint his eyes.

Er'ril stepped beside him. "What's wrong?"

"I must have made a wrong turn. I don't remember this crossroad."

"What are you saying?"

"I'm saying we're lost. There are many parts of these ruins I haven't explored. Some sections are unstable and apt to fall. Some parts are where beasts of the underground rule and guard against intruders."

"And where are we now?"

As if in answer, a sudden loud hissing bloomed from all around them. Elena whimpered beside Er'ril.

Bol lowered his lantern. "How fast can you run carrying Elena?" he whispered to Er'ril.

"Why?"

Bol peered into the darkness. "I didn't know they had stretched their territory so far. The winter cold must be driving them to these lower regions."

Er'ril listened to the growing hissing. "Serpents?"

Bol shook his head. "Worse. Much worse. Rock'goblins."

THE TWO SKAL'TUM BEAT THEIR WINGS THROUGH THE COLD NIGHT air as Kral struggled to his feet. One of his knees protested the motion, and he grabbed for Rorshaf's withers to steady himself. The war charger sidled closer to him. Though the horse's eyes were wild with fear and its coat slick with sweat, Rorshaf stayed by the downed Kral, ready to protect.

The skal'tum behind him chuckled, the sound of its laughter like rocks rattling through a wash during a flash storm. "My little bird broke hisss wing. Come and I will fix it."

Kral heard the scrape of bony wing and claw approaching his back. He stared at his empty hands—weaponless. He had lost the ax when he was thrown from the horse. It now lay in the dirt near the feet of the second skal'tum. He needed another weapon but had none. Unless . . .

The second skal'tum crept closer toward him from the front. "We have had a long trip here. We could use a little meal before we tear apart the cottage and find our true prey."

Both of the skal'tum now hissed sibilantly. Green oil dripped from the claws of the skal'tum in front while it stared at him like a dog salivating for a bone.

Kral's hand settled on one of his packs. He picked the strap loose and flipped open the covering.

"Now what doess our little man think he hass?" the beast behind him asked. "Another shiny blade to prod at us? You cannot harm us, soft one, but only whet our appetites."

Kral reached into his pack and grabbed his "weapon" by a long ear. He pulled free the decapitated head of the skal'tum he had slain in the town. He raised it high for both creatures to see. "Do not trust so fully your dark magick! I have learned how to thwart your foul protections."

The sight of the head, its long tongue hanging slack from its dead lips, had the desired effect on the beasts. Kral guessed the two skal'tum had seldom seen one of their kind slain in many centuries. The shocking revelation caused both of the beasts to flap back from him in trepidation. He hopped forward, his horse following at his whistled command. He swung the head toward the skal'tum in front. It backed far enough away from Kral that he could reach the ax.

He quickly wiped the ax's edge through the thick blood that dripped in globs from the severed neck in his hands. "Blood of your kind smeared on a blade will render your dark protections useless." He raised the blade, praying his ruse would hold. "I do not need the sun to kill you!"

His words shook the skal'tum. Both near exhaustion themselves, neither seemed willing to test his claim. He mounted and, using his knees, guided his horse to the side. Now both skal'tum stood in front of him.

"We will kill you, little man. Mark our wordsss. When the tale of what you have done reachess our tribe, you and all your kind will be meat upon our fangss."

"We will be ready for you! Your blood will flow like rivers down our mountains," he assured the creatures as he swung his horse around and signaled Rorshaf to his fastest speed. Fear ignited his mount, and Rorshaf's iron-shod hooves thundered across the cold ground. Trees flew past to either side. With a net of limbs blocking the sky overhead from a winged assault, Kral allowed himself to breathe again.

As he and Rorshaf raced through the wintry night, thunder

rumbled from overhead. The storm was about to break. Kral watched lightning arc across the black clouds as two emotions warred in his heart: relief at having survived, and shame for what he had done. He kicked Rorshaf to a faster speed, as if he could run from his ignoble act. Froth foamed from Rorshaf's lips as he obeyed his master and sped through the woods.

It was not the abandonment of his companions in the cottage that caused his heart to weigh like a stone in his chest. Though he had left them to the beasts, his heart knew he had done all he could to buy them time to escape the cellar and reach safety. He had done his best, risking his own life.

No, what caused his heart to ache and his throat to choke was that he had lied, spoken an untruth! And for no other reason but to save his contemptible hide!

He yanked on Rorshaf's reins. His mount reared, wild-eyed, foam flying from the bit, and pulled to a short stop. Suddenly lightning and thunder crashed above Kral, as if the heavens above screamed for his lying heart. A freezing rain began pelting through the pines to strike his upturned face.

No man of his clan had ever allowed a lie to escape his teeth. With the spittle of his foul tongue, Kral had doused the fire of his family clan. For that blasphemy, he could never return to his mountain home.

A man forever lost, Kral howled into the face of the rain.

24

ELENA CLUNG TO THE SWORDSMAN'S JERKIN AS THE HISSING OF THE goblins crept around them. Now what? She had seen too many horrors this past day. She buried her face into Er'ril's leather jerkin. A rumble of distant thunder echoed from above, silencing the hissing but not for long. As the crackling roar died away, the menacing noise resumed, itching at her ears. She peeked an eye open and stared down the hall behind them. Were there darker shadows sliding toward them?

Uncle Bol spoke behind her. "I smell rain down this hall."

She glanced back toward her uncle.

He peered down the hall leading to the left. "And I think the hissing is less this way, too."

"Then let's go," Er'ril said.

With her ear pressed near his chest, Elena heard Er'ril's heart pound in its bony cage. She concentrated on the rush of blood through the warrior's heart, letting it drown out the hissing.

"Toss away the torch," Bol said. "You'll need that arm of yours to carry Elena. We must hurry. They may let us pass through their halls unmolested if we don't dally."

Elena allowed herself to be hefted into the air by Er'ril's iron-muscled arm. She held her arms around his neck to maintain her perch. "Swing to my back," he said.

She did as he asked and wrapped her legs around his waist. He kept his one arm hooked in her leg. "I don't need you to hold me," she said right into his ear. "If you lean over just a bit, I can hold on by myself."

Er'ril grunted acknowledgment and let go.

She tightened her knees and adjusted her weight. She held her place firm; it was not unlike riding a horse. "I'm set," she said.

Placing a hand on the pommel of his sword, Er'ril nodded to Bol. "Lead the way." Elena's arm across his windpipe strained his voice.

Bol raised his lantern, slipped into the hall on the right, and led the way at a slight trot. Er'ril followed with a strangled "hang on" tossed back at the girl.

Elena pushed her cheek against his neck and held tight, careful not to choke her mount completely. Her nose filled with the scent of him: horse and a rich muskiness, like a hint of the loam of his home plains. A picture of him as a boy running in the fields of his Standi home passed through her mind's eye, legs strong as they leaped irrigation ditches, chest wide as it drew the air yellowed by the dusty pollen of the spring fields. What if they had met as children? Would they have been friends?

Before she could ponder the strange effect his smell had on her heart, they entered the new hallway. The hissing grew louder as the walls around them echoed the threat. The noise seemed to creep into her skull and bounce around inside. She stared over Er'ril's shoulder as he trotted after Uncle Bol and the lantern.

Though they moved quickly, the pace was not so hurried as to trip a foot on a crumbling stone or bump a head on a fallen roof beam. It was this fast yet steady pace that kept Uncle Bol from death. From her perch, Elena could see the forward edge of the lantern's light as it raced ahead of them, illuminating obstacles. As she stared, the lantern light sliding along the stone floor suddenly vanished ahead as if swallowed by a hungry darkness. It took her a moment to realize what lay ahead. "Watch out!" she called to her uncle, who still hurried ahead of them.

Her words struck his ears at the same time the sight reached his eyes. He skidded to a halt, his arm swinging to keep him from falling. His toes teetered at the edge of a precipice. Er'ril came near to colliding into his back and sending him tumbling into the black pit ahead, but the swordsman was agile and instead pulled Uncle Bol from the edge.

Elena dropped from Er'ril's back. All three stared at the yawning precipice. The hall had been split by an old crack and a shifting in the rock of the foothills; the edge of the lantern light barely reached across the gap to where the hall continued on the far side—much too far to leap.

Another crack of thunder echoed from the storm overhead. The thunder's bark rang clear from the distant hall. Uncle Bol was right. A way to the surface did lie at the end of that hall. But with the pit between them and the hall's continuation, it might as well have been a thousand leagues away.

The thunder seeped away, and the source of the hissing became clear. The noise rose like steam from the precipice, as from a furious teakettle ready to explode.

"Rock'goblins," Bol muttered.

Behind them now, a thick-tongued hissing answered its brethren from the pit.

Uncle Bol turned to face Elena. She had never seen such despair in his eyes. "I'm sorry," he whispered to both her and Er'ril.

Elena barely heard his words. From the hall behind them, she saw inky shadows shift and squirm toward their light.

"KRAL!" NEE'LAHN CALLED THROUGH THE STORM-SWEPT WOOD. Limbs lashed about her horse, and a hard rain beat down, stinging her face. She continued through the wood toward where she had heard the thunder of passing hooves. She coaxed the stallion forward.

Behind her followed the mare and its rider, Rockingham. Though the steed was tethered to her stallion, the man made no effort to leap from his mount and flee. Apparently the prisoner had no desire to traverse these woods on foot with monsters loose this night.

"He's dead," Rockingham said sourly. "Let's find a thick-boughed tree and weather this storm out."

"No."

"He can't have survived the skal'tum."

"He did it once."

Rockingham pulled his shoulders up and hunched against a sudden wet gust. "Not this black night."

"I heard him."

"You heard thunder."

Nee'lahn nudged her stallion forward, leading the mare with her. Her senses were keen. It was *not* thunder she had heard. "Kral!" she called again, the wind ripping the name from her lips.

As if in answer, a light bloomed in the wood far ahead. Her first thought was that they had circled back around and that the misty light came from the old man's cottage. No, they were too deep in the wood, too far from the cottage. She sat straighter on the horse and peered forward, trying to pierce the veil of rain. The light, a soft azure glow, appeared to be bobbing up and down. Was some-one hailing them? Maybe Kral?

She reached a hand to the trunk of a tree and allowed her eyes to drift partially closed, searching through the rough bark and down to the heart of the tree, to its very roots that entwined with the other trees of the dark wood. She hummed a song of the nyphai low in her throat, a song of inquiry. Who lay ahead, friend or foe? But her only response was a rumble of irritation. How dull the roots of these trees, like men snoring in dream, compared to the symphony that once played in her own forest home. Only a single feathery answer returned—elv'in.

Startled, she let her fingers drift from the woody bark. Just an old nightmare, she thought. These trees here were lost in the past. The elv'in had been gone from these shores for a thousand ages. They had disappeared long ago, sailing their wind ships beyond the

Great Western Ocean to a faraway land, from which they had never returned.

Still, even this mention of the ancient elv'in stirred a worry in her chest; it was such a cursed name to find among these storm-drenched limbs.

Her curiosity inched her stallion in the direction of the light. The trunks of trees, moving between her and the light, winked the glow into and out of existence like some cryptic signal. Finally, an especially fierce gale blew down from the peaks, and a wall of rain swept over them. The light blotted out. Nee'lahn stopped her horse and waited, unsure where exactly the light had last stood.

As she held her breath, her eyes searching, Rockingham slipped his gray mare beside her chestnut stallion. "I don't like this. We should go. No telling what manner of beast might be loose this night."

She raised a warning hand. "Hush!" Her ears strained. She thought she had heard the snapping of a twig nearby.

"Wha—?" Rockingham's question was strangled to silence by a large hand clamped over his mouth.

Nee'lahn flinched in her saddle as she saw the huge shape swell up and pull Rockingham from his perch. A knife flashed into her hand from a sheath on her wrist. Whoever had grabbed Rockingham was on the far side of the horse, hidden from view.

From the corner of her eye, she saw the glow reappear on her right, farther in the forest. She ignored it, her attention focused on the commotion behind the mare. A face suddenly appeared over the withers of the horse. The rocky planes and thick beard of the face were familiar. "Kral?" she asked in a hushed voice.

"Down," he whispered at her, a hand motioning her to dismount.

Nee'lahn slipped from the horse's back. She darted to Kral and Rockingham. The garrison man was rubbing at his neck, his eyes narrowed with anger.

"Tether the horses," the large man whispered in her ear.

"Why?"

He pointed toward the light. "The horses draw attention. You two were making enough noise to attract a deaf cliffcat. On foot, the storm should hide our scent and cover our footfalls."

"Who's over there?"

"I'm . . . not sure." Kral quickly swung his face away. "But on this foul night, we should heed caution."

Nee'lahn's brow crinkled. The mountain man was acting oddly, but his words were sound.

"I'm not going anywhere," Rockingham said, planting his feet.

"You're right," Kral said. He grabbed both the man's wrists in one hand and bound them with rope. "You're staying here with the horses." Kral tossed an end of the rope over a high branch of a winter oak and caught it again. He pulled it taut, dragging Rockingham's arms so far up that he danced on the tips of his toes. Kral tied the rope around the bole of the tree.

Rockingham began to protest, but a gag stuffed into his mouth silenced his words.

"Is that really necessary?" Nee'lahn asked, surprised at the savagery in Kral's behavior. "He hasn't caused us any trouble."

"What about the skal'tum?" Kral said. "How did they know where to find us?"

She remained silent, unsure.

"Come, the sun's rising," he said. "I'm returning to the cottage and ridding the valley of those beasts, as I did with the other." He nodded toward the light. "But first I will know who else moves through these woods on a stormy night."

Nee'lahn thought of mentioning what she had heard from the tree voices, but Kral's actions made her uneasy, reluctant to open her worries to him. Besides, what was the need of speaking of the elv'in kind? They were creatures of old stories.

"It would be best if you stayed with the horses, too," Kral said.

"No." The word escaped her mouth before she could stop it, but she didn't take it back. "I'm coming with you."

Kral hesitated as if to protest, then merely shrugged and turned away. Nee'lahn followed his wide back as he slipped away. For such a huge man, he seemed to float across the forest floor. Silent and sure, he sped toward the distant light, ax clenched in one fist. Nee'lahn, a creature of the forest herself, still had to press hard to keep pace with the man. The storm, with its sudden buffeting winds and wet embrace, hindered her, while the rain sluicing through the bower overhead ran off Kral's body as if off rock.

Not a word was uttered as they continued, but inside Nee'lahn a thousand concerns fought. Even after his battle with the skal'-tum in the town, Kral had come away from the fight winded but unfazed, with his calm resilience intact. Now, though, his words had a bite to them, and his actions were as sharp as the edge of his ax. Even his shoulders seemed tight and bound in iron.

If Kral had not been so strange, she would have perhaps stayed with Rockingham and the horses and might have been able to keep Rockingham from being trussed up like a beast. But the way Kral's brows brooded over his sunken red eyes scared her—not for herself, but for others he might encounter. Not all things this night needed to be met with blade and muscle.

Nee'lahn came abreast of the mountain man and watched the light glowing past the last scattering of tree trunks. Whoever cast this light into the storm deserved to attract more than just blind fury. She edged ahead of Kral, determined to see first if Kral's ax might be needed. She sped ahead of the giant, her lithe feet danc-ing across the fallen leaves and twigs in silence. The ways of the forest paths were part of her nature. Behind her, she heard a whisper of ire from Kral.

The slightest smile edged her lips until she reached the last of the trees and saw who and what brought light into this dark wood. *No!* Instinct took hold of her heart as her dagger again appeared at her fingertips, snatched from her wrist sheath. She flew into the circle of light.

The tall, slender man, twice Nee'lahn's height but half her weight and dressed in only a thin white shift tucked into billow-ing green trousers, twisted a long thin neck to face her. He stood in a ring of mushrooms with one arm raised high, bearing aloft the source of the glow. A bird, perched on his raised wrist, glowed a bright azure from its feathers. Startled, it beat its wings twice, and the light waxed brighter with its motion. A moon'falcon!

The falcon opened its beak and screeched.

"No, Nee'lahn!" Kral called behind her as she raced forward with her dagger held high.

She ignored him, a scream of rage escaping her lips.

The elv'in must die!

ER'RIL PUSHED THE CHILD BEHIND HIM AND UNSHEATHED HIS SWORD. He faced the dark hallway. Hissing black shapes slid toward them. Bol stood with the girl and held his lantern up. Its light cast the trio in an island of illumination. With the precipice at their heels, retreat meant only another form of death.

"I don't understand," Bol muttered behind him. "The few times I've encountered signs of the rock'goblins, I merely had to run away. They've never pursued me."

"Maybe they've grown bolder," Er'ril said. He saw a few of the shapes slip toward the edge of the light. The lantern's glow seemed to hold them back, like some magickal shield.

One of the shadowy figures broke away from the others and dragged forward. It stood just outside the light, clinging yet to the blackness. A glimpse of red eyes and a baring of needled fangs reflected the traces of the lantern's glow. Er'ril found the tiny hairs on the nape of his neck raising at the sight. The creature's shape echoed night terrors of his own childhood when blankets were pulled tight to chin as the house creaked at midnight.

"They won't hold much longer," Er'ril said. "Do you have any weapon, Bol?"

"No, only the light." The old man stepped forward, flashing the lantern ahead.

The sudden movement of the light caught the bolder goblin by surprise. It stood exposed in the bright light, no taller than a goat. Its skin, which had appeared black in the shadows, was now revealed to be a scaly white, like the underbelly of a dead fish. A filthy oil sheened its surface. Huge red eyes stared, unblinking, at them. Then it hunched back from them with a sharp hiss, exposing the fangs of an asp. A tail, with a single black horn brandished on its tip, whipped from behind the goblin to coil and writhe in threat.

Er'ril grimaced, not at the sight of the single beast cringing in the lantern's glow, but at what else the spreading light revealed. The hall before them was crammed with hunching, squirming forms. Even the walls and roof were festooned with goblins hanging from claws dug into the crumbling blocks of stone.

The single goblin nearest them darted back into the shadows. The bulk of its fellow creatures also shied from the encroaching light, but not in full retreat.

"What do you make of them?" Er'ril asked Bol. "My sword cannot singly force a pass through their mass. What of wit'ch magick?" Er'ril forced himself not to stare at the little girl cowering behind Bol.

"No, Elena is dry. And like her male counterparts, it takes sunlight to renew her power. She cannot help us."

"Then can these rock'goblins be reasoned with?"

"I know not. They are a skittish lot, having only rare contacts with others."

"And what happened to those others?"

"Their skulls and bones were found, well cleaned."

Er'ril stared as the goblins began a slow creep back toward them. He motioned Elena toward one wall and had Bol stand guard before her. Er'ril needed room to maneuver. He raised the tip of his sword.

He watched for any sign that the beasts had gained enough confidence to attack. But they continued to hover at the edge of the lantern's light, as if waiting for a sign of their own. The goblins seemed determined to keep the intruders from leaving, but unsure what to do with them otherwise.

"What . . . are they doing?" Elena asked from behind her uncle.

Her voice was surprisingly steady. Maybe she was too naive to properly appreciate their predicament.

"I'm not sure, honey," Bol said, "but we'd better be quiet."

With their words, a commotion seemed to be stirring among the mass of goblins. It started far down the hall and commenced toward them—a furious hissing and a squabbling of clicking tongues.

Er'ril tensed, his sword arm rock steady, his eyes narrowed with concentration.

Suddenly another goblin burst from among the mass to reveal itself in the lantern light. Like the goblin before, this one stared up at him with huge red eyes, its tail thrusting toward Er'ril cautiously. But in its tiny hands was clasped an object that flashed in the lantern light. The goblin slunk forward, its hands raised toward him as if offering a gift. Er'ril backed a pace and pointed the tip of his sword at the creature.

The other goblins filling the hallway had silenced their hissing and stood stone still. The goblin standing before Er'ril peeled its long fingers open to reveal a single sculpted lump of metal, so large it took both of its tiny white palms to support it.

Er'ril gasped. The metal glinted like gold in the lamplight. He knew this object and its shape and knew it was not gold that shone in the light, but iron forged from the blood of a thousand mages. He had hidden it among the ruins of the ancient school over a century ago for safekeeping against rogues and thieves during his traveling.

It was the ward of A'loa Glen.

Stunned by the unexpected revelation, Er'ril allowed his guard down and moved too slowly. The goblin with the prize darted forward, not at Er'ril, but past him. Before Er'ril could react, the goblin snaked behind him and flew to the lip of the yawning precipice. The creature paused a moment, peering over its shoulder at him.

"No!" Er'ril dropped his sword and lunged a hand at the beast. The ward must not be lost! Again he was too slow. The goblin leaped into the precipice and tumbled into the black maw, still clutching the key to the lost city.

Er'ril dashed to the edge, falling to his knees, and searched the chasm. Nothing but blackness stared back at him. "Bring the light!" Er'ril commanded.

"Look, they're leaving," Bol said.

Er'ril allowed himself a quick glance. The mass of rock'goblins were slinking back from them, disappearing into the gloom of the dark halls: one less threat. Swinging his attention back to the precipice, Er'ril repeated, "Your lantern! Shine it here!"

"Why? Let's get out of here. We'll backtrack to the surface," Bol said as he stepped to the chasm with the lantern.

"Lower it into the pit."

Bol bent with a sigh and leaned his lantern over the edge. The light spilled into the darkness to illuminate a narrow cliff only a few spans down. Crude hewn stairs led from this ledge deeper into the chasm. Just at the edge of the lantern's glow, a goblin could be seen jumping down the steps. It was soon beyond the reach of the light.

"We need to catch that little toad." Er'ril pulled to his feet and picked up his abandoned sword.

"Why? Let him go, Er'ril. We need to get Elena to safety."

Er'ril slammed his sword into its scabbard. "If we're to have any chance of reaching A'loa Glen and the Blood Diary, we need what the goblin carries. It's the key to unlocking the path to the lost city. Without it, the ancient spells woven around A'loa Glen are impregnable. I must retrieve the ward."

Bol's brow crinkled as Er'ril's words sank home. "How did they find it? And why show it to us and run away?"

"We were herded here." Er'ril pointed to the now empty hall-way. "By exposing the ward, they no longer need to push us. They expect that it will now *pull* us."

Elena had wandered to stare into the precipice. "Pull us where?"

Er'ril stepped beside her. "Down there."

KRAL LUNGED AFTER NEE'LAHN. WHAT HAD IGNITED SUCH FURY IN the usually quiet woman? Rain lashed in swirls through the small clearing among the trees. The lone occupant, a man as tall as Kral but thin as a wind-whipped sapling, glanced toward Nee'lahn with the mildest pursing of his lips, as if only slightly curious why this woman was racing toward him with an upraised dagger. His hair, tied into a long braid that draped down his back, was cast in shades of silver, but surely not from advancing age since the smoothness of his face suggested otherwise. His blue eyes, though, which settled only briefly on Kral, suggested time had worn away both youthful fears and wonder. The eyes seemed bored.

The only light in this stormy glade swelled in waves from a bird, a falcon aglow with a deep azure light. Perched on the tall man's bony wrist, the bird's response was more vocal than that of its bearer. It screeched through a sharp beak at Nee'lahn, mimicking the tiny woman's own declaration of rage.

A gust of rain stung Kral's eyes. He blinked. In that fraction of a heartbeat, the bird vanished from the stranger's wrist. In a streak of light, not unlike the bolts striking between clouds, the bird dove to Nee'lahn and knocked the dagger from her hand. Before Nee'lahn's shocked feet could even stumble to a stop, the falcon had returned to its perch.

Nee'lahn stood panting, her fine hair plastered in welts across her face. "This is not your land!" she yelled above the thunder. "Your kind do not belong here."

By now, Kral had reached her and placed a hand upon her shoulder. Unsure who this man was but trusting Nee'lahn's instinct, he stood by to support his companion. He felt her quiver under his palm, as if her emotions boiled within her, threatening to explode. "Who is this man? Do you know him?"

Nee'lahn's quaking calmed as he spoke. "No, not him. But I do know his people—the *elv'in*!" The last word was spat at the stranger.

The stranger remained silent, unconcerned, as if he did not speak their language. Kral tensed as the elv'in man suddenly moved, but he only reached a long finger to ruffle the feathers of his falcon. This seemed to calm the bird, and it settled deeper on its perch, less taut.

"I have not heard of his clan," Kral said, his words for some reason whispered.

"You could not. Even before the race of man appeared on these shores, the elv'in were myth, long vanished across the mists of the Great Western Ocean.

"Then how do you know them?"

"The trees have long memories. Our most ancient roots were young when the elv'in still walked under the boughs of the Western Reaches. The most hallowed trees still sang the stories: songs of war . . . and betrayal."

"But they sing no longer," the stranger said, speaking for the first time, his voice like the chiming of bells. His eyes, though, were still on his falcon, his head bent slightly in study.

"Because of you!" Nee'lahn began to shake again.

He shrugged.

"You betrayed us." Tears appeared on her lids.

"No, you destroyed yourselves." For the first time, a spark of anger glinted in the blue eyes of the stranger, a sudden storm in a summer's sky. He swung to face them both fully, high cheekbones sharp on his white face.

Kral squeezed Nee'lahn's shoulder, attempting to bottle the swelling rage inside her. Through his touch, Kral sensed the truth in Nee'lahn's words. She believed her accusations. But Kral also had the impression that the stranger was not lying either. He believed his own assertions of innocence.

Kral spoke into the tense silence. The storm raging in plays of wind and thunder above seemed calm compared to the quiet war waging here. "I do not understand. What happened between your peoples?"

Nee'lahn turned to Kral. "Once, a long time ago, the spirit trees of my home, the koa'kona, grew everywhere on this land, spreading from the Teeth across the vastness of the Western Reaches to the Great Western Ocean itself. Our people were revered as spirits of root and loam. And we shared our gifts freely."

The stranger snorted. "You ruled as if all the other races on the land were mere tools to aid in the growth of your precious trees. Your rule was a tyranny."

"Lies!"

"At first, even we didn't recognize how unnatural your spread upon the lands was. We aided you, using our gifts of wind and light to help your trees grow. But then from the winds on high, we began to sense the corruption that this marching spread of your people had upon the land: Swamps drained, rivers diverted, mountains fell. The beauty of life's variety was thwarted by your people's single-minded creep. So we held back our gifts and tried to speak reason to your ancient elders. But we were reviled and cast out from our homelands."

"But not before cursing us! You seeded the Blight upon your winds and cast the rot of root and leaf upon us. Our trees began to wither and die across the land until only a small glade, protected by the new magick of the human race, survived the purge. You destroyed us."

"Never! We held life precious, even your own. It was not we who cursed your trees and brought the Blight, *but the land itself.* Nature fought your spread to protect its diversity. You were cast down by the land itself. Do not blame us."

Kral saw Nee'lahn's eyes grow wide; reason and rage fought within her gaze. "You lie," she said, but this time her voice was tinged with doubt. She turned to face Kral. "He lies, doesn't he?"

Kral shook his head. "I sense only truth, but only in the faith of his words. He believes what he says. That does not mean that what he believes is true."

Nee'lahn raised her fists to her temples as if to squash the doubts now rooted therein. "Why? Why then have you returned?"

"When we were banished, elemental wards were placed upon

these lands by your ancients to keep us from these shores. With the death of the last tree, the strength of the wards faded, and the paths here opened again. So I was sent."

"Why?" Kral asked.

"To retrieve what we had lost, what we were forced to leave behind."

"And what is that?" Nee'lahn asked. "We kept nothing of yours."

"Ahh, but you did. You hid it in this valley, a vale still named as we named it long ago—Winter's Eyrie."

Both Kral and Nee'lahn voiced the same question. "What?"

He raised his falcon high. "Seek out what we have lost." The bird burst out from his wrist in a streak of moonlight and soared across the drowned glade. *"Seek out our lost king."*

Book Four

MOONLIGHT AND MAGICK

25

TOL'CHUK LUMBERED BEHIND THE OTHERS, HIS SHOULDERS HUNCHED against the pelting rain. The storm had struck as soon as they had cleared the mountain heights and entered the rimwood forest of the lower highlands. Spears of lightning crashed in jagged bolts across the night sky, illuminating the dark forest ahead in sharp bursts of blinding radiance.

In one of these bursts, he saw Mogweed and his wolf-brother almost a league down the path. Even with the storm's howl, his companions had traveled lightly once they reached the forest's edge. Woods were their home, and even though this was not their own forest, the familiar canopy of woven branches and bushy undergrowth seemed to ignite renewed vigor in their limbs. The injured wolf, even burdened by his splinted leg, raced among the trees, while Tol'chuk, racked by rib-cracking coughs and a nose clogged with dripping slime from the constant dampness of the weeks of travel, found himself slipping farther and farther behind the others.

Tol'chuk dreamed of his own dry caves with a roaring fire in his family hearth. He bowed his head and dragged a forearm across his raw nose. The first winter storm had always marked the Sulachra, the ceremony of the dead, in which cured goat dung was burned in family hearths to honor the spirits of the departed. He pictured the caves billowing with the sweet smoke and the females waving fans of dried toka'toka leaves to cast the mingled odors out into the storm. Lightning was supposed to open cracks in the dome of the sky through which the smoke would seep to the next world, letting the dead know they were still remembered. Tol'chuk coughed, an echo of the thunder above, and wondered who would perform the Sulachra for his dead father. And if no smoke arose for him, would he think he had been forgotten?

As Tol'chuk plodded down the path, the tapping of his thigh pouch on his leg brought a sudden realization. He stumbled to a stop, his palm cupping the Heart of the Og'res in the pouch, and remembered the Triad's words. The spirits of the og're dead, including his father, had not made the journey to the next world. They were trapped here, in the heartstone!

This realization opened a hole in Tol'chuk's chest into which a profound hollowness swelled. The Sulachra ceremony was a sham! The smoke had never reached the flared nostrils of the spirits. The dead had never reached the next world.

Tol'chuk's hand fell away from the pouch, from the gem. The Sulachra had been a time when all the og're tribes united for a brief few days in a communal act of homage. It was a time of peace and contemplation, a short respite from the tribal wars. It united the og're people with its grace. But now, with the knowledge of the lie behind the act, the beauty of the ritual was forever fouled for Tol'chuk.

In just a heartbeat, he had become less an og're. He glanced ahead at the dark wood spread before him. So many leagues still to cross on this journey. What else would he learn on this trek? Who would he become?

Thunder mocked him from above as lightning split the dark roof of the world. In the flash of illumination, Tol'chuk realized he had lost Mogweed and Fardale. His traveling companions had disappeared among the black, glistening trunks.

Alone among the trees, Tol'chuk felt as if he were the only living creature for a thousand leagues. Between the rumbles of thunder, the forest lay silent around him except for the rattle of rain on leaves and the brief whistles of wind through pine branches. Not a tor'crow cawed, not a frog croaked. Tol'chuk wiped at his nose and sniffed loudly, just to interrupt the forest's silence. I am here, he said with each sniff. I am not dead.

He marched on. As he took his first step forward, he saw a glow blossom into existence on his right. How had Fardale and Mogweed gotten so far? He adjusted his course toward the light, his legs as heavy as the tree trunks around him. These swampy woods addled his sense of direction. The light, like an island in a storm-swept sea, became his beacon. With his eyes fixed on the glow, Tol'chuk trudged forward.

The lonely wood fired a craving for the sight of others, some reassurance that all living creatures had not been swallowed up by this black forest. As his legs increased their lumbering pace, he wondered how his companions could enjoy this cramped and closed world of heavy limbs and choking undergrowth. Where were the open views across a thousand leagues? Where was the parade of snowy peaks spread far and wide? Here, he could barely reach a hand forward to keep a branch from slapping his face or see much beyond the tip of his nose. Even the tunnel to the chamber of spirits had not felt this confining.

As he marched, he noticed he was gaining ground on the glow's position. The others must have stopped and were finally resting. Hopefully they had found a dry spot to weather out the remainder of this night's storm. Besides the desire for companionship, the thought of a dry shelter hurried his pace.

Soon he spotted the motion of dark figures within the glow. His heart gladdened at the sight of others. He was not alone. As the light swelled momentarily brighter, he saw three silhouettes limned in the azure glow. His feet stumbled to a halt.

Three? Who had his companions met?

Suddenly the glow shot away, streaking like a fiery arrow into the wood. Perhaps he should stay hidden. But what if the others were in trouble, met up with some brigand or marauder? He was not familiar with the tricks of the forest floor and knew that the only reason the others were unaware of his location was because of the blanketing noise of the storm. To sneak closer and survey the situation firsthand was beyond his skill. Too many snapping twigs and branches would betray his approach.

Seldom creatures of deception or cunning, og'res relied on brute force for both offense or defense. Though only a half-breed, Tol'chuk knew this part of his heritage held true.

So he took the single course open to an og're. He wiped his nose, swelled his chest with damp air, and crashed forward in a loping run that had surprised many crag'goats among the peaks. The speed of an og're was their tribe's only deception. Few creatures were aware of how quickly an og're could move when necessary. And these few creatures, like the hunted goats, never lived to tell.

It was the suddenness of his speed, even though accompanied by a shattering roar of cracking branches and sapling trunks, that caught the three in the glade unaware. Three faces swung to face Tol'chuk as he burst into their tiny clearing—three faces of startled strangers.

None of these were his companions!

He realized his lonely thoughts had hidden from him the possibility that a different group of travelers might be huddling in the stormy forest. Tol'chuk stood stunned as the others momentarily stared wide-eyed back at him. The largest man, almost as massive as an og're himself, was holding an ax, while a tiny female gasped with a hand over her mouth. A waifish, silver-haired man stood frozen nearby, eyebrows high up on his forehead.

The thin man, like a version of Mogweed stretched close to breaking, was the first to move. Only a slight pursing of his lips and a relaxing of his posture spoke his lack of alarm. He raised a single finger, pointed it at Tol'chuk, and spoke with bells in his voice. "It seems I'm not the only one straying far from home this stormy night."

With the man's words, Tol'chuk felt a pull on his heart, as if from hooks imbedded deep in his chest, from the chunk of heartstone at his thigh. This meeting was not chance. He stared at the small blond woman with her hulking friend. Tol'chuk spoke in the common tongue, "Who be you?"

That he could speak seemed to stun the ax man and the tiny woman. She even took a step away. Only the gaunt man seemed unimpressed.

"Who be you all?" Tol'chuk repeated.

The wraith of a man spoke, waving his hand to encompass the group. "Seekers like you, og're. The wit'ch draws us to her like moths to the flame."

Tol'chuk wiped his nose, confused, the ache in his heart beginning to dull. "I do not understand. What wit'ch?"

The man smiled, but there was no mirth in his voice. "The wit'ch who will destroy our worlds."

MOGWEED CROUCHED BY THE OPENING IN THE HILL. THE TUMBLE OF stone blocks near the entrance to the ancient tunnel was covered in wet moss and a flaky lichen. A gnarled oak growing on the slope above the black opening wormed roots through the soil to drape across the entrance like bars to a prison. From the size of the oak and the thickness of the lichen growth on the stones, this tunnel was as old as the forest itself. He noticed this whole valley seemed littered with crumbling stone and the remnants of ancient walls.

Perhaps it was an abandoned mine. Mogweed had heard that the Teeth were pocketed with ore and jewel mines like old cavities. The thought of diamonds and gold drove Mogweed closer to the tunnel entrance.

Bending near the opening, Mogweed crinkled his nose at the smell from the hole. It reeked of old animal droppings and the muskiness of bear. But the scent must be old because the growth of root across the entrance was too thick for a bear to pass. Even

Fardale had had a hard time squeezing through to explore the tunnel.

If no dangers lurked there, it would be a safe haven to wait out the brunt of the storm. He heard his brother snuffling deeper down the tunnel. "Did you find anything?" he called.

Of course, his brother could not answer. Even discounting Fardale's wolf form, it still took direct contact, eye-to-eye, to speak the spirit language of his people. But the voiced question helped dispel the misgivings that grew like webs around his heart as he sat out in the rain among these foreign trees. He could swear just moments ago he had heard a scream from somewhere not too far away. But the thunder and rain muffled the scream, and now Mogweed was unsure if it was just the howling wind he had heard.

And where was the og're?

Mogweed was a tiny bit shocked at the pang of worry that accompanied this quandary. He should be relieved that the lumbering beast that could break him in half with a shrug was not here. But by now Mogweed had grown confident that the og're meant him no harm, and here in the dark forest, alone, Mogweed would gladly welcome the appearance of his sharp-eared, rocky face.

Mogweed stood back up and studied the slopes around him as lightning lit the surroundings. He had known Tol'chuk was lagging behind. The phlegmy illness plaguing the og're had been getting worse. A day's rest beside a warm fire in a dry shelter was what they all needed.

Adjusting his oilcloth slicker, Mogweed again crouched to watch for the reappearance of his brother. Luckily, Fardale's keen wolf sense had discovered the tunnel. It was what they all needed, especially the sick og're. As he bent to lean on a root and peer into the darkness, a rivulet of rain that had pooled on his coat's collar tipped and ran down his neck in an icy trail. Shivering down to his toes, Mogweed called, aggravation thick in his throat, "Hurry up, Fardale, before I freeze to death out here."

Suddenly a brilliant crack of lightning burst behind Mogweed.

Its radiance reflected off a pair of eyes only an arm's length from Mogweed's nose. With a sharp cry, Mogweed tumbled back. As his backside landed square in a frigid puddle, the realization that the eyes were amber and slitted struck him. They were the eyes of his brother.

He watched Fardale poke his wolf head between two roots. If a wolf could express amusement, this one was certainly doing so.

"Fardale, you piece of cold dung!" Mogweed rolled to his feet. His fury and embarrassment blazed away his chills. "Give a warning before pouncing on a person."

His brother's eyes glowed. *The hungry sparrow fixed on a worm gets eaten by a hawk.*

"Yeah, well I don't have your sharp nose or night eyes. The senses of a man are so dull, why do they even bother wasting room on a face with noses and eyes?" Mogweed wiped at his wet bottom with a scowl. "So is it safe?"

An image formed behind Mogweed's eyes as Fardale climbed from the tunnel: *A nest lined by dry feathers and high in the crook of a tree.* Fardale limped on his splinted leg to join his brother.

Mogweed sighed. "Finally I can get warm, and maybe dry these clothes. Seems like I have been damp forever."

Tol'chuk's image formed in Mogweed's mind. Fardale's eyes glowed toward him.

"I don't know where he is," Mogweed answered. "If we light a fire in the tunnel, the flames should guide him here."

Fardale's stance seemed hesitant, questioning, as if thinking of leaving Mogweed here and searching after the slow og're.

"He'll get here in his own time," Mogweed insisted, suddenly nervous at the thought of being left alone again. "Besides, Tol'chuk isn't likely to encounter anything an og're can't handle."

His words seemed to settle the wolf, but Fardale's eyes kept wandering to the ridges and slopes around them. Satisfied his brother would stay, Mogweed tossed his bags between the roots, then after much squeezing and squirming, followed them into the tunnel's entrance.

An ankle-deep carpet of blown leaves and pine needles greeted Mogweed on his arrival. Grimacing at the mulchy mess, he bent and retrieved his pack from where it lay partially buried. As he shook his bag clean of clinging leaves, he heard a low growl rumble from outside the tunnel. At first, he thought it just thunder, then recognized it as a warning from his brother.

He swung around in time to see a streak of light, like a flaming arrow, descend into their small valley between steep ridges. The light aimed straight for his brother. Fardale had his nose raised toward it, and a continuous growl flowed from his throat.

What was it? Mogweed squeezed closer to peer between the roots. The streak of light suddenly banked and aimed away from his brother—directly toward him! Mogweed tumbled back as what now could be seen as a glowing bird dove toward his face.

From the bird's beak, a piercing scream preceded its flight.

Throwing himself backward into the deep mulch, Mogweed watched the creature dive between the roots and into the tunnel. With a yelp, he covered his head with his arms. The beast flapped and sailed over his body, sharp talons brushing the back of his hand as it passed.

Then it was gone, sweeping away into the depths of the tunnel.

Mogweed sat up, stunned. Fardale squeezed between the roots to watch its glow disappear down the dark corridor. Once it had faded around a distant turn in the tunnel, Fardale swung and sniffed at Mogweed's scraped hand. Mogweed was unsure whether he did so out of sympathy for his injured brother or simply to inspect the scent of the bird.

Fardale's nose tickled the path the talon had taken across Mogweed's hand, his breath hot upon his brother's wound. Seemingly satisfied, Fardale pulled back. He darted around and trotted down the tunnel several steps.

"Where are you going?" Mogweed asked.

Fardale glanced over his shoulder at him. *A she-wolf crouches and protects her litter from the hidden snake in the grass.* His brother then loped after the glowing bird.

"Wait!"

But Fardale did not even slow. Soon Mogweed was alone again. Out of the rain and with the entrance somewhat protected by the drape of roots, he should be relatively comfortable and safe. Still, his heart thundered blood through his ears as he strained to listen for his brother's padding footfalls. Mogweed's hands kept clutching at his neck, protecting his throat.

The strangeness of the bird had spooked him. As a denizen of the Western Reaches, he was familiar with most winged creatures. But the likes of that bird were unseen in his lands. Maybe they were common here in the human lands, but somehow he sensed the bird was a foreigner here, too. The bird seemed out of place with this forest, a creature of another world.

As he waited, pondering the bird, the storm lulled and the constant background rattle of rain quieted. At least the worst of the storm seemed to be blowing itself out. With the disappearance of the rain, a new noise arose. Maybe it had always been there, with the patter of rain masking it. Or maybe it had just started.

The sound did not come from outside his hiding place, but from somewhere down the tunnel—where both the bird and his brother had vanished.

The noise raised the tiny hairs on his arm.

Fardale's final words to him now seemed foretelling: *A she-wolf crouches and protects her litter from the hidden snake in the grass.* The noise, a soft hissing that rose and fell as if the tunnel itself breathed, flowed toward him from deep in the tunnel, like a thousand unseen snakes.

Suddenly a sharp howl pierced the soft hiss. It was a howl of pain, a howl Mogweed had come to know—Fardale's howl.

A deep silence followed, and it weighed on Mogweed's heart like a stone.

"I KNOW NOTHING OF A WIT'CH," TOL'CHUK SAID, EYING EACH OF THE three strangers. Though the large man bearing the threatening ax should have drawn most of the og're's attention, it was the gaunt man with the braided silver hair who kept Tol'chuk wary. The man's persistent sneer hovering below hooded eyes silently warned at a danger sharper than an ax blade.

"This be none of my concern," Tol'chuk continued. "I bid you well on your journeys." He rested a hand over his fanged lips in an og're gesture of peaceful intent, though he was unsure if they would understand the motion. Backing from the trio, he maintained his guard.

"Wait," the small woman said, struggling to overcome her initial fear. She wiped strands of streaming hair from her wet face. "This is a black night, full of danger. Beware these woods."

Tol'chuk paused his retreat. He noticed the woman give the skinny man a brief glance with her warning.

"There are beasts, black of heart, loose in the woods," she continued, "hunting for friends of ours. Be careful."

Tol'chuk thought of his own companions traipsing blithely through the wet woods. "I, too, have friends in these woods. What sort of—"

Suddenly a piercing howl broke through the slowing patter of rain. All eyes swung in the direction of the cry. As quickly as it had pierced the night, the sound faded away.

"Wolves," grumbled the ax man.

"No, one of my friends," Tol'chuk said, recognizing the voice of his wolf companion. "Fardale be attacked. I must help him." The og're started in the direction of the howl.

"Hold, og're," said the thick-bearded man, hefting his ax higher. "If you would have me, I will join you. It may be one of the foul beasts that we drew into the mountains that attacks your party. If so, you will need my help."

"Yes," said the small woman. "Kral is right. Allow us both to accompany you."

"No, Nee'lahn," the large man said. "It's too dangerous."

"Nowhere in this wood is safe this night. I'm coming."

Tol'chuk balked at accepting their assistance but had no time to argue. Without a word, he turned and lumbered in the direction of the howl. He noticed the gaunt man followed.

Nee'lahn noticed, too. "Elv'in, you are not welcome. Be gone on your dark pursuits and leave us be."

"Oh, I was not coming to help you," he said as he strode after them. "It just so happens this is the path my moon'falcon flew."

"Your pursuits are folly. No king of yours was left among the lands."

"So your kind has always claimed."

"Quiet!" Kral barked. "Enough of your bickering. You'll draw the beasts upon us. From here we proceed in silence."

Tol'chuk wordlessly thanked the bearded man. Why did these races need to spout continuously? Even Mogweed, with no other to talk to, carried on tiresome monologues, as if the sound of his own voice brought him pleasure.

With a nagging worry for his talkative companion, Tol'chuk led the party over the ridge and down the next slope. Due to the steep grade, the slope was tricky to maneuver, but piles of crumbling rock dotted the way ahead, offering footholds among the slippery cascade of wet leaves and mud. The party quickly maneuvered from stone to stone down the ridge to the floor of the hollow.

Once safely off the slope, Tol'chuk stood hesitantly. It had sounded as if the cry had come from somewhere nearby, but the woods fouled his senses. Where should he go? Suddenly motion caught his eye. He twisted and saw Mogweed, his back to Tol'chuk's party, struggling among the roots of a large black oak as if the tree itself were attacking him. After a heartbeat, Tol'chuk recognized the characteristic black eye of a cavern opening beyond the man. Mogweed was blindly fighting his way out, dragging his pack after him. It ripped loudly on a snagging rootlet. As his pack snapped free, he was flung around to face the group. At the sight of the cluster of strangers, Mogweed's mouth dropped open, and he scooted back to the pile of roots.

Tol'chuk stepped forward. "You be safe, Mogweed. These folk will not harm you."

Mogweed swallowed several times, trying to free his tongue.

He jabbed an arm toward the hidden cavern entrance. "Far . . . Fardale is in trouble."

"I heard your brother's cry," Tol'chuk said. "What happened? Where be your brother now?"

"A bird . . . Some cursed glowing hawk lured him deeper into the tunnel."

"The moon'falcon!" Nee'lahn cried behind Tol'chuk, her voice sharp with indignation. "It was the elv'in's bird! See, I told you. He is not to be trusted."

"My pet did not harm your friend," the elv'in argued, "unless he was foolish enough to threaten the bird. My falcon is simply trained to survive—like all elv'in."

As Tol'chuk swung around to face the others, he found the eyes of the woman called Nee'lahn narrowed with hate as she stared at the thin man, but before she could utter another word, the bearded mountain man rumbled at them both. "I do not care about old quarrels." He stabbed a finger at the thin man. "You, elv'in, what is this tunnel? And—"

A palm snapped up, interrupting Kral. "First of all, my name is Meric, of the House of Morning Star, not elv'in. And I know nothing of this tunnel. My falcon flies upon the trail of our lost king. He chose this subterranean route, not I."

"He lies!" spat Nee'lahn.

"I am not here to sway you." Meric twisted on a narrow heel and strode toward the entrance to the tunnel. Mogweed danced out of his way. Apparently, like Tol'chuk, his companion sensed the palpable danger emanating from the man.

Tol'chuk, though, followed Meric, feeling responsible for Fardale. The present fate of his companion was partly his fault. He should not have lagged so far behind the others. If he had been with them, perhaps he could have stopped whatever had attacked Fardale. Few things pierced an og're's protection.

Ahead, Meric bent in half to enter the tunnel, slipping between the shield of oak roots with nary a struggle. Tol'chuk, though, realized the century-thick roots would bar his way. He pulled at a few of the roots, but even an og're could not uproot an ancient oak gripping firm to rock and soil. From between the roots, he saw Meric pull a clear stone from his pocket and rub it between his palms. Then he blew upon it, as if bringing a dying ember back to life, and a greenish light burst from the stone. With the light held before him, Meric disappeared down the tunnel.

Tol'chuk sensed someone at his back. Kral, the mountain man, spoke from behind his shoulder. "Let me chop a way inside."

Tol'chuk stepped back to give Kral's ax room to swing.

"Stop!" Nee'lahn flew forward, raised a tiny hand, and pushed the huge ax aside. "This tree did no harm." She placed her palms reverently on the roots, as a child might touch an elder. After bowing her head for a single heartbeat, she merely pushed the roots aside, as if sweeping back the leather flap to one of Tol'chuk's home caves. Having tested the tenacity of the roots with his own muscle, Tol'chuk was awed by the power behind those small hands.

He was not the only one impressed. Tol'chuk heard a grunt of surprise from Mogweed, who huddled under his shadow. "A nyphai," Mogweed said with wonder in his voice. "I thought all the tree singers were long dead."

Mogweed's words were ignored, though Tol'chuk noticed his companion studied the small woman with a measuring glance, his eyes narrowed.

"Nee'lahn," Kral said, drawing Tol'chuk's attention, "considering your view of the elv'in, perhaps it would be best if you returned to Rockingham. The og're and I can handle this."

The small woman seemed about to argue, but Kral continued. "Besides, Rockingham has been trussed up for some time now. I'm sure his wrists are sore."

Though Tol'chuk did not understand of whom Kral spoke, the look of concern on Nee'lahn's face suggested Kral had won her over. Still, Tol'chuk had his own concerns. "But the wood be not safe for a female alone," he said, slightly surprised at his own heartfelt worry for the tiny woman.

"Thank you for your concern, og're," she said coldly. His consideration seemed inadvertently to offend her. "But among trees, I have no fear."

Mogweed spoke up, his voice faltering as he stared at the black tunnel. "I . . . I can . . . go with her for her safety."

Kral swung around before anyone else could speak. "It's decided then." Hunched, the mountain man entered the tunnel first, squeezing past the roots that were already bending back toward the opening. He marched, back bent, down the stone tunnel.

Tol'chuk followed, crouching on the knuckles of one arm to climb inside the passage.

"Be careful," Nee'lahn called. "And beware the elv'in."

Tol'chuk did not answer, fearful of again insulting the woman, and only followed Kral's back.

Soon the weak light of the night forest faded behind them. Even the eyes of an og're had difficulty judging the shades of darkness. He heard Kral grunt as he tumbled into unseen obstacles. "That Meric and his light can't be too much farther ahead," Kral said as he paused to rub at a bruised shin.

Tol'chuk stayed silent. A buzzing noise, so faint even his sharp ears could barely discern it, kept him distracted from Kral's observations. He poked and rubbed inside one of his ears, unsure if the noise came from inside his head or from the tunnel.

Kral continued, and the scrape of his boot on rock obliterated the sound. Tol'chuk followed, ears straining. As they rounded a corner in the stone tunnel, his ears no longer had to strain. The buzzing noise was now loud enough to be heard even over the scuff of Kral's boot.

The mountain man stopped and listened. "What's that noise?" Kral whispered.

Tol'chuk by now could discern a faint glow coming from around the next corner. "There be a light," he said softly and pointed ahead.

Kral crept forward, now careful not to scrape his heel on the crumbling rock. Tol'chuk tried to imitate his stealth, but his claws would not cooperate. He sounded like a scuttling cave crab.

As they neared the corner, the light ahead grew brighter as the source flowed toward them. "Someone comes," Kral breathed.

"Be it Meric?" With Tol'chuk's words, a small stone, glowing a greenish light, rolled around the corner and bounced to the tip of Kral's boot. "The elv'in's stone," Tol'chuk said.

Kral bent and picked it up. He turned to pass the crystal to Tol'chuk. The buzzing had now grown to a distinct hissing around them. Kral pointed to a smudge on the stone's glowing surface. "Blood."

26

THE HOWL SHOOK ELENA, ECHOING FROM SOMEWHERE BEYOND THE chasm. Even Uncle Bol seemed upset, mumbling something about there having been no wolves in these parts for ages. The wolfish cry split through the hissing rumble of the rock'goblins like a knife thrown through fog. It buried itself deep in Elena's heart, rupturing her pocket of resolve. She stood on the steps that led from the first ledge, unable to goad herself deeper into the chasm.

The gloom of the gorge danced with visions of tortured beasts and rending teeth. She trembled with her eyelids stretched wide, aching from the strain to see what lurked just beyond the black veil. She expected at any moment for claws to reach out and pull her into the darkness, never to see light again. Even the lamp held by her uncle did little to cast back the smothering gloom.

A hand clamped down on her shoulder. "Careful there, sweetheart." Uncle Bol pulled her back from the edge of the narrow stairs. "The edge is weak, just crumbling stone held together by age. I don't trust it supporting even someone as light as you. Stay close to the wall."

She teetered back to the sheer wall.

Er'ril stood four steps down from her, where he had stopped when the howl echoed to them. His sword pointed into the darkness beyond the edge of the narrow stairs. The flickering lamp-light cast weaving shadows across the planes of his face, sometimes creating a wicked appearance of sunken eyes and dead lips. Elena shivered at the sight; then the lamp steadied and the rugged, road-worn warmth returned to his face, eyes alight with danger.

He caught her gaze upon him. "We must be quick if we are to catch up with our thief," he said.

Uncle Bol nodded, and Er'ril swung his sword forward and followed its tip down the dark stair.

"Uncle," Elena whispered as she stayed close to his lamp, "if those goblins want us to go this way, like Er'ril said, what do they want of us?" Behind her breastbone, a fear she fought to keep tightly bound wiggled free. After all that had happened since the sun set yesterday, she suspected she knew the answer to her own question. Her fears were confirmed by the concern shining from her uncle's eyes. It was *Elena* the goblins truly coveted.

But, of course, he denied it. "Honey, there's no reading the thoughts of these sunless creatures. It's most likely just mischief. They're known for their thievish hands and wily ways."

Though she didn't believe his words, she nodded anyway; Uncle Bol needed no further worries. Swallowing a dry lump like an old crust of bread, she even offered him a weak smile.

Uncle Bol nudged her forward after the swordsman. Er'ril had by now crept farther down the stairs, almost to the edge of the lantern's reach. There at the last strand of light before the sea of darkness, he had stopped. His face was turned toward them, a look of puzzlement wrinkling up his normally smooth features. But his eyes were not on them but stared at something behind Elena. His words quaked the fear in her chest. "Something comes." His sword pointed to the darkness behind her.

She and Uncle Bol spun around. The blackness behind them now had a glowing eye. A spark of light swung in slow swoops, searching.

"Who—?" Uncle Bol began.

Er'ril hissed him quiet.

The eye of light stopped its wavering and stood fixed in the wall of darkness, then darted toward them.

Er'ril slipped like a ghost beside Elena and shoved her back. All three ducked to the wall. Elena, protected by the two men, cringed. What new horror now?

Then it was upon them. Elena gasped, not with horror, but with awe. A bird aglow with a light the color of sunshine on water swept before them, wings spread wide, plumage bright with a soft radiance. As it winged closer, subtler hues of rose and copper could be seen playing across its feathers. It hung in the air before them, slightly rising and falling with unseen currents of air, wings flexing as it rode the darkness. Eyes like pebbles of coal studied them where they hugged the wall.

"Amazing!" Uncle Bol said, his voice low with wonder. "I thought them long dead to our lands."

Er'ril still had his sword raised toward it, ever cautious. "What is it, some cave bird?"

"No, it is a creature of the upper world. It traps moonlight in its feathers, giving it light to hunt the darkest night."

"In all my centuries of travel, I have seen many sights, but none such as this."

"It is from before your time, Er'ril, long before even your oldest ancestor."

"What is it then, Uncle?" Elena asked. By now the worry of danger from the intruder had faded. The men had relaxed their guard on her and allowed her to push between them to get a closer look at the bird as it continued to hang above the well of the chasm. She stood near the edge of the stair—but not too near, mindful of her uncle's warning.

"I believe it's a moon'falcon. I have only seen them described on ancient, crumbling parchments." Her uncle's words took on a far-away tone, as if he was searching deep within himself. "The nature of the beast is spoken in some texts as a glorious creature of noble intent and in others as a fiend of foul omen."

Her uncle continued droning on, but Elena heard little past the naming of the bird—moon'falcon! Drawn by its beauty, Elena found her hand reaching over the stair's edge. If only she had a crust of bread to lure it to her as she did the fat goose on the pond near Maple's Corner. Or maybe a piece of meat, she corrected herself, for surely from its hooked beak and sharp talons this was a hunting bird. But what did it hunt in so dark a cavern?

She reached even farther toward the bird, leaning slightly. The falcon banked on a wing tip and swung toward her. Moonlight flashed brighter as it beat its wings and pulled higher above her. She stretched her arm up, following its flight. She could almost reach it, her fingertips close enough to brush the azure light it shed. Cooing sounds of comfort slipped from her lips. She prayed for it not to fear her.

"Careful, Elena," her uncle warned as the bird slipped a breath lower.

Elena's hand was now awash in its glow. Delight crowded the traces of fear from behind her breastbone—until the falcon screamed.

The bird had seemed about to alight upon her outstretched hand; then its intended roosting spot had *vanished*.

Elena's hand was gone!

A cry escaped her own throat, mimicking the falcon. The screeching bird fluttered upward. Elena ignored the creature, her attention focused on her arm. Beyond her wrist lay only darkness, as if the chasm's blackness had swallowed her hand.

Yanking back her arm in fright, she expected a flood of blood and pain. But as she pulled her arm to her chest, her hand reappeared, attached to her wrist as usual.

She groaned. The skin of her hand, bright in her uncle's lamplight, again flowed a ruby red. Whorls of deeper red, almost black, swirled across its surface.

A sob escaped her throat. Not again! She held her hand out to her uncle in supplication, her eyes begging him to take it away. With her arm held up to her uncle, the falcon swooped in a streak

of moonlight and landed upon her blood-colored hand. The suddenness of its weight almost caused her arm to drop. But before
the bird could be dislodged, its black claws dug deeply at her
palm, fierce enough to pierce the skin for a heartbeat. Blood
welled like fat tears around the talons of the falcon. With an effort
she steadied her arm, and the bird loosened its tight grip, its claws
slipping from her flesh. The claws now shone silver in the lamplight. Wonder at the bird's beauty momentarily muffled her
shock.

The falcon cocked its head from side to side as it studied her
fingers. A sudden thought that perhaps it was considering one
of them as a meal flitted across Elena's mind. But it merely bent
its head down and rubbed its crown of feathers on her trembling hand.

Satisfied, it suddenly perched straighter on her hand, spread its
wings wide, and screeched a cry of triumph across the cavern,
light bursting brighter from its flared plumage.

"So what do your ancient texts say of that?" Er'ril asked Bol.
He nodded to the falcon perched on the child's wrist. After its
raucous outburst, it had quieted down and begun simply to preen
its feathers with a hooked beak. Er'ril was unsure what bothered
him more, the bird's behavior or actually witnessing a wit'ch
ripening to power. His eyes kept drifting to the girl's red hand. He
had accepted the old man's claim of Elena's heritage, but to see it
proven still startled.

"As I said," Bol scolded, drawing Er'ril's eyes from the child's
hand, "concerning the moon'falcons, the scrolls speak different
tongues—some bright, some dark."

"And what about her hand? I thought mages required sunlight
to initiate a quickening. How did she manage to renew her Rose
in this pit?"

Bol scratched behind an ear with a finger. "Perhaps the bird's
light."

"Moonlight?"

"I remember reading a text of a long dead alchemist which supposed that moonlight was merely reflected sunlight." Bol waved the fingers of one hand dismissively. "Of course, the alchemist was burned for such blasphemy. Still, one wonders."

Both men's eyes settled on the bird. Elena caught the direction of their attention. "Can I . . . may I keep him?" she asked, her eyes aglow with reflected moonlight from the bird's feathers.

"It's a wild creature," Bol answered. "I don't think I, or anyone else, can control its heart. It makes its own choices, and for some reason, it has chosen you."

"Do you think he'll stay with me?"

Bol shrugged. "Who can say? But I'm afraid, honey, that the bird may just be spooked by the dark halls. It probably wandered into these tunnels to escape the storm outside and became lost. Once out in the forest, I expect it will take to wing again."

Er'ril turned his back on the two, his eyes again studying the dark stair. Enough about some stray bird. Rare or not, it did not bear on his pursuit of the iron ward. The thieving goblin was by now far down these stairs and likely impossible to find among the warren of halls and passages. Further pursuit was probably futile, but Er'ril could not forsake his trust. The ward, one of only two, had been bestowed on him by the Brotherhood as an honor to his family . . . and for his sacrifice. He felt an itch at the stump where his right arm once sprouted. His eyes closed with the memory. The price of the ward had been a costly one.

He shuddered, opened his eyes, and raised his sword. No, he would not leave the ward to these slinking, hissing creatures. "We should continue. The trail grows cold."

Bol nodded and picked up his lantern, which he had set down on the stair. "Well, at least we now have two sources of illumination," he said, raising his lamp and nodding to the moon'falcon. "Perhaps we can better light this cold trail."

"If we wait much longer, even the midday sun won't help us." Er'ril swung forward and led the way down the stair. His boots stomped on the rock, followed by the lighter tread of the others. As much as he regretted the delay due to the bird, Er'ril found Bol's words proved true. With the increased light, the mud and grime now glistened with the growing dampness, warning of treacherous footing. The light also revealed small prints with wide-splayed toes patted into the thin layer of silt.

Er'ril pointed to the prints with the tip of his sword but kept silent. Bol nodded. To see evidence of the creature they pursued hushed the party. Here was proof that what they chased was not an illusory phantom, but a creature of bone and blood. As they continued in silence, the air itself dampened with a thickening mist. Soon Er'ril found the dense air difficult to breathe; each lungful had to be bit and swallowed.

Bol whispered behind him, his breath wheezing between his words. "Are you . . . sure . . . there's not another way to . . . unlock A'loa Glen's magickal walls? Do we really . . . need this ward? Perhaps Elena's magick—"

"No!" Er'ril cracked at him. "I must . . . we need the ward."

"I don't want to do any magick," Elena said, bolstering Er'ril's words, her voice sour with dread.

Her uncle patted her on the head, trying to reassure the child, but instead raising a sharp chirp of warning from the falcon. The bird's chest puffed out, and its black eyes needled toward the old man's fingers. Clenching his knuckles, Bol pulled his hand back. "I guess I'm outnumbered."

Er'ril increased the pace down the stairs, worried that further delay might fade the feeble track they followed. But another concern sped his pace. With enough time, the old man might eventually convince him to abandon his pursuit. His mind already dwelled on Bol's words. Perhaps there *were* other ways into the lost city. Perhaps Elena's wit'chings *could* pierce the magickal veil around A'loa Glen. Maybe they *didn't* really need the ward.

Gripping the hilt of his sword until his wrist ached, Er'ril marched down the steps. The ward was his!

"Slow your pace, Er'ril. My bones are not as agile as yours."

Bol's words had a strained edge, and the old man's breath rasped in the thickened, damp air. "This rock is as slick as a salamander's back."

Er'ril slowed his pace. Not so much at the old man's request, but because the last of the stairs had appeared out of the gloom ahead, lit by the twin fires of bird and lamp.

They had reached the bottom of the chasm.

He raised a warning hand to keep Bol and Elena from following until he checked what lay ahead. With his back gliding along the wall, he slid down the last of the steps and crept to the limit of the lamplight with his sword slicing the way forward. Gloom forced his eyes wide.

At the bottom of the stairs, a wide floor of tumbled rock and littered rubble spread ahead. A thin path wound through the debris. Barely discernible on the far wall of the chasm was a rip of blackness far blacker than the dark rock. Was it the entrance to another tunnel? Er'ril guessed the narrow path led to that spot.

As he studied the way ahead for hidden attackers among the scattered boulders, he heard the scuff of boot on rock behind him. The light brightened as his two companions disobeyed his command and crept closer.

Bol stepped to his shoulder. "Well, what do you think?" he whispered.

Er'ril restrained the sharp retort on his tongue. Why couldn't they simply mind his directions and stay on the stairs? He kept his eyes focused forward. His gaze settled on the distant tunnel. With Bol's lantern now closer, the improved light illuminated the opening in the far cliff wall.

It was a tunnel opening, not like the man-made halls of the old school, but a natural fissure in the rock. A crack in the rock face started at twice the height of a man and split wider as it reached for the floor. Sudden motion near the wide entrance to the tunnel caught his eye.

Er'ril tensed.

He saw a small, dark shape dart down the last of the path. It paused at the entrance of the tunnel. Somehow Er'ril sensed that it stared right back at his own face, laughing at him. Then the diminutive figure bounced into the fissure and was swallowed away.

"Hurry!" Er'ril said, his voice thick with threat. "We're close! But watch the shadows. I don't trust these goblins."

ELENA ALLOWED THE FALCON TO CLIMB UP TO HER SHOULDER. ITS claws dug through the thin fabric of her shirt and pinched her skin as if refusing to let even the wisp of the woolen cloth stand between it and Elena's flesh. It nestled close to her neck, but as if obeying the swordsman's warning, its head kept swiveling back and forth, studying the chasm floor ahead.

Without further instruction, Er'ril led the way into the tumble of rocks and boulders. His heavy boots thudded forward down the path. Bol gently nudged her to follow, though she noted his hands kept well away from the bird's beak. She also noted that her uncle's breathing had become alarmingly raspy in the damp, heavy air. Even she found herself having to suck air through her mouth to keep from feeling suffocated. She glanced up to her uncle, who offered a weak smile. His color seemed more ashen, but maybe it was just the lantern's light making his face appear so pale.

"We'd better not let Er'ril get too far ahead of us." He nodded for her to proceed ahead while he kept watch on their back.

Elena marched after the retreating swordsman, who set a furious pace across the flat ground. Without the fear of breaking a neck on slippery stairs, the need for a cautious gait had vanished. Elena almost had to run to keep up with Er'ril.

Glancing over her shoulder, she noticed her uncle lagging farther and farther behind. He walked hunched over, wiping at his brow with the back of a hand. Was his hand trembling? Maybe she should call for the swordsman to slow down. Just as she was working up the courage to speak, Er'ril raised his hand in warning.

She was relieved he was calling a break in their hurried march. She closed the distance to Er'ril. "My uncle—" she said, pointing behind her. She swallowed another mouthful of air, surprised how short of breath she was herself, and continued. "—he needs to rest."

The swordsman made a noncommittal grunt, his eyes studying a group of large boulders clustered like dragon's eggs to the right of their path. "Stay here," he said and started toward the boulders.

She stood, shifting from one foot to the other. She twisted her neck. Uncle Bol was still several spans away, and he walked with one hand clutching his left side. He slowed even further once he realized they had stopped. Grimacing, Elena crept after the swordsman.

He must have heard her footsteps or maybe noticed a shift in the light. He swung to her. "Listen, lass. You need to stay put. I must check the boulders ahead for any ambush, and I don't need you to slow me down if there's trouble."

"But it's dark over there. My light will let you see better." Tears threatened at the thought of abandonment. She glanced far back to where her uncle had stopped and was leaning on a large rock.

"No, if there are any of those goblins out there, your light will signal my approach like a hundred flaming brands. I go alone. Return to your uncle."

She nodded acquiescence and pushed back her shoulders to show she wasn't scared of anything. Her lower lip trembled slightly and ruined her effort at bravery.

He gave her a tiny smile. His usually stark features cracked in lines of sympathetic amusement, lines well worn into his face. She realized his face must once have smiled easily, though that had clearly been a long time ago. "We all fear, Elena," he said. "Sometimes we have to put it aside and go on. Don't let it control you."

"Are *you* ever frightened?"

He stared at her wordlessly for the longest time, then merely shrugged. His eyes seemed to look far away, and his voice was small. "Since I lost my brother, I don't think I've ever felt completely safe."

She touched him on the elbow. "Me, too," she said meekly.

Her words seemed to puzzle him, then realization dawned behind his eyes. "We'll find your brother."

"I miss Joach so much."

"Well, we're not going to find him down here. We need to forge ahead. Now go help your uncle—it looks like he could use a shoulder to lean on—while I check the boulders ahead."

She nodded, her trembling calmed. He studied her for a moment, then swung on a heel and continued toward the maze of boulders, his sword raised. She watched him duck and disappear behind a rock the shape of a small cottage. Waiting for several heartbeats, she searched for any sign of the swordsman. Nothing moved, but the shadows clung everywhere among the boulders. Anything could be lurking there, hidden from sight. Standing with the moonlit bird, she realized how she must blaze like a star to any eyes watching from the cluster of rock.

A shiver passed down the back of her neck, as if someone lightly waved a finger over the tiny hairs of her nape. She suddenly felt hidden eyes staring at her. She backed from the line of boulders, toward where her uncle was waiting.

Was that something moving in the shadows below the rock shaped like a broken barn? As she moved, all the shadows shifted with the movement of her light. The shadows themselves seemed alive, wriggling with foul intent. Maybe they had swallowed the swordsman and now wanted more.

Her feet began retreating faster. Her heel struck a loose stone, and a yelp escaped her throat as it skittered away. It wasn't a stone! She watched it scuttle from her, its claws ticking open and closed. The creature—some sort of cave crab—vanished into the shadows.

Her flesh crawled now with imaginary cave creatures. She sped away toward where her uncle had last stood. A medium-sized boulder blocked her view of Uncle Bol, but his light shone like a beacon just beyond.

"Uncle Bol," she called as she rounded the edge of the boulder. She spotted her uncle just a few steps away and skidded to a stop. His lantern lay on its side, and her uncle sprawled beside it. He lay limp on the cold stone.

Shock froze her feet for several heartbeats, her breath trapped in her throat. Uncle Bol! She could not face the thought of losing another of her family. She even took a step away, as if fleeing from the sight would undo it. Then she saw his chest move up and down. He wasn't dead! He still breathed, but consciousness had fled him. Relief almost cut the cords holding her upright. Her knees buckled slightly, but she fought to keep her feet. She half stumbled, half fell down beside her uncle. The falcon squawked a warning at the sudden motion, flapping its wings in agitation. Moonlight bloomed brighter on her uncle.

She reached for his hand. His skin felt cold and oddly moist. His cheeks were pale, like those of a corpse laid out for viewing. She found herself patting his hand and mumbling, "Uncle Bol, wake up. Don't leave me here. Please, wake up." She reached to his face next and laid a hand on his brow. He was hot. The touch of her hand on his feverish forehead stirred him. A low moan escaped his throat, rising like steam from a boiling pot. Even this soft noise sounded loud in the quiet cavern.

Uncle Bol rolled his head from side to side as if suffering a nightmare. But her touch did not awaken him further. She rubbed his cheeks and massaged his wrists, but nothing drew him to consciousness. She glanced around her as a sob escaped her lips. She needed help. Where was Er'ril? She feared calling to him, afraid of what else might answer her summons from these shadowed rocks.

As she listened for any sign of the returning swordsman, she heard the soft tinkle of flowing water. Hadn't there been a spring-fed stream near here? She studied the surroundings. It should be just past that pillar of rock!

She returned her attention to Uncle Bol. Maybe a bit of water on his lips might help. But did she dare leave him?

Her uncle settled back down as if his foul dreams had slipped away, but his breathing had a more ragged edge to it now, a throaty gurgle that caused her to clutch at her own neck. She could not just stand and watch him die. She found her eyes drifting toward her right hand, where whorls of red hues seemed to be swirling faster with her agitation.

Could her magick aid her uncle? Her mind's eye drew up the picture of her parents buried in flames. No, she dared not risk it. She lowered her hand. She needed to go for water. If she ran, it would only take a moment to reach the small stream.

Before fear could keep her frozen forever, she darted away. Again the falcon spat a squawk of protest and dug his claws deep into her shoulder to keep its perch. Elena ignored the pain and ran.

Her feet flew with the knowledge that her goal was so close. It was for that reason that when she saw what stood by the stream, she could not stop in time and fell to her knees, scraping them savagely on the coarse rock. A scream locked in her chest at the sight. Her falcon, jarred from her shoulder by the sudden stop, flapped up and circled above.

The stream lay an arm's length away, but something else had reached it first.

She watched the shaggy beast raise its head from where it had been lapping water. Huge yellow eyes reflected back her falcon's light. She knew this type of beast. She had seen hunters from the highlands carrying their pelts to town. It was a wolf.

It growled at her in warning but did not approach any closer, apparently as cautious about her as she was of him. It took a few steps back, limping on its right front leg. The remains of some sort of bandage hung from the injured limb. It was hurt. She saw that one of its ears was torn, shredded and matted with blood.

She remembered the howl they had all heard earlier. She guessed this was the creature that had voiced that pain.

Both stared at each other warily. The wolf had stopped growling and now just stood, slightly wobbly, on three legs. She studied the traces of the old bandage. The wolf could not have done that itself; it must have been cared for by someone. She knew some woodsmen used wolves to aid their hunting. Was this someone's lost pet?

As she realized the wolf was not going to leap at her throat, she allowed herself to breathe again. She leaned away, meaning to retreat, then paused. Fear kept her ready to bolt, but the swordsman's words about not letting fear control one's actions kept her crouching in place. Maybe the wolf needed help, like her uncle.

And another thought occurred to her. Maybe its keen nose could even lead them all out of here! Elena pictured her sick uncle. They needed a way out quickly. If she could coax the wolf . . .

Taking a chance, she bit her lower lip and crawled a step forward to the stream. Using both hands, she cupped a scoopful of cold water and held it out to the wolf. Surely it would take this gesture as a friendly one. The wolf's eyes narrowed slightly with suspicion.

She forced her arms not to tremble as she held her position firm. At that moment, the falcon flapped down and gently landed on her shoulder.

The wolf eyed the bird, then looked again at the offered water. It took a step forward.

"Come on," she whispered. "Don't be afraid."

The wolf padded another step toward her, its nose now so close she felt its hot breath on her fingers. It craned its neck forward. A tentative tongue slipped from between exceptionally long fangs to touch the water. Though wanting the water, its eyes never left hers. The yellow eyes, she now noted, were odd. The irises were slitted up and down, not round, more like a cat's eyes than a dog's.

As she stared in fascination and awe, its eyes suddenly dilated black and darted to her right. It pulled its neck back with a growl.

"Get back, Elena! Now!" She glanced over her shoulder to see Er'ril stepping from around a boulder behind her, his sword raised in menace toward the shaggy wolf. "Run behind me." Er'ril lunged at the wolf with the sword.

Without thinking, Elena threw herself in front of the swordsman's weapon. She knocked his blade aside with the flat of her hand. "No!" As her right hand made contact with his sword, a flash of ice blew out from her palm to swallow Er'ril's sword.

Er'ril gasped and shook the frigid weapon from his hand. The iron sword crashed with a clang to the stone, and like a glass vase, it shattered into a thousand frozen pieces.

Elena watched the swordsman's eyes settle on her face. He wore an expression of red-cheeked anger mixed with shock. "My sword!"

"I didn't mean to do it," Elena said in a small voice, hiding her right hand behind her back. The realization that she had just destroyed their party's only weapon dawned on her. Tears rose to her eyes. "I'm sorry."

Behind her, she heard the wolf growl.

ER'RIL GRABBED THE STUNNED GIRL AND SWEPT HER TO THE SIDE, PRE-pared to do battle with the huge wolf. The beast was injured, so perhaps he still had a chance of driving it away with a swift kick or the strike of a fist.

The wolf, though, was not growling at them, but had his back turned and faced toward the dark trail they had traversed earlier. The wolf's hackles were raised, and a long, steady rumble flowed out to the darkness.

"Something's coming," Elena said.

Now Er'ril could hear the scuffle of disturbed shale and a more familiar noise—hissing. "Goblins." He pulled Elena away.

The wolf backed toward them, sloshing through the small stream.

Elena pointed to the beast. "He knows, too. They're probably the ones who injured him."

Er'ril ignored her words and pushed Elena ahead of him as he retraced the route back toward the fissure. "We need to get to your uncle and keep moving. Without a weapon, we have no chance of breaking out of here. We need to keep ahead of them."

Elena was staring back. "The wolf is following us."

Er'ril spotted the wolf, too. It kept a wary distance away, somewhat hidden, and clung to the shadows of the boulders. It kept pace with them, padding silently.

"He's protecting us," Elena said.

"No, he's just following the light."

"He has an old broken splint on his bad leg. Someone must have lost him."

The girl was right, but there was no telling if the wolf had gone feral on its owner. The splint looked old and weatherworn, as if the creature had been traveling some distance with it. Wild or not, it did not seem an immediate threat, and if the goblins should attack, its long teeth might prove useful, perhaps buying them time to flee. So Er'ril let it follow behind—as long as it kept its distance.

Once the old man and his lantern came into view, Elena dashed ahead to kneel beside her uncle. Er'ril joined the girl, noticing that Bol's chest still rose and fell. He placed a finger on the old man's neck. The pulse was weak.

He straightened and searched the darkness. After they had fled the stream, the hissing had faded. At least the goblins were again keeping their distance.

Elena raised her eyes to Er'ril. "Is he going to die?"

"I don't know. He's an old man."

"What can we do?"

"I can carry him."

She eyed his single arm with doubt in her eyes.

"He's light. I'll manage."

Elena nodded, resting a palm on her uncle's chest. The hand glowed a rich ruby in the double light. Er'ril recalled the strength of the power that had frozen his sword. He had barely dropped it in time to keep his hand from being consumed by the ice. She had powerful magick, but her control was weak. Still . . .

"There is one other way," he said. "But there are risks."

She brightened. "What?"

"Your magick."

Hope died in her eyes. She sagged her head. "No. I can't make it do what I want."

"You kept me from harming the wolf."

"Maybe, but I didn't mean to destroy your sword. The magick is wild."

"In my time, young mages were always fouling up. I had a brother, Shorkan. He came to his Chyric power the same age as you. Once when he was young, he burned down our kitchen as he tried to light our hearth with his magick."

"He got better, though, right?"

He nodded. "With practice and training, he became a great mage."

"But who can train me?"

Er'ril knelt beside her. "I was my brother's liege man."

"What's that?"

"His protector. Each mage was assigned a liege man to keep them from harming themselves with their early magick. I was beside Shorkan during his initial training, pulling him out of many scrapes. We liege men were not privy to the higher arts but were instructed in the lessons of control—how to manage the flow of power. We learned these lessons to assist those in our charge." Er'ril tried not to wince as he picked up her red hand. "I can perhaps help you."

"Really?"

"I will try. But what you must do to help your uncle, though it is a simple thing, requires a subtle touch of magick."

"Will this save him?"

"I don't know. What I'm going to teach you is not a true healing—that is beyond my knowledge. What I can show you is how to pass a small drop of your magick to your uncle. This will boost his spirit and maybe allow him to escape this fainting illness."

Elena stared at him with doubtful eyes. "What if something goes wrong?"

"Then he will die."

Her eyes twitched wide with fear. She stayed silent and hugged her arms around her chest. After several silent moments, she finally spoke. "But Uncle Bol could die if I don't try."

Er'ril nodded, impressed with the resiliency of the child. Her hand trembled as she unclasped her arms and studied the whorls of color on her ruby palm, but a determination and resolve shone forth from her eyes.

She stared directly at him, her jaw tense. For the first time, he saw in that small face the woman she would become. Bright green eyes, a wash of red hair, strong lips. She would grow to be a woman of fair beauty—if she lived that long. "Show me what I must do," she said.

He knelt and beckoned her down beside him. "It requires blood."

She withdrew from him slightly.

"Fear not; this is small magick. Just a drop." Er'ril pointed to the sheathed dagger Bol had given the child.

Elena reluctantly withdrew the wit'ch's dagger from her waist. Its silver glowed in the bird's light like a sliver of the moon.

"Pass me the dagger," Er'ril said.

The child did, more than willing to relinquish the weapon.

Er'ril took one of the old man's hands and laid it on his own knee. Then, using the knife, he poked a small hole in the tip of Bol's thumb. Thick blood welled like a black pearl from the wound. He offered the knife back to Elena. "You must do the same."

He saw her wince and clench her fist away. Her expression sparked a sudden memory of the small boy sacrificed to forge the Blood Diary. He, too, had worn the same shocked look when faced with his first cut. Er'ril stared at the small girl and prayed she wouldn't share the boy's fate.

"You must do this. Your uncle performed the initial cut in christening your dagger. This next must be by your own hand."

She nodded and fought to unclench her fist and reach for the knife. With a surprisingly steady hand, she raised the blade above her red thumb.

"Just a nick. Too much blood will be hard to control."

She took a deep breath, darted one quick look at him, then stabbed the tip to her thumb. He noted she was careful not to dig too deep. Once done, she sheathed the knife casually, as if she had just buttered a slice of bread. Her eyes remained fixed on the blood seeping from her injured thumb.

"Good girl. Now place your wound atop your uncle's." As she reached to do so, he stopped her hand. "When you make contact, you will be able to . . . able to feel your uncle."

"Feel?"

He scrunched up his brow. How could he describe something he had never experienced? "My brother once told me it was like suddenly becoming that person. You don't sense their thoughts, but simply know what it's like to wear their skin."

Her eyes narrowed—whether with worry or doubt, he couldn't tell. "Then what do I do?"

"As soon as you feel this contact, allow no more than a breath to pass, then you must immediately sever the connection by removing your thumb. The longer you stay connected the more magick will flow into your uncle. You must not let more than a heartbeat of magick seep into him."

"Won't a little more help Uncle Bol heal quicker?"

"No. This is raw magick, not a controlled spell. Only the chosen, like yourself, can be a vessel of so much power. No more than a drop can be risked."

"What if I give him more?"

"Do you remember my sword?"

ELENA PICTURED THE SWORD ENCASED IN AN ICE SO COLD THAT IT made iron brittle. She stared at her uncle spread out on the rock floor. She would not let that happen to him.

She remained kneeling, fixed and afraid to move, fearful of harming any more of her family. From the corner of her eye, she spotted the wolf buried in the inky shadow of a nearby boulder. His amber eyes glowed from his hiding place, reflecting back the moonlight from the falcon on her shoulder. The swordsman held her uncle's bloody thumb toward her, staring. So many eyes were on her.

She closed her own eyes and took a huge breath, willing herself calm. She opened her eyes and looked only at her uncle's face. He— the man who had regaled her with countless tales by firelight— needed her. And now she was living in one of his fanciful stories.

As she stared, she suddenly realized how much her uncle looked like her own mother, with the same cheekbones and set to the eyes. And his nose, broader than her own, was so like her brother Joach's. So much of her family was in the lines and planes of his face. As this thought dawned on her, her heart grasped some sliver of hope. If she saved him, perhaps in some measure she could keep a small piece of each of them alive.

She lifted her face to the swordsman.

He wiped away a tear from her cheek.

She pushed his hand away. "I'm ready."

Holding out her uncle's hand, he reminded her, "Only a single drop."

With a final deep breath that sounded more like a moan, she pressed her thumb on her uncle's wound.

At first nothing happened, and she almost cried with a combination of relief and hopelessness. Then she felt a part of her drawn through the wound into her uncle. She still saw out of her own eyes, saw how her touch seemed to tense her uncle's body, felt the falcon fly from her shoulder with a startled cry, and saw it perch on a spur of rock. Yet at the same time, she felt the tickle of beard on her neck and how her joints ached in protest to tensed muscles. She also felt the cold stone under her back as she lay sprawled on the rock.

Mostly, though, she sensed her heart straining to beat, struggling and quivering; but she was unable to tell if this was her own heart or the shadow of her uncle's. She was lost somewhere between the two. The line between Elena's awareness and her uncle's sensations blurred.

Fear and the swordsman's warning caused her to yank her

thumb away. As soon as contact was broken, she snapped fully back into her own body. Shaking her head loose of cobwebs, she sat back on her heels, suddenly feeling very small and, for some reason, starkly alone.

A groan drew her attention outward to where her uncle was struggling to sit up. He raised a shaky hand to his forehead. "What happened? Did I fall asleep?"

He seemed to be much better. His color had pinkened and his breathing sounded clear. But Elena knew better than to expect that he was healed. She had felt his heart. Uncle Bol was still sick.

She hugged her uncle but found no words. Er'ril, though, related all that had happened to her uncle.

Once the swordsman had finished explaining, Uncle Bol took Elena by the shoulders and held her at arm's length so he could study her. "You saved me with your magick. I feel about ten years younger, ready to take on a battalion of goblins."

His smile was infectious, and an embarrassed grin appeared on her face.

"See, I told you that Fila's strength was in you." He pulled her back to his chest in a fierce hug. As she lay within his embrace, she listened to the old man's heart. She remembered the straining beat, the weak flutter of his pulse. Each beat made her shiver, afraid it would be his last.

Of what use was this magick? How could it save a world when it couldn't cure an old man? She suddenly felt the weight of the last two days without sleep. She allowed her uncle to hold her up.

As she slumped in his embrace, a rumble of hissing arose around her again, sibilant and demanding—rock'goblins. Her uncle pulled her to her feet. When would she be able to rest?

"Hurry," Er'ril called. "The beasts grow impatient, and the path stales."

As Elena followed, her feet dragging as if they were full of sand, the moon'falcon flitted across the cavern to alight on her shoulder again. From the corner of her eye, she noticed the wolf trailing in the shadows on her heels. What made these creatures of the field trust her?

She glanced to her ruby hand, the wound on her thumb gone.

And what of the unknown spirit who had granted her this magick? Why did this spirit trust her, too? She was only a farmer's daughter; what strength of substance did these creatures all see in her?

Tears suddenly appeared in her eyes, but she wiped them away before anyone noticed them. She did not want this responsibility. She sniffed back her tears. Was there no one to whom she could pass this duty?

She stared at Er'ril's wide back as he marched ahead. Her liege man, he had called himself. In her heart, Elena knew the magick was her burden to bear, but maybe she did not have to bear it *alone*. This thought dried her tears. Maybe there was someone she could lean on, someone she could trust.

"My liege man," she whispered to herself, allowing her tongue to taste the words.

27

KRAL PASSED THE RADIANT GREEN STONE TO TOL'CHUK AND WIPED
the blood from his fingertips onto his trousers. The strange hissing
had faded to a whisper, then vanished. The resulting silence
weighed like the heavy air before a summer storm. He left the
og're to examine the elv'in's stone and crept farther down the
crumbling stone hall.

The greenish glow from the small gem lit the black hall, swamp-
ing the walls in an unnatural sheen. Ahead, strings of moss and
rootlets festooned the ceiling, while the floor was littered with ancient rock that ground to powder under his heel.

Kral slapped aside a root trying to lodge in his beard. Ducking
his head, he rounded a corner. Tol'chuk and the light followed.
The hall ended just ahead with a large chamber beyond. Kral motioned for the og're to stop and wait.

He unhitched the ax from his belt, and with its leather-wrapped
hickory handle firmly in hand, he slunk forward. The greenish
glow lighted the dried blood still on the ax's blade. It shone a purplish black, like a bruise on the iron. He ground his teeth at the reminder of his dishonor, the lie that had passed his tongue. He
tightened his grip on the weapon. Maybe fresh blood would help
wash away the foulness upon his blade and heart.

Kral reached the entrance to the large chamber and crouched with his back against one wall of the hall. He darted a quick glance into the room ahead. The room had once been a great hall of some kind. Vaulted ceilings spanned into the darkness above, and on the walls, faint frescoes whispered with echoes of a distant past. The hall must have been a meeting chamber: The walls were pocked with the openings to many other passages. The chamber was so large that even the sharp green light from the stone could not pierce to the far wall of the room.

Kral stayed crouched and searched for any sign of the elv'in. The strange man must be near, since his glowing stone had rolled back to them, but as much of the floor as Kral could see lay empty. Maybe he was deeper, beyond where the light reached. Kral stood and waved Tol'chuk closer to him so the stone could light the chamber more fully.

The claws of the og're scraped loudly as he lumbered up to Kral. They entered the hall together.

"I smell . . . something odd," Tol'chuk said. The og're had his nose raised and splayed wide.

Kral stopped and eyed the room ahead. With the better lighting, a splash of wet blackness could be seen staining the gray stone. He pointed. "Blood."

The two stepped forward together, but the og're's eyes kept wary watch on the walls around them, rather than on the floor. Kral allowed him to keep guard and knelt to confirm that what lay on the floor was indeed blood. He dipped a finger to the stain and raised it to his nose. It smelled of musky iron. A smeared trail disappeared into the hanging blackness at the deep end of the chamber.

"The blood is still warm." Kral straightened up. "Meric must not be far."

The og're seemed to be ignoring him. His grinding voice just warned, "The smell . . . it grows stronger."

Kral sniffed. He smelled nothing but dust and mold. Impatient, he nodded to the trail of blood.

They followed the path into the darkness. Within five steps, Kral realized why the light from the stone had failed to penetrate to the far wall of the chamber. There was no far wall. Beyond the floor ahead lay only open space, as if some monstrous god had cleaved away the back half of the chamber, leaving a deep gorge ahead.

Kral walked to the lip of the chasm. The blood trail led over this edge and into the tumble of rocks below. He glanced at the smeared path again. Had Meric dragged himself here, seeking safety below, or had his bloody carcass been hauled and dumped? And what had attacked him?

Tol'chuk hissed. "They come. The smell!"

A strange odor suddenly hit Kral's nose like a blow. The odor of festering wounds enveloped him. Kral raised his ax. "What is it?"

"Not it, them!" The og're raised a claw and swept across the room.

From the passages all around them, pairs of red eyes—like hundreds of angry red stars—reflected the light back toward them.

A hissing arose around them.

Kral backed a step, his boot's heel slipping over the lip of the cracked floor.

Suddenly the hissing blew toward them with a fury, and the pack of beasts raged from the tunnels.

ROCKINGHAM RUBBED HIS SORE WRISTS AND CRACKED HIS NECK TO loosen his bones. A mixture of anger and relief fought in his breast. "I thought you had left me to the crows," he said sourly.

Nee'lahn kept in one hand the knife with which she had sliced his bonds, obviously still wary of him. "I would not have done that. Besides, we need the horses." She gathered the reins of Mist and of Er'ril's stallion. Kral's huge war horse glowered at her as she approached.

Rockingham took a moment, still massaging the muscles of one arm, to appraise Nee'lahn's companion. The man stood as tall as Rockingham, and as thin. His lanky brown hair hung loose, not tied back in any typical fashion of this region. An outlander, Rockingham guessed. The angles of the stranger's face were sharp and his narrowed eyes even sharper. He wore a hunter's coat of sewn leather over gray leggings and jerkin. Strange fashion for these parts.

"Who is your friend?" Rockingham finally asked Nee'lahn.

Nee'lahn finished checking the security of the packs on the horses. She wiped a hand over her forehead, sweeping back stray hairs. "Kral is helping him find his lost companion."

The stranger stood silent, as if trying to fade into the wet wood around them. Rockingham faced him. "What's your name, friend?"

"Mogweed." His voice was edgy, nervous.

"You're not from these parts, are you?"

He shook his head.

"Where do you hail from?"

He stayed silent.

Rockingham recognized when someone was trying to work up a fabricated story. This man had secrets. He liked that. A person with something to hide could be coerced—if only Rockingham could discover his secret.

"I . . . I come from the southlands," Mogweed finally said.

Rockingham nodded but did not believe a word. Even Nee'-lahn must have sensed the lie on the stranger's tongue, because she glanced up with a sour expression on her face.

What was this man doing here in these drenched woods? What did this stranger want? The desire in a man's heart was the price of his soul. If he could just discover that . . .

As Rockingham studied Mogweed, the stranger suddenly tensed and cringed down. A heartbeat later, the horses began to nicker in agitation. The war charger stamped an iron-shod hoof.

Then both he and Nee'lahn heard it at the same time. The beating of heavy wings approached from the deeper valley. It came from the direction of the cottage. Neither had to speak the name of what flew this way.

"They must not have found the girl," Rockingham said.

"Hurry!" Nee'lahn urged. "The cavern's not far from here. It's too small for the skal'tum. We'll be safe there. Kral is already inside."

Mogweed must have known of the shelter she mentioned. He gripped at Nee'lahn's sleeve. "No, it's not safe. My brother—"

"Trust us," Rockingham said and caught the reins to the gray mare that Nee'lahn tossed to him. "Nothing in those caves can be as bad as what hunts us now."

Mogweed hesitated. His eyes searched the wood as if seeking a way to bolt. Like a frightened deer, Rockingham thought.

Nee'lahn spoke to the man, slipping her sleeve loose from his grip. "This is of no concern to you, Mogweed. They seek us. If you flee, I doubt they would follow."

As Nee'lahn swung atop the stallion, Mogweed's eyes continued to sweep the dark forest. Fear shone in those strange amber eyes.

Nee'lahn spoke again. "I know who you are, Mogweed. You're from the Western Reaches, like me. But you're not a man. Your slitted eyes speak what your tongue does not. You are si'lura."

Rockingham choked on her words. "Shape-shifter!" He backed from the man. So this was the stranger's secret. He scurried atop his own mount, wishing to escape a creature of such foul legend.

Nee'lahn spoke again. "Si'lura, it is easy for you to hide here. Just shift into a woodland beast and disappear. This fight is not yours."

"No," the man said, his eyes wild. "You do not know me. I cannot change! I am trapped in this form."

His words seemed to surprise Nee'lahn. She paused in her saddle, her eyebrows arched. The noise of the beating wings grew louder. She reached a hand toward the shape-shifter. "Then come with us or flee; we cannot wait."

Mogweed took a step away, then stopped. Just as Nee'lahn began to pull her arm back, he darted forward and gripped her hand. She yanked him up behind her seat.

Nee'lahn kicked her horse to a gallop and led the way. For a moment, Rockingham thought of fleeing in the opposite direction to gain his freedom. He listened to the beat of wings on cold air and shuddered. He spurred his own horse to follow. To land in the hands of the Dark Lord's lieutenants after failing to retrieve the girl was pure folly.

He thundered after Nee'lahn. He needed the cursed child.

Rockingham stared at the back of the man seated behind Nee'lahn. His initial shock of the si'lura had waned. What was there to fear from a shape-shifter who couldn't shift? He was just a man then—a man with a secret and a need, a man who could be manipulated. Rockingham recognized a key when it landed in his lap. Perhaps with such an ally he might yet unlock his bonds and escape both his present captors *and* the wrath of the Dark Lord.

He kicked his horse to narrow the distance between the racing mounts.

The clapping of wings echoed from the valley walls in pursuit.

If only he had enough time . . .

Tol'chuk knew these beasts. The og're tribes were often plagued by runs of rock'goblins through their lower caverns and tunnels. Rarely were they more than mere nuisances: stealing bright objects, breaking stoneware, fouling corridors with both their stench and spoor. Never had he heard of them brandishing weapons.

As these goblins swarmed up toward them, though, flowing from the surrounding tunnels like a flash flood down a dry gully, each of the small creatures bore a wicked blade that glinted green in the stone's light. Each goblin alone posed no threat—not to an og're, or even to the large mountain man beside him. But these were not lone beasts.

Tol'chuk remembered a spreehawk he had seen as a child. It

had made the mistake of chasing a gingermouse to its warren home. Alone in a field, the mouse would have made a nice meal; but when its brethren had boiled from the many neighboring burrows, the hawk had become the prey, set upon by the tiny teeth of hundreds of mice. All that was left of the mighty hawk were cleaned bones and a hooked beak; even the eyes had been plucked empty. This memory flashed across his mind's eye as the swarm burst from the tunnels.

Now he was that hawk.

Kral growled something low in his throat, unintelligible. He had his ax hefted for battle.

Useless, Tol'chuk reasoned. The og're did the only thing he could. He scooped the large man beside him in one of his massive arms and hauled him up in a firm embrace. Shock at his action stunned the mountain man for a blink, then the man began to thrash, believing himself attacked. With Kral in his arms, Tol'chuk leaped into the black gorge.

To the mountain man's credit, Kral did not scream, only froze in the og're's embrace as they plummeted. A jutting rock crashed into Tol'chuk's shoulder, tumbling him to the side. Tol'chuk fought for balance and barely kept his feet under him as he smashed onto a ledge of stone. The force of their combined weight crushed the og're to the rock. Air exploded from his chest as he struck the floor, though he was careful to protect the human man, cushioning Kral from the impact with his own body.

Kral rolled off him—to the great relief of Tol'chuk's bruised lungs. The mountain man pushed to his knees and glowered at the og're, his eyes red with rage. "What do you think you do, og're?"

"There be no hope above. There lay only death."

For a moment, a flash of regret crossed Kral's features, as if he had welcomed the fight—or maybe just the outcome. "I make my own decisions," he finally said, his voice straining high. "Don't do something like that again."

"I be . . . sorry." Tol'chuk struggled to sit up. The effort must have shown on his face.

"You're injured."

"Not bad. Og'res be thick boned."

Kral's voice now had a trace of concern. "It was a foolish act, leaping blindly."

"I saw . . ." His mouth struggled with the common tongue. "I spotted this ledge from above, man of the mountains."

Kral looked doubtfully at him.

"Og're eyes pierce the dark better than humans'." By now, Tol'chuk had managed to get his feet under him. He pushed upright but swayed.

Kral placed a hand on the og're's shoulder to steady him. His other hand still clutched his ax. He had not dropped it, and Tol'chuk doubted even death would ever pry the weapon from his fingers. Ax and man seemed one.

The mountain man stayed quiet until Tol'chuk took a few deep breaths and his feet steadied. "I owe you an apology," Kral finally said in a calmer tone. "And I owe you my life. I misjudged you sorely."

Tol'chuk fingered a bruised rib. "Your people always have."

"I won't repeat that mistake."

Tol'chuk clapped him on the shoulder. "Then I will try to . . . try to warn you before I push you off a cliff again."

A crack of a smile broke across Kral's features. "You are a strange og're."

"More than you know." He released the man's shoulder. "But where now? I jumped . . . but did not think where to jump next."

Kral retrieved the glowing stone that had slipped from the og're's fingers on impact. Luckily, Tol'chuk thought, it had not rolled from the ledge. The mountain man held up the stone. "Whatever we decide, we had better hurry. The elv'in's light fades."

Tol'chuk noted that the stone, which before had stung his og're eyes to look at directly, now caused no discomfort. "The goblins will not let us rest, either," he added. Stepping to the edge, Tol'chuk searched the terrain below.

"Do you see a way down?" Kral asked at his shoulder.

"I see the chasm's floor. It be too far to jump."

Kral had backed to the wall and ran a hand along the stone. "The cliff is rough. There are many handholds and protruding rock. We could try climbing down."

Tol'chuk turned to Kral. "I see a fall of boulders below us. If we could scale to there, we could climb to the chasm's floor."

Kral nodded and seemed to be weighing the various risks, his eyes far away. Suddenly he pointed his ax to the far end of the chasm. "Are my eyes casting phantoms in this gloom, or is that a light yonder?"

Tol'chuk swung around and stared where the mountain man pointed. Yes, a glow—two lights!—bloomed in the distance. He watched the lights bob. The twin flames approached the same wall upon which their ledge rested, but much farther down the chasm floor.

"Goblins?" Kral asked.

"No, goblins do not like light. It weakens their blood." Tol'chuk remembered how the og're tribe kept powder pots burning to keep the rock'goblins from sacred areas of their caves.

"Then who?"

"I know not."

"You said your og're eyes were keen in dark places. Can you make out any details?"

"The distance be great," he said and strained his eyes toward the light. He caught occasional glimpses of shadows moving in the glow but failed to make out any details. "No, nothing. It be too—" The og're tensed.

"What?" Kral's voice rose with concern.

The og're raised a claw. Odd images formed in his head, yet the touch was familiar: Fardale. The wolf-brother was below, attempting to tell him something: *A wounded cub finds protection. A strange scent sparks a trail.* A few other images half formed in his head but were too fleeting to register fully.

Only one other image coalesced: *Blood flows with sparks of lightning.*

Tol'chuk did not understand the meaning of this last image, but the wiry hairs of his back ridge bristled.

"What do you see?" Kral asked impatiently.

"Not see, feel. Something strange be happening down there."

"How do you know this?"

"A friend . . . a brother . . . be down there. Not alone."

"What does he tell you?"

Tol'chuk shook his head. "He be too far away to be clear."

As they watched, the twin lights vanished into a distant tunnel below.

"We must follow," Tol'chuk said, his voice suddenly strained.

"Why?"

"I . . . I do not know," Tol'chuk lied.

Kral's brows lowered suspiciously.

A twinge of guilt stabbed Tol'chuk, but he did not offer further words. How could he describe the sudden pull on his heart? Tol'chuk knew that if he uncovered the heartstone hidden in his pouch it would be shining bright enough to eclipse the feeble glow of the elv'in stone.

The Heart of his people was calling him forward.

He must follow.

Mogweed fought to keep his seat atop the galloping horse. How strange to ride the back of another beast. He had never seen such a thing. Once, from the safety of their forest home, he and Fardale had spied on the herds of wild steppe horses grazing on the plains north of the Western Reaches. Doe-eyed mares guarded by fiery-eyed stallions had spread in dappled colors across the yellow steppes. He could not imagine those horses mounted and controlled by leather and iron.

How strange the peoples of these lands were. Did they control all the beasts of the field? He remembered how the tall, thin man claimed to control the glowing falcon and how the hunters had leashed the snarling sniffers to their will. What drove other races to control living things? Among the si'lura, where other beasts' shapes were theirs to experience, the thought of capturing and enslaving creatures of the wild seemed foreign.

But if he wore this human form much longer and the will of man consumed his own identity, he might begin to understand. Then he, too, like the horse beneath him, would forget what it was like to run free. As he clung to the waist of the nyphai woman, he prayed he never would.

The horse suddenly jolted under him. He clutched tighter to Nee'lahn, not trusting his legs to hold him atop the stallion. Mud and decaying leaf had betrayed the horse's footing.

"This steed will not drop you," Nee'lahn said, wiggling to loosen his grip on her.

He relaxed his hold a bit, but maintained a wary watch. How could he trust an enslaved beast? He kept his eyes and ears alert.

Years of accumulated humus muffled the thunder of the horses' hooves as they raced up another ridge. The beat of wings still echoed from the hills around them. He could tell—even with his dull human ears—that the sound swelled rapidly.

The nyphai woman must have realized this, too. "We will make it," she said, though it sounded more as if she was trying to reassure herself.

The other horse pounded abreast of them, the mare's legs less burdened than the double-weighted stallion's. It lurched to the top of the ridge first. Rockingham pulled his steed to a stop and pointed. "There is a clearing ahead. Is that the one?" he yelled into the wind. Rain had begun to lance again from swollen clouds. "I see no cave."

"It is there, hidden," Nee'lahn answered as the stallion clambered to the ridgeline and swept past the stopped rider. "Hurry!"

The pair of horses more stumbled than galloped down the steep hillside. Sodden branches kept trying to bat Mogweed from his perch. He found he could only keep from screaming by squeezing his eyes closed. Thunder again pounded from above, only barely drowning the hammering of his own heart. In brief gaps in the thunder, he realized a keening whine flowed from his own lips.

Just before panic threw him from the horse's back, the crashing ride came to a sudden stop. Mogweed dared to open his eyes. Before them lay the small clearing. Afraid the horse would again begin its wild race, he tumbled off the mount and took several steps away.

Nee'lahn pointed to the cavern opening, guarded by the roots of the sentinel oak. "There's the cave," she said to Rockingham as he pulled his mare to a stop beside her.

"Hush!" he answered her, a hand raised in warning.

Mogweed's quivering legs tensed to run.

"What?" Nee'lahn whispered. Her eyes searched the clearing.

"Listen." Rockingham jumped from his horse and motioned her to do the same.

Mogweed forced his human ears to strain. He heard nothing but the spat of rain on leaves. Even the thunder had died away. Mogweed sensed, though, from the pressure in the air, that it was but a lull before the true storm that was about to break.

"I hear nothing," Nee'lahn said, tethering their mounts. She looked confused, then her eyes flew wide. "The wings! I can't hear them. Run!"

Rockingham was already running.

But it was too late. As they all darted toward the cavern opening, two huge figures dove on widespread wings to crash to the dirt before them. Claws sank deep in the mud, leaving raked furrows as they came to a stop.

Mogweed screamed at the sight of them. He sank to his knees in fright. Twin sets of red eyes studied him. Wings of black bone folded behind shoulders, and a foul stench of rotted carrion flowed from them. A sick malevolence could be tasted in the air. Never in his worst nightmares had he imagined beasts so foul.

"Little mice, where do you ssscurry to?" one of them hissed as the other laughed sibilantly. "Do you think you can escape the hungry cat?"

By now the horses were whinnying in terror behind them. The

mare thrashed against its lead, but both rope and tree held firm. The stallion, though, snapped its lead and dashed across the clearing, its eyes rolled white in panic.

Quicker than an eye could follow, one of the two beasts pounced on the fleeing horse and sank its claws into its back. Fangs and claws ripped the stallion's belly open, spilling red entrails across the cold mud. The monster then released the horse, allowing the stallion, not yet dead, to stumble away, dragging its bowels behind it. The attacker laughed at the sight, bloody foam on its lips. Before the horse took more than a few wobbly strides, its neck stretched taut with pain, the creature again lunged and swallowed the horse within its stretched wings. Thankfully, the wings blocked the sight as the monster savaged the horse. But the pitch of the horse's scream passed through the wings to them all. Mogweed covered his ears. At that moment, he wished for his own death, just so he would never have to hear such a noise again.

Then, just as the scream reached its highest peak, it abruptly cut off, and the beast stepped away from its kill. What lay steaming on the frigid ground now bore no resemblance to a horse: just a mound of raw meat, broken bone, and ripped bowels.

Mogweed pressed his face to the ground, his gorge rising in his throat. Nausea overcame his horror. He emptied his belly on the ground.

As his stomach stopped convulsing, Mogweed felt the creatures' red eyes on his back.

"Sssee, at least one of you knowsss how to bow before your masters," one of them laughed.

The other spoke as Mogweed raised his face. It was the one who had attacked the horse. Blood stained its face black, while its fangs glowed white upon its lips. "Now where isss the child we sssseek?" It pointed to the cooling mass of shredded horse. "Or would sssomeone like to be my next ride?"

Nee'lahn answered. But her words did not comfort Mogweed. "We will tell you nothing, dogs of the Dark Lord."

An angry hiss spat toward her from the nearest beast.

Rockingham, though, spoke quickly behind her. "You know me, O Lords of the Black Blood."

Nee'lahn swung to the man, her eyes afire.

He ignored her. "I will tell you where the girl hides."

28

Er'ril tried not to push the old man to a faster pace. If Bol collapsed again, more time would be lost than a slower pace wasted. So he kept the march to a sedate walk, even as his heart pleaded for speed.

Yet, as Er'ril watched the gray-bearded elder, he realized his concerns for the man's frailty might be a false worry. After the girl's ministrations, Bol seemed remarkably revitalized. His heels no longer dragged through the shale, and his breathing and humor had greatly improved. Er'ril might even have braved a quicker gait had Elena not kept darting sharp looks toward her uncle. In her eyes Er'ril saw wary concern, mistrust in her uncle's sudden vitality. It was this suspicious look, not his own appraisal, that slowed Er'ril's march toward the far wall of the chasm.

Even Bol protested the crawling pace. "The cave crabs are making better time than we are. Listen to that hissing. The rock'goblins grow impatient."

"No, Uncle. They keep their distance. And besides, the wolf guards our backs."

Er'ril noted Elena placed much confidence in this dog of the wood. She had even insisted they wait when the wolf seemed to smell something in the dank cavern breeze and paused in his lurking pursuit, nose raised. He had stood gazing with those strange amber eyes into the darkness, then continued to follow. Only then did Elena allow them to press forward.

"A wolf at our backs!" her uncle huffed. "That does not offer much comfort."

"We are not going any faster," Elena said in a tone that did not brook argument. The moon'falcon on her shoulder flapped its wings in a single snap, punctuating her statement as if irate that anyone should question the human it had chosen.

Even though he and Bol wished for a quicker march, Er'ril kept the pace steady. He suddenly realized he trusted Elena's instinct in this matter more than her uncle's or his own, and this thought stumbled his feet. He trusted a *wit'ch*.

Er'ril thought back to hundreds of other young mages fresh to their apprenticeships. Many had grown haughty and willful after the first taste of their magick, full of their new power. Time had eventually tempered most of those proud souls as they realized there were limits, dangers, and responsibilities that went along with donning the white robes.

Er'ril watched Elena. She kept one hand on her uncle's sleeve, restraining his pace, as her eyes swept across the cavern, noting where the wolf padded in shadows, studying the trail ahead. Her keen eyes settled on his own as he studied her. She did not look away. She had learned much of magick in a stunningly short time, learned its capability for destruction and salvation, its wildness and its control. But most of all she had already had a taste of its responsibility.

He judged the stubborn and weary set to her eyes. There lay a willfulness not born of pride and conceit, but of lessons taught in fire. In just two days she had learned more of what it meant to be a mage than had many an apprentice after years of schooling. Maybe not in the knowledge of spells and cords of magicks, but in something more essential—the consequences of power.

Yes, wit'ch or not, he did trust her.

He broke from her stare to continue toward the fissure in the far wall. Ahead lay mysteries and other dangers, and without his sword, he would face them with an empty hand. Yet, oddly, he found a small comfort in the wit'ch behind him.

He led the way across the uneven track, warning the others of patches of slippery mud or treacherously loose rock. The hissing of the rock'goblins harried their trail, but not one approached close enough to their island of light to reveal itself. Only shadows and the creep of the dark wolf moved about them.

"Almost there," Bol commented as they neared the fissure.

Did the old man's voice have an edge of fatigue? Er'ril eyed him. He seemed to be breathing fine, and his color still remained ruddy.

"And to think I always liked exploring these old ruins." He made a rude noise with his lips. "After this night, I am well rid of these dank and dripping halls."

"We'll be out of here soon," Elena said aloud, then added a softer, "I hope."

Er'ril reached the entrance to the dark fissure. "Pass your lamp up here, Bol." Unencumbered by his sword, he could light the way forward; he sensed that more danger lay ahead than behind.

Bol handed the lantern to him, and Er'ril checked its oil with a frown. "Whatever game these goblins play, they had better be quick," he said. The lamp was almost dry. Er'ril twisted the flame lower to slow the consumption of fuel. With the addition of the falcon's moon glow, the lamplight could be spared.

He raised the lantern to the yawning gap in the chasm wall.

Before entering, he studied the way forward. From across the chasm, he had thought the fissure to be a natural crack in the rock face. But with his light now illuminating the interior, he discovered his mistake. Arches stood between walls of rough-hewn rock, marking the way forward. Neither nature nor the gods had created this passage, and from the handiwork, this was not the work of humans either. The pocked and scraped surface of the raw rock bore the distinct scratch marks of ancient claws, and on the first of the arches, crude images of goblins tangled together.

Er'ril fingered one of the gouged tracks on the wall. As his finger touched the wall, the hissing from the trailing goblins suddenly stopped. By now their noise had become so constant that when it ceased, the silence was like a clap of thunder on the ears.

"I suspect we are nearing the end of their game," Bol whispered, though his voice still rang loud in the now quiet chasm. "I think we need not worry about the lantern's oil."

"Come," Er'ril said and led the way into the tunnel. "I tire of this chase."

After only a handful of steps into the tunnel, they passed under the first arch. On closer inspection, Er'ril noticed the tangle of goblins carved on the arch were in various acts of sexual union. The entire span was one continuous orgy of profane intimacies in every possible contortion, including some that Er'ril had never imagined or wished to imagine.

Er'ril noticed the girl's eyes grow wide as she realized the content of the artwork. She blushed and looked away.

The only comment from Bol as he leaned closer to inspect a pair of male goblins sharing one of their females was a simple, "Interesting, very interesting."

With both men's eyes on the arch, Elena was the first to notice a change in the tunnel. "There's light coming from up ahead," she said.

Er'ril turned and finally noticed a weak shimmer flowing around a curve in the tunnel ahead. He shaded his own lamp to better judge the light. In the deeper darkness, the meager glow took on a sharper brightness. Though the light was diffuse, its color and quality seemed to awaken a memory in Er'ril. Where had he seen such a silvery, pure glow?

"I thought the goblins shunned light," Er'ril said.

"Yes, bright light," Bol answered. "Some say their eyes are attuned to a different type of illumination, allowing them to move through the dark paths of the mountains' hearts. Some say it's the emanations of elemental rock magick that attract and light their ways. For this reason they plague many crystal mines and infest many sacred cavern systems. Rock magick draws them as a lodestone draws iron.

"My iron ward," Er'ril said, suddenly realizing. "It is carved from elemental magick. I hid it very well. But if they can sniff magick—"

"Not sniff, *see*. Some say—"

Er'ril shook his head. " 'Some say, some say'—enough of this prattle! The source of that light should be bright enough to blind even a desert warrior of the southlands. The answer to what the goblins are doing with such a light lies ahead." Er'ril moved down the tunnel. "And elemental magick or not, I mean to get my ward back."

He followed the silvery trail. As the light grew around him, its sheen kept nagging at him. Where had he seen such a light? Its purity seemed to suck the drab color from the surrounding walls, revealing the spirit of the rock underneath. The glow even drew a certain beauty from the rudely carved arches. Where—?

A sudden memory intruded and stopped his feet. He now remembered where he had seen a similar sight! A shiver passed through him. He shook his head. It was impossible. Not here. Maybe it was just a trick on his eyes after the hours spent in this black hole with only the yellow flame of the lamp and the cold blue light of the falcon to guide them. The purity of this light could not be what he suspected.

He found his legs hurrying.

"No," Elena said from farther back in the tunnel. Concern for her uncle rang in her voice. "We do not race. What lies ahead can wait."

No, Er'ril thought, it cannot. Yet he heeded her and slowed his pace. He would trust this wit'ch.

"WHAT'S GOT YOU SO RILED?" BOL ASKED AS THEY CAUGHT UP WITH Er'ril.

Elena watched her uncle for any sign of deterioration. She did not trust her magick's balm, and she prayed he would last long enough to reach a true healer. Like the lamp's dwindling oil, she knew her magick would eventually leak away and leave her uncle hollow again, susceptible to his weakened heart. But right now he still seemed hale and strong.

Uncle Bol reached a hand to the swordsman. "Slow down, Er'ril. The girl's tired. She can't keep up this pace."

A whisper of a smile slipped to Elena's lips. Here she was so worried about him that she had never thought he might be harboring the same fears for her. "I'm fine, Uncle. But we should still proceed with caution."

"Elena is right," Er'ril said. "Something odd lies ahead. Whether it means us harm or not, I'm not sure. But we should conserve our wind and strength for the worst." Er'ril continued down the tunnel toward the light, his lantern raised.

Uncle Bol waved Elena forward, and since the tunnel was wide enough, he walked beside her. "I saw that look on your face," he called to Er'ril's back. "You have a suspicion of what lies ahead."

"There you are wrong, old man."

"Old? You're five or six times my age. Now out with it. What do you suspect? What is bothering you?"

"Just bad memories."

"Of what?"

"Don't you find the . . . the quality of the light strange?"

Her uncle narrowed his eyes to stare ahead.

"I think it's pretty," Elena answered.

Er'ril shook his head in such a way that Elena felt foolish for her words. But it was beautiful! The light seemed to wash everything clean, and as they continued deeper into its glow, the very air seemed less heavy and damp, as if they were walking into a spring morning after a long winter's night.

"It's not natural," her uncle said. "It isn't elemental magick, either: It's much too strong. Maybe some type of conjured light? Though I have never heard of sorcery performed by goblins, little is known about the species." He pointed to the grotesqueries carved into an arch they passed. "For instance, I would never have guessed at their . . . their imaginative appetites."

"It is magick," Er'ril declared. "I can practically smell its stink."

"Surely not. As I said, elemental magick is a subtle working. Nothing elemental could generate such a power."

"It's not elemental," Er'ril said. He spoke between clenched teeth. "It's Chyric!"

Uncle Bol tripped to a stop. "Nonsense! Down here? Once Chi abandoned our land, no such pool of power survived in these parts. Maybe at A'loa Glen, but not here."

Er'ril turned to Elena's uncle, his face tight. "I have seen a light of this character once before."

Elena spoke up. "Where?"

The swordsman remained quiet. His eyes did not even brush toward her.

"Where?" her uncle echoed.

After a further pause, he answered, his voice low. "When the Book was forged."

"What? Are you sure?"

"I would not forget." His eyes took on a faraway look as he remembered another time and place. "It was my assignment during its cursed binding. Look for the sign, Shorkan told me: a flash of blinding white light. Then I must close the Book and end the spell." His eyes focused back on Uncle Bol.

"The light . . . you can't mean . . . ?"

"I can never forget it. Not even after five hundred winters. It burned through my eyes to sear my mind. The light is the same, rich with Chyric energy."

Her uncle scratched at his beard and murmured, "Odd. Perhaps there is another explanation."

"The cursed goblins can keep their explanations and secrets. I just want my ward."

"Maybe that's it," Elena said. "Maybe your ward-thing plays some role."

Her uncle's eyes sparkled with her words. "The girl's right! It's so obvious."

Er'ril's face just frowned deeper. "It is of no matter."

"No, Er'ril, it is. Why did the goblin show you the ward and run? Why have the goblins not attacked us and only driven us forward? That is unlike them. What do they want?"

Er'ril's eyes glanced at Elena, then quickly away.

Uncle Bol must have caught his look. "That's what I thought. It had something to do with Elena."

She cringed. She had suspected as much herself, but to hear it voiced aloud stung. Please, she prayed, don't lay this at my feet. She had so much to be blamed for already—her parents, her home, Aunt Fila, Joach.

Uncle Bol continued. "But I was wrong."

Er'ril's brows rose with a doubt Elena felt, too. "Then what do the goblins want?" he asked.

"It's so obvious!" He reached a hand and tousled Elena's hair. "Yet if she hadn't added her insight, I would've never seen it."

"What?" This was echoed by both Elena and Er'ril.

"Not *what, who*?"

Er'ril's nostrils flared in exasperation. Elena just waited. As Elena had warned the swordsman at the supper table—only last night, though it now seemed like ages ago—Uncle Bol would only let his stories flow at his own pace.

"Out with it, old man!" Er'ril finally blurted. "Who do they want?"

Her uncle rolled his eyes as if it was so simple. "Why, you, of course."

Elena kept one ear cocked to the two men's argument. She hoped in her heart that Uncle Bol was correct. If the rock'goblins wanted them, let it not be because of her.

"You are daft, old man!" Er'ril said. "Me? They want me? I've never even encountered rock'goblins before—not once during the hundreds of winters I have wandered the land. What would they want of me?"

Bol ran a comb of fingers through his beard and shrugged. "The answer lies ahead."

Elena, relieved that the burden of responsibility for their

plight was taken from her shoulders, had let her gaze wander back behind them. She spotted a darker shadow close to one wall; the wolf still followed. Poor creature, he was probably just as scared and lost as they were and was trusting them to find a way out of this maze of tunnels. She prayed he hadn't misplaced his trust.

"Then let's get going," Er'ril said. "If they only want me, maybe they'll grant you both free passage out of here."

"No, we leave here together," her uncle said.

"The wolf, too," Elena added, but except for a distracted pat on the head from her uncle, they ignored her words.

She walked beside Uncle Bol as they set off once again down the tunnel. Er'ril led the way, still carrying the lantern even though he extinguished the lamp's flame to conserve its fuel since the silvery light had now grown sufficient to light their way. The only other illumination came from the moon'falcon drowsing on her shoulder.

As they continued down the tunnel, she kept an eye on the wolf trailing behind them. The beast would wait until they had worked a fair distance along the tunnel, then dart forward to his next hiding place, trying to disappear into shadows. But the light grew around them. As shadows grew fewer and fewer, the wolf could no longer completely vanish into the blackness.

Now that Elena could see more of their lingering companion, she studied him more closely, almost walking backward. She was surprised to see that his coat was not solid black as she had first supposed, but actually streaked with lines of browns and golds. His fur glowed lustrous in the light, and his eyes were chunks of shining amber. She also noticed that his limp seemed to be worsening. His head bobbed in pain as he placed weight on his injured forelimb. Poor thing!

As she watched, she felt the wolf's eyes on her and knew he studied her, too. For a moment, those yellow and gold eyes met hers across the tunnel. As eye met eye, she suddenly felt light-headed, and her right hand grew warm and tingled. She suddenly tasted the wild wood of his home and sensed his heart beating to run free under the forest's dappled shadows. Her eyes grew wide with these sensations, and the tunnel walls faded around her. An image formed: *A baby bird falls from a nest and tumbles toward the ground, but just before crashing, its tiny wings spread and it flies. As it sweeps up, the small bird grows into a huge eagle, its wings blocking the sun, swallowing the world.*

Just as quickly as the image had appeared, it broke apart. The tunnel reappeared and wrapped around her again. All she now saw were those amber eyes of the wolf glowing toward her. Elena's foot stumbled on a loose rock.

Uncle Bol caught her before she fell. "Careful, honey," he mumbled.

She barely heard his words, her eyes still on the wolf. What had just occurred? She rubbed her eyes. The wolf still stared at her from where he crouched, his eyes narrowed. Somehow she knew the wolf was aware of what had just happened to her—the sensations, the image of the baby bird. Elena watched the wolf's lids slip lower, shadowing those strange amber eyes.

No! It was more than that, Elena suddenly knew. The wolf did not just *know* of these visions, he had *sent* them to her!

But how? Why? What did it mean?

She grabbed at her uncle's sleeve, pulling him to a stop. "The wolf . . . the wolf . . . he . . ."

"Shh, Elena. We're almost to the end of the tunnel."

Elena saw Er'ril glance toward the wolf at her words. The swordsman's face tightened with menace, as if suspecting the wolf might be attacking. As he saw that the beast still crouched well away from them, his eyes swept to her in question. But Elena found her tongue twisted by Er'ril's stern face. How could she put into words what had just happened? With her silence, the swordsman returned his gaze forward.

Uncle Bol's eyes had never budged from where they stared at the blinding light shining through the arch of stone marking the exit to their tunnel. "It's so beautiful," he said softly.

Elena finally noticed how bright the light had grown around them.

Uncle Bol nodded Er'ril forward. "Let's see what lies ahead."

The swordsman again led the way, but more slowly, hesitantly, as if fearful of what he might discover. Elena noticed as she tried to follow that her feet were just as reluctant to move. It wasn't fear: Somehow the light itself, now so very bright, seemed like a strong wind in the tunnel. She found she had to push against it to continue farther down the hall toward the arch.

"Most interesting," Bol said behind her. Her uncle leaned forward to press on, like a man in a gale.

Er'ril had a hand held before his eyes, pressing outward, as he approached the arch.

Elena glanced behind her to see if the wolf still followed. She caught him just darting ahead into this bright section of the tunnel. Now there were no shadows to hide in at all. Still, he kept his nose close to the ground, ears laid back flat to his head. As he pushed into the light after them, she saw him suddenly stop.

His body twitched. He took another hesitant step forward. As he moved, the light bathed over him, and his flesh seemed to ripple. He took another step, obviously in pain, his neck tight and bunched. Elena gasped. The wolf's form now flowed like thick syrup. The light seemed to be blowing the shape of the wolf away from the arch. What was revealed underneath was not wolf, but something that flowed in streams and channels. Melted wax, Elena thought.

The only part of its body that remained untouched were its eyes. The same amber eyes stared at her from a mass of rippling, flowing flesh.

Stunned, she watched it try to slide farther toward them. But movement seemed to take too much effort, and somehow Elena knew it was excruciating. Lines of pain seemed to flow through its rippling tissue. It backed away a step, then another. As it retreated from the light, the wolf form grew back into place—ears, limbs, tail, fur—until Elena could not tell that anything had happened.

The wolf stared after her as she followed her uncle deeper into the light, toward the arch. But she knew it was *not* a wolf. She watched it back another step away. Its eyes never left her face, and a deep sadness enveloped her. But whether this came from the wolf or from her own feeling, she could not tell.

"Sweet Mother!" Er'ril said behind her. Elena twisted to see if the swordsman had also witnessed what had happened to the wolf-creature. But the swordsman had his back to her. He had reached the exit to the tunnel, standing with one hand on the last arch of stone. He stared beyond the opening at something in the next chamber.

She watched him sink to his knees. "No, Sweet Mother, it can't be! Anything but this!" he cried. "Not here! Not after so long!"

29

"WHERE ISS THE CHILD?" THE SKAL'TUM REPEATED, STEPPING CLOSER
to Rockingham. It held a haunch of horse thigh in one claw and
tore into it.

Not able to suppress a cringe, Rockingham took a step away,
nearer the nyphai woman. Nee'lahn's scowl marred her soft lips.
He held up a hand toward Nee'lahn. He knew she might burst
forth at any moment with something to ruin his scheme with the
skal'tum—like the fact that he had no idea where the foul wit'ch
was! Curse those without deceit. How did they live to an old age?
He pressed his open palm toward her, willing her silent.

She ignored him. "You are the lowest of beetles digging into
dung," Nee'lahn hissed, obviously believing he was about to betray them. And he would, if betrayal would allow him to live; but
the time was not ripe for that quite yet.

He risked removing his eyes from the skal'tum and turned to
face Nee'lahn fully. He forced his voice into a deep-throated tim-
bre. It was said among those of Blackhall that the Dark Lord's
lieutenants had difficulty hearing in the lower ranges. Their sharp
ears, like a firebat's, heard best in the higher pitches. Whether this
was gossip or fact, Rockingham still kept his voice quick and
silent. "Hush! If you wish to live, let me handle this. Trust me."

"Trust you!" she said too loudly. "I would sooner trust the Black Soul himself."

"If you don't wish to be dinner, keep your tongue still."

The cowering figure of Mogweed sidled closer to Rockingham. The shape-shifter's eyes were still fixed on the steaming mass of bone and gore that was once a proud stallion. The remaining mare nearby had stopped yanking on its lead and just stood shaking. Its eyes rolled white with fear, but it kept quiet. Smart horse, Rockingham thought.

Mogweed leaned into their conversation. "If this man knows these beasts, perhaps it would be best if we heeded his counsel."

The tiny woman dismissed the shape-shifter's words with a shake of her head. "He knows nothing. He—"

"Exactly!" Rockingham said, determined to keep her from further voicing aloud how little he actually knew. He drilled her with his eyes and spoke low, his hushed words more an exhalation than speech. "I *don't* know. That's just it. I can't reveal anything useful to them—only save our hides. I have no wish to fall into their capture. Death at their claws would be pleasant compared to being dragged before the Dark Lord in disgrace." His glance took in the ravaged horse. That was merciful compared to what could occur within the bowels of Blackhall's dungeons. He forced his eyes to pierce Nee'lahn to silence. "Let me do my job."

And what he did best was survive—by his wits and his tongue.

She glowered at him but kept her lips pressed tight.

He turned to face the skal'tum, who had finished cracking the bone of the haunch and stood sucking at its marrow. The beast knew they were trapped and seemed to enjoy drawing out the tension. The other creature crept closer, its eyes fixed on Rockingham. "I hear gnatss buzzing, but no answers. Tell us where the girl hidess."

Rockingham straightened his riding cloak, trying to appear confident and calm before the towering bulk of the twin skal'tum. He cleared the tension from his throat with a cough, then began. "Like you, great lieutenants of the Black Heart, I, too, am on the trail of the wit'ch-child."

"You have failed. Word has reached Blackhall. We were dispatched to correct your misstake."

Rockingham spread his palms wide as if in shock and hurt. "It was no mistake of mine. The fault lies at the feet of the old maimed one, Dismarum. He would not heed my desire to use force and blade to nab the girl, instead relying on tricks and deceit. That was his downfall, and alas, our failure! This child is steeped with wicked cunning. She eluded the darkmage's many traps."

"And where were you during all thiss, little man?"

He rested his hand upon his heart. "The Black Heart gave me to the darkmage. I had no choice but to do Dismarum's bidding— as mistaken as it was. Yet once Dismarum failed and used his arcane magick to flee from his disgrace, I was free to pursue the girl. And so I do."

"Then why iss she yet free?"

"She's quick and protected by strong allies and stronger magick."

"She iss a child."

He jabbed a finger at the closest beast. "A *child* who killed one of your own. You would do best not to underestimate her skill— as did your unfortunate brother."

The other skal'tum, his claws still red with horse blood, sprang closer. Rockingham fought to keep from backing away. Now was a crucial time to show strength. "You lie to us, man of weak flesh," the skal'tum said. "We have met the killer of our brother. It was no girl. He even knew the breaches of our black protections."

Curse that hill of a man! Why was everyone so free with their tongues? Consternation laced with fear coursed through his veins, but he kept his face fixed in a look of benign disinterest as his mind spun on threads of deceit. He sharpened his voice to answer the creature. "And who did you think *gave* this man your secrets?"

This thought gave the skal'tum a pause. It glanced to its companion, then back to Rockingham. Its voice was less malignant. "Yet she iss still not captured. Here the blame lies solely upon you."

"Ah, true she is not yet chained at your feet, awaiting the master's pleasures." Rockingham could not stop a shiver from passing through his body at the image of what pleased his lord. His tongue stumbled, but he continued. "Bu . . . But . . . I have harried her and driven her before me like a leaf before a storm, and now have her boxed and trapped. I have only to retrieve her."

"Where?"

Rockingham pointed to the root-shrouded entrance to the tunnel. "She is trapped, too deep for you to reach by digging. You will never get to her before dawn's light." Both skal'tum glanced to the eastern horizon; their wings twitched in a protective gesture. So some things gave even a skal'tum pause. Rockingham allowed the ghost of a smile to play upon his lips. "Only I can coax her from her hole."

"If she iss sso fierce, how can you, a wisp of a man, hope to drag her here?"

"I have something she wants." Rockingham nodded to Nee'lahn, whose face was frozen in distaste and hate. The next lie was crucial. "I have her beloved sister."

He watched Nee'lahn's eyes grow wide with shock. His smile grew full. Sometimes even the righteous fell into step with his deceptions by pure chance. Her look of hate and open-mouthed shock seemed so genuine. He swung to face the twin skal'tum. "I am actually glad you arrived so opportunely. Now I can leave her in your capable care as I flush our quarry out of her warren."

Rockingham waved Mogweed from Nee'lahn's side and indicated he should approach. The si'lura stood still. Rockingham saw him tremble. "With you two minding the sister," Rockingham said to the skal'tum, "my guard and I can pursue the girl with quicker feet."

He again waved to Mogweed. This time the shape-shifter broke the ground's hold on his feet and stumbled to Rockingham's side. He stood almost too close, like a clinging shadow.

One of the skal'tum slipped closer to Nee'lahn. To her credit, she did not even shrink as it loomed over her. She only glared at Rockingham.

"Keep her safe," he said. "She is vital to capturing the wit'ch."

"We will do our duty," the skal'tum near Nee'lahn said.

"And you do yourss, little man," said the other.

Rockingham bowed his head in acknowledgment, hiding his grin of success. Then he hooked the shape-shifter's elbow in his own and guided the stunned man to the black tunnel entrance.

From behind them, the bloody-clawed skal'tum who had shredded the horse called to them, "If you betray uss, do not think because you are the master'ss creation we will not tear your limbss from you and feast upon your eyess."

Rockingham's shoulders twitched up to his neck at its words. He did not understand what the creature meant by "the master's creation," but considering how easily he had duped them, there was no fathoming what mistaken ideas filled their alien minds. He pushed Mogweed through the drape of roots and into the tunnel.

He then turned to face the skal'tum again. "Trust me," he said loudly to them. Then his eyes settled on Nee'lahn, but he quickly tore them away. Betrayal was a dinner best served cold. Still his heart did quiver a beat. He seemed to remember a woman who had once looked at him with similar eyes of hurt and rage. But who? He squeezed between the roots and followed Mogweed onto the carpet of leaf and rot that spread into the entrance of the tunnel. And when? He could almost pull up the woman's image from his past—even a scent, daffodils, and sunlight on golden hair—but like a flutter of butterflies, the memory broke apart. He shook his head; probably just some whore he had bedded and was too drunk to remember. But in his heart, he knew he was wrong.

Mogweed cleared his throat, drawing his attention. The shape-shifter's eyes were wide and almost aglow. "Where do we go now?"

Rockingham scowled and pointed. "As far away from those monsters as possible."

Mogweed did not move until Rockingham shoved him onward. The shape-shifter mumbled, "But . . . but no one has come back who went this way."

Tol'chuk scrambled down the last of the boulders to reach the chasm floor. He glanced up to where Kral still struggled atop a precariously perched granite slab. It teetered under the mountain man's feet. Tol'chuk had left the glowing stone with Kral to better light the mountain man's climb, but the elemental magick in the stone had faded to a whisper of its former glory. The stone, since it had to be carried in one hand, was more a burden than an aid in the mountain man's journey down the tumbled wall of the chasm, but Kral clung to it like a drowning og're to a log.

"Go to your left!" he called to Kral. "The climb be steeper but craggier. Easier to find footholds and clawholds."

"I don't have claws," Kral grumbled but took his advice and swung to the other side of the fall of boulders.

Tol'chuk waited. He could do nothing else. He studied the mountain man's progress. Kral was a skilled climber, as he supposed all mountain men must be to survive above the snow line of the Teeth. Even with the weak eyes of his kind and one hand burdened with the stone, Kral was managing the last of the dark cliff face with surprising speed and skill.

Still, his descent was not fast enough for Tol'chuk's taste. The og're shifted his feet with impatience. To wait patiently after so much exertion was hard. His back muscles ached, and a ripped claw on his right hand pulsed with pain. Even his legs—two trunks of muscle, tendon, and bone—quivered at the sudden cessation of activity. But worst of all, he still felt a strong pull on his heart to continue the pursuit of Fardale. Ever since the wolf-brother's images had slipped into his skull, the occasional pangs as the Heart of his people called him forward still tugged on his spirit, mostly when he stopped or rested—like now.

He fought to distract himself, to ignore the drive to abandon the mountain man on the cliff and strike out on his own. That was not the way of an og're. One tribe member did not leave another in danger, a sentiment ingrained into the bones of all og'res—even a half-breed. A noble trait, Tol'chuk thought, but unfortunately it was also the chief reason the clan wars among the tribes had been historically so vicious and protracted. To injure one member of a tribe was like attacking the whole. No affront was left unanswered, no threat left unchallenged, until the entire male population of one of the two warring tribes was destroyed. Tol'chuk scowled at his sour thoughts. Except for religious ceremonies, there had never been a time when all the og're tribes had united. And considering the drive of his people and the honor code of the warriors, he doubted they ever would be.

Sometimes honor and loyalty, he realized with a sigh, were not such noble traits.

Still, he did not abandon Kral, even as the hooks dug deep into his heart to pull him onward. He could not ignore countless generations of og're blood flowing through his veins. Honor and loyalty, though the sentiments had killed thousands of his fellow og'res, were still as much a part of him as bone and tendon. He waited.

Thankfully, Tol'chuk did not have much longer to wait. Kral, with his chest heaving, hopped off the last boulder to land beside him.

"I hope we are making the right choice in pursuing this path," Kral said, forcing words out between gasps. "We'll never climb back out this way."

Tol'chuk shrugged his massive shoulders. "We will find another way back up." He led off in the direction where Fardale and the lamps had last been seen. He heard a slight groan as the mountain man forced his legs to follow. Kral could probably use a rest after the climb, but Tol'chuk did not want the wolf-brother to get too far ahead of them. If this subterranean system was the same as Tol'chuk's tribal cavern, with its warren of twisting and branching tunnels, then with only a little distance, Fardale could be easily lost to him. He urged the mountain man onward. "Speed be our best chance to keep ahead of the rock'goblins."

"Also the best way of running right back into them," Kral added, but he kept up with the og're.

They proceeded in silence, conserving their breath for the hike across the uneven terrain. As they trudged, the air grew thick as goat's milk. Tol'chuk's huge chest drank without difficulty. An og're was built for the deep caverns buried under the mountains. Kral, however, had lived among the high, snowy peaks and was accustomed to the thin air blowing through the Teeth. This stagnant damp air was not making his journey easier. The large man labored to keep close to the og're.

Tol'chuk kept one ear turned back toward the mountain man, listening to his graveled breathing. Kral voiced no complaint, but Tol'chuk knew that a rest would be needed shortly. He searched across the length of the cavern. A cluster of boulders lay across their path ahead. If they could at least reach there before stopping, Tol'chuk thought, then they would be close to the tunnel into which Fardale had vanished. The urging from the heartstone of his people, though, made him reluctant for even this brief delay. Now that Tol'chuk was moving, he did not want to stop.

Kral coughed behind him, rattling and hoarse. Tol'chuk bunched up his brow. Just a bit farther, he thought. He marched on, listening to the mountain man for any further sign of exhaustion.

Tol'chuk, keenly attuned to Kral's breathing and to the slippery terrain of loose rock, did not notice a shadow detach itself from a boulder and step toward him until the figure stood directly in his path.

"I'll have my stone, please," the figure said.

Kral rounded the wide body of Tol'chuk with the light. In the greenish glow, the figure was revealed to be the one called Meric, the elv'in man. His white shirt, torn, was marred by mud and by darker stains that could only be blood. His green pants were ripped, and a scrap of his shirt was wrapped around his upper thigh. Blood trailed down his leg. A black bruise stood out on his white cheek. He repeated his demand, his hand held out. "My windstone." Though his words were casual and his manner disdainful, his hand trembled slightly.

"We thought you dead," Kral said. He still clutched the stone in a fist, obviously wary of the elv'in. "The blood, the trail over the cliff. How did you survive the jump to the first ledge?"

"I didn't jump to any ledge." He still held one hand out but used the other to wipe away a strand of silver hair that had escaped his long braid. "I leaped to here."

Kral glanced up into the blackness through which they had jumped, climbed, and trudged to reach this spot. "Nee'lahn warned of your lies," he mumbled, but his eyes returned to study the thin man.

"I do not lie."

Tol'chuk's voice rang with suspicion. "Not even an og're could survive such a fall."

"I did not fall." Disdain rang in his voice.

"What did you do then?" Kral asked. "Fly?"

"No, the elv'in may be masters of wind and air, but not even we can achieve flight. The elemental magick is not that strong. I could not fly, but through the use of elemental power, I could control my plunge to this chasm floor. I slowed it, spread its energy into a glide to here."

"And you waited for us?"

A slight scowl twisted his lips. "I tended my wounds." He pointed to his legs. "Those creatures caught me off guard, and I took several stabs before I was able to escape. As I stanched the blood, I saw the glow of my windstone at the top of the cliff. I watched you jump and climb here—and waited. Not for you, but for my stone." He thrust his hand farther toward Kral. "Please return my property."

Kral still kept the rock in his palm. "This is the only light. We have a friend to find."

"As do I."

Kral and Meric stared at each other.

"We can go . . . together," Tol'chuk said. "If the goblins attack again, we will need everyone."

"I'll keep the stone," Kral said.

"You will kill its light. I can warm its glow back to bright."

Kral clutched the stone tighter. Tol'chuk noted that the glow had waned rapidly since leaping into the chasm. The mountain man hesitated, then slowly reached out and pressed the crystal rock into Meric's palm. He held the stone and the elv'in's palm in his large hand as he spoke. "We stay together. Swear it."

"We do not swear lightly among my people, man of the mountains."

"Neither do we." Kral's hand tightened its grip. "Now swear."

Meric's eyes narrowed with threat, and he spoke between clenched teeth. "I give my word. I will help you find your friend."

Kral maintained his grip for a heartbeat, his eyes boring into the elv'in. Then he nodded and released his hand.

"We must go," said Tol'chuk.

"Where?" the elv'in asked.

"We seek our friend in the tunnel yonder," Tol'chuk said. "He be with others who have lights."

"Lights?" Meric asked, his voice swelling with hope. "Did one float upon the winds? It could be my bird."

Tol'chuk scratched the bristled hairs atop his head. "No."

This brought a frown to Meric's thin lips. "You saw no other light?"

Tol'chuk shook his head. The elv'in seemed distraught with the news. "Why be it so important to find this bird of yours?"

"He scented royal blood. I could tell when I entered this valley."

"I do not understand."

Meric ignored Tol'chuk, scanning the dark chasm. Kral explained. "He claims his bird is like a hound on a trail. It seeks their lost king."

"Descendant of our king," Meric corrected. He rubbed his retrieved windstone and blew on it. The stone bloomed brighter, highlighting the silver hair and white skin of the elv'in. He faced them. Old hate burned in his words. "Our queen was allowed to leave when we were banished from our lands, but our king was kept hostage."

Kral waved a hand to encompass the chasm and lands beyond.

"How do you know a descendant still survives after so many centuries?"

"The king swore he would keep the line alive in our lands."

"But what if he couldn't?"

"I said he *swore*, mountain man," said Meric, venom in his voice. "And our promises are kept."

Sensing a growing tension, Tol'chuk changed the tack of the conversation. "This hawk—"

"Moon'falcon," the elv'in corrected, swinging his eyes away from Kral.

"Yes, this bird," Tol'chuk continued, "how can it seek someone it has never met? Even a sniffer needs a scent."

"It is not so much a scent as a bond. The eggs of moon'falcons are bathed in royal blood. Bird and blood are linked. This falcon is a direct descendant of the moon'falcon originally bonded to our king. Descendant will know descendant. It will only alight on someone with our lost king's blood."

"But I saw it with you," Kral said.

Meric sighed heavily, as if this were all so obvious. "I am of royal blood, the fourth son of Queen Tratal, the Star of the Morning. It is our people's dream to reunite the two houses of our race—the present queen's line and the ancient king's line."

Kral burst forth with a hoarse chuckle. "So, Meric, you're also a matchmaker seeking a husband for one of your sisters." He laughed again. "To reunite your noble houses! Gads, I'm glad my clans left that all behind. We bow to no one."

Meric's face reddened at Kral's ridiculing attitude; his thin lips pulled thinner and his eyes spat hate. Tol'chuk sensed currents running deep in this thin man that if brought to the surface would be more of a danger than a hundred goblins. Tol'chuk decided it was time to end this conversation. Besides, the compulsion to continue the journey was again beginning to throb in his chest. "There be a tunnel ahead. My friend went in there. Maybe your falcon went that way, too."

The blood slowly drained from Meric's face as he turned to

him; then he gave a slight shrug. "I will go with you—as I swore."
He darted a narrow-eyed glance to Kral. As his eyes settled back
on Tol'chuk, he continued, "I will let the bird hunt a bit longer."

"Then we go." Tol'chuk led the way before Kral could say
something to further aggravate the elv'in. Meric stayed close to
Tol'chuk, allowing Kral to trail behind.

The silence wrapped around them as they forced their way
through a tight set of stubborn boulders. Tol'chuk had to hoist the
smaller men over some of the bigger rocks. Kral would only let
him do this with much frowning and a reddening of cheeks. The
independent mountain man bristled at needing help, but he was
not too proud to recognize the reality of the situation. In brooding
silence, he allowed himself to be hauled up and pushed to the top
of the steepled rock.

Meric, on the other hand, accepted Tol'chuk's aid without even
a nod of thanks. He had a palm held out for assistance even before
Tol'chuk offered, as if he were well accustomed to being cared
after by those stronger of limb. Tol'chuk lifted him, surprised at
how light the elv'in was, as if his bones were hollow like some
long-legged wading bird. He pushed Meric high enough for the
elv'in to reach an arm up to Kral. Kral ignored the arm and just
stared into the darkness. After realizing the mountain man was
not going to help, Meric grasped a spar of rock and pulled himself up.

This was all accomplished in silence. Tol'chuk's arms and legs,
busy with the climb, allowed his mind to ponder the elv'in's words.
Something bothered him, but he could not quite place a claw on
the scrambling bug of his concern. The quiet hike through the
boulders allowed him to review what he knew of the elv'in. His
thoughts backtracked to their first meeting, and by the time they
had cleared the nest of rock, he finally remembered what bothered him.

He turned to Meric. The elv'in was hunched over, breathing
heavily after the passage through the stones. Even Kral leaned on
a neighboring boulder, massaging a kink from his left thigh.

"When first we met in the clearing in the woods, you mentioned nothing of a king's descendant. Only something about some wit'ch. What be that all about?"

Meric nodded, trying to catch his breath. "Yes, the other reason I was allowed to seek the king. Our oracles spoke of a wit'ch in this land who would appear in the same valley as our lost king. This wit'ch will draw protectors from all the lands like moths to a deadly flame, and she will grow to ravage our ancient homes. So besides seeking our king, I am to search for signs of her."

"Why?" asked Kral, stepping forward, limping slightly on his left leg.

"To kill her."

30

Elena watched her uncle step to Er'ril's side. The swordsman had sunk to his knees at the threshold to the next chamber. He held his face away from the light shining forth from the room. On Er'ril's cheek rested a single tear, glinting like a jewel in the radiance.

"What is it?" Uncle Bol said, placing a hand on the swordsman's shoulder.

Er'ril did not answer, but simply pointed into the next room.

Elena crept within her uncle's shadow. She peered from around his back into the face of the light. The source of the radiance stood in the center of a crudely circular chamber. The room was otherwise empty and unadorned.

"Amazing handiwork," her uncle said, squinting into the chamber. "But what troubles you so, Er'ril?"

Er'ril shook his head and stayed silent.

Elena slipped from around Uncle Bol's back to better view the chamber. In the center of the room, resting on the bare floor, stood a crystal statue that fountained forth with silvery light. Even though the stone of the statue was the well of this pure light, Elena found the radiance did not blind her to the features of the sculpture; actually, the opposite was true. The light seemed to drape and fold around the statue, adding a certain detail and substance to the work.

"The artisan who created this piece was one of astounding skill," Uncle Bol said, his words mumbled as his eyes kept drifting with concern toward the swordsman. "Surely this is not the work of goblins. The smoothness of the stone, the fine details around the eyes and lips, are nothing like the crude carvings on the arches."

Elena found herself silently agreeing with her uncle. It was a thing of exceptional beauty—though a *cruel* beauty.

The statue was that of a small boy. Elena judged him to be no older than ten winters. The figure knelt with one hand resting on the floor, the other arm raised high, as if in supplication. The boy's face, contorted with pain, was also turned to the heavens. The reason for the boy's agony was clear.

"See how the sculptor chose to mix his materials for dramatic effect?" her uncle said, laying a hand on her shoulder. "The boy is crystal, but the sword is silver."

Elena nodded. From the corner of her eye, she saw Er'ril wince at the mention of the sword. Like Er'ril, she did not like this feature of the sculpture.

Thrust through the back of the crystal boy, piercing chest and heart, stood a silver sword. Its pommel protruded a handspan above the boy's back, its point buried into the rock of the floor. The boy seemed to be struggling to escape his fate, as if still unaware of the fatal nature of the sword's blow, only aware of its pain. His face, innocent and lost, searched the heavens for release from the agony. His eyes stretched wide, pleading for an answer as to why this had to happen.

Elena found her own eyes welling with tears as she stared at the boy's face. An impulse struck her to go out and comfort the child, try to relieve his suffering. But she knew it was only a statue. The pain expressed here was from an era long ago, but the sculpture was so fine, the agony reached up from the ages to touch her own heart.

"It is a shame the statue is marred," her uncle said sharply; as a scholar of ancient histories, he had always hated to see bits of antiquity damaged. He scowled now as he pointed. "One of the goblins must have broken it when dragging it here."

Elena could not fathom at first what her uncle meant. Then she realized the boy's left arm, which was raised toward the roof of the chamber, was missing its hand, as if it had been chopped off with an ax. How odd she hadn't noticed that immediately. Still, as she studied the piece, somehow she felt her uncle was wrong. The statue was not damaged, just unfinished—like a sad song ending a few notes short of its completion, the ear still waiting.

Her uncle had by now turned again to Er'ril. Uncle Bol's face was stern, his lips iron hard, and his cheeks sunken with determination. "Enough of this foolishness, Standi! What so troubles you about a bit of sculpted crystal?"

Er'ril remained silent with his shoulders humped in sorrow. When he finally spoke, his voice was low and directed to the rock floor. "It is my shame," he mumbled, "my shame given form."

As Er'ril bowed his head, he now knew in his heart that Bol's earlier words were true. The goblins had not herded them here because of the girl but because of him. Somehow the rock'goblins knew of his shame and had driven him here to face it.

If that was what these creatures wanted, then he would grant them what they asked. Knowing he did not deserve to hide from it anyway, he finally raised his eyes again to stare at the statue. The boy's face, carved in such fine detail, burned with bright light, and his own mind flamed in memory. He could never forget that face—and never should, he thought. In some small manner, he could at least honor the boy's sacrifice by not forgetting him.

As his eyes rested on the small raised face, he remembered the room in the inn and the night the Book was forged. So much of that night had come home to him again in the past day. First Greshym reappearing on a street, black with dark magick. And now this: a sculpture of the boy mage who had been sacrificed on the point of Er'ril's own sword so the Book could have its blood. The players of that fateful night were again being drawn together.

The mystery of why all this was happening and why he had been lured to this chamber finally penetrated the shameful ache in his heart. He pushed to his feet. He had lived with the memory of his foul act for centuries. Though the sight of the statue had shocked and thumbed this old bruise to life, an anger now began to build in his breast, burning back his throbbing guilt. He straightened his back. Whoever had sculpted the statue had much to answer—and Er'ril was determined to be the one to pry those answers forth.

Bol spoke up as Er'ril stepped into the chamber. "Out with it man! What is wrong?"

Er'ril nodded to the statue. "That is the young mage whom I slew the night the Book was forged." He saw Bol's eyes widen with his words, and even the girl shied from him; but he did not look away this time. His voice held steady. "I do not know what game is being played here. But I mean to end it."

Er'ril strode closer to the statue. As he approached, the pain on the boy's sculpted face seemed to worsen, as if the statue recognized him and feared meeting him again. Just a trick of the light, he thought. He reached a finger and touched the hard crystal surface. For a moment he expected it would burn or in some way harm him, revenge for his previous crime, but the stone was merely cool and smooth, its surface slightly damp with dew from the moist cavern air.

Er'ril found his finger brushing the boy's cheek. He had forgotten how very young the lad was. And how small—Er'ril towered beside the kneeled statue. Surely the child had not deserved this fate. Er'ril tried to find words to ask his forgiveness, but he had never learned the boy's name.

"It had to be done," Bol said softly behind him. "I read the old texts. Innocent blood had to be shed."

"But did I have to do it?"

"We all have burdens we must carry in life: my sister Fila, Elena, the boy. These are dark times, and if we pray for a future dawn, we must get on our knees, no matter how tired our bones or how sore our joints."

"I am done with praying. Who listens?" He placed his palm on the boy's raised and anguished face. "Who listened to this boy?"

"The path you have walked has been one full of heartaches and sorrow, and I will not say where you walk next will be any easier. I can only tell you this—it is the *one* path that will redeem all you've done and justify all who were sacrificed. Do not lose your heart, Er'ril of Standi."

Er'ril let his hand slip from the boy's face. "It is too late. My heart was lost long ago."

"No." Bol reached a hand and squeezed Er'ril's shoulder. "It may be hiding, grown hard over hundreds of winters, but down this path I wager you will find your heart again."

Er'ril's face tightened. He had no wish to find his heart again. That would be a pain he could never bear.

Elena's small voice suddenly rang with alarm. "Listen!"

Er'ril raised his head. A familiar noise was again flowing toward them—hissing.

Goblins approached! Er'ril glanced toward the tunnel. No sign yet of the beasts. He glanced around the chamber. There was one other tunnel opening onto the chamber, and from there, too, flowed the sibilant hiss of goblins.

"They have us boxed," Bol said.

"And we're too exposed out in the open," Er'ril said. "Our best chance is in one of the tunnels."

Bol turned to Er'ril. "We have no chance of fighting them. We don't even have a weapon. They drove us here for a reason, surely not to kill us. They could have done that at any time."

Er'ril swung from Bol's side and stepped again toward the statue. "I am not trusting to the logic of a rock'goblin. All I know is we need a weapon." He slipped to the back of the statue. Leaning forward, he grasped the pommel of the silver sword and pulled on it. For a moment, it stayed caught within the grip of the sculpted crystal, and Er'ril feared he did not have the strength to yank it free, but as his muscles knotted tighter, the sword suddenly slipped free as if a ghostly hand had simply released its hold.

Er'ril staggered backward, sword in hand. Steadying himself, he raised the weapon up. Its long blade shone so bright the silver itself seemed to be forged of glory. "Now we fight. Enough of slinking shadows and hissing threats."

"That won't be necessary." The voice came from behind him.

Er'ril twirled around, his sword shearing through the air to point at the speaker. From the other tunnel stepped a hunched figure. Crookbacked and gray with shaggy hair, the speaker raised his face toward the light. It was a man. He stepped toward them. He wore only a loincloth, foul with mud and filth. His chest was scarred with the raking of many claws, and he limped on the club of a twisted foot. His right arm had been torn off at the elbow and now ended in a scarred mass of pink tissue.

"Who are you?" Er'ril asked.

With his words, a rush of goblins burst into the room from the tunnel behind the man. They clustered around the man's legs like nervous shadows. Elena had crept closer to Er'ril by this time. He heard her squeak beside him and glanced to see red eyes staring out from the other tunnel. They were trapped.

He faced the decrepit man again. "Who are you?" he repeated, his voice thick with threat.

The man pushed back his muddied hair to reveal a gaunt face pocked with scars. His nose had been torn and had healed crookedly; one eye was gone. He smiled to reveal a mouth barren of teeth. "You do not recognize me, Er'ril?" The man cackled, his laugh bright with near-madness; his hand twitched as if it had a will of its own.

"I know none such as you, creature of the cave," he said with disgust.

"Creature of the cave?" The man tittered again. His hand climbed to his hair and picked at something there. He dug it out and examined it a moment, then pinched it between nails grown long and yellow. "Your brother was never so rude when last we met—him begging for a boon."

Er'ril's eyes twitched with surprise. Shock held his tongue. Who was this madman?

Bol spoke into the silence. "You live among the rock'goblins?"

The man waved a dismissive hand. "They fear me. They call me 'the-man-who-lives-like-rock' in their clicking and hissing tongue."

"You know their language!" Bol's voice rang with wonder.

"I've had plenty of lonely time to learn."

Er'ril had by now overcome his shock. He cared little for the rock'goblins and their speech. "You spoke of my brother," he finally said.

The man's bright eyes settled back to Er'ril. "Oh, yes, Shorkan was always a mixture of delight and frustration. Such a pity we had to lose him." His eyes shifted to the statue. "We lost so much that night."

"Enough of this foolery, old man. Who are you, and why have we been herded here?"

The man sighed heavily. "I was once called Re'alto, Master Re'alto by my pupils. Do you still not recognize the headmaster of the school?"

Er'ril could not stop a gasp from escaping his lips; his sword point dropped to the floor. Master Re'alto! Impossible, but Er'ril spied a vague resemblance under the scars and filth. How could this be? How could the headmaster still be alive? All the mages had been thought destroyed the night the school was purged by the skal'tum and dog soldiers. The boy was supposed to be the only survivor. "H-How?"

The man stayed silent as his strained smile faded to a sad frown. A certain lucidity entered his bright eyes. His voice lowered with the weight of memory. "On that night . . . I sent your brother after the boy in the apprentice wing and tried to escape. I meant to flee myself, but the dreadlords caught me. Luckily, they decided just to play with me." He pointed to his shredded arm and scarred chest. Suddenly the old man looked dazed. He searched around himself as if he had lost something. His eyes fixed on a tiny goblin, much smaller than the others. He snatched the squirming creature up by one arm. "Aren't they cute when they're young?"

Er'ril's mouth sneered in disgust. He had never respected the headmaster, having thought the man too craven and whining. But now . . . "Master Re'alto, enough of this nonsense. What happened?"

Er'ril's words snapped him back. He dropped the goblin, as if surprised to be holding it. He wiped his hand on his loincloth and continued. "I . . . I still lived when word reached my dreadlord captors that Shorkan had escaped with a boy. They left me for dead, as I was thick with their poisons. I dragged myself off to one of the deepest cellars, and from there, I knew a way into the underground caverns."

"You abandoned your school."

The man's voice grew stern. "I am no sea captain to die with his ship! The school was lost. All that roamed the halls were the screams of the dying and the dogs of the Dark Lord." The old man wiped at his brow as if to erase the memory. "I just wanted to die in peace, not fill the belly of a dreadlord. So I dragged myself here." He waved his hand to encompass the chamber.

Bol spoke next. "Yet you did not die—not of your poisoned wounds or age."

Master Re'alto's eyes settled on the statue. His eyes became lost and the old man began to hum to himself, rocking slightly on his feet.

When it was clear no answer was forthcoming, Bol cleared his throat.

Re'alto blinked at the noise, then spoke, his voice a whisper. "No, I didn't die. Instead *he* came back."

"What do you mean?" Er'ril asked.

"The boy needed me. Somehow he knew where I was and he appeared, rich with Chyric power. His light healed me, and as long as I kept near the light, its magick kept the years from aging me. He needed a guardian, someone to watch over him." He pulled his eyes from the statue and spoke to them in a conspiratorial tone, as if afraid the statue might hear. "At first I balked at his request, but I had so poorly kept my school from harm." The man sagged with exhaustion. "How could I refuse?"

"How do you know all this?" Bol asked. "Does the statue speak to you?"

Re'alto's one hand fluttered about his head as if waving the thought away. "No, he speaks to me in dreams. He is the only thing keeping me sane down here."

Bol turned to Er'ril, his eyes full of doubt, questioning the man's current sanity.

Suddenly the man sprang straight and screamed at them. "Keep her away!" The goblins erupted in angry agitation around his feet.

Er'ril glanced beside him to see Elena reaching a hand, her ruby-stained hand, toward the statue. She seemed only curious. The man's words froze her. "You'd better leave it be," Er'ril said to her.

The moon'falcon on her shoulder squawked at him, but she dropped her hand and slipped closer to Er'ril.

As she retreated from the statue, the man calmed down, and after a few breaths, the goblins settled to a low hiss. "She must not touch it," the man said.

"Why?"

"The boy waits only for you, Er'ril, no other. We have both been waiting a long time for this meeting."

Er'ril's eyes narrowed. "For what purpose?"

The scarred man pointed with his one good hand toward the boy's raised limb. The statue's arm ended at the wrist. When Er'ril just stared at him in ignorance, Re'alto started to jab vigorously toward the statue. "To complete the statue, you fool!"

What was he talking about? Er'ril thought. The man clenched his fist and shook it at him. Then, like the bursting of a log in a hot fire, Er'ril suddenly understood! He spat toward the man. "So that's why you stole the ward?"

"About time you figured it out," Master Re'alto said, then continued to mumble something else, as if he was arguing with himself. Suddenly he raised his head and yelled at Er'ril. "You were always so thick-headed!"

Before Er'ril could respond, the old man swung to face the plague of goblins behind him. He clucked and hissed at them. One of the goblins near the back darted away. Re'alto spoke with his back to Er'ril. "Their sense for magick is strong. That is how they found me. The light scares them, but the magick attracts them. They think me some sort of god."

Down the tunnel, a commotion arose. A goblin pushed through the others. Its hands were clutched together, laden with something heavy. Its tail flagged back and forth in agitation as it stepped up to the old man. With its head bowed, it offered what it held in its clawed hands. Re'alto accepted the gift with a hiss and a snort.

The goblin slunk away, and Re'alto turned to Er'ril. "It was easy for them to find where you had hidden the ward. The boy spoke to me in dreams, and I sent them to fetch it. We knew you would come back for the ward, so we just waited. When word reached me that you had arrived, I had that little goblin use it to lure you down here."

"Why didn't you fetch me yourself and save us all this game of chase?"

The headmaster frowned and rolled his eyes. "I must not leave the light's touch. It's not safe for me." He held the ward out to Er'ril. "I have waited long enough. Finish the statue."

Er'ril stared at the ward. He had risked so much trying to retrieve it, but now that he knew to what purpose he was meant to put it, he balked. The chunk of metal melded out of the iron distilled from the blood of a thousand mages glinted a fiery red in the silver light. Er'ril studied it and knew what he had to do.

The ward was forged into the shape of a fist—a small boy's fist.

Er'ril handed his sword to Bol, whose eyes were wide with questions. With his hand shaking, Er'ril took the ward, the iron fist almost slipping from his numb fingers. He clenched it tighter, his fist wrapping around the smaller fist. He stepped to the statue.

"Only you could do this, Er'ril," the headmaster of the school said. "Your hand took his life."

Er'ril reached and balanced the fist upon the empty wrist of the statue. It fit perfectly. When his fingers slipped free of the ward, the fist remained in place. He stepped back. With the statue complete, a new nuance shaped the sculpture. Where before the boy had appeared plaintive and his face pained with supplication to an uncaring heaven, with the fist raised high, the piece was transformed into one of defiance. The boy's face now shone with the agony of responsibility, the fist raised in rage and determination.

It was no longer a boy who knelt, *but a man.*

As Er'ril stared, tears in his eyes, the crystal face swung to stare back at him, gaze meeting gaze.

Behind him, Elena cried out in surprise, and a rattled gasp escaped from Bol. But Er'ril's ears only heard the mumbled words of the old headmaster, his voice bordering between exaltation and madness. "Only you could do this, Er'ril of Standi. Your hand took his life. *Only yours could give it back.*"

31

Mogweed hugged the stone wall of the tunnel as Rockingham fought to light a brand made from a dried branch and a torn piece of Mogweed's shirt. The si'lura feared the thin man, with his quick movements and suspicious eyes, but found he could not help but respect the man's tongue—and few had ever commanded Mogweed's respect. Not even his own brother, with his stout heart and loyalty, had earned more than a sneer from him; this man, however, was worth studying. With only his words and his wits, Rockingham had won them freedom from the claws of the winged beasts. Fardale would have fought them with teeth and muscle, and only won them all a savage death.

There was much Mogweed could learn from this man.

"Blast this thing!" Rockingham cursed as he struggled, trying to ignite the oiled shirt with his tinderbox. He struck the flint again, and at last a thick spark jumped to the tinder. "Finally!" He blew the spark to a weak flame. Soon the shirt blazed, blooming like a rose in the gloom; the sudden light cast dancing shadows across the thin man's features and stung Mogweed's eyes. "Collect a few more branches and strip that shirt. We may need to replenish our torches. I don't know how long we'll be down here."

Mogweed glanced the length of the tunnel, first in the direction of the wood where the skal'tum waited, then toward where his brother had vanished. Fardale's howl still echoed in his head. "Where do we go?"

"We kill time. Dawn is near. The skal'tum will only wait so long before the sunlight chases them to shadowed roosts."

"Are you sure?"

Rockingham shrugged. "Just in case, we can use the time to see if there's another way out of here—an exit well away from those beasts."

Mogweed's respect for the man flared higher. He always seemed a step ahead, his mind cunning even in the face of such monstrosities. "We need to be careful," he said, trying to be of use. "There is something down here, something that hisses. I think it attacked my brother."

Rockingham raised his flaming brand. "Creatures of the dark usually fear fire. As long as we go slowly and keep the torch blazing, we should be safe."

Mogweed nodded and followed the man deeper down the tunnel. Their muffled steps echoed around them. Moss and roots hung in drapes from the low roof. As they crept farther along, Rockingham's torch occasionally caught a dry tendril of hanging rot, igniting it with a hiss and a crackle. Each time that happened, Mogweed's heart jumped to his throat. The hiss reminded him of the sound that had drawn Fardale away.

After a stretch of silence, Rockingham whispered, "Ahead there. I think the tunnel ends."

Mogweed's feet stopped. He could not follow.

"It's a room," Rockingham said, continuing, unaware his companion had halted.

Darkness quickly wrapped about Mogweed's shoulders as Rockingham and the torch slipped farther away. The gloom began to whisper wordlessly in his ear with a voice of its own. Mogweed knew it was only his imagination, but still the blackness could not be ignored. His fear of the darkness clashed with his fright at what might lie ahead.

But a larger fear finally drove Mogweed onward. Ever since beginning this journey, Fardale or the og're had always been at his side or close by. Now with his wolf-brother surely dead and Tol'chuk lost among the tunnels, the thought of being down here alone, with only his own heart and mind for company, finally freed his legs. His feet whispered across the stone floor to close the distance to the torch.

"Yes, it's a large chamber," Rockingham said, examining the room from the tunnel's mouth. "Lots of other tunnels lead from here, though. Who knows which way leads out—if any of them do."

Mogweed furtively poked his head into the room. There was no sign of Fardale, or any of the others. His ears strained for evidence of the hissing that had flowed through the tunnels earlier. It was difficult with his heart thundering blood past his ears. "Maybe," he mumbled, "whatever is down here already ate its fill."

"We can only hope so, but can't count on that," Rockingham answered.

"What should we do?"

"There are too many ways out from here. We run a good chance of becoming lost. I say we wait here until sunrise, then try to sneak back out the way we came."

"What about the woman?"

"Nee'lahn?"

"Yes."

Rockingham's face took on a pained expression, but Mogweed could tell it was mostly feigned. "Her life wins us our freedom."

Genuine sorrow winced for a beat in Mogweed's breast, but he quickly pushed it away. He lived. That was all that mattered. Besides, the nyphai race had always been cold to his people.

The silence became awkward after only a few moments. Neither wanted to dwell on this last thought. Words were needed to free them from the memory of Nee'lahn's violet eyes.

"You're truly a shape-shifter?" Rockingham asked. He had settled his back to the wall so he could rest and keep a full view of the chamber.

Mogweed's head bowed slightly, suddenly shamed by his heritage—or at least by the reputation of his people, as undeserved as it might be. "We are called *si'lura*."

"And you can just change your shape whenever you want."

"Yes, once I could."

"How wonderful that must be."

Mogweed raised his head, shocked to hear such a thing stated by a man. Humans had always hated them. Surely the thought of shifting disgusted them.

"To shed an old form and pull on a new one; I wish I could do that sometimes: simply walk away from an old life and start a new one. New face, new body." Rockingham's eyes drifted inward at some private memory. His eyes quickly focused back. "That would be one way to get out of my present predicament," he said with a slight laugh.

This man was odd, nothing like the people Mogweed had expected to find on this side of the Teeth. In his wood, humans had always been the hunters, the terror of the forest paths. He wanted to know more of this strange man. "What is this predicament you speak of?"

Rockingham stared at him, his eyes judging and suspicious. Then he sighed and grew resigned. "What does it matter if I tell you? I was sent to fetch a girl from the valley here—a child the lord of this land suspected was a wit'ch."

A tentative smile crept to Mogweed's lips. Surely the man jested with him. He had heard stories of wit'ches, but everyone laughed at such tales.

Rockingham caught his expression. "This is not a fireside fable. The Dark Lord was right. She is a wit'ch."

Doubt thick in his heart, Mogweed wondered if the man was using the trickery of his tongue to try to fool him. "This is the girl the winged monsters asked about?"

"Yes, but she escaped me, and the master will not let that go unpunished. I must either run far away, beyond the Black Heart's reach, or retrieve the girl."

"Where is she?"

Rockingham's features hardened. "How in the Mother's foul grace do I know? If she's smart, she's out running with her tail tucked between her legs and won't stop until she crosses the Great Western Ocean."

"But if you could catch her, you'd be safe?"

"Not only safe, the Dark Lord would shower gifts upon me— gifts of magick and riches."

Mogweed's mouth dried. He slipped beside Rockingham to lean on the wall, too. "Magick? This lord of your people, he has skill in this?"

"Oh, yes, I'd say he has skill." Rockingham shuddered. "He can do some . . . amazing things."

"He must be greatly revered."

Rockingham looked at Mogweed, his face wide with shock, then burst out laughing. *"Revered!"* he said between gasps. "You know, I never heard anyone use *that* word in connection with my august lord." He clapped Mogweed on the shoulder. "I like you, shape-shifter. You have an interesting view of life in our lands."

Mogweed did not know how to respond to this praise, unsure if he was being mocked.

"What brings you to these lands anyway—a shape-shifter who can't shift?"

"We . . . I seek a cure. Books mention a place called A'loa Glen, where powerful magick still resides." Suddenly light dawned in Mogweed. He stood straighter and faced Rockingham. "Is that where your great lord reigns?"

Rockingham's eyes suddenly looked sorrowful, and he shook his head. "I hate to tell you this, friend, but A'loa Glen is a place of myth. I have traveled much of these lands. Such a city does not exist."

The man's words were like stones tossed against Mogweed's chest. It didn't exist? His voice choked in his throat. "Are . . . are you sure?" He glanced at his body: the thin arms, the wan skin so weak that clothing had to be worn to protect it. He couldn't be stuck like this forever! "You must be wrong!"

"I don't wish to hurt you, and would let you have your dreams, but such a place truly was destroyed long ago, sunk under the sea."

"Then how am I to free my body?" This question was not meant for Rockingham, only for his own crying spirit.

Still the man answered, his voice a shrug. "My master could do it, I'm sure. His magick is without equal."

Mogweed's heart tensed. He grabbed at this hope and clutched it to his chest. "He would do this?"

"My lord is not one to grant wishes easily. But who knows? If I presented you to him as a friend . . ." His voice suddenly soured. "But that's impossible. I could not show my face in that court, not after failing him."

"But if you had the girl!" Mogweed said. His mind ground on this new hope. Maybe all was not lost. "You mentioned a shower of gifts—including magick."

"Of course, with the child we could ask for anything. But I see no girl here."

Mogweed sagged. There had to be a way!

"But who knows?" Rockingham said. "I still might come across this girl. And with you helping me, perhaps we could yet catch her."

Mogweed's fists clenched with the hope. He turned to Rockingham, his lips determined, his voice just as sure. "I *will* help you." For a moment, Mogweed thought he caught the hint of a sly smile behind Rockingham's eyes, but then in a breath the man's face seemed guileless again, open with invitation. Mogweed added, but now with less certainty, "I will help you catch the girl."

"YOU MEAN TO KILL THIS WIT'CH?" KRAL ASKED THE ELV'IN, struggling not to reach across and throttle Meric's thin throat. He knew the elv'in referred to the girl Elena. What was this madness concerning the child? He had been with her almost an entire day, and she seemed no different than any child of her age: no magick, just a scared wisp of a girl.

"What concern is it of yours, man of the mountains?" Meric said as he followed the ridged back of the og're across the last of the chasm floor. Their destination lay just ahead—a fissure cleaved into the chasm wall. "If I should slaughter the wit'ch, I would be ridding this valley of a plague."

"This is not your land, elv'in. You will not kill anyone of this valley on the whim of prophecy."

Meric twisted to face Kral. "Do not try to stop me, or you will discover how swiftly an elv'in can kill."

"You threaten when you should be begging forgiveness," Kral said and thumbed his ax free of its catch at his belt. Without his even glancing at it, the ax's haft dropped snugly to his palm, the handle cold in his hand. If a fight was what this elv'in wanted, he would be glad for the challenge.

Meric's eyes glanced to the ax, and his face closed darkly, his eyelids hooded with threat.

Though the man seemed slight of muscle, Kral recognized a snake when he stepped on one. The ease and sharpness of this fellow's movements suggested hidden dangers, like the folded fangs of the pit viper. Kral tightened his grip, leaving his thumb free to pivot his weapon. He waited. In the ways of the mountain, he would let the elv'in make the first move.

And Meric did—with amazing speed.

The elv'in vanished from where he stood and appeared crouched atop a nearby boulder. A blade so fine and thin it seemed more shadow than substance now stood in the man's fist. The elv'in had jumped too quickly for Kral's eye to follow. Only a whine of warning in the back of his skull had alerted Kral to the motion of his opponent.

The warning sounded again, and Kral barely had time to raise his ax and deflect a thrust toward his belly. He did not even see the attack, only reacted instinctively. His ax struck the sword with such force that Meric's sword arm flew backward. The elv'in stumbled back a few steps, catching his balance, his face bright red with exertion.

Kral judged that these lightning movements taxed the elv'in.

No man could move with such unnatural swiftness for long. The elv'in must be drawing on some strange elemental powers in his blood.

Meric panted between clenched teeth.

Kral hoped he could survive until the man tired. He carried the ax in both hands now, and the muscles of his arms bulged with tension. Meric squinted one eye at him and raised the tip of his sword.

Suddenly the character of the light in the cavern blew apart. The weak elv'in's light was engulfed by a blood radiance. Both combatants swung to the source of it.

Tol'chuk stood fully upright, towering over the two men, with an arm raised high above his head. In his hand rested a stone the size of a bull's heart. It blazed forth with a blinding radiance, as if the og're's rage was given form. "Stop!" he boomed into the cavern, his voice echoing to the walls. "You swore oaths! You be brothers now. Among og'res, brother does not kill brother!"

It was not Tol'chuk's words or even the blazing red stone that dropped Kral's ax arm. It was the pain laced with shame in the og're's expression. Suddenly Kral's face flushed with a shame of his own. Meric also lowered his head, and the sword vanished from his hand. Where it had disappeared to, Kral could not say. No scabbard hung from the el'vin's belt.

"Why do you fight?" Tol'chuk said, lowering his arm. "Over this wit'ch? Kral, you speak and act as if you know this female."

Kral could not lie, at least not again. He kept his voice low. "I suspect I know who the elv'in speaks of. She is but a child."

Meric spoke next. "Child or not, she is a monster. I will kill her. All who aid her are creatures of evil and will die beside her."

"I know this child. I saw what tried to kill her—there lie your monsters! Those who help her have shown themselves to be honorable and of noble spirit. I will gladly stand by their side and die if need be."

Kral's words shook the tight resolve of Meric's features. "But the oracle of Selph warned—"

"I care not for the words of some soothsayer," Kral said.

"Words of prophecy are often spoken in such twisted tongues. Only rock speaks plain and true."

Tol'chuk's crystal had begun to fade. He folded it into a pouch on his thigh. "I agree with the mountain man," he said, his expression sour with memory. "Oracles do not always speak plain."

Kral added, "And innocent blood once spilled cannot be returned. The child has done nothing to warrant a knife to the heart. I will judge her by her actions, not by prophesied words from across the sea."

Meric, his face held stolid, swung his eyes between Tol'chuk and Kral. "Your words are spoken from your hearts," he said. "I will give them thought."

"So, wit'ch or not, you will not harm the child?"

Meric stared at him, darted a glance to Tol'chuk, then spoke. "I will hold my sword—for the moment."

Tol'chuk clapped his hands together. "Good. We go."

Kral nodded and hitched his ax.

Meric turned on a heel and followed the og're. Kral studied the man's back. Behind his eyes, Kral's skull still buzzed with echoes of a distant warning. As a man of the mountain, one with the rock, he had probed Meric when the elv'in had promised to stay his hand, judging for the truth behind the man's words. Nee'lahn's final words to Kral had been proven correct: Meric was *not* to be trusted.

The elv'in had lied.

32

Elena gasped and backed against the wall of hewn rock, her eyes wide on the awakening statue. As her shoulder struck stone, the moon'falcon flew from its perch with a squawk and winged away, a streak of light fleeing from the miracle before them. From the corner of her eye, she saw it flash into the tunnel exiting the chamber, escaping back the way they had come. A few goblins jumped at the bird as it flew, but a piercing screech retreating down the tunnel told her the falcon had escaped.

Yet even the loss of her bird did little to sway her attention. Before her eyes, crystal stone melted to liquid light—first the sculpted head, then the boy's body. Like a rose whose petals were opening to the sun, the sculpture stretched up on legs of radiance.

As stunned as Elena was by this miraculous event, one other sensation intruded—pain. She clutched her right hand to her chest. It blazed with a fire as radiant as the boy's light, as if the ruby color in her skin had become a flaming glove too tight for her hand. Tearing her eyes from the boy, she stared at her hand. It looked the same. No flames engulfed the fist held to her breast.

She tucked her hand within the folds of her shirt, trying to stanch the ghost fire. In the shadows of the cloth, the burning skin faded to a bruised ache. Holding her hand there, buried close to her heart, she realized that it must be shielded somehow from the boy's light. Still, a part of her tingled with an insane urge to rush to the source of the light and merge that power with her own. She trembled. A strange combination of attraction and repulsion fought within her breast. Yet, remembering the madman's warning to her not to touch the statue, she kept her feet in place and her hand hidden.

She glanced to where the scarred man named Re'alto stood among his goblins, and found him staring at her. Goblins pranced in agitation about his legs, their tails lashing back and forth. The change in the statue had obviously spooked them. One goblin tried to scramble up the headmaster's leg, digging gouges in his thigh with its sharp claws. The man did not move except to bat the beast away. Blood ran in thick rivulets down his leg, but still his eyes remained fixed on her.

He seemed to know he had caught her eye. From across the distance, he mouthed a word to her. Though no voice spoke, she knew what word his mouth formed, his lips twisted with hate: *Wit'ch.*

She cringed from his sneer and mad eyes, trying to pull back into the rock itself to escape his loathing. Fortunately, Uncle Bol slipped to her side, stepping between her and the madman's gaze. He placed an arm around her shoulders. Relieved, she hid within his embrace.

"It's as if Chi is here," her uncle mumbled beside her, his eyes never leaving the statue. "You can feel a trace of the ancient spirit in the air."

Elena sank deeper into his arms. She, too, sensed the echo of some force from ages past. This spirit called to her blood, urging her forward. Yet her hand still ached and throbbed with remembered flames, a warning to stay away.

She heard her uncle mumble something. The tremble she heard in his voice drew her attention from her thoughts. Uncle Bol wore a sad smile, his eyes shining moist in the light. "I wish Fila were here to see this," he said as he hugged her tight.

His words and touch awakened the sorrow Elena had boxed

away in her heart for all those she had lost—her mother, her father, her aunt, her brother, and in some ways, even herself. Through tears, she stared toward the center of the chamber.

Er'ril remained frozen before the statue, as if he had become the sculpture instead. The swordsman's eyes also shone bright in the light, but not with awe or wonder: His face was etched with lines of shock and horror. As Elena watched, Er'ril sank to his knees, his face now even with the boy's. "I'm sorry," he said so hoarsely Elena barely heard the words.

The statue reached toward the swordsman with its iron hand. The sculpted fist opened, and the boy placed the metal palm on Er'ril's shoulder. Its touch sent a shiver through the man. "No," the boy said, his voice a wind whistling through a crystal flute. "I am the one who is sorry. I failed you all."

ER'RIL WATCHED THE BOY'S PAINED EXPRESSION DEEPEN. HE WAS SURE his own face mirrored the boy's. Er'ril's voice cracked with tears. "I killed you, slaughtered you upon my sword." In his mind's eye, he pictured the spill of blood welling across the oiled wood.

The boy's grip on his shoulder tightened, and his voice gained substance. Er'ril even heard the accent of the boy's coastal home. "I have not much time to speak. Unleashed of the crystal, my spirit will soon dissipate. But know this, Er'ril of Standi, you did not kill all of me. I still live. Your blade only cut from me that which every good man would wish killed in themselves."

"Your words make no sense. I remember you lying dead on the floor of the inn."

Crystal lips smiled sadly on Er'ril. "Have you never discovered the truth of what happened that night?" The boy seemed to pull inward. "So much time has passed, yet so little wisdom has been gained," he said softly. "I should never have failed my brothers."

"Fail? It was the foul traitor Greshym who played black tricks on us all. You were but an innocent pawn in his games."

"I wish it were so, knight of the Order. But you are wrong.

Greshym and your brother did not shirk their duties. When the spell was cast and the magick unleashed, we all finally knew what was truly asked of us. At first, we had thought our deaths would be the only price. But as the magick swirled, we learned the cost was much steeper." The boy choked on his next words. "I saw and panicked. The other mages stood their ground while I fled."

Er'ril pictured again the ring of wax, his brother Shorkan yelling in shock, and the boy fleeing his place in the circle. "What happened? What was so direly asked?"

The boy's voice lowered to a strained whisper. "For the Book to be forged, we all had to make a sacrifice. The pure and good in each of us had to be drawn out and imbued into the Book." The boy's voice cracked to a stop.

Er'ril stayed quiet and waited for the grip of old memories to loose their hold on the boy's tongue.

"B-but more was asked! When all that was good in us drew to the Book, we would *not* die!" The boy glanced to Er'ril, his eyes wide with horror. "The evil and foul in us would yet *live!*"

His words chilled Er'ril. He remembered Greshym's ruined face cowled in shadow on the streets of Winterfell—a sickness walking in the form of his old friend. "I saw Greshym," he mumbled, "draped in the robes of Gul'gotha: a darkmage."

The boy lowered his head. "That was the final price. For us to forge a book to defy the Dark Lord, a part of us had to be given to him. A balance had to be achieved. For our goodness and light to become the Book, a debt had to be paid. That which was foul and sick was gifted to Gul'gotha, a tool to be used as the monster saw fit." The boy's iron hand tensed on Er'ril's shoulder. "I could not pay that price."

"So you ran."

"I was too late. The splitting of my spirit had started and could not be stopped. As I broke the warded ring around us, that which was evil in me broke through and attacked you."

Er'ril remembered the shaggy, fanged creature. "The beast I slew in the inn," he said, "that foulness came from you?"

The boy nodded. "While you fought, I fled through the breach in the ring, denying the Book my goodness. In my panic, my spirit, imbued still with Chyric energies, sought a familiar place. I found myself back at the school and sensed that a mage yet lived—Master Re'alto, dying of wounds here in this subterranean hold. I cured him and held his life with my magick. I sensed there would come a time when I could undo the damage my fear created and absolve my shame. So I crystallized my spirit, hid it here with a guardian, and waited. I knew you would come. When you slew my evil half, we were linked, you and I, by bonds of time and place."

"For what end? What do you want of me?"

"We must both finish what your brother Shorkan started. The Book is not complete. I must join my spirit with the others to complete the spell started five hundred winters ago."

"But how?"

"You must take me to the Book—" The boy swung to face the girl. Elena cowered against the wall. "—with the wit'ch. All must be brought together."

Er'ril pulled his shoulder free of the boy's hand. "The Book is far from here. To carry your statue—"

"You will not have to. You have brought me a talisman." The boy held up his iron hand, which had once been the ward of A'loa Glen. He clenched it back into a fist shape. "You must carry this to pierce the magickal veil around the sunken city. But I will make your ward more than a lump in your pocket. I will—" The boy suddenly winced with pain. His image seemed less fluid, thicker, like clotting blood. It seemed more an effort for the boy to move now. "I cannot hold my spirit free of the crystal much longer. Time runs short. I must move into a new vessel or return to crystal form."

"What must I do?" Er'ril had a hand raised as if to help, but his hand hovered, unsure what to do.

"I will join the ward." The boy held the iron fist toward Er'ril. "This will be my new vessel. Once I join, I will not be able to speak to you again."

"But I have—"

"I must leave you." The boy's voice had grown faint. His light faded along the edges, and the crystal lost its sharpness. The boy's image blurred. As Er'ril watched, the light and substance that had once been both boy and statue began to draw into the iron fist. The boy's voice came back to him, as if far away. "I can answer only one more question, swordsman."

Er'ril's mind whirled with a thousand questions. There were countless answers he had wanted for five centuries to hear. As he fought his tongue free of the tangle of questions, each vying to be asked, one question slipped from his lips. For endless winters, he had regretted never asking this before. He would not lose his chance now.

"Boy, what is your name?"

The boy remained quiet for a moment. Er'ril saw a single tear slide across the boy's cheek, a tear of thanks. "De'nal. My name is De'nal."

"I will not forget." Er'ril bowed his head.

When he raised his eyes, the boy's form had faded to an insubstantial haze, crystal giving way to pure power. The iron ward hung in the air and drew the energies of soul and magick into itself. Just before the light fully faded, he heard De'nal's voice whisper in his ear, "You are forgiven."

Then, in the last spark of light, a mere nimbus around the iron fist, Er'ril saw the ward fall to the floor. As iron struck rock, the light vanished and blackness swallowed all away. In the darkness, Er'ril allowed himself to weep for a boy slain on his sword so long ago.

Book Five

THUNDER

33

Tol'chuk stared into the fissure and scratched at the ridge of bone above his eye. He could have sworn he had spied a wisp of light flowing from far ahead, a radiance of unusual character. The language of the og'res had over a dozen words describing the quality of light in tunnels and caves, yet Tol'chuk found his tongue unable to describe what he had seen. When he had finally reached the mouth of the fissure, intrigued by the radiance, the light had suddenly blinked away. Tol'chuk continued to stare. Was the darkness playing tricks on his tired eyes?

He knew, though, that his eyes were sound and his sight sharp, and one other factor gave substance to the reality of the glow: With the vanquishing of the light, the pressure upon his blood to pursue this path had suddenly vanished. He suddenly felt no compulsion from the Heart of his people to continue. This intrigued him more than the light itself. What had happened?

Behind him, Tol'chuk heard the plodding tread of Kral and Meric as they caught up to him. Tol'chuk sighed. The og're had hurried forward, tired of the heavy-edged silence that encased his two companions.

"So where's this light?" Kral said. The mountain man placed one hand against the chasm wall, his chest heaving deeply in the thick air.

Meric ran his palm across his shredded shirt, trying to put some semblance of order to the scraps that hung about his shoulders. The black stain along his pant leg had grown, his wound beginning to weep again. Meric stood leaning all his weight on his uninjured leg, too short of breath even to speak. His eyes, though, spoke of his waxing irritation with their situation.

"The light be gone," Tol'chuk said. He stood staring into the tunnel ahead, unsure where to go next, his heartstone offering no direction.

"You said your friend went this way," Kral said. "Maybe he found a way out."

"I feel no breeze," Tol'chuk said. "I smell no *nelodar*."

"Smell what?"

"Og're word. Air outside a cave, clean of tunnel smells," he mumbled, suddenly distracted. Tol'chuk squinted his eyes. The shadows deep in the tunnel, along the left wall, had seemed to shift toward him for a moment. Tol'chuk tensed as he studied the path ahead. The shadows continued to lie still. Maybe he was mistaken—then he noted movement again! A growl of warning burst from his thick chest.

"What is it?" Kral said, his ax already in his hand.

"Something comes."

Meric hobbled beside them, his thin sword now also pointed down the tunnel. "Goblins?"

Tol'chuk was not sure and left the elv'in's question unanswered. The three stood across the fissure mouth.

"Can you make that foul light of yours any brighter?" Kral hissed at Meric.

The elv'in raised his green stone to his lips and blew across its surface. Like an ember of coal in a fading hearth, it flared brighter. Meric held the stone higher, casting its light deeper within the tunnel.

With the increased illumination, two eyes reflected back the light from a cloak of shadows—eyes of amber.

"What is it?" Kral whispered.

A stone's throw down the tunnel, it stalked fully into the light. It glared at the light and growled at them.

"A wolf!" Kral tensed and shifted his ax for a better grip.

Tol'chuk placed a claw on the mountain man's arm. "No, it be my friend."

The og're's words reached the wolf, and its growling waned to a low rumble that showed the beast to be wary of the others.

Tol'chuk called to his wolf-brother. "It be safe, Fardale. Come."

Fardale padded forward slowly, still careful. His eyes met Tol'chuk's, and images flowed into the og're's skull.

Tol'chuk heard Meric complain, the sound seeming to come from a distance away. "We came all this way and risked our lives for that? Your dog?"

"Fardale be not a wolf," Tol'chuk answered in a distracted tone, trying at the same time to interpret the thoughts of the si'lura. "He be my bloodbrother. We share heritage."

The images from Fardale fought to sort themselves in Tol'-chuk's skull. A seed of understanding slowly bloomed. Something miraculous had happened down this tunnel, but the details were unclear. *A light that burned. Flesh that flowed like a river.* The images were mixed with sorrow and pain, as if something Fardale had fiercely desired had slipped from his grasp. Heartache and wonder were etched on the images from his brother in blood.

"Where are the others?" Meric asked beside him. "You said they had lights."

Tol'chuk nodded. "Fardale, where be they?"

The wolf twisted his nose and looked back the way he had come, indicating with his nose the direction of the others.

"Looks like they kept on going," Kral said. "And so should we. We found your wolf. Let's find our way out of here."

Fardale's eyes settled back on the og're. Tol'chuk spoke. "Did the others find a way out?"

One image formed in Tol'chuk's mind: *goblins.* Hundreds of goblins. Fardale sent him an image of a wolf retreating down a tunnel as goblins scurried past in such a frantic hurry that they ignored the slinking wolf.

"Well?" Kral asked. "What are we waiting for? The wolf is not going to answer you."

Tol'chuk broke his gaze from Fardale to face Kral. "He did. There be goblins ahead. They have trapped the others."

Kral nodded to the wolf and snorted. "He *told* you that?"

"There be much in these lands you have yet to learn, mountain man."

"Perhaps, but what I *do* know is that we need a way out. If goblins are busy that way, we'll try another way. Maybe the far wall of the chasm has a way up."

"You would leave the others to the goblins?"

"It is no concern of mine." Kral waved Tol'chuk's words away. "I have friends who are in danger above. That is where my responsibility lies."

"But Fardale has sent me pictures of the others. They be of your race and be guarded only by a warrior with one arm. You would leave them to such weak protection?"

Tol'chuk's words forced Kral's eyes wide. "One-armed!" Kral glanced to the wolf with a new measure of respect in his gaze. "It cannot be. Down here? Did your wolf tell ... send ... do whatever the blasted thing it does ... about the others?"

"The warrior guards a female child and a whiskered old man."

"Sweet Mother above, it has to be them!"

"Who?"

"My friends. We must hurry!" Kral started down the tunnel, edging past the wolf. Fardale also swung around to follow.

Tol'chuk took a step in pursuit when a voice raised behind him. "I will not go with you," Meric said.

Kral spun on a heel. He still had his ax gripped tight. "You swore an oath."

Meric shrugged. "I have kept my sworn promise to aid you until the og're's friend was found." He pointed to the wolf. "There he is. That is *all* I swore, and I am now free of my word. I will take my light and search elsewhere for my bird—alone. I find your company tiresome."

"You monster!" Kral spat. "We need your light."

"It is no concern of mine," Meric mocked, using the same words Kral had spoken but a breath ago, even the same disdainful tone.

Meric took a step away from the fissure mouth. "I will give you one thing to help you on your way . . ."

Kral waited, his brows bunched like thunderheads.

Meric smiled, but there was no mirth in his eyes. "I give you my best wishes."

Kral howled in rage and lunged toward the elv'in.

Tol'chuk caught the man across the chest as he tried to barrel past him. "No! Do not shed blood." Kral tried to plow his way forward, but Tol'chuk did not budge. It was said an og're could take root in rock and hold his place. "Meric be a free man, not a thrall. He has honored his word to us."

Meric nodded toward the og're, but his lips still sneered at Kral.

"We cannot hope to help my friends without a light," Kral argued. "You would have them die for this one's convenience."

"My eyes be sharp in the dark," Tol'chuk said. "I will lead you to your friends. The others have lights. If we reach them, then we will not need the elv'in's stone."

Kral still seethed, far from convinced by the og're's words.

"I will be going," Meric said from behind. "Good luck, og're. I wish *you* well."

As Tol'chuk struggled against the renewed effort of the mountain man to pass him, his og're eyes spied a glint among the shadows filling the tunnel ahead. "Wait!" he said. "Look!"

All eyes swung down the tunnel. As they watched, the glint became a glow, and the glow grew to a distinct light, an azure radiance that wafted up and down and swung in wide swoops.

"It is my falcon!" Meric cried, as the bird flew closer.

In a streak of brilliance, the moon'falcon swooped over Tol'chuk's head and landed upon the elv'in's raised wrist. The bird held its wings slightly spread as its breast fluttered in exhaustion. Its light waxed and waned slightly as it danced upon its perch.

"He can now spare his stone," Kral mumbled sourly at Tol'chuk's shoulder. "He's found his louse-ridden bird and can use *its* glow to light his coward's way out of here."

Meric must have heard the mountain man. He spoke as he

studied his bird and picked a loose feather from its wing. "No, I will still keep my stone."

Kral swore and dove forward. Tol'chuk still succeeded in restraining him, but only halfheartedly. Even Tol'chuk found the elv'in's actions more than a little petty. Kral's words had been fair and correct. Meric did not need the stone, while they needed it sorely.

The elv'in's next words restored the og're's faith in the thin man. "I *will* keep my stone, but I will also go with you."

"Why?" spat Kral. "I suspect this sudden change of heart and charity. Why help us now?"

"I offer no charity." Meric fingered the bird's crown of feathers. He nodded to the falcon. "The bird's nails have silvered. It is the sign." Meric tried to keep his voice in its usual detached tone, but his excitement could not be hidden. "He has found our lost king."

NEE'LAHN KEPT HER BACK AGAINST THE TRUNK OF THE OLD ELM. Her fingers delved the crannies of its bark. Nearby, she heard the mare nicker with fear as it hid at the edge of the wood. The horse had skittered into the forest as far as its tied lead would allow, attempting to blend into the trees' shadows.

What the mare shied from loomed near Nee'lahn's shoulders.

She tried to ignore the skal'tum's towering figure. The creature still licked its lips with a long black tongue. The other skal'tum, relieved of guarding her, had its turn to feast on the remains of the slaughtered stallion. The sound of snapping bone and sucking lips drove her eyes far from the sight.

Her fingers worked the bark harder with her nails; the pain kept her from running in terror from the creatures. The beasts had not even bothered to tie her up, confident that escape from them was impossible. And they were right. They moved as quickly as striking snakes, and their eyes were sharp in the dim moonlight. Escape for her was impossible.

As she waited, her eyes kept drifting to the root-shrouded entrance to the tunnel. Rockingham had betrayed her, but as much as she hated the scoundrel, at least he had been able to help the si'lura escape. And if Rockingham found Kral and the og're among the twisting tunnels and could warn them, they too might be able to find another exit to the caves and slip away from the claws of her captors. Her life could at least buy these others their freedom—or so she hoped.

She sighed as her fingers worked. For as long as possible, she must maintain Rockingham's lie. Let the skal'tum think she was the sister of the child they sought. It kept her alive and kept the beasts here—away from the cottage. She hoped Er'ril and the girl had been able to escape the old man's farm and had run far away from here. The longer she helped maintain the ruse the better their chance of escape. So she bit her tongue and waited.

Beside her, the skal'tum must have caught her eyes on the tunnel. "Fear not, little one, your ssisster will come." It laughed at her. "Such a ssweet reunion. I may even let her taste your heart."

She did not answer the creature, just ignored it, refusing to let her fear show. They might kill her, but she would offer them no sport.

Her nails finally dug through the last of the elm's bark to reach the meaty pulp. She rested her fingers there, the tree's cool flesh soothing her torn flesh. She stood there. Lightning played upon the peaks of the nearby Teeth. Thunderheads brewed. The storm that the black clouds heralded would be one to shake the roots of the world. She closed her eyes on the warring sky and began her preparations. She reached toward the tree's spirit.

When the skal'tum came for her, Nee'lahn planned on giving them no sport—but she would give them a fight!

34

Elena crouched in the blackness of the cave. The darkness was so profound she felt it press against her skin. If not for her uncle's arm around her shoulder, she would have thought herself sucked to another plane where light had yet to be imagined. Never had she experienced such total darkness. Her eyes stretched wide, seeking light.

Her uncle slipped his arm from around her shoulder, breaking her tether with the world. Now only the rock under her feet remained to convince her the world still existed. Her only solace was that the burning in her right hand had completely faded with the light. She hugged herself tight, suddenly wishing the moon'falcon had not abandoned her. Its light would be most welcome.

As if the gods had heard her, brightness suddenly burst back into the chamber. Blinded by the explosive return of light, it took a moment for Elena's eyes to blink back the glare. Her uncle raised the lantern. He had flamed the wick back to life and twisted the oil key to a bright glow. He held the lamp high.

In the lantern's light, so much duller than the crystal radiance, Elena saw Er'ril crouch down and retrieve the iron fist from the stone floor. He studied the ward for a moment, a strange expression locked upon his face, then carefully placed it into a pocket of his shirt.

As Er'ril straightened and stood, movement drew Elena's eyes to the back half of the chamber. A cry rose to her lips. The mass of goblins squirmed and roiled around the prostrate form of the mad headmaster. Re'alto lay facedown on the stone floor, his good arm thrust toward where the statue had once stood. He did not appear to be moving—or breathing. A single goblin crept up and lifted Re'alto's hand. The arm hung limp within its claws. The goblin dropped the hand and scooted back in fear.

Er'ril by now had also spotted Re'alto. He took a step toward the former headmaster.

Uncle Bol spoke from beside Elena. "Don't, Er'ril. He's dead. The boy's light was all that sustained him. With the magick gone, his life has fled. From the way those goblins are acting, I suggest we leave him undisturbed."

Er'ril nodded and retrieved the sword he had left with Bol. The sword, though no longer bathed in the light of the statue, still seemed to shine with more than lamplight. Lines of radiance danced across its surface.

"We should try for the passage through which we entered," Er'ril said. "There are fewer goblins."

"Be warned," Uncle Bol said, "that any aggression on our part could ignite their wrath. They have just seen their statue vanish before their eyes, and Re'alto, whom they worshipped, lies dead at their feet." Uncle Bol nodded to where several goblins huddled together, pointing claws toward them. "I believe we are being blamed for their losses."

"Then the sooner we vanish, the better." Er'ril nodded for Elena to approach him. "We need a distraction," he said. "Something to spook them away for a heartbeat and buy us time to slip free."

Elena nodded but could not fathom what the swordsman thought she could do.

Her uncle seemed even less sure of Er'ril's plan. He kept his voice hushed and his eyes quick upon the goblins surrounding them. "I don't think it's a good idea to scare them in their present state, Er'ril. The creatures are stirred up enough already. A panic could—"

"We will be meat in their bellies if we don't hurry." Er'ril lowered to one knee beside Elena. He kept his sword raised toward the clutch of rock'goblins. "Now, child, I showed you the way of healing with your uncle. You now need to learn another small bit of magick."

Elena balked, her mouth going dry. She felt a fist squeeze her heart. Wild magick scared her more than the fangs and claws of the goblins. "Is there no other way? Maybe Uncle Bol is right. We could just let them calm down and maybe they'll go away."

The hissing around them had increased to a screeching pitch. As she watched, more goblins flowed into the room from the two passages. Their musk bittered the air with their fear. The goblins closest to the collapsed body of the headmaster began stamping their left feet on the stone floor. Soon others took up the cadence, the sound echoing around the cave. The beat throbbed, and the eyes around them burned.

Uncle Bol whispered, "Maybe Er'ril is right."

She found both men staring at her. Her heart beat an intimate harmony with the goblins' stamping. Still, she freed her tongue from the roof of her mouth. "I will try."

"Good girl." Er'ril passed his sword to her uncle. "Keep the sword in sight. They seem to respect it." Once Uncle Bol had awkwardly raised the tip of the blade, Er'ril turned to Elena, reached out, and gripped her right hand. His urgency and tension flowed into her from the tightness of his fingers, yet he kept his voice calm. This she appreciated more than his sword. "This will work, Elena. Trust me. Magick is closely associated with light. You saw this with De'nal's statue and experienced it when sunlight or moonlight ignited your powers. You know this in your heart, don't you?"

She nodded.

"One of the easiest workings of magick is simply revealing its presence."

Er'ril must have sensed her confusion from the way her eyebrows scrunched together. "Magick runs hidden through your blood and body. Only the red hand marks you as a wielder of spiritual power. Magick, like the flame in a lantern, desires to flow free from you, to reveal itself to those around you. But like a lantern door closed upon the flame, your body hides this truth. Yet I can show you how to open your door and let your light shine forth."

Elena remembered what could happen when her magick "shone" through her. Both of her parents had been burned by its flame. "I will kill everything around me," she warned.

"No, I do not ask you to cast your magick out. That *can* kill unless done in a controlled manner. I can't teach you that. All I ask is that you open yourself and let others see what is inside you, see the flame within."

"Why? How will that help?"

"Goblins fear the light and can sense magick. If you reveal yourself to them, they may be baffled or awed enough to allow us to escape."

Her eyes studied the goblins writhing around them. She saw the headmaster's body picked up and carried on the backs of several larger goblins. It was done with a touching reverence. Others cleared a path so the body could be removed unmolested from the chamber. The goblins seemed to have held the headmaster in great respect, or at least the magick that dwelt inside.

This thought must have occurred to Uncle Bol, too. "It just might work. It seems they worship magick," he muttered as Re'alto's remains were shuffled away.

"How do I do this?" Her voice trembled, as did her shoulders.

"Easily," Er'ril said. "Since you are not allowing magick to pass from you, a blood ritual is not even needed." He raised his palm to her cheek and rested it there. His eyes looked down into hers, and she felt a quaking in her knees that had nothing to do with the fear around her heart. "Just close your eyes and search inside, as you did with your uncle's body."

She did as he asked, squeezing shut her eyelids, but terror kept her close to the surface. Her ears stayed keen on the stamping and hissing around her, and her nose filled with the acrid scent of goblin bodies. She did not understand what was asked of her and shivered.

Suddenly his arm wrapped around her body. He held her cheek pressed against his chest. "Shh, ignore all that is around you. Shut off your senses." The odor of the swordsman's oiled hair replaced the stench of the goblins in her nose. His whispering filled her ears, pushing back the echoes of the chamber.

"They're finished with Re'alto," she barely heard her uncle say. "If you're going to do something, do it quick."

His words should have panicked her, but Er'ril's arm tightened about her, pulling her away from her fears. She allowed herself to drift within his embrace. His breath, warm and calm, brushed her cheek. "See yourself," he said. "See the woman in the child, like the oak in the acorn. Find your strength and you will find your magick."

His words and heat created waves of sensations in Elena that she could not express. She did not even try, allowing herself simply to be, to put aside all she knew about herself and just exist. As she floated in a place without thought or substance, a light grew within the darkness. No, that was not true. The light did not grow, she just drew near it, closed in upon it like a swallow swooping to its nest. The radiance had not appeared out of the darkness: It had always been there!

From a far place, she heard Er'ril's voice. "Open your eyes and show us. Show us your flame, Elena."

She now understood. Pushing Er'ril's arm from her, she stood up. She did not have to hide who she was! Once on her feet, she opened her eyes and unbound her heart, opening a door that had been closed since she was young and had learned the world does not want to see one's true self. She put her inhibitions aside and spread her arms wide, encompassing both the chamber and the world. She revealed herself without shame or remorse. Both who she had been and who she was now—but most important of all, who she would become!

Like a window opened on the sun, her magick blazed forth, driving all shadows from the room.

ER'RIL'S FIRST IMPULSE ON SEEING THE GIRL AWAKEN WITH POWER was to snatch the sword from Bol's stunned fingers and drive the blade through her heart. He even found the sword in his hand. But he fought against this deadly impulse, his knuckles white upon the blade's hilt. Even Bol backed a step away from the child. The old man's mouth sagged open in surprise, her light etching his features in stark lines.

Such power, Er'ril thought. He had never imagined. Even a mage freshly renewed to Chi did not shine with such brilliance. Elena stood with her arms wide, her body bursting with a shattering light. Shadows were not even cast by those who stood— instead the light seemed to bend around them, folding all within its heart.

Yet the child within the light frightened Er'ril. She was no longer a scared youngster clinging to those around her, confused and wary of her power. A confidence shone forth from her face and body that came close to eclipsing her inner light. The release of her radiance had cast her to a place without fear or doubt. Such was not the face of a child or even just a woman, but something close to a goddess. Er'ril spotted flares of increased brilliance in a halo about her body as if the stars themselves fought to be near.

As wondrous as she was, Er'ril found his eyes fixing on a single feature of the girl. Her lips, full and parted slightly, smiled on sights beyond Er'ril's vision. In that smile, Er'ril saw the woman she might become: a wise, strong woman no man could control. Er'ril found his breath thick in his throat as he stared. Something stirred in his chest, something he had thought long dead: *hope*.

This effect on his heart shook him more than her power. She is but a child, he told himself. Yet he knew he was mistaken. Three faces stared out from this one shining visage—the child Elena, the woman Elena, and something that was not Elena, that was not even from this world.

Just then, a goblin wobbled up to Er'ril, its eyes glued on Elena, and bumped into his leg. It clung to Er'ril's pant leg for a moment, like a ship seeking a safe harbor. Before Er'ril could knock it away, it loosened its grip and stumbled toward the girl. Er'ril meant to bring up his sword and stop it, but the goblin suddenly crashed flat upon its face. Its tiny form quivered for a breath then lay still upon the rock floor—too still. Dead, thought Er'ril.

He tore his eyes from the girl and saw that the chamber floor was littered with a sea of collapsed goblins. He watched other rock'goblins drawn forward from the tunnels by the light. Like blind moths, they stumbled into the chamber's brilliance; but within a few bumbled steps, they weakened and fell crying to the stone floor in a tangle of limbs. Others grew wise to what was happening and fled back from the light, disappearing down the tunnels.

"The light," Bol said from nearby. "It slays them. Is Elena doing that?"

Er'ril found he needed to speak to keep himself distracted from the child. "I don't think so. The light is a mere reflection of her magick. It's not a force that should harm."

"Goblins shun light." Bol waved his hand over the piles of deceased creatures. "Maybe for a good reason. Maybe light is inimical to their nature. This much light, this much power, is perhaps deadly."

Er'ril's eyes were drawn back to the girl. Their words must have pierced the glow around Elena and reached her ears. Her lips were no longer smiling.

ELENA HAD HEARD HER UNCLE SPEAK. THOUGH HIS WORDS SEEMED like birds fluttering from far in a forest, their meaning reached her. Her eyes focused back to the chamber. She saw the goblins piled around her, necks and limbs twisted in unnatural angles. There were so many! She had killed hundreds of the poor creatures. She cried out, and the light shining from her crashed to the rock and vanished. She stood quivering—an island in a dark sea of dead goblins.

Now only Uncle Bol's lantern lit the chamber. He came to her, bringing the light. She shied from its glow. The inner light, the core of who she was, had killed; now this small brightness accused her of her foul deed. Elena swung from the lantern's glow and accosted the swordsman. "You said it wouldn't harm them," she cried in a voice that threatened a flood of tears.

Her words wounded him. His eyes winced and his lips frowned. "I'm sorry, Elena. I did not fully understand the nature of these creatures or the brilliance of your magick."

She covered her mouth with her hands. The brilliance of her magick! His words sickened her. The goblins had done them no harm except maybe harangue them a bit, and they had also played a role in returning the ward to Er'ril. For their effort, she had brought them death. Her eyes saw many smaller figures tangled among the larger goblins. She had even slain their children.

She moved her palms to cover her face. She refused to see any more.

Uncle Bol placed a hand on her shoulder. "It's not your fault, honey. We didn't know. If anyone is to blame, we are. We were the ones who asked you to do this."

She shook free of his grip and lowered her hands to glare at him. "You don't understand!"

Her uncle's eyes widened.

A bitter laugh slipped from her. "I enjoyed the power! I never felt so whole and free. I basked in my magick, let it roll through me and freeze away all doubt. And while I embraced this light, joyful in its glow, it slew those around me."

"Honey, it's all right. You didn't know."

She turned her back on her uncle. Not just because his words failed to offer any solace, but because she was afraid he would see the truth in her eyes. She had already said too much. Sobbing, she fell to her knees on the floor.

What she had not told her uncle and was even afraid to face herself was that she *had* known. Somewhere deep within her being, she had sensed the death around her, felt their lives snuff out like blown candles. And she had not cared, could not care. She had ignored the bodies crashing at her feet as the magick within her screamed, impossible to ignore. Her heart sang for its release, for the force to flow out into the world. Its song of power so filled her ears, it drowned out the cries of the dying goblins.

Er'ril came and pulled her to her feet, his sword still in his fist. He must have sensed what raged within her. "Raw magick is seductive," he said. "Do not let it fool you."

She tried to pull away, but his arm was strong with hard muscle. He lowered his face until he stared into her eyes. His voice was fierce. "You are still Elena. Do not let your magick define you. It is only a tool." Then his words softened to a whisper. "It speaks with its own voice. That voice, I know, can be hard to shut out and can often seem like your own soul—but you don't have to listen. You are still Elena: daughter of your parents, sister to your brother, niece to your uncle. You are blood, not magick."

She nodded. His words gave strength to her legs. She allowed herself to be led to Uncle Bol, whose eyes shone bright with concern, and let him wrap his arms around her. She sobbed into his chest, but this time her tears healed rather than ripped her apart.

As she sank into his embrace, the hissing that had been silenced by her magick began again. Only now, no fear etched its surface. Elena pushed from her uncle's arms. The three of them stood among the dead.

"We had better get out of here," Er'ril said.

It was too late. The goblins burst from the tunnels. With the light gone, they now sought the vengeance denied them by the glow of the wit'ch. For the first time, Elena heard a goblin scream.

Er'ril burst forward to meet the rush of beasts, pushing his companions back to the wall. His sword sang among the goblins' writhing bodies. Never had he wielded a weapon with such a fine edge. Its blade sliced bone as easily as air. As he whipped his sword to all sides, goblins piled before him, but others leaped over the carcasses of their brethren to press the attack.

From the corner of his eye, Er'ril saw Bol batting his lamp at the few goblins who tried to get near Elena. The swinging lantern bounced wild shadows across the chamber walls. The old man held his own. The goblins were still wary of the child, as if expecting her to explode with light again. Silently, Er'ril hoped Elena might try but knew he could not ask it of her. She remained too shaken.

He pressed on. If the goblins would let up for a breath, he might be able to forge a path to the nearest tunnel.

They did not. Instead the battle became fiercer. Fearing the girl's power, the goblins targeted Er'ril with their rage. Goblins attacked from so many sides Er'ril could not stop them all. Claws ripped his chest; teeth tore at his legs.

As keen as the edge of his blade was, the hopelessness of the situation touched his heart. He faltered. Goblins swamped him, knocking him backward. He crashed to the stone floor, his head striking hard enough to raise points of dancing light before his stunned eyes. Five goblins straddled his chest and legs. Three pinned his sword arm to the rock. Teeth buried into his forearm.

Biting back the pain, Er'ril struggled under their weight. If only he had his other arm, he thought uselessly, then perhaps he would still have a chance of freeing himself. He heaved against the mass of goblins, determined to roll loose. As he struggled, he felt the ward ripped from his pocket. Curse them, one of the beasts was trying to steal the iron fist again.

He thrust his head up to see which of the thieving creatures was yanking on his pocket. With his neck straining, he eyed the breast pocket of his shirt where he had hidden the ward.

No goblin claw lay there. Instead he saw a sight that almost startled him enough to fling the goblins from his body. Crawling free from his pocket like some metal spider was the iron fist, fingers splayed and digging for purchase. With the fist in sight, Er'ril felt a stabbing jolt at his stumped shoulder. At first, he thought a goblin claw had gouged him. But no, once before he had felt such a burning sting—long ago, when he had lost his arm. It was the sting of magick! As the pain swept away, a new sensation bloomed at his stump. Er'ril could feel his missing arm!

His frantic eyes searched his empty shoulder and told his heart the limb was still gone, but Er'ril would swear he sensed the phantom of an arm now linked to his shoulder.

An arm that ended at the iron fist!

He now felt the cold metal of the ward that gloved his ghost hand. He flexed the iron fingers. Sweet Mother! The boy De'nal's words came back to him: *I will make your ward more than a lump in your pocket.*

Stunned by the sight, he stopped struggling. Taking advantage of his sudden stillness, one of the goblins lunged for his throat, fanged teeth bared to rip. Reflexively, Er'ril reached with an arm that had been gone for centuries. The iron hand flew up and clamped upon the thin neck of the goblin. The bones of its throat cracked under the vice of iron as he squeezed the life from the attacker.

The other goblins saw what happened and piled away from him. They backed in a tangled mass. Er'ril rolled to his feet, sword in one hand. His other hand, the one of sculpted iron, still floated in the air, clutching the limp goblin. He willed the metal hand to open, and the goblin dropped dead to the stone. As Er'ril moved his phantom arm, the iron ward swung through the air seemingly on its own, but Er'ril knew it was not so—he controlled it as he would his own hand.

The rock'goblins shied from the floating threat, their large black eyes narrowed with fear.

But for how long?

Er'ril's question was answered immediately. A new stream of

goblins flowed into the chamber, and their numbers bolstered the others' courage. With an angry hiss, they lunged from all sides. Even their wariness of Elena had faded. Er'ril saw them accost her and her uncle,

Er'ril backed to help them, but even with the aid of his iron hand, he found himself hard-pressed by the mass of attackers. Limping from a deep gash in his left leg, Er'ril struggled toward his companions. Savagely, he ripped into the beasts with silver sword and iron hand, digging a bloody path through the goblins.

Yet even this was not enough.

Stone, now slippery with blood and gore, betrayed his feet. He slipped and tumbled to his knees, an opportunity the goblins snatched up with bloody glee. The beasts engulfed him, swarming up his back, clawed nails digging and ripping. He was again pressed to the cold rock. As teeth tore at his neck, a cry of defeat escaped his throat.

35

KRAL FOLLOWED THE LAST OF THE GOBLINS TOWARD THE END OF THE tunnel. Swinging his ax, he cleaved the skull of a large one that had twisted around to block his path. Kral tried to pull his blade free, but it was caught in bone. He stopped and wiped his wet brow. He and the others had fought their way down the tunnel from the fissure mouth. Strangely, little true resistance had been offered. The goblins had mostly ignored them as they ran. The beasts seemed as determined as his party to reach the tunnel's end.

Something there had the creatures riled.

From the flickering glow ahead, Kral saw that the tunnel ended a stone's throw away. A large chamber lay beyond, and hundreds of goblins, living and dead, crowded the floor of that room.

"They could not have survived," Kral growled, thinking of the small girl and the one-armed swordsman. He yanked his ax free of the dead goblin.

"Do not despair," Tol'chuk said. The og're raked a goblin from his leg and smashed it on the tunnel wall. "Goblins hate light. Where there be light, there be hope."

Suddenly the glow ahead flared brighter. A goblin aflame with burning oil danced in agony across the chamber floor. It ignited two other goblins who mimicked his prance.

"Someone yet fights," Meric said, pushing past them. The thin sword in his hand dripped black blood.

On the elv'in's heels, the wolf sped forward toward the chamber, its injured limb forgotten. A snarl flowed from its throat.

His ax now free, Kral followed. Tol'chuk kept the few straggling goblins from their backs.

The party burst into the chamber, a war yell upon Kral's lips. Still the goblins ignored them, so focused were they on a battle at the far wall. Kral saw the old man from the cottage sloshing burning oil on another goblin while the child hid behind him. But the most intense fighting was just ahead of the pair. A tall pile of goblins writhed upon someone crushed under their weight.

Like a surging wave, the pack of beasts swelled up as the fighter pushed to his knees. For a moment, he seemed about to break free and regain his feet, but then another surge of goblins drove him back down—yet not before Kral saw who fought. Er'ril's face, clenched with effort, one eye bloody and swollen, flashed for a moment before being engulfed again.

Roaring, Kral hacked his way forward; the moon'falcon circled above, a piercing screech issuing from its beak. The others threw themselves against the sea of creatures, but it was like fighting a surging surf. As soon as one onslaught was battered back, a second would strike them. Soon the party split into two. Tol'chuk guarded Kral's back while the wolf and elv'in spun together in a dance of death. The tides of battle pulled the two pairs farther and farther apart.

"Help the old man and the child!" Kral yelled to Meric. The mountain man slashed the neck of a goblin with such might its skull flew across the room. "We'll go for the swordsman!"

Kral didn't know if the elv'in had heard him over the screams of the wounded and dying, but it seemed Meric did shift slightly in the correct direction. Satisfied, Kral swung toward Er'ril. Over his shoulder, the mountain man heard the crack of bone as Tol'chuk kept guard. Kral smiled grimly. An og're, he thought, was as good as having a stone wall at your back. It left Kral free to focus his ax and muscle on the battle ahead.

The mountain man pulled in his rage and began forging a path toward Er'ril, his ax a blur, his motions more instinctive than planned. His mind retreated to a place of memory, to lessons learned long ago.

Kral had mastered the art of the ax from Mulf, an ancient grizzled warrior of the Teeth. It was said that the old man had fought during the D'warf Wars and had held the Pass of Tears by himself for a full day and night. As a lad of only eleven winters, his eyes full of future glory, Kral had sought the elder in his cave high in the Teeth. When he had first caught sight of Mulf, Kral's hopes died in his heart. Mulf, back bent, looked as ancient as the roots of the mountains. His beard, white as early snow, hung so low the old man had to tuck it into his belt to keep from tripping. How could this decrepit wreck teach him anything? Mulf had seemed too weak even to heft an ax, let alone wield it in battle. But after his first lesson with this ancient teacher, the young Kral had found himself seated on his backside in muddy slush, a large bruise on his forehead from where Mulf had clubbed him with the butt of his ax handle. The last thing the youngster remembered was the ax's blade slicing for his head. But in a motion too quick for his eye to follow, the old man had flipped the ax around a thumb and only wood struck his skull instead of sharp iron. That cold morning, ice chilling his backside, Kral learned the first of many lessons from his sharp-eyed teacher—do not underestimate your opponent.

And today he did not!

The goblins might be small of stature, but they were fierce, all muscle and sharp edges. Kral did not let his arm slow or his eye stray from the flurry of claws. His wariness kept more than one goblin's knife from his chest. As he neared where Er'ril fought, the goblins flashed spiked daggers like those that had assaulted them atop the chasm and driven Kral and Tol'chuk over the cliff.

He knocked aside a blade by slicing through the goblin's wrist. The beast howled. Its knife, a claw still wrapped around the hilt, tumbled away. Kral swung his face from the spurt of blood jetting out its amputated wrist—not in disgust, but simply to keep the hot blood from blinding him. Another knife-wielding goblin attacked from the opposite side. There was no time to swing his ax around, so he borrowed his old master's trick and slammed the butt of his ax handle into the beast's eye. Bone cracked under his wood, and the goblin collapsed to the rock.

Kral stepped over the creature and continued his march of death.

ER'RIL SANK UNDER THE MASS OF THE BEASTS, WRESTLING WITH MORE than just the goblins. A part of his spirit was ready to surrender to the struggle—it seemed like he'd been fighting ever since the forging of the Blood Diary. Yet, in his bones, the stubbornness of his Standi roots would not let him truly succumb to despair. No, the centuries of winters weighed heavier upon his shoulders than these slathering goblins. He had already sacrificed so much, waited for so long—he would not die here, not this way!

With a scream on his lips, he kicked goblins from his legs and used his iron hand to throttle beasts that tried to rip his throat or face. His sword arm, when not pinned under the flailing bodies of the creatures, cleaved an area clear for breaths at a time, but never long enough for him to regain his feet or see how Bol and Elena were faring. A wall of rock'goblins continually surrounded him.

Yet, he did not relent, refusing to listen to the whispers of despair.

For a moment, he heard a cry and the word *child* shouted out from across the room, but the hissing and screaming quickly drowned out the voice. But who could have shouted? Had he imagined it?

In a streak of light, he saw the moon'falcon swoop across the cavern roof. The cursed bird must have returned, confused by the tunnels. He thanked the gods for this small blessing. Its sudden light gave the goblins a pause, and he managed to free his arm. Swinging his sword in a savage arc, Er'ril drove the beasts back.

Standing once again, he saw a sight that froze his heart.

A goblin twice the size of a man loomed just a span away. Its arms ran with blood; its fanged mouth grinned with death.

Er'ril stumbled back. Suddenly a jabbing pain blasted up his right leg. His limb gave out. As he fell, he saw a goblin with a dagger drive its blade a second time into his thigh. Knife hit bone, and his vision swelled tight with pain. He flailed and kicked himself free of the knife. Kneeling up, he blindly thrust out his phantom arm. His fist clamped around the knife-wielding creature's throat and squeezed the life from it. He swung the dead goblin, which still hung in his iron fist, and knocked other goblins from his side. He used its limp body as a shield.

Still Er'ril was not quick enough.

A knife buried into his back. Pain blacked his eyes for a breath. When his vision cleared, he saw his iron hand empty, his shield gone. Goblins, several of them armed, loomed before him.

Pain and rage narrowed his eyes. His own death finally lay nearby, a death he had been denied for centuries.

He raised his sword. At times during his long life, he would have welcomed death, wanting that final peace—but not now! Others were counting on him—the girl, the old man, even the child De'nal. He raged against this death.

Pushing onto his already wounded left leg, he ignored the flare of agony in his back and spat blood on the floor. He clenched his sword in a hard fist.

Just as he raised his weapon's tip in invitation, the wall of goblins burst apart, and he saw the hideous king of the goblins rip through its brethren to stalk before him. The creature lifted two of its smaller kind and threw them across the chamber. Er'ril's sword arm trembled. Did he have the strength to face this monster? It towered over Er'ril, twice his height and even broader of shoulder.

Suddenly a familiar voice erupted. "Thank the rock, you still live." Er'ril knew that voice. He saw Kral step around the huge creature. The circle of goblins, now broken, shattered into cowardly pieces and fled. Er'ril's head swam as he twisted his neck. The chamber was now emptying of goblins. He saw those who yet lived slink and hobble from the room, except for the giant, deformed beast before him. Er'ril saw Kral place a hand on its arm. The mountain man must have recognized the horror in Er'ril's eyes. "His name is Tol'chuk. He is a friend."

"What . . . what . . . ?" Er'ril was too dazed to form his question.

"He's an og're. He helped rescue you."

Kral's words reminded Er'ril of the others. He stumbled around, and saw Elena sliding from behind her uncle's back. Bol's clothes hung in shreds; blood splotched his face and chest. As the moon'falcon swung in a loop overhead, the old man offered a weak smile. Er'ril saw two others still moving among the dead goblins. The wolf who had been stubbornly following them nosed the twisted remains near Bol and Elena. Beside the dog stood a tall man with silver hair tied in a long braid. A needle-thin sword hung loose in the stranger's one hand, almost as if he had forgotten it was there. The man's eyes searched the cavern.

Er'ril tipped slightly forward, suddenly dizzy. Before he fell on his face, Kral was there, an arm around his shoulder. "Easy, there. You took some deep wounds."

Elena's voice rang from across the room. Er'ril saw her stretch her right hand to the wound on her uncle's cheek, the red of her hand matching the blood on his skin. "Uncle Bol's hurt, too," she called to them. He heard the tears behind her voice.

Er'ril saw the thin stranger suddenly tense near the girl. The man's sword, forgotten and limp in his hand before, now rose and pointed at Elena. "The mark!" he shouted at her, his eyes staring at her hand. "The mark of the wit'ch!"

Kral suddenly released Er'ril's shoulders. "No!" the mountain man bellowed. Er'ril's legs were too weak to hold him up. The stone floor rushed toward him. He saw Kral lurch toward the thin man but knew the mountain man was too far away. "No, Meric! No!"

Er'ril's vision blurred as the silver-haired man lunged toward the girl, quick as a forest cat. Elena barely had time to turn her head as the sword aimed for her heart.

Before the sword struck, a cool blackness pulled Er'ril away.

36

ELENA SAW THE SWORD DIVE FOR HER CHEST, AND HER ARM SHOT UP in a warding gesture. The figure of her attacker was a blur of motion her eye could hardly follow. Only his sword, held steady and firm as it swept toward her, glinted fine and sharp-edged in the weak light. A cry rose in her throat, but fear trapped it there. She opened her mouth in a silent scream.

Yet a cry did reach her ears—a piercing wail of rage. As the sword lunged, a streak of lightning came between her and the weapon's tip—the moon'falcon! She saw the bird impaled upon the blade, its screech still echoing from the walls.

The impact of its tiny body seemed to travel up the sword and stun the attacker. The man halted his sword thrust, his feet stumbling beneath him. He held his sword out, the weapon shaking in his hand. Its tip hung less than a thumb's width from the thin shift over Elena's chest. The moon'falcon, speared through the breast, fluttered its wings feebly, its beak agape with pain. The man stood, his eyes fixed on the bird, eyelids wide with horror.

Suddenly Kral bowled into the man, knocking him to the side. Both men collided into the rock wall. The sword tumbled from the stranger's hand and struck the stone with a loud clatter.

The choked sob finally escaped Elena's throat, and she fell to her knees beside the weapon. The moon'falcon, still stuck upon

the blade, beat a single wing. She reached a small hand and lifted
the bird's head. Its black eye stared into her. The glow caught in
its feathers was quickly dying away.

Tenderly she cupped the tiny body and pulled it from the blade.
Maybe her magick could help it, like it had Uncle Bol. As the sword
slipped free of its breast, the moon'falcon dimmed and ceased to
breathe. She was too late! Elena clutched the bird to her breast.
Her tears were the only thanks she could give it now.

"It protected her!" the silver-haired man who had attacked her
gasped. "It gave its life for her."

Kral crouched over the man, one hand at the swordman's thin
neck. The mountain man's other hand pointed to where Er'ril had
collapsed to the rock floor. "Bol, see to Er'ril."

Her uncle nodded. As he crossed to Er'ril, Uncle Bol gave wide
berth around the hulking monster nearby. It crouched upon its
haunches but made no move as her uncle passed. It seemed more rock
than flesh—an og're, the mountain man had claimed. Nosing near it
limped the wolf, which Elena knew was more than just a dog of the
forest. It remained close to the thick-boned behemoth. As she stared,
both their eyes turned to her. She noted with a skip of her pulse that
their eyes were the same: yellow orbs split by black narrowed slits.

Kral called to the og're. "Tol'chuk, help me with this traitor
Meric." Then his words settled on Elena. "Lass, are you harmed?"

Elena twisted to face her attacker. Silver-haired with sharp blue
eyes, the man called Meric met her stare. "I . . . I'm fine," she said.
"Why did he attack me? Why did he kill my bird?"

Before Kral could answer, Meric spoke, his voice as stinging as
his eyes. "Your bird?"

Elena refused to shy away from the accusing look in the man's
eyes. She still cradled the broken falcon in her palms. "I found
him in the caves. He landed on my arm."

"The moon'falcon was this man's creature," Kral said. "He
claimed—"

"The wit'ch lies!" Meric interrupted. "The bird would shun
one of such foul blood."

Elena shifted her hand to hide her shame farther under the falcon. By now, the og're had shambled over to them. Kral climbed from Meric's chest and passed the man into the og're's care. Elena scrambled back.

"Hold him firm, Tol'chuk. I will not have him attacking the girl again."

The og're then spoke. Its capability of speech shocked Elena: She had not fathomed an intelligence above that of a draft horse behind its thick brow and piggy eyes. Its voice was that of cracking stones. "Meric will not harm her." The og're released the claw clasped to the man's shoulder.

Kral darted forward to stand between Elena and Meric. "What are you doing? Did one of those goblins club you in the head?"

"He won't harm her. He can't."

Elena noticed Meric made no aggressive move toward her. His sword still lay at his feet; his shoulders sagged.

Tol'chuk spoke again. "The moon'falcon landed on her. Meric's tongue may claim this a lie, but his heart saw it dive, casting its life aside for her own. The truth cannot be denied."

Kral twisted his head to stare at Elena. His eyes shimmered with understanding. "You can't mean . . . ?"

Meric answered, his words strained. "Here stands the blood of my people. The wit'ch is the lost descendant of our king."

Meric sank to his knees and picked up his sword. His motions and face were so defeated that even arming himself did not raise a word of alarm from Kral. Meric held the shaft of the blade in both thin hands. With a strength Elena had not thought he had, the man snapped the sword across his knee. "I came to find a king and instead found a queen." He presented the broken sword toward Elena. "My life is yours."

Elena blinked several times, confused by his strange words.

Uncle Bol saved her from having to respond, but not with words of solace. "Er'ril dies! I need help!" he called from across the cavern.

All eyes swung to her uncle. Elena saw the swordsman's body

clench, his neck thrown back, his eyes open and blind. Breath spasmed from a chest struggling to keep life in its body.

The dead falcon slipped from Elena's fingers.

Er'ril swam through a sea of blackness. He struggled against its pull, but he tired quickly, his limbs becoming leaden with his effort. Darkness thickened around his limbs like sap in winter, and he sank beneath its surface.

As he drifted down, he surrendered his struggle against it, not so much because he was resigned to his fate, but simply because he was practical. He had wasted his energy in this fight. As he pulled his energies back into himself, his eyes began to see various hues flowing through the blackness engulfing him. The strongest stream was the brackish green of a stagnant bog. One word came to his mind: *poison*. He somehow knew the goblin's blades had been dipped in dire alchemies.

Words from far away itched his ear.

"What does she do?"

"Put the dagger down!"

"I feel no beat of his heart."

"He's dead."

"No!"

Er'ril knew all this should mean something to him, but darkness penetrated his mind and curled into his skull. It spoke with a voice, too. It whispered release. He listened.

The voice consoled him, and the blackness laced with green ice worked through his blood toward his heart. Why had it grown so cold?

As even this question faded from his awareness, a new voice intruded. He tried to push it away but was too weak. ". . . fight it. Hold on. Please, don't leave me." Did he know that voice? He let the currents of blackness carry him away. It mattered not.

He drifted . . . at peace.

Then a blazing radiance thrust through the blackness to grab him with piercing claws. At its touch, ice and fire fought in his blood. He writhed within its grip. Never had he felt such agony. Every injury he had ever suffered, every pain he had ever endured, came back to him in one searing lance of fire. He screamed as the claw wrenched his body from the sea of blackness into a burning brilliance. No! It hurt too much! He tried to fight his way free of its hold, to dive back into the cool darkness, but it would not let him.

The light burned through him, driving the wisps of blackness from his skull. The streaks of green poison stopped their spread but were not driven out. Like river asps, they swam and hid, waiting to strike when the light should fade.

Brilliant spots of color began to dance across his vision, swirling in slow spirals. He found his eyes could blink. Each swipe of lid slowed the whirling until the hues became faces.

He saw Elena bowed over him, Bol at her shoulder, Kral beside him.

The mountain man was the first to speak. "You saved him! Healed him!"

Elena's face was pale, her skin drawn tight to bone. Echoes of pain swam in her moist eyes. She pulled her hand from his own. Er'ril saw her palm bright with blood. Her thumb had been sliced deeply at its base. He saw the dagger in her other hand. It was the wit'ch dagger Bol had christened in the cottage.

"No," she answered Kral, her voice a cry of sorrow and frustration. Her hands clenched. "I couldn't heal him!"

Er'ril tried to sit, sure he would fail. The measure of his strength surprised him. Wobbling and with the aid of Kral's hand, he did manage to push himself up. He teetered as shards of darkness spun through his vision, but these faded with several deep breaths.

Beside him, Er'ril spotted the iron ward on the stone floor. Once again it was just a carved lump of ore. He felt no phantom link to the metal. He picked it up and held the small fist in his own as he fought to calm his spinning head.

Kral kept one hand clamped to Er'ril's shoulder. "*See!* He is cured!"

Elena shook her head and let her uncle tie a bandage around her wounded hand. "My blood bought him time," she said, her words grown hard. "Nothing else. He needs rest and a healer, or he'll yet die."

Kral still seemed to doubt her. "He lives now. That is what matters. But the goblins could change that unless we get free from here."

"How? Where?" Bol asked. He had finished tying the bandage. His eyes were strange upon his niece. "We can't go back to the cottage with the skal'tum waiting."

His words sobered Kral. "And with us carrying Er'ril, climbing out is impossible."

Er'ril's tongue swam thick in his mouth. "L-Leave me."

They all ignored him. No one even looked in his direction.

The og're, who hovered just at the edge of Bol's lantern light, spoke up. "My wolf-brother says he may scent a way."

Er'ril twisted his neck to where the og're now pointed. The wolf had his nose to the other passage exiting the chamber, the tunnel from which mad Re'alto had come. The dog stood, his nose raised, and sniffed the sighing breeze of the passage.

"He says he scents a familiar trail," the og're continued, "the scent of his brother Mogweed."

THE SCUFF OF TREAD ON STONE PULLED MOGWEED FROM HIS DROWSE. He opened one eye, not rising from where he sat, thinking that perhaps Rockingham was pacing again. But Mogweed was wrong. The man sat with a branch in his lap as he worked on fastening a strip of cloth to one end. Their torch was jammed into a crevice in the floor. Its flames danced light across the walls. The torch, only half burned, should last until dawn, but Rockingham prepared another, always wary.

Mogweed straightened his slump and drew Rockingham's eyes.

"So the sleeper awakes," Rockingham said in his usual mocking tone. "Morning nears. But you could still—"

Holding up a hand, Mogweed stopped his words. "I thought I heard something," he said, and with a wince, unbent his limbs and stood.

"I heard nothing."

"Your ears are not as keen as mine." Mogweed crept along the wall and paused at each tunnel mouth, his head held cocked as he listened. He heard nothing. Perhaps the noise was just the trace of a forgotten dream.

At the mouth of the fourth tunnel, he heard it again: a soft scrape on rock. He froze. The sound repeated. Mogweed waved Rockingham over. The man slipped soundlessly beside him. When the scuff whispered from the tunnel again, Mogweed raised his brows in question to the man. Rockingham shook his head. The man still could not hear it.

Through Mogweed's mind ran horrible pictures of what might have attacked his brother. Fardale's howl still rang in his ears. He backed from the tunnel.

"What did you hear?" Rockingham asked. His voice, though whispered, seemed so loud.

"I don't know. It's too far away." Mogweed hunched his shoulders. "Maybe we should see if the skal'tum are gone." He glanced longingly toward the way back to the surface, then back to the tunnel. His mind could conjure worse things than the monsters above.

Rockingham stood listening by the opening. "I think I hear it now, too."

Mogweed backed another step.

"I think I just heard someone's voice!"

Monsters seldom spoke. At least not the ones of Mogweed's imagination. Rockingham's words drew him forward again. He pushed aside the memory of Fardale's howl and listened. Then he heard it, too. Snatches of conversation echoed up from below, too far away to be heard distinctly, but clear enough that they could recognize the cadence as the common tongue, not some flesh-rending beast's. Mogweed's heart began to beat faster. Strength came in numbers greater than two; with others, he had a better chance of surviving this night.

A sudden bark of laughter erupted from below. Rockingham and Mogweed's eyes met. Relief surged through Mogweed at the noise. The ebullient outburst was welcome among these dark tunnels. But Rockingham's eyes narrowed with warning, and Mogweed's heart clenched.

"I know that laugh," Rockingham said sourly, "that boulder-grinding guffaw. I had hoped the beasts of the tunnel had feasted on Kral and by now spat out his bones. Apparently the beasts have a more refined palate than I had hoped."

"He is strong," Mogweed argued. He remembered the huge, bearded man and the thickness of his arms. "And he has an ax."

"Shush!" Rockingham drilled him to silence with his glare. He continued to listen to the echo of voices.

Mogweed heard someone speak. As those in the tunnel approached, the words traveled clearly now. His sharp ears even detected the exhaustion and bewilderment in the speaker's voice. "You're saying Elena is descended from this Meric fellow's king."

Rockingham, too, must have heard subtle nuances to the speaker's words. "It's Er'ril!" he hissed in recognition. "What misfortune is this!"

"Is he another warrior?" Mogweed whispered, his heart singing with hope. He pictured two men the size of Kral—with himself hiding behind their wide backs.

"He guards the demon child," Rockingham said. His eyes gleamed in the torchlight.

At first, Mogweed did not know who he meant. Then it occurred to him. "Do you mean the girl the winged beasts seek? The one for whose capture your king will grant us many gifts?"

A girl's voice rose from below. "I think I see a light ahead. Look!"

Rockingham darted away, pulling Mogweed with him. "It is she!" he said with delight.

"What are we going to do?"

Rockingham's brow crinkled as his mind worked on the puzzle. When he spoke, his voice was sure. A smile without warmth marked his lips. "Stay silent about what lies above. Let me do the talking. I only ask one thing of you. Do this to help me, and you will be richly rewarded."

Mogweed's eyes glowed with imagined treasures. His gaze flickered down to his own body. To be free of this form, that was worth all the gold in the world. His tongue wet his dry lips. And if he performed well enough here, there was no telling how vast his reward might be. Perhaps he could both break the cursed hold upon his body *and* still keep the gold. His eyes rose again to Rockingham. "What must I do?"

Rockingham leaned to his ear and whispered as Mogweed nodded. It *was* but a simple thing—and the reward so ripe.

ELENA FOLLOWED THE RIDGED BACK OF THE OG'RE UP THE STEEP TUNnel. Close behind her, Bol helped Er'ril hobble along while Kral and his ax guarded their backs against a renewed assault from the rock'goblins. Beside her, like a thin shadow, marched the man called Meric. She did not know what his claim of common ancestry might mean, but her mind was too cluttered with other worries to give this one much thought. Her eyes kept drifting back to the swordsman.

Er'ril needed to rest as soon as it was safe. He walked with his head hung as if it was too heavy for his body, and his breathing wheezed. The poison in his blood could resume its attack at any time.

Her uncle caught her staring. "He's doing fine, honey. Er'ril is strong."

His words raised the swordsman's head. Er'ril nodded to her. "I'm fine, child. When the Book was forged, I was gifted with longevity and quick healing. You may not have cured me, but you have given me enough time to heal on my own." He stared directly into her eyes. "You did save me, Elena—don't doubt that. Your magick can kill, but it can also heal."

Elena noted a subtle distinction absent from the swordsman's words. Her magick truly killed, but it did *not* truly save. It was not a fair exchange.

Bol tried to bolster Er'ril's claim. "And your magick gave me the renewed vitality to climb out of this hole. I would've hated for this pit to be my burial tomb."

Elena smiled weakly at her uncle. Worry etched the warmth from her lips. Her uncle did not understand. Her magick was only a cork in the bottle holding the dregs of her uncle's essence. When her magick faded, so would his life.

She continued to follow the og're's back. She kept her eyes forward, suddenly afraid to look behind, fearful of those grateful eyes.

The og're stopped. "A chamber be just ahead," the creature called from over its craggy shoulder. "A torch burns. My wolf-brother has gone ahead to spy what awaits there."

The others now all crowded close.

"Do you see anyone?" Kral called from the rear.

"I see Fardale at the mouth of the tunnel," the og're passed on. "A figure stands beside him." A long pause, then Tol'chuk spoke, his voice relieved. "It be Mogweed and another man—no goblins."

"Then let's get out of this foul stone dungeon," Kral said.

The og're led the way to the chamber. As the huge creature stepped out of the tunnel, Elena finally had a clear view into the torchlit room. She saw the wolf sniffing at a man in hunter's colors. The beast wagged its tail, but the hunter ignored the wolf and had eyes only for her. When she caught the man staring, he quickly tore his eyes away.

She moved aside to allow the others access to the chamber. As she shifted, she saw another figure in the room, holding a torch. She gasped and backed into Kral just as the mountain man bowed into the room.

"What is it, girl?" he said in irritation. Then his eyes spotted the torchbearer, too. "What're you doing here?" his voice growled.

Rockingham nodded to the party. "Waiting for you."

Kral swung his eyes over the room. "Where's the nymph? What have you done with Nee'lahn?"

All eyes were on the two. Rockingham raised his face to the others beseechingly. "I don't deserve these accusations. I left the young lady with the horses. It was too dangerous for her to accompany us down here. So Mogweed and I, at our own peril, came down to investigate. You were all gone for too long a time." His eyes ran over the party. "But now I can see why. It seems we're all back together again—with a few newcomers." Rockingham bowed to the og're.

"We should go," said the og're. "I smell something foul, and the sooner we leave these tunnels, the better."

"You probably smell Rockingham," Kral said. "But you're right. Let's go."

The mountain man organized the party. He sent Rockingham ahead with the torch, the wolf and Mogweed at his side. Kral went next with Elena beside him, both to protect her and keep a wary eye on Rockingham. Bol, Er'ril, and Meric kept close to their backs, while the og're watched their trail for whatever fouled the tunnels with its smell.

Rockingham set a fast pace toward the surface, and no one asked him to slow down. He kept a constant flow of conversation on the way up. "Dawn is fast approaching. It would be best if we used the remaining darkness to clear out of this valley, maybe try for the highlands or even the mountains." His words droned on for the entire length of the march.

Everyone was too tired to ask him to quiet down.

"Nee'lahn will be so happy to see you all," he continued. A sharp laugh burst from his lips. The man seemed positively giddy.

After so many close calls, Elena knew she should feel the same way, but her feet dragged under her. Soon a layer of dead leaves and crumbled branches mulched under her feet. She brightened like a sailor seeing a seagull as land approached: Here were signs of life from above! Everyone's feet now sped across the slippery bedding. She glanced to her uncle. They shared the first true smile in what seemed like ages.

Her feet felt light. She danced a bit ahead of Kral. She spied a drape of roots ahead in the torchlight. It was the mouth of the tunnel!

A grinding voice rose behind the party. "Something be wrong," the og're called. "The smell worsens. Wait."

Not now, Elena thought in despair. We are almost out!

The wolf also sensed something amiss. A growl flowed from its throat.

"Goblins again?" Kral bellowed to Tol'chuk.

"Not sure."

Kral faced the others. "Meric, take Elena out of here. I'll join Tol'chuk. We'll keep whatever threatens from your backsides."

Meric nodded and pushed her forward.

She hesitated, but Kral waved her on and urged her uncle and Er'ril to follow closely. Er'ril seemed as if he was going to stop and aid Kral. But the mountain man pointed to the tunnel's end. "Get out. In your condition, you'll just be in the way."

"Be careful," the swordsman said hoarsely as he passed.

Meric urged Elena ahead with more insistence. "Hurry. We must get to the safety of the forest."

Elena needed no other invitation. She flew with Meric close behind.

Ahead, Rockingham still stood where he had stopped when the og're had called out. When he saw them coming, he waved for the wolf and Mogweed to hold their spot while he crept to the drape of knotted roots and squeezed through. Mogweed knelt and wrapped his arms around the wolf's neck to hold the dog from bolting.

Once through the twist of roots, Rockingham swung around and held the torch as a beacon. He waved to Elena. "Come on. Those tunnels are a death trap."

She raced toward him, passing Mogweed, who stared nervously in both directions. The wolf continued to growl as she sped past. Mogweed had a tight hold on its ruff. She reached her hand to Rockingham, just as it dawned on her the wolf was growling toward the forest—not back down the tunnel!

Her eyes met those of the man who had killed her parents.

She froze with her arm outstretched and knew her mistake when Rockingham darted his hand out and grabbed her wrist. He yanked her toward him.

Elena screamed and fought against his grip. The others rushed toward her, but Mogweed tripped in the mulch as he tried to come to her aid and fell in a tangle with Meric. They blocked the tunnel long enough for Rockingham to drag Elena through the roots.

One of her hands clutched at a rootlet as she was pulled out, but it broke in her fingers.

With surprising strength, Rockingham threw her into the clearing beyond the tunnel.

She hit the wet mud and leaves and scrambled around to face him, ready for his attack.

A voice yelled from behind her. "Elena! Beware!"

She recognized Nee'lahn's voice and spun on a heel.

Twin skal'tum stepped from under the woven eaves of the surrounding forest. Elena fell to her knees.

"Welcome back, little mouse," said one of them.

"Time to play," said the other.

37

AT THE GIRL'S FIRST SCREAMS, ER'RIL BROKE FREE OF BOL'S SUPPORTing arm and almost pushed the old man aside. That bastard Rockingham had played them all for fools! Er'ril's feet wobbled under him as he fought his way forward, cursing his poisoned muscles.

Ahead, Meric threw Mogweed off him, untangling their limbs, and dashed down the tunnel. Meric had no weapon, but this didn't slow his flight toward the tunnel's mouth. The wolf, freed from the jumble too, sped at his side.

Er'ril frowned as their swiftness mocked his hobbled tread. He tripped over Mogweed when the huntsman tried to stand. "I'm sorry," the man mumbled as he cowered from Er'ril's angry face and scooted aside.

From out in the night rose cold laughter, sibilant and full of malice. Er'ril's blood frosted at the noise. He had heard such a sound many times drifting across old battlefields long forgotten by man. Skal'tum strode this night. Only death followed their foul laughter.

Meric and the wolf pushed through the shroud of roots ahead and vanished into the night. Er'ril and Bol struggled in pursuit, finally reaching the tunnel's end. Both men's breath now heaved through clenched teeth. Er'ril grabbed for a handhold, determined to continue. But before he could crawl out of the tunnel, strong fingers snagged his shoulder and held him.

"No!" boomed a voice at his shoulder. It was Kral. The mountain man pulled him from the exit. Er'ril saw Bol also restrained by one of the giant man's fists. "You're both too feeble. Stay. Tol'chuk will guard you."

Er'ril wrenched his shoulder to break the mountain man's hold but found himself too weak. He could escape neither Kral's grip nor the truth of his words.

Kral roughly shoved them aside and elbowed his way through the roots. Tol'chuk stepped up behind them. The og're's eyes practically glowed in the passage. Er'ril was not sure whether Tol'chuk was here to protect them or to keep them from interfering.

"I'm going out," Er'ril said and reached to the roots. He expected the og're to make some motion to stop him.

Instead it was Bol's hand that stayed him.

The old man gripped his elbow, not to restrain, but simply to let his own urgency flow into Er'ril. "It suddenly makes sense." The old man squeezed his arm. "Kral is right. This is not *our* fight."

His words shocked Er'ril into pausing. He had not thought Bol a coward. He snapped his elbow from the old man's grip and swung his face to Bol. "Elena is in danger!" Er'ril spat out. "At your word, I am her guardian. You ask me to abandon her?"

Bol's eyes squinted with anguish at his words; claw marks blackened his cheek. "Of course not," he said. "Just know this: What occurs this night was meant to be." The old man waved him on.

Er'ril grimaced at the delay and shoved through the roots. In his haste, he snagged his jerkin on a branch. Ripping his leather free, Er'ril stumbled away from the tunnel's mouth. Bol squeezed after him, but Tol'chuk simply tugged at the roots. His arms strained with bulging muscles, but the old oak held firm to the rock. Twice the girth of a man, the og're could not pass.

"This is not your battle either," Bol consoled Tol'chuk.

His words satisfied the og're as little as they had Er'ril. Tol'chuk continued to rip at the roots.

Er'ril ignored them both and swung to the clearing.

In the center of the space, battle lines were already being drawn.

To one side, Rockingham had his back pinned to a thick oak. Before him, the wolf growled with its hackles raised. The animal meant to keep the man from further mischief. Better to tear out his throat, Er'ril thought grimly—end his mischief forever.

But Rockingham held little of Er'ril's true attention. The larger battle building in the center of the clearing drew his eyes.

A pair of skal'tum had Elena caught between them. With their backs to her, leathery wings trapped the child within folds of bone and skin, keeping her from those who sought to rescue her. The child's eyes were wide, tears staining her cheeks. She trembled, cringing when a wing brushed her skin. Er'ril knew the murder of the goblins had so unnerved her that she feared to use her powers to free herself.

Others sought to save her.

The twin skal'tum faced three opponents.

Meric stood to one side, eyes red with fire. No weapon lay in his hand, yet a nimbus of light danced across his body. Though the air in the clearing stood quiet, ghost winds whipped Meric's silver hair, now undone of its braid. The sky above matched his fury, and hulking clouds sped, as if toward this spot. Lightning etched the bellies of the thunderheads, revealing spouts of blackness reaching for the ground. Dawn might be near, but the black skies spoke of a night without end.

On the far side of the clearing stood the small figure of Nee'lahn, her shoulders against a large elm, her arms raised in a stance of defiance. She threw her head back, as if about to sing forth to the warring skies. The mighty elm, towering above her, swept its branches up and spread its limbs to those same skies, the tree matching the small nyphai's defiant pose.

Closer to Er'ril, Kral stood with his mighty ax in one hand. As thunder rumbled into the clearing, his teeth shone in the flashes of lightning, feral as a bear's. Kral shifted his ax. "Now I will wash my shame!" he screamed at them and the skies. "In your blood!"

The skal'tum faced the three. Whispers of nervousness swept through their wings, stanching their earlier laughter. Their black lips pulled back to expose white fangs. Angry eyes weighed the degree of threat from the small figures who challenged their might.

Bol spoke into the tense silence that descended over the clearing. Even the thunder accompanying the flashes of lightning held its rumble in its deep throat. Er'ril knew when next the thunder spoke it would howl with battle. Bol snatched at Er'ril's sleeve. "The elementals!" he hissed. " 'Three will come.' So it was written." Bol stabbed a finger around the clearing. "Kral, Meric, and Nee'lahn. Rock, wind, and the fire of life. Three will come! Not to my cottage, as I had thought—*but here!*"

"Three who will die," Er'ril answered. "They cannot pierce the dark magick of the dreadlords." He pulled free his sword, but his arm shook as he tried to raise its tip. Poison screamed in his muscles.

"You and your Brotherhood have always judged the elementals too lightly. The outcome is not foretold." Bol used a single finger to push down Er'ril's weapon; the swordsman was too weak to stop him. "This is not our fight," the old man repeated.

Er'ril tried to will the iron fist in his pocket back to life. Maybe his phantom arm had the strength his other arm did not. But the fist failed to stir. Either its magick was spent, or it believed the old man.

Behind him, Er'ril heard Tol'chuk wrestle with the tangle of roots. The og're growled his frustration.

Er'ril clenched his fist around his sword. His heart echoed the og're's sentiment.

In the clearing, the battle began without him.

NEE'LAHN SAW ONE OF THE WINGED BEASTS LUNGE A HUGE CLAW AT where the elv'in stood. Or rather where he had *once* stood. The claw grasped empty air as Meric flew backward. Nee'lahn would have sworn his feet had not moved. Meric then crossed his arms over his chest and lowered his chin. The nimbus of light scintillating from his body flared brighter; from the heavy clouds, a slender spear of lightning lanced the reaching claw of the beast.

Thunder cracked the air.

The skal'tum screamed and yanked back its arm. Though obviously paining the beast, its claw remained flesh, not a charred ruin. Its dark magick had protected it from true harm. The second skal'tum held its position near the frightened child.

Nee'lahn knew she must draw one of them away and give Elena a chance to run. The wit'ch must not die! The rebirth of Lok'ai'hera rested with this child. Nee'lahn remembered her dying elder's prophecy: *Green life sprouting from red fire—a fire born of magick.* Nee'lahn eyed the trembling girl. She must not die.

Nee'lahn's bare toes dug under the thin soil to the roots of the elm. She had called the tree's spirit to her earlier. All was prepared. She lowered her eyelids slightly, sang to the old forest, and drew its power to her.

As her mind sang, her song joined others, and her spirit merged. She became the elm. She became the forest.

The wit'ch must be free!

She swung her arms out toward the skal'tum with the injured hand. The elm above mirrored her motion, and its longer limbs grabbed the skal'tum in thick arms hardened by centuries of snow and wind.

The skal'tum struggled, and Nee'lahn gasped at its strength. She battered it with limbs and tried to drag the creature from Elena's side, but the beast's claws dug deep into the mud and rock. It budged not an inch.

Nee'lahn dug her toes deeper into the soil herself. Sweat beaded her forehead; her throat burned with her silent song. She had not thought it would strain her so, but she had never tried to wield so much power. The elemental magick that ran in her blood was also a part of her. Using it now meant burning a part of her, like a log fueling a fire. Her breathing labored as she fought to hold the foul creature.

She knew she could not do this herself. Her eyes spotted Meric.

The glow about his body had returned after pulling the lightning down. An ally stood ready. His lightning alone did not harm the beast, and her grasping branches also failed to budge it. But maybe together? She bit her lip at the thought. Elv'in and nyphai had not joined spirits since the land was young. Could they bridge the chasm of ill blood between them?

Meric faltered as he drifted closer to the skal'tum. The elv'in seemed determined to give his life for the child. Nee'lahn had trouble reconciling the nobility demonstrated here with the ember of hate in her heart. She bit her lip. Could she trust him?

The skal'tum wrenched in her grip, and she felt the elm's branches break. Pain shot through her. She slipped to one knee. Meric's eyes swung to hers, his face tight with strain.

His lids narrowed, and she knew his thoughts flowed with the same consternation.

But it was time to ignore heritage and forge a new alliance.

She signaled Meric with her eyes; he nodded slightly.

Another bolt from above struck the beast. The skal'tum writhed but still remained unscathed. Its pained thrashings shook it partially free from the elm's grip.

But Meric's bolt gave Nee'lahn the time she needed to alter her song. Her fingers clawed toward the sky. Roots erupted from the soil and snared the legs of the beast, wrapping tight and digging into its morbid flesh. Nee'lahn fought the beast's hold on the mud. If she could free its claws, the branches could drag the creature from Elena's side.

Meric struck again. But this time, his bolt failed to reach the ground, striking the air over the skal'tum. Meric wavered on his feet. His hair hung limp to his shoulders, the ghost winds gone.

He tired as much as she. Their faces had grown pale; their breath had grown ragged. The release of such power had ravaged them both.

Nee'lahn found herself on both knees now. Her muscles quivered with effort. Several of the larger branches began to bend back to the tree—no longer striking toward the skal'tum. Meric's next attack was only a flash of light, without even a snap of thunder.

The second skal'tum noticed their faltering attacks and swung to aid its partner, ripping a root loose. Nee'lahn gasped with the pain and fell to one hand.

They were doomed to fail.

AS THE SKAL'TUM FOUGHT TO FREE ITS BRETHREN, KRAL SAW AN opening, an exposed flank. He charged with his ax raised. He knew he could not kill it, but he hoped to draw its attention to himself and keep it from aiding the other skal'tum tangled in the roots.

Arcing over his shoulder, his ax swung toward the beast's flesh.

Kral gasped as his blade cleaved the tender belly of the skal'tum and gutted the beast. Black innards spilled forth from the wound like a foul tongue from a dying mouth.

Man and beast stood frozen at the sight. Kral's ax dripped blood down its hickory shaft. The skal'tum stared with huge black eyes at its sliced belly.

Then its gaze swept up to Kral. Its eyes narrowed, and with a screech, it flew at him.

Kral barely had time to raise his ax and block a rake of razored claws at his throat. He was much too slow to stop the other claw from grabbing his calf. The skal'tum snapped the bone of his leg.

Pain had yet to reach his awareness as the beast yanked him into the air. Before the agony of his broken limb could drive him into blackness, Kral hardened his heart against the pain.

He was a rock. Rocks did not feel pain.

Hanging in the beast's grip, Kral bent at the waist and blindly swung his ax toward the wrist that held him. The iron blade shuddered slightly as it passed through the bone of the creature's arm. He was allowed only a moment of satisfaction before he fell and struck his head on the ground.

Dazed, he rolled away from where he thought the skal'tum stood, hugging his ax to his chest. Blood flowed from a wound on his forehead, obscuring his view. He rolled to his one good knee,

unable to stand, and swiped his ax before him. It encountered nothing. He rubbed the blood from his eyes and saw the skal'tum clutching the stump of its arm, trying to stanch the black river spurting from its wound.

Kral stared at the creature's injured belly and arm. His weapon had truly pierced its dark magick! But why? How? He silently thanked the gods of his people. Whatever the reason, he now had a chance to wipe the shame from his heart. With a coward's tongue, he had fled from these beasts earlier. This time he would show his courage!

The beast finally realized the futility of its effort to halt the bleeding and dropped its wounded arm. Blood hung in thick clots from the severed wrist. It again stalked toward him, more cautiously this time, wings raised in wary readiness.

Behind it, Kral spotted Elena's face glowing in the flashes of lightning. She was caught in a claw of the other beast. Her captor still struggled to free its legs of the entangling roots and its wings of the clinging branches.

Before he could help her, Kral needed to dispatch the beast who now approached so carefully.

Kral eyed the creature, looking for weakness. It still had so many weapons: a clawed hand, two daggered feet, and a mouth of ripping teeth. And the beast was now alert, thinking instead of reacting. It would not again act rashly and underestimate its quarry.

Kral knew what he must do. He had to draw the beast closer.

He took a deep breath and stoked himself for the fire ahead. Once prepared, he released the magick from his heart. He was no longer rock. Stone melted to flesh once again. The pain from his fractured leg now flowed free. It stabbed and burned through his blood like a fire through dry brush, tearing him apart. His vision blacked, and he fell to the mud.

He fought to stay conscious, but the pain argued against it.

Through the fog of agony, he heard the skal'tum cackle as it leaped at its injured prey. "I will enjoy feasssting on your bowelsss, mountain worm," the beast hissed.

Kral forced his eyes open. He lay on his side and saw the crea-ture's toes dig into the mud only a breath away from his nose. He twisted his head up in time to see the beast lunge its teeth for his throat. Kral ignored the agony spearing from his leg and threw himself into a roll, bringing his arm and ax up in a wide swing.

Only one chance, he thought. He felt his ax bite, but what?

When he came to a stop, he saw the skal'tum lying sprawled an arm's length away. *Its head lay even farther.*

Thank the gods!

Kral rolled again to one knee, but now it took all his effort to keep at bay the darkness that howled for him. He saw that Nee'lahn and Meric fared no better. The nymph lay curled in a ball by the base of her tree, one hand stretched up to the elm's trunk. The tree's limbs still moved, but they offered little restraint. Meric had collapsed to his knees, obviously spent. No glow traced his figure.

As Kral watched, he saw the surviving skal'tum snap the last of the roots from its limbs and brush off the feeble branches. It was free. And Elena still lay within its grasp. She fought against it with weak fingers; Kral saw her tears.

From the numb glaze coming to her eyes, Kral knew she was succumbing to the same darkness that hounded him. Yet where Kral's darkness burned, hers promised the coolness of escape.

Do not lose heart, he silently willed to her.

Kral raised his ax a final time. He could not cross the clearing and reach the other skal'tum. But his ax could!

He would have only one throw.

As he hauled back his arm, he prayed that the gods grant him this one wish. Closing his eyes, he wrenched his arm forward, drawing on all the muscles in his back and shoulder. He opened his eyes; the ax flew from his hand.

The blade flipped in slow circles through the air.

The fate of the child was now beyond his grasp. His heart knew its duty done and allowed the blackness to swell. With a groan, Kral's vision blurred, and he fell to the mud.

ELENA SAW THE AX FLY TOWARD HER. SHE DID NOT STRUGGLE TO ES-cape its path. She simply closed her eyes. Let it strike her. Let the horrors end.

A sharp rush of air passed overhead. The claw that clasped her shoulder tensed for a heartbeat, then dropped away. Surprised at the sudden freedom, her knees buckled under her own weight.

"Run, Elena!" Er'ril called to her from across the clearing.

His words took several heartbeats to penetrate her skull. Her head twisted to see what remained of her captor: It still stood above her, but the long hickory shaft of Kral's ax protruded from its chest like a third arm. The blade had buried itself fully in the creature's chest. Black blood dribbled from slack lips.

It still stood, one claw gently fingering the ax's leather-wrapped handle. A cough bubbled up from its chest and cast forth more blood. It sank to its knees, as if crudely mimicking Elena's pose. She was transfixed by the flow of black rivers from its lips.

"Get back!" Er'ril called.

"Elena, honey—run!" Her uncle's voice broke the strange spell the skal'tum had upon her. She found her feet moving and hob-bled across the sodden leaves. Yet she could not draw her eyes from the horrible creature's death.

The skal'tum's wings sank to the mud. Its eyes searched the clearing and stopped when its face found Rockingham. A single claw raised and pointed to the man. It spoke with specks of black foam accenting its words, "Blood speaks to birthright. *Nai' goru tum skal mor!*"

Elena felt a flow of power pass over her from the beast. The hairs on her neck stood quivering.

The beast fell backward, the haft of the ax pointing to the cloud-choked sky. Its chest heaved one last time, and a gout of blood fountained from nose and mouth. Then it lay still.

All eyes were on the dead skal'tum when Rockingham began to gasp and clutch at his throat. The man ignored the growling wolf and stumbled into the clearing. His face had reddened to a pur-plish hue, his eyes bulged out. He raised a hand to where Elena stood. "H-h-help me."

His body suddenly snapped back, stretched taut. With his spine arched at such an impossible angle, Rockingham balanced on his toes. He screamed a single word to the sky—a name. "Linora!" Then a sharp crack echoed across the glade, and like a puppet with its strings cut, Rockingham collapsed dead to the mud.

Elena stared numbly at the man who had killed her family. She had thought to feel some satisfaction, but only an emptiness yawned behind her breastbone.

Silence descended over the valley. A wind moaned through the wet wood.

The wolf padded over to Rockingham and sniffed at him. Its hackles were still raised.

Her uncle spoke behind her. "Look there, I think Kral still breathes."

"He lives?" the swordsman said, amazement thick in his voice.

Elena tore her eyes from Rockingham's corpse and turned to where Kral lay.

Uncle Bol knelt by the mountain man and pulled Kral's head from the mud. Leaves smeared one side of his craggy face. Kral's eyes fluttered open, and he let out a shuddering breath. He coughed. "Did I . . . did I kill it?" he said with a weak tongue.

"Yes," her uncle said. "Now don't move until we splint your leg."

"Let . . . let me see the girl."

Her uncle waved Elena over to them. She rushed to the moun-tain man's side, elated to find even a single death cheated this night.

Kral's eyes glowed with relief at the sight of her.

Er'ril accompanied her. The swordsman knelt beside Kral. "You saved us all." He waved his hand to indicate Meric and Nee'lahn, who were now just starting to rise on shaky feet.

"We all did," Kral mumbled. "With the help of the gods." He pushed up enough to see where his ax protruded from the dead bulk of the beast. He sighed and sank his forehead to the mud. Elena heard him mutter a prayer of thanks.

Er'ril touched his shoulder. "Your ax flew true. Your arm's strength saved this foul night."

"But it did not save my craven heart," Kral mumbled to the ground.

"What is this you mutter?" Er'ril asked. "You slew them bravely."

"No, the gods did. My blade should not have cut through the beasts' dark magick. It was the work of the gods, not my arm."

"No, Kral, it was no god's hand that pierced their black protections. Your blade was anointed in the blood of the creature you slew in Winterfell. Its black spirit bathed your ax. A weapon so treated will slice through their magick."

Kral's head swung up as Er'ril spoke, his eyes suddenly focused and sober. He reached and clutched the swordsman's knee. "What is this you speak?"

Er'ril seemed confused by the fervor in Kral's eyes.

The mountain man's hand slipped from Er'ril's knee. Kral's eyes narrowed with a pain that was not just physical. "I thought it a ruse, a lie."

"What lie?" Er'ril asked.

Kral hung his head again. "My tongue spoke falsely to escape the beasts at the cottage. I told them I knew of a way to pierce their skin's shield—that my ax could kill them."

Kral's pain held the swordsman's tongue.

Uncle Bol spoke to fill the hard silence, placing a hand on the mountain man's chest. "But it ended up being the truth. You did not lie."

Kral's eyes continued to shine with pain. "In my heart, I did."

Uncle Bol looked to Er'ril for help. He only shook his head, unsure what else to say. Kral's eyes began to close again, his breathing hoarse with pain.

Elena found herself placing a hand on Uncle Bol and Er'ril. She guided them aside and knelt by Kral. He had saved her. She would not let him carry this pain in his heart. Too many others had already given too much for her safety. She could erase this one debt.

As she knelt, Kral's eyes opened a bit wider in acknowledgment of her presence, but deep sorrow still resided behind his pupils.

She raised his chin with a finger, then moved the finger to his lips. "No lie passed your tongue, man of the mountains. Your heart protected you, as you protected me. Do not let guilt sully your brave actions. Your heart held true." She bent and placed a small kiss on his lips, then repeated in a whisper, "No lies passed these lips."

Her touch and words softened the lines drawn deep on his brow and around his eyes. His body visibly relaxed. "Thank you," he muttered softly, and his eyes drifted closed. His breathing resumed a more peaceful rhythm.

Er'ril squeezed her shoulder. "You may have just saved his life. His guilt would have sapped his will, and Kral's heart must be strong, free of doubt, to heal his wounds."

Elena fell back to Er'ril's chest. The swordsman's words were a balm on her soul, too. A long sigh rattled in her tired chest. Er'ril placed his arm around her and helped her rise.

Uncle Bol wandered over and knelt by Rockingham. The killer lay on his back in the mud, his limbs twisted at odd angles. Her uncle placed a hand on the man's neck.

Elena waited. She suddenly had an urge to pull Uncle Bol away. Rockingham had killed her parents. She did not want anyone else near him. She opened her mouth, then closed it, knowing how foolish her words would sound.

"I feel no beat of his heart. He does not breathe," her uncle said. He stood with a groan, one hand supporting his lower back. Turning to them, he wiped his hands together as if to remove any traces of Rockingham's foul touch. "He is dead."

Elena allowed herself to relax. It was over. Dawn was near. She suddenly had a heartfelt need to see the sun again.

Her uncle smiled at her.

She returned it, shyly at first, then stronger. This long night neared its end.

As she smiled, her nose warned her before her eyes. A stench of open graves swelled across the glade. Her nose curled from the smell, trying to shut out the noxious odor.

When Elena saw what rose behind her uncle, she screamed.

38

Mogweed heard the girl's terror and retreated farther down the tunnel. Whatever created such fear had to be far worse than any goblins. Maybe he could find another way out. But fear of the dark passages and of hidden cave creatures kept him hovering.

Near the tunnel's mouth, Tol'chuk stood by the drape of roots, still unable to free himself from the passage. The sounds of battle had ignited the og're's blood. He tore viciously at the iron-hard roots of the oak. Several of Tol'chuk's claws had ripped and now bled.

Mogweed saw the og're shake with a blood rage. Suddenly Tol'chuk swung from his attack on the roots to face Mogweed. The og're's eyes glowed, not with the amber of his si'lura heritage but with the red fire of an og're. He pointed a ragged claw at Mogweed.

"You!" Tol'chuk boomed, funneling his anger toward him. "You knew!"

Mogweed felt the air thicken as the og're's rage enveloped him. His eyes grew wide with the memory of the og're tearing the sniffer to bloody tatters when they first met. His tongue froze in his mouth.

"You knew what lay beyond the tunnel, yet your tongue be silent!"

Mogweed fought his throat and lips, trying to find words to deny the accusations. He could not.

Tol'chuk thundered down the passage, filling the entire tunnel. Mogweed covered his head with both arms. He felt the steam of the og're's hot breath. He cringed, awaiting the rip of teeth.

"Why?" Tol'chuk hissed in a small, deadly voice, much more chilling than his booming rage. "Why did you betray us?"

Mogweed knew he must speak. In his present fury, Tol'chuk would certainly kill him. But what could he say? He *had* betrayed them. Only Rockingham would know the words to escape this fate. Mogweed pictured the man's snide demeanor. Yes, Rockingham would know, and as Mogweed thought of him, he suddenly knew, too. Rockingham had taught him something. *Why deny?*

Mogweed focused his breathing to a slower pace and swallowed several times. He tried to ignore the pungent smell of the heated og're. "I did know about the winged beasts," he finally admitted, his voice squeaking.

Tol'chuk's breath rushed at him. "You confess it?"

"Yes." Mogweed closed his eyes. He pictured himself as Rockingham. "But I was forced to. Nee'lahn's life was held hostage on the strength of my silence."

"You sacrificed all of us for the one?"

"No, they only wanted the girl. They swore safe passage for the others."

Tol'chuk remained silent at his words.

Mogweed pressed his advantage, as Rockingham had done with the skal'tum. "I knew nothing of this girl child, but the nyphai are friends of my people—of your people, too. Si'lura and nyphai have been allies of the forest since ages lost in the past. I could not let Nee'lahn die for the sake of a female human child. Humans have hunted us, slaughtered us like mere animals. Why should I trade the life of a friend for an unknown enemy? So I agreed."

"You could have warned us," Tol'chuk said, but hesitation and doubt now laced his ire.

Mogweed struck harder. "My tongue does not make false promises. Though the pact was a foul one, I made it in an attempt to save the life of an innocent. Once spoken, I would not go back on my word. Would you? Is that the way of the og're people?"

Tol'chuk sagged to the tunnel floor. "No, it be just such a betrayal by one of my ancestors that started my journey and cursed my people."

Mogweed sensed he should keep quiet.

"I apologize," the og're said after a period of silence. "The road of honor can often be difficult."

"Your words are spoken with respect," Mogweed said solemnly, bowing his head, though his heart soared with laughter. "I accept your apology."

From down the tunnel, the girl screamed again.

ER'RIL PULLED THE SCREAMING CHILD TO HIS CHEST. A GRAY TEN-tacle, thick as a man's thigh and laced with splotches of red, whipped from behind Bol to wrap around the old man's waist and chest.

Gods above! Er'ril stumbled back, yanking the girl with him.

Large suckers, like tiny mouths, glued to the old man's clothing and skin. Before Bol could raise a hand against the creature's hold, he suddenly spasmed in its grip. His mouth opened in a cry that never sounded. Then he fell limp.

The tentacle thickened and lifted the old man's thin frame. It flung his body, like a rag doll, to the forest's edge. As the tentacle unwrapped, Er'ril saw what had killed Bol. Horned daggers, poking from each of its sucker mouths like hundreds of spearing tongues, pulled from the man's flesh. A steaming red oil dripped from the tip of each horn: *poison.* The horns retracted.

Elena moaned as Er'ril guided her backward toward the forest's edge. She sank to the mud, her eyes fixed on her uncle's collapsed form.

With his one arm, Er'ril tried to hold her up, but his weak muscles were racked with the strain. Elena slid in his grip. He fought to drag her back from the beast, his boot heels slipping in the mud and dead leaves.

Er'ril stared in horror at what awaited them if they failed to reach the trees.

Rockingham's chest had split open like a chiseled melon, and a cauldron of black energies swirled forth. From this void, the tentacle had wormed into the world.

It continued to throb and undulate as it dragged farther out of the swirling densities.

Now Er'ril understood how the Dark Lord had tracked them. Rockingham was not a man, at least not any longer, but a construct of black magick. Er'ril had heard rumors of such creatures. He was a *golem*, a hollow shell created from the dead heart of a suicide.

He tugged the child farther from the emerging creature, gaining small strides.

Like a malignant birth, parts of the beast pushed through the black magick billowing from the dead man's chest. What followed the tentacle was more than a creature of nightmare. Er'ril could never have imagined a beast so foul of form. His mind fought against accepting what he saw.

The tentacle was not an arm of the beast, but a tongue. As it shoved into the world, its blubbery mouth appeared, puckering and swelling around the poisoned tongue. As its lips pulled back, a ring of jagged teeth gleamed like broken glass. Rows of teeth continued deep into its throat.

Above the mouth waved hundreds of tiny stalks, each longer than Er'ril's arm, tipped with black orbs the size of hens' eggs. Er'ril's instincts told him these orbs were not eyes, but some other organ of sense beyond this world's comprehension.

A keening wail, like the cries of slaughtered rabbits, flowed from the creature.

It lurched and rolled into the clearing.

Elena slipped from Er'ril's weakening arm and fell fully to the mud. He tried to move her but was too weak. He searched for help. Across the clearing, he saw Meric hauling Nee'lahn along the edge of the forest. The elv'in struggled to circle around the beast toward them.

Suddenly, Elena jerked under Er'ril's touch. Her feet scrabbled to push her up. The shock of her uncle's death had faded enough for her to become aware of what crept closer. Er'ril helped her stand. "Hurry," he cried in her ear. She obeyed him.

No longer needing help, Er'ril waved Meric back from them, knowing the elv'in bore enough burden with the nyphai. Meric's eyes settled on the girl now moving on her own. He nodded to Er'ril, then limped with Nee'lahn into the cover of thick trunks and twining branches.

Er'ril and Elena retreated toward similar safety.

By now the beast, as tall as two men and longer than four, had fully entered this world. Its body resembled a large slug, gray skin glistening with a mucus that steamed hot in the cold night. Streaks of black and red, like slashes in its flesh, decorated its sides. Lining its bulging torso were suckers larger than swollen pumpkins.

Suddenly its body shuddered and gave one sharp spasm.

Elena screamed.

From the torso's suckers, ten jointed legs burst forth, armored like some massive insect. The legs lifted its bulk off the mud. Only its tongue still draped to the ground, curling and twisting like a snake in nettles.

Knowledge of this beast's nature suddenly gripped Er'ril's heart. He had never seen such a creature, but he had heard it described long ago. Though ages had passed, he had not forgotten. Here stood a creature from the volcanic lands of Gul'gotha. In the burning sulfur pits of their homelands, these creatures burrowed to lay their eggs among poison and fire.

Er'ril's mind fought against this knowledge. He prayed he was wrong.

But what happened next confirmed his fears.

The beast's back bowed up and spasmed again. Its skin tore

open along its sides, and wet wings shook free. Bone and webbing spread from one side of the clearing to the other.

Er'ril drove Elena faster.

Now he could not deny this beast's name. Even the structures of the wings were similar to those of its smaller offspring.

"A mul'gothra," he huffed under his breath as he pushed the girl.

It was a birthing queen of the skal'tum.

39

Elena ran with Er'ril toward the protection of the forest, her loss still choking her heart. She kept her eyes far from Uncle Bol's body, knowing she must resist the allure of paralyzing grief—if not for her own sake, then for the swordsman who would not forsake her but would instead die at her side.

As she ran, a savage rain began to lash down from the warring skies. Streaks of lightning played between the clouds, while crackling rolls of thunder shook from the peaks of the Teeth.

Elena darted looks behind her, expecting to find the beast at her throat already. *Mul'gothra.* Though the swordsman had only mumbled the word, her mind had caught it. It somehow fit the creature.

Across the dark glade, the beast stalked toward them, slightly weak on its jointed legs, like a chick new from an egg. It shook its wings, rattling bone and leather. Cold rain ran in steaming streams across its hot skin.

It sensed her stare. Its stalks waved in her direction as a low cry of recognition hissed from its mouth. Words crept through its hiss like a whispered scratching from a grave. "Come. It is useless to run, child." The words flowed from deep down its dark maw.

Elena knew it was not the mul'gothra that spoke or even a creature in its belly. What spoke crouched in a web far from this rain-swept clearing: something far more sinister than the squealing horror crawling toward her, something from blasted lands and sunless pits.

Deep inside, she knew who spoke.

It was the Black Heart, the Dark Lord of the Gul'gotha.

Its foul words flowed again from the mul'gothra's throat. "The world will scream unless you submit. I will destroy all you hold dear. Your name will be a curse to all ears. That I promise you—unless you come to me. Join with us, now."

Elena ignored the words as she ran, trying not to hear but unable to block them as they wormed into her skull.

"Come hear how loud the screams will be if you resist. Thank you for leaving me such a choice tool to work with."

Elena's feet stumbled in their pursuit of the forest's edge. What did the foul one mean? She stopped, half turned toward the creature.

Er'ril tried to urge her on, but she shook free of his poison-addled grip. The swordsman seemed not to hear the words spoken to her.

The beast twisted to the side, its many feet churning the mud. Its new target was clear. One of her party still lay sprawled in the clearing, like abandoned refuse: *Kral.* The mountain man lay prone across the wet leaves. Not even the rain woke him to the looming monster.

The mul'gothra crept toward him. Its gray tongue snaked closer.

Elena swung her head away, not wanting to watch. As she shunned the sight, her eyes ended up on the crumpled form of Uncle Bol. His face was turned to the sky. Rain struck his open eyes.

Her heart ran cold. Stripped of all family—as if the flesh had been stripped from her bones—all that was left of the young Elena was a core of brittle hardness. So many had died—and in her name!

She tore her gaze back to Kral and took a step toward the beast.

She could stomach no further sacrifice. She was through resisting. Let all the horrors end. Please, no more, her heart sobbed.

Before she could take a second step, a streak of darkness shot past her knees and raced forward. The wolf flew to stand between Kral and the mul'gothra and howled at the monster, a cry that sliced through thunder and rain. The swiftness of the dog's appearance must have startled the winged horror. It skittered back from the snarling wolf.

The stalks waved frantically. Then its tongue snapped out and batted the dog aside. The impact sent the wolf tumbling through the rain to strike the trunk of an oak. Elena saw him struggle to raise his head, legs pushing at the piled dead leaves. Then the wolf collapsed—unconscious or dead, Elena did not know. His pink tongue hung from slack jaws.

The mul'gothra again stalked toward Kral.

No! She stumbled forward.

"Elena! Stop! You cannot help him!" Er'ril tried to snatch at her, but his poisoned blood slowed his moves. She slipped his clutch. "Stop!"

She ignored the swordsman's call. The beast would make short work of Kral and all of her friends. She ran forward now, her heart dead in her chest. The only way to keep her friends clear of its rending teeth was to give the Dark Lord what it wanted. Let her own sacrifice save the others. Let this night end.

No more would die in her name.

Her eyes tight with dry tears, she lunged to the mountain man's side just as the tip of the mul'gothra's tongue brushed the crown of Kral's head. She skidded to a stop in the mud and kicked aside the tentacle. She stood in a small pool of rainwater as the beast towered over her. Elena raised her arms, her head thrown back. Rain sluiced onto her face and ran cold through her hair. "No more," she called in a strangled voice. "I am yours."

As it leaned toward her, she saw down its puckering mouth. Its stench clenched her stomach. She fought her rising gorge. Deep in its throat, coiling and thrashing, was a nest of other tongues. But the tongue that spoke was none of these. "Smart child. It is useless to resist. Your heart knows its master."

The mul'gothra crouched down on all its legs, like a spider about to bite. Elena wanted to stand brave, but her knees began to buckle. One of its tongues slithered from the gaping mouth and throbbed toward her. Its tip touched her boot, then crawled up her body. Like a foul lover's embrace it slid under her soaking shirt and wrapped around her chest. Its touch burned. She felt its suckers kiss at her skin.

"We shall create things that will shudder the world," the voice said, but Elena knew this was not spoken to her as much as it was whispered to the Black Heart's own desires.

Her knees finally gave out completely, but before she sank to the mud, the tongue tightened its hold and lifted her into the rain. The suckers that had kissed now bit as they held.

Elena closed her eyes. Let him have his wit'ch. Let him have his prize. He would never have her soul. Death stalked all those around her. Perhaps it would claim the Gul'gotha, too.

"It is a long flight," she heard it say.

She closed her mind, shut out the world, and sought a place within her where she would not hear the rattle of wings or the pounding rush of her own heart—somewhere to hide. She retreated, flying far away from this dark glade.

The Dark Lord's next words stopped her flight. "But the mul'gothra is weak. It must first feed."

Elena's lids flew open, and she saw the beast whip another tongue from its long gullet to wrap around Kral's neck.

Her body screamed. Ice ran cold in her veins. No! Her silent cry echoed to all corners of her being, awakening that which slept curled around her heart. The world dimmed. Not even a flash of lightning penetrated her darkness. Ice reached her heart—and a fire exploded within her.

"*I said no more!*" she shrieked. Her voice reached the clouds overhead. Thunder answered her. "*No more!*" she screamed again.

Her tormented shriek tightened the grip around her chest, trying to press her silent. Her words were still ignored. From down a narrow tunnel, she saw the tentacle dragging Kral's limp form toward the mouth and teeth. Her vision squeezed to the point of a needle. A cold fire raged inside.

For the past two nights, she had reacted, lashed out, been blown this way and that, like a dead leaf in a whirlwind.

No longer.

She would no longer be ignored.

If the Dark Lord wanted a wit'ch, let him have a wit'ch, one flowing with magick!

Touching the fire within her, she opened herself to her power and let the cold flames glow through her skin. The energy raged within the shell of her body. It sought a crack to run wild into the night. It screamed for blood.

So be it!

She reached to the mouth of the mul'gothra and sliced her right hand on a razored tooth of the beast. As her blood poured free, her magick rushed out.

She struck with a hand whorled in red fires.

The beast screeched and dropped her to the mud.

Landing on her feet, she saw the mul'gothra had released Kral, too. The beast backed from her, scuttling away to the far side of the clearing. At her feet, the amputated end of its tongue convulsed and twisted like an axed snake.

Her heel kicked it away.

Elena again stood in a small pool of rainwater, her head raised to the heavens, her eyes cold on the mul'gothra and the malignant beast inside. At her toes, the water froze to ice and spread. The pool became a frozen pond. Mud at its edges cracked as her cold fire spread farther. Rain turned to ice around her, striking her cheek with sharp bites. She ignored the rain's stinging kisses and stepped toward the beast.

"I told you—*no more!*" She took another step. Kral lay behind her. Determination burned through her: None would touch him now.

"I will have you, child, whole or not." The mul'gothra spread its wings in challenge.

She heard another voice behind her—Er'ril's. He sounded so far away. "No, Elena! You aren't ready! Come back to me! Run!"

She ignored him. No longer would she listen to others.

This night she would *no* longer be a pawn in a game of ages and lost bloodlines.

No leaf in a wind.

No child.

Elena reached a hand toward the beast. Blood dripped from her wounded palm, steaming and hissing as its hot touch met frozen mud.

This night she would be a *wit'ch*.

"You should have listened," she warned, ice in her words.

The beast cringed back a moment. Then, like a coiled viper, it lunged. As it raced toward her, hundreds of tentacles burst from its throat, tangling the air with their thrashings.

Elena stood still as it hurtled toward her. She closed her eyes and clenched her right hand into a fist. She let the fire build within her bloody fingers. The power swirled tighter and tighter upon itself. Her arm trembled with the energies warring within her fist. They became a cold sun in her palm.

The ground shook as the mul'gothra thundered toward her.

She felt the foul heat of its stench on her face.

Her fingers opened, like a rose at dawn.

The force of an exploding star burst from her palm.

ER'RIL WAS BLOWN BACK BY THE FORCE OF THE MAGICKAL EXPLOSION. His back struck a tree. He shakily managed to keep his feet.

Tears had frozen in his eyes. He blinked his lids to warm his vision and saw a sight that stopped his breath.

The mul'gothra had been blown back from Elena's throat. It lay on its back. She had killed it!

No!

He saw a wing twitch. Then in an explosion of muscle and wing, it rolled back to its feet. It swung to the child again. A screech flowed from its black throat.

Elena still stood with her arm raised above her head, fingers splayed wide.

Er'ril swore at the sight.

Her hand was no longer red! With her magick spent, she had no protection.

He stumbled toward her. As he wobbled on his feet, Elena slashed her arm down, fingers pointing at the mul'gothra.

Lightning cracked with such fury from above that Er'ril fell to the muddy ground. He raised his eyes in time to see a thunderhead dive from its place in the heavens. It swallowed the monster in its black grip.

She had called the very sky down upon the creature! Er'ril had never imagined she had such power.

Her magick was not spent, he realized. It had just been cast out into the world—and now it returned. Within the captured thunderhead, he saw her magick glow with the fire of blue ice.

Suddenly a gray tentacle shot out from the churning mists of the black cloud. It sailed for Elena's outstretched arm.

ELENA DID NOT CRINGE. A SMILE OF WICKED DELIGHT PULLED HER lips tight. The power sang to her heart. She felt the bonds linking her blood to the magick, and she knew what she must do.

Her eyes hardened at the grasping tongue.

Her magick whispered in her ear. It told her the cloud that wrapped around the mul'gothra also stood in her hand. She clenched her fist closed.

The cloud shrieked with tormented winds, than shrank, collapsing around the mul'gothra. As it closed around the beast, all its stored moisture changed from mist to water. As the mists cleared, Elena saw a huge bubble of water mold around the thrashing mul'gothra. The beast was drowning.

Elena somehow knew the Dark Lord had fled back to his hole buried under Blackhall. He had left this shell behind.

The mul'gothra still fought its death as the magick sang inside Elena. Her power wanted more. *More!*

A part of her recognized the gasping creature as a mere tool of the Dark Lord, knew its death was nothing to bring such joy, but another part of her sang with the magick swimming in blue scintillations across the surface of the water.

Power still waited to be used, screamed in her ear with its need. Elena heeded the call.

She stared at the drowning beast and clenched her fist tighter. Before her, the bubble of rainwater blew to ice, freezing the beast in its heart, like a fly caught in amber. The towering crystal of ice crashed and sank partly in the mud. Blue fire skated across its surface, a trace of power.

It sang so sweetly. It begged. *More!* Her blood thrilled with its song.

How could she deny it? It would be like denying her heart.

She tightened the muscles of her forearm until they bulged. Her fist now clenched so hard her nails dug into her palm. She did not feel the pain and squeezed tighter still.

Her smile grew ecstatic.

The wall of ice exploded. Like Er'ril's sword in the caves, the frozen beast inside shattered into thousands of pieces. Ice and beast blew away from her, leaving her untouched. The forest behind the beast did not fare so well. Trees were tumbled for a league into the forest. A jumble of ice boulders and sections of mul'gothra spread in a fan from where she stood.

Elena's fist fell open at the sight of such massive destruction. She fell to her knees, then to her palms. What had she done? Her mind pictured the struggling, gasping mul'gothra, argued that it was dangerous and had to be killed. And she knew this to be true. Such a beast would have ravaged her valley home. Yet she also knew how she had felt as she lashed out—joyous with its dying, elated at its death.

Worst of all, as she stared at her hands, so white against the black mud, a part of her desperately craved the light of dawn— not for its warmth, but only for the sun's ability to ignite her power again.

Here she recognized the wit'ch in her, calling out. Elena could not dismiss this as the voice of her magick. No. It was her own heart singing for the power.

But what about the woman who could not stop the tears from flowing down her cheeks at the death of a living creature, a misused tool killed so savagely by her hand? This was her, too.

Who was she?

What had she become?

Boots appeared in the mud before her eyes. Er'ril knelt down beside her. He lifted her chin with his fingers. His touch was warm on her skin. Her magick had left her so cold.

He pulled her to his chest and said no words.

There were none to heal her heart.

40

ELENA PULLED THE DEERSKIN PARKA TIGHTER AROUND HER SHOULders, trying to squeeze every pocket of frigid air from underneath the coat. The first clear morning since they had arrived three moons ago drew her from the home caves of Kral's clan. Snowy peaks, tinged a rosy hue by the dawn, reached for the blue sky. The sight took her breath away in streams of white as the cold bit at her nose. She buried the lower half of her face in the furred collar of her parka.

A morning this clean made her wonder if all that had happened to her was nothing more than a bad dream. Here, she awoke to the sound of giggling children and the prattle of cookwives preparing a morning meal of warmed oats and raisins. Cinnamon spiced the air as well as the food. Pottery clinked with spoons. Voices raised to shout greetings, not warnings.

Yet Elena had only to walk a handful of steps to be reminded that this peaceful world was all an illusion. In a side cave, Er'ril rested on a bed, wrapped in down-filled blankets. The bones of his face shone through his skin. He was a skeleton of a man now, his muscles wasted by a raging fever. The poisons had reached his heart at the same time the party had reached Kral's home. The swordsman had collapsed at the head of the pass.

If not for the broad back and strong legs of the og're Tol'chuk, Er'ril would not have even made it that far. Even the surviving horses—Kral's Rorshaf and her dear Mist—had been too exhausted to safely carry the injured man up the last of the treacherous mountain trails. But with Tol'chuk's help, the limp form of the plainsman finally reached Kral's home caves.

Not until an entire moon had passed did his fever finally break. Only the steamed leaves boiling in pots, prepared with care by Nee'lahn, and Er'ril's own strong spirit kept death from his cave those long days. Elena had spent many nights sitting beside his bed, mopping his brow with cool mineral waters from deep in the caves, listening to him moan and tangle his sheets. Once, he had opened his eyes straight at Elena and screamed, "The wit'ch will kill us all!" She had cried and run from the room, even though she could tell from his glazed eyes that he was deluded by the poisons in his veins. It had taken her many days before she could return to his cave.

This morning, after sneaking Mist a bit of dried apple, Elena had visited Er'ril and found him sitting up in bed, conversing with Kral. The mountain man's lower leg was still clamped between splints, but he managed to hobble through the caves with a crutch of hickory wood under his arm. The wolf had sat by Er'ril's bed, ears perked as the two men spoke. Elena still had trouble fathoming the animal as a shape-shifter and could not resist scratching him behind an ear and patting his head. She had done so as she entered the small cave. The wolf had wagged his tail, and Er'ril had offered her a smile. His color, though pale, had glowed with the warmth of life instead of the ashen shades of death. Returning strength had shone from his eyes.

Elena had mirrored his smile shyly, but now out in the crisp air, she smiled more fully. He would live.

Snow crunched under her boots as she climbed the ice-crusted trail that led from the sheltered caves to the windswept Pass of Spirits. Across the Teeth, the thin spires of smoke from the hearths of other clans of the mountain folk rose to greet the morning. Twelve in all, she counted as she wound up toward the pass.

It was these people who had offered them shelter and a place to hide. Winter had closed the pass with a mighty blizzard just as the party limped into the safety of the Teeth. They planned to weather out the bite of winter among Kral's clans: to let their trail grow cold to the dogs of the Gul'gotha, to let their wounds heal, to let time dull sharp memories that sapped spirit and muscle, to forget for a while and rest.

A long journey lay ahead, but none of them spoke of it. That was for another time—for when that bloody night finally lost its hold on their hearts and tongues. Now, they simply existed, basking in firelight and warm company. Few words were spoken.

Only one decision had been made. When winter thawed, they would all go with Elena and Er'ril on the journey to A'loa Glen.

Each voiced a different reason: Meric to guard his king's bloodline, Nee'lahn to honor the words of a dying prophet, Kral to seek his vengeance, Mogweed and Fardale to break a curse, and Tol'chuk to answer the demands of a glowing stone.

Yet one unspoken reason lay in each heart—ties of blood now bound them all.

Elena let the sun melt this knowledge from her as she continued toward the Pass of Spirits. Though the cold burned her chest, she knew she must make this journey for all who had died in her name, to show them who she had become.

She would make it for her mother and father, for her aunt and uncle, and for a brother who had vanished off the streets of Winterfell.

She wiped a tear from her eye before it froze and continued up the steep path, wondering what had become of her brother Joach.

"COME HERE, BOY," GRESHYM GROWLED OVER HIS SHOULDER AS HE threw open the wardrobe and unhooked the white robe inside.

The wit'ch's brother shambled over to him. Joach's eyes did not blink, and saliva foamed at the corner of his mouth. He stared at Greshym, awaiting his order, but no awareness glowed from his pupils. The spell of influence still held the boy in its thrall.

Greshym stared sourly at the boy's sunken face and wasted figure. He kept forgetting to tell the boy to eat. He frowned. It would not do to let him die. The boy might yet prove useful.

Greshym slipped the white robe over his head and pulled its cowl lower over his face. He threw a blue sash across his shoulders to indicate he was under a vow of silence, not wishing to be disturbed as he crossed the passages to the Praetor's chamber. With a final tug on his robe, he checked the fall of his garments in a mirror, then frowned and lowered his head farther to keep his face deeper in shadows.

Satisfied, he turned to the door of his dormitory cell. "Follow," he ordered the boy as he swung the door open.

Joach shuffled two steps behind him as he entered the passage. The hall was empty, but Greshym was careful to keep his face hooded. Too many eyes prowled these halls. The boy's naked face would raise no inquiring looks. He appeared as any other servant, maybe slightly more slack jawed. A dullard, they would suppose, and politely refrain from mentioning the boy.

Greshym followed a path well-known to him. He had no need to raise his head to check directions. He climbed the stairs near the kitchen and followed a dusty passage to the other wing. Twisting and turning through the various halls, he entered the oldest section of the Edifice. Now the dust of crumbling stone and cracked mortar marked their steps' progress in puffs of ancient decay. Reaching the stairs to the western tower, named the Praetor's Spear after its lone occupant, Greshym stopped to clear dust from his nose, smearing the cuff of his white robe.

The boy bumped to a stop at his heel. Mucus dripped from his nose.

"Stay," Greshym ordered the boy. Once satisfied that he was obeyed, Greshym hauled himself alone up the countless flights of stairs as they curved along the inside of the tower.

He passed two guards along the way. They had been alerted of his arrival by their master. Greshym did not even wave a hand of acknowledgment as he huffed past them. He spied the deadness behind their eyes. Both were under a spell of control similar to the boy's, though of a delicacy and fine webbing beyond Greshym's skills. So subtle was the working that the guards themselves and the brothers of the Order were unaware of the master's touch among their own.

Greshym reached the last landing and approached the iron-bound oaken door. Two guards stood with sheathed swords. Their eyes did not move as he approached. Greshym raised his hand to rap on the wood, but before his knuckles could touch oak, the door swung inward on its own.

"Come," a voice from within ordered. Greshym cringed from the sound of the Praetor's voice—not in fear, but in simple recognition that the tone was the same as his own when he ordered the boy Joach. *He thinks me nothing more than a servant.*

Greshym stepped into the chamber of the Brotherhood's esteemed leader and saw the Praetor standing by the western window. Through the glass, the black finger of the tower's shadow pointed toward the distant coast. The Praetor stared beyond the sunken remains of the once proud city of A'loa Glen and out to the sea, past the islands of the Archipelago that dotted the water like the backs of huge sea creatures. Greshym knew where he stared.

Greshym waited. The door closed behind him and latched shut. Now away from the prying eyes of his other brothers, Greshym pushed back the hood of his robe.

There were no secrets here.

Greshym stayed silent. The Praetor would speak when ready, so Greshym simply studied his stiff back. Only a few individuals knew the identity of the Praetor. As leader of the city and the Brotherhood, he had given up his name to don this cloak of responsibility. That had been a long time ago. None but Greshym still lived to remember that day.

The Praetor finally swung away from the window. His eyes were the same gray as his brother Er'ril's. "I feel her gaze," Shorkan said. "The wit'ch stares toward the Book."

"She will come here," Greshym said. "The Book calls her."

As Praetor Shorkan turned back to his vigil, wraiths of black
energies caressed his skin and mocked the white robes of his sta-
tion. "We must be ready for her. The Black Heart must have his
wit'ch."

ELENA ROUNDED THE LAST OF THE TWISTING PATH, HER HEART
lighter as the pass spread wide before her. She stepped to the Pass
of Spirits with a prayer of thanks on her lips. An errant gust tried
to tug the hood from her face, but it quickly tired of its play and
died away. The wind was calm this morning, but she knew that
by evening it would howl through the Teeth as if pining the loss of
the sun.

She studied the pass. Snow had fallen this last night, and not a
single print marred the spread of virgin white. Elena regretted
having to ruin such a sight with her plodding boot prints, but her
goal this morning still beckoned. With a sigh that plumed into the
air, she crossed into the pass and began the short march to its crest.
A thin scree of ice caked the surface of snow, cracking in protest
with each step. The scrunch filled her ears.

By the time she neared the highest point of the pass, she was
forging through snow up to her knees. A sweat had built under
her inner linens, and she knew that when she stopped it would
rapidly chill her. Still she pushed on until she crested the tallest
point of the pass.

She stopped and stared east. Short of breath, damp, and sure to
grow cold, she did not regret the climb. The mountains opened up
before her, and the full face of the sun bathed her in its radiance.
The morning was so bright and clear that Elena swore the glint at
the curve of the world was the Great Ocean itself. The lands
spread below her in sweeping vistas. She could see winter had
reached its snowy grip far into the foothills and valleys. Yet, beyond that, among the distant plains, a hint of green glowed in the
dawn, like a promise of spring.

Elena pulled off her rabbit-fur mittens and lifted her hands to the sunlight. They glowed in the dawn—one white as the snow, the other whorled with the reds of sunset.

It had taken her a long time after that foul night to finally renew. Though not injured like the others, Elena had sustained a deeper wound in that dark glade. She had needed this time of rest and contemplation to heal.

Because ever since that dark night when she had knelt in the mud in Er'ril's arms, a question had consumed her spirit: *Who was she?*

Elena stared at both hands now and raised them to the world.

Was she the *red* of the wit'ch or the *white* of the woman?

She now knew, and in the Pass of Spirits, she showed the world.

She touched her palms together, intertwining her fingers.

This is who I am.

And as Elena looks toward the distant sea beyond the horizon with her legion at her back, I must end this story.

My inkwells have run dry, my wrist aches, and I must find a vendor who is not too steep on his price of ink and scroll. So please let me end my story here. Let me rest. What I write next—the journey to the lost city—even I dread remembering.

So here I end the story.

The legion is formed, and the path is drawn.

The dark journey begins tomorrow.

ABOUT THE AUTHOR

JAMES CLEMENS was born in Chicago, Illinois, in 1961. With his three brothers and three sisters, he was raised in the Midwest and rural Canada. There, he explored cornfields, tadpoles, and frozen ponds, dreaming of worlds and adventures beyond the next bend in the creek.

Eventually, pretending to grow up, he went to school at the University of Missouri where he graduated with a doctorate in veterinary medicine in 1985.

During one especially icy Midwestern winter, the lure of ocean, sun, and new horizons eventually drew him to the West Coast where he established his veterinary practice in Sacramento, California. Presently, he shares his home with two Dalmatians, a stray Shepherd, and a lovesick parrot named Igor.